the FEMALE VORTEX (Civil......)

Foreword

Riverton was a quiet agricultural village where a strange thing happened one night. The farmers, having penned their sheep, kenneled their dogs, and hung up their smocks, went to bed. But when they awoke in the morning the pastures had been filled with row-upon-row of small terraced houses. Surrounding these houses, massive factories had appeared and were noisily making steel for industry, steam trains for India, textiles to clothe Africa, coal to pollute the atmosphere, and chemicals to poison the world. And the sky was hiding behind thick black smog that was to persist for two hundred years.

To claim one of these 'two-up and two-down' terraced houses, and receive a small sum of money in exchange for labouring twelve hours a day, excitedly they hurried from farms and fishing quays. In their bundles, they carried the controlling tenets of God and Bible. But these ambiguous concepts, like the immigrants' ingrained frugality, were about to be tested.

For those settlers to the new towns and cities quickly discovered that the promised land of milk and honey was actually yielding only beer and bread. Those who prospered had some education or were callous and quick of wit. Nevertheless, the evolution of manual labour as a commodity contributed to a stability that could only be dreamt of in the old days of subsistence farming. The creation of factories sheltered the workforce from climate conditions, best described as brutal, and the fixed exchange rate between employer and employee created equilibrium the envy of the world. For example, in 1872 the unemployed in Riverton numbered less than 2% of the male population. Of course, if they didn't work, they didn't eat, and the thought of starvation was the perfect stimulus.

But the descendants of those farmer and fisher folk – and who managed to survive beyond childhood - settled into a routine as rigid as the spring-wound clock on the long wooden shelf above the black-leaded fire grate. Female shop assistants were bred, housewives darned socks, and the men went to the pub on Friday night and kicked the shit out of each other.

Factory life was, the new underclass agreed, better than wallowing in mud, or suffering frostbite – or worse - at sea. The workshops provided heat during the long hours; rented houses had backyards, running water and flushing lavatories. It was no longer necessary to bury it, and, with a further nod towards hygiene, communal bathhouses were built with dark green walls and cleansed with putrid disinfectant. But there were downsides: dogs and cats were allowed to roam the streets, defecating and copulating like rabbits in spring. The lavatory pans were a godsend, ideal for drowning resultant kittens and puppies.

The incidence of street rape and robbery, at first endemic, was moderated by the introduction of gas-lit streets, shift work and prostitution. But the stinking back

FEMALE VORTEX
(civilization?)

by

Bernard W Roberts

Published by

ninagiotti@btinternet.com

A catalogue record of this book is available at the British Library

i

The *Female Vortex (civilization?)* was first published by Nina Giotti alleyways remained unlit, convenient locations for interacting with other men's wives (in theory, unmarried women were still under God's and mothers' control. In reality: please read on).

Committees were formed and later legitimized by central governments. Slowly, systems evolved to keep the plebs quiet. And entrepreneurs rushed to meet their needs and wants. In Riverton, there was a butcher, a baker, and an undertaker – the latter prepaid by instalments. One shop recharged wireless batteries (for sixpence), another hired out magazines (again for sixpence). There was a herbalist, three beer shops, two back-entry bookies, a dog racing track and a dancehall. And Riverton also had two pubs and three pie shops. They thought they had it made.

But then, in 1914, most village men between the ages for 18 and 40 went to war. During that four-year war, religion prevailed and churches prospered. God was still considered an all-seeing entity - and on our side! He quenched the sexual urges of those young (and old) women left behind, but couldn't protect the millions who perished on the battlefields and at sea. Of course, some men survived the war, but often not in one piece; and Riverton was not immune from these spectacles.

With trade unions making unreasonable demands on mill owners' huge profits, at the beginning of the 1930s, unemployment had climbed to more than 17%. But by the time Frederick O'Flaherty was born in 1934, things were looking up. And this trend continued until 1939 when war was declared on Germany, and demand for armaments and barbed wire created the illusion of economic growth.

Frederick O'Flaherty was born in Riverton, but his ancestors had arrived from Ireland, Scotland, Wales, and the Isle of Man. His father, Joseph O'Flaherty, had a more clearly defined lineage. He had been born and bred in County Mayo where he and his fifteen brothers followed the family tradition of digging up the peat bogs at Ceide Fields. Unlike his siblings, Joseph was romantic, and word of amorous women living on the other side of the Irish Sea reached his ears.

It was Thursday evening, 7 August 1930, when confirmed bachelor Joseph O'Flaherty arrived in England. Carrying his worldly possessions in a brown paper bag, he was looking for sexual fulfillment. It was his good fortune, as Mrs O'Flaherty now recounts (contentiously), that he met her the very next day.

Although the church was not licenced to sell liquor at its weekly shindig, Father O'Keefe had, as usual, erected a collapsible table from which to sell his homemade brew. Delores Higginbottom, as she was then known, was working as a barmaid (unknown to her father, the priest and her mother had a close relationship). Those in the know argued Delores's employment was nepotistic, others, not in the know, invoked the Peter Principle. But the criticism was cruel and fuelled by jealousy: the poor girl had had very little education and, at twenty-five, little prospect of finding a husband. However, a spark was ignited when she handed Joe more money in change than he had handed her for the purchase of a jug of ale. Later, lying in the presbytery, they fell into each other's arms.

Being Catholics, neither Joseph nor Delores believed in contraception (at that stage). And that Friday night, or the next (but she did admit it could have been any evening of the following week), she conceived. With what some would consider undue haste - and not being familiar with her promiscuous past - Joe agreed to her father's demand. They were married four weeks after she missed her period.

Delores's father was employed by the council as a wage clerk, and being responsible for calculating overtime earnings for grade two staff, wielded considerable influence above his station. As a consequence, he was able to get his new son-in-law a job with the tramways department on £2.10.8p a week. Delores's mother also wielded some influence through her connections with the Holy Name Church, and was instrumental in Joe and Delores securing a 'two-up and two-down' terraced house on Primrose Street at a subsidized rent of two shillings a week.

Siobhan, weighing-in at nine pounds, was born on Mayday 1931. After that date, Mrs O'Flaherty always went to bed with a Dumas Cap wedged inside her vagina. Uncomfortable, it was better than the alternative, she argued with herself. But it was not foolproof, and, as a consequence of wear and tear, the second child, Frederick (Fred), was born three years later, quickly followed by two more boys, Riordan and Patrick. Although Father O'Keefe baptized all four children in the stone font of the Holy Name, it was only Fred who later questioned the integrity of religious indoctrination.

In 1940, the call to arms came again, and most Riverton men between the ages of 18 and 41 volunteered to serve in the armed forces. Being colour blind, flat-footed and overweight, Fred's father was turned down for war duty (it was not racial prejudice: the Irish were not excluded). He was happy in his work as a tram conductor, and, when turned down by the army, his celebrations lasted three days and nights.

By the end of 1942 the enlistment age had widened from 41 to 51. Overnight, Riverton's socio-sexual landscape changed: most sexually active men had disappeared. But their young and middle-aged spouses remained. There were, of course, social opportunities for lonely female souls: gossiping at the corner shop, pushing the pram in the public park, or a visit to picture house (with Grandma minding the kids). But these distractions were no substitute for sex – and God was no longer the force He was in 1914.

In July 1944, American airmen arrived in nearby Wallington. Pictures of bronzed young men in stylish beige gabardine uniforms, soft hats, and dancing shoes filled the front page of the weekly Riverton Times. The local girls were excited by rumours that these men, referred to in the press as GIs, were willing to exchange silk stockings and chewing gum in return for just a grope.

News of this USAAF installation reached the ears of the Riverton battalion serving in France. Being paid a fifth of what those American GIs were being paid – and sweating in thick khaki uniforms, tin hats and hobnail boots – the swaddies felt acutely disadvantaged. Although there was considerable unrest, much to the relief of Colonel Crispin Pettigrew, only three Riverton men went AWOL. Those three knew they had married whores but were, like many men, possessive. But nobody in the battalion worried when they learned a prisoners-of-war camp had been built in Riverton itself, a few hundred yards from those lonely and hungry terraced streets. Mistakenly, they thought the Italians would be kept behind bars.

Frederick (Fred) O'Flaherty, as recorded above, was born into this community, and this is the true story of his rise and fall.

SUNDAY 3 SEPTEMBER 1939

The pages of this morning's newspapers were filled with foreboding. It seemed inevitable that the Hitler-led wars in Europe would one day cross the English Channel. But Fred's mother had more pressing matters on her mind: her husband's drinking!

After saying Seven Hail Mary's, she went to the Holy Name. The church was unusually busy and, after mass and queuing for fifteen minutes, she reached the confessional box. Naturally, the details of the exchange between Delores and Father O'Keefe remain secret. But Father O'Keefe was so incensed that he could be heard effing and blinding.

Although his very-long relationship with Delores's mother ended in 1938 - the same day her father caught them in the act of fellatio in the sacristy - the priest still felt a sort of paternal guardianship.

Dolores arrived home just before eleven and passed on Father O'Keefe's message. With the threat of excommunication hanging over him, Joe sat quietly listening to the BBC on the wireless. At eleven-fifteen, Chamberlain began his much anticipated speech, but even when he announced 'this country is at war with Germany', Joe remained impassive.

Like most married men, there were moments when Joe wished he'd remained single, and this was of them. The wet nappies draped over the fireguard were filling the house with steam and a mix of ammonia and methane gases. The four children were shouting, arguing, fighting, and driving him crazy. And, he reflected, the financial demands of the four children were a drain on his weekly wage. Those former thoughts of digging peat on the rain-soaked Ceide Fields were suddenly transformed to sun splashed afternoons. Leisurely evenings spent with his fifteen brothers drinking Guinness in Mac's Bar on Ballycastle's Main Street. If only…

And then there was the wife, perspiring and bent over a sink full of yet more nappies and releasing her own particular odours. Until this day, open criticism of his lifestyle had only come from Delores – and then as suggestions, not orders. But it was the way she said it, rather than what she said. The criticisms by his in-laws had been less direct but not entirely veiled. And his father-in-law never failed to remind him that without his help, he wouldn't be working on the trams. The criticism by the church was at an entirely different level. He decided he would do something about it, like reapplying for the army.

MONDAY 11 SEPTEMBER 1939

Fred, with an unexplained desire to learn things new, was looking forward to the start of his first year at St. Aloysius School. Not yet six, he was reading books from the library, and commenting on current affairs. His family found this phenomenon strange and perplexing: after the age of 14, neither of his parents had read anything other than a newspaper.

However, Fred was not happy at being accompanied to school by an irritable Grandma on his first day. But, as Mrs Higginbottom forcibly explained, his mother was otherwise pre-occupied. Malleable by nature, he held her hand.

Fred's mother, Delores, was again accompanying her near neighbour, Ivy Porter, to the Infirmary for her monthly electroshock treatment. When she wasn't threatening to throw herself under a tram, Mrs Porter was doing handstands on the street, her heels against the wall, her skirt tucked in her knickers.

Fred's father objected to his wife accompanying the woman to the hospital, saying Mrs Porter should be locked-up in the lunatic asylum.

The above is a brief introduction to Frederick O'Flaherty's family. But, as you know, neighbours and events can also influence a child's development. This biography, then, would be imperfect if it failed to identify and examine some of those formative and external influences.

With Tommy Timpson and Harry Piddel, six-year-old Fred was rolling marbles in the gulley where the cobbled roadway abutted the raised flagged pavement. Mrs Ivy Porter, who lived three doors away from Fred's parents' home, stood on the doorstep of her terraced house. Dressed in a heavy brown dressing gown with pink carpet slippers, she took the cigarette from her mouth, threw it into the road, and shouted:

"Fred, come here; I want to show you something." Fred looked across, unsure how to respond to this strange demand. And he was within hitting distance of a large multi-coloured marble. "Come on, I've got something to show you."

She led the boy into the house, passing through the parlour where a large, brown, corduroy settee dominated the small room. In the sparsely furnished back room, she asked him to sit down. He did as he was told, and sat on the three-legged stool beside the black fireplace. Fine grey ash spilled out onto the hearth.

"I won't be a minute," she said, leaving the room.

He listened to the woman's heavy footsteps on the wooden staircase that was partitioned from the living room. He wanted to run out and be with his friends in the street but thought that would be disrespectful. There was a movement in the ash, and, for a moment, Fred's attention was on the contrasting black beetle. He watched it slowly crawl out of the ash and onto the tiled hearth, but, with the sound of Mrs Porter's returning footsteps on the stairs, it quickly disappeared back into the grate. The tall woman reappeared carrying a sword inside a long silver and ivory-

10

inlaid scabbard. But Fred was uncomfortable sitting on the unbalanced stool; afraid he might fall into the hearth, he stood up.

"Our Jack broke the leg on that stool. He's a stupid fool," she said. "Let's sit in the parlour. It's more comfortable there."

She led Fred back into the front room.

"Sit down," she said, and Fred sat in the soft chair in the corner of the room. Sitting on the settee, she placed the sword across her knees.

"This belonged to a German officer. Mr Porter brought it back from the war when he came home on his last leave. Come here, Fred. You can touch it. Come on; don't be shy. It's a real sword that killed people. It's still got blood on it!" Slowly, she withdrew the long sword and placed it with its elaborately decorated scabbard across her knees.

Fred was hesitant. He had overheard his parents discussing Mrs Porter and the electric shock treatment she was undergoing for repeatedly threatening to walk in front of a tram. His mother was sympathetic, blaming Mrs Porter's husband. Fred knew his mother regularly accompanied Mrs Porter to the hospital where she witnessed her being strapped down, gagged and her hair standing on end. Fred's father, Joe, always questioned how Mr Porter could be the cause of her depression when he was 'hundreds of bleedin' miles away fighting for King and country. She's just a nutcase, and if she stands in front of my tram, I 'ope we soddin' get 'er.' His response was always the same whenever her name was mentioned. Fred had also often heard his mother say Mrs Porter left the hospital looking like a zombie. But that was the impression the local children had of her – even on non-hospital days.

"Come here, Fred," she said, softly, encouragingly.

Fred looked for signs of violence in her eyes, but saw only kindness. He stood up but stopped short of where the woman was sitting. She reached out and took his hand, drawing him gently towards her. He stood by the woman's knees but was confused. He'd seen pictures of soldiers with fancy swords, but they were Japanese. He was uncomfortable being alone and so close to this grown up in her own home.

"Touch it."

Fred ran his hand over the inlaid patterns on the sword's handle but couldn't see any traces of blood on the highly polished blade. Smiling, and staring at Fred, she ran her hand down the flat side of the long blade.

"They chopped heads off with this," she said, widening her eyes and pulling back the sides of her mouth.

She slid the sword back in its scabbard and put it down on the brown linoleum-covered floor.

"Can I go now, Mrs Porter?"

"Yes, Fred, but don't tell anyone you've seen the sword. It's our secret."

A few months after this incident, Mrs Porter moved house to Daffodil Street, another rented property just three streets away. The houses were almost identical, and although neighbours couldn't understand her reasoning, it seemed to be in keeping with her irrational behaviour.

WHIT SUNDAY 1 JUNE & MONDAY 2 June 1941

Three of the six retail shops lining the main road between Primrose Street and Daffodil Street were no longer trading. The owners of these three shops had been enlisted and were now fighting the Germans in Europe.

Mortise locks and double padlocks secured the menswear shop and adjoining bicycle shop. And their remaining stocks were still displayed behind large plate-glass windows. The third shop, situated on the corner of Primrose Street, once sold secondhand goods. However, its remaining stock having no value, the front door had been left inadequately secured. And, within an hour of Isaac Goldman locking up, the shop was ransacked. But an old, high-backed, lounge chair remained. While the arms and back of the green vinyl-covered chair were in good order, the seat had collapsed, exposing four rusty coil springs.

Although Joe had thought for a few minutes about reapplying for the army, he decided against the idea. Instead, he became an Air Raid Warden. But, tired after his eight-hour shift on the tram and three pints of bitter beer at the Bull's Head, it was always a struggle for him to get ready for his warden duties.

Reluctantly, he put the webbing strap of his first aid kit over his left shoulder and the strap of the gasmask case over the other. Delores helped him slide the armband up his left sleeve. Having checked the battery of his torch and tested the whistle, he put the tin helmet on his head. It was this last act that gave him a sense of importance. As a warden, he had authority to enter a house if an internal light was visible from the street. He also had permission to reprimand any person lighting a match on the street.

At the junction of Primrose Street and Main Street, and with a bucket of sand at his feet, he leaned against the wall of the former second-hand shop. Filling his pipe with tobacco, he looked around: the blackout seemed to be complete. All the streetlights were off, and all the windows, as far as he could see, blacked out. Wispy grey clouds were floating across the night sky, occasionally revealing the pitted face of the full moon. He was entranced by the beauty of the moonlight glinting off the two sets of tramlines running along the middle of the road.   He felt proud at his connection with these examples of modern engineering.   But he was also reminded of what his co-worker had told him about Riverton.

Archie, the regular driver of the circular-route tram on which Joe collected fares, had, he once explained, filled several notebooks with the history of Riverton.   On the first few rest periods (before the pubs opened), Joe liked to sit with him, having a smoke while listening to his tales of olden days. It was without a hint of self-importance that Archie told Joe how the Romans had built this road and that it ran east to west.   Fascinated at the recollection, Joe looked down as the moonlight glanced off the shiny cobbled road.   He was surprised how, after all those hundreds of years, the cobbles had retained their shape and polish.   At that very moment the town clock struck midnight.   It was a magical moment for Joe. And, as he counted the clock's chimes, he thought back to his youth and those long days of digging up the peat on the wind-blown bogs of Ceide Fields.   'No, sir,' he said aloud to himself, there were no pubs in County Mayo selling Chesters bitter beer. No pubs with the beauty of the Bull's Head with its cushioned seats, electric lights, polished wood counter and the likes of big-breasted Edna honestly filling pint pots to the rim.

Thinking about his moments of leisure, Fred decided it was time for a smoke. At that very moment, the whirring sound of the air raid siren began hooting up through the musical scales. But Joe, knowing that they were always erring on the side of caution, struck a match. 'Bliss,' he thought, while subconsciously recognizing that he had just broken an ARP cardinal rule.

Reflecting that another warden may be in the area, he walked through the open door of the former second hand shop and, placing his upturned helmet on the chair's springs, carefully lowered himself. Whether the German pilot, flying at 10,000 feet, had seen the ignited match is debatable, but what is not in contention is the fact that the pilot was using Knickebein radio beams to guide his payload. And the Luftwaffe had a proven accuracy record, with each bomb landing within 100 yards of the midline of the beam.

Joe inhaled deeply on his pipe, wondering what was making the whistling noise. Fortunately, he was still sitting in the chair with its high back to the window when the bomb landed. All the plate glass windows of the six shops shattered into tiny fragments, and Joe and chair were thrown violently across the room. It was some minutes before he was able to rise to his feet. He staggered through the dust and looked out: the explosion had ripped up hundreds of cobbles and water was gushing out of a massive crater in the road. Twisted bicycles and shredded menswear lay scattered on the pavements. But his heart missed a beat when he saw the twisted tramlines standing upright in the middle of the road.

Delores had responded promptly to the siren, hurrying her four children downstairs where, huddled beneath a grey blanket, they crouched under the stairs. Fingering her rosary beads, she had just finished reciting the *Apostle's Creed* and said the fist line of *Our Father* when the crown-topped chimney crashed through the slate roof before bouncing off the double bed.

It was in the darkness under the stairs that Delores first realized that her eldest son was destined to be somebody special when he grew up.

"Don't worry, Mam. If they bomb the house, I'll rebuild it," seven-year old Fred said, patting his mother's back.

11 NOVEMBER 1942

Although in his third year at St. Aloysius R.C. School, Fred was still fearful of teachers wearing all black or black and white habits. In particular, he and other children complained about the teaching methods of seventy-six-year-old Sister Margaret.

"She always shouting, waiving a long rod and accusing me of copying," Fred had said, responding to his mother's questioning.

Sister Margaret had been recalled from retirement due to the shortage of teachers caused by the war and related conscription. She had always been a strict enforcer of discipline but her impatience with slow learners and copycats had grown exponentially with age. She was not responsive to complaints and spoke to parents in the same derogatory way she spoke to her pupils.

Collecting Fred from school, Delores confronted Sister Margaret.

"Of course I shout," the Sister replied, defiantly and with her face close to Delores's. "He's a clever boy, but too clever for his own good. He's got to learn not to copy. He must be smuggling papers into class because his answers are exactly as written in the textbook. We don't know how he does it and he won't tell us."

"He's got a good memory, Sister." Delores replied, stepping back a pace.

Avoiding further confrontation, the nun asked how she came to have such a lovely Irish name. Delores explained that her husband came from County Mayo.

"Oh, County Mayo!" Sister replied. "The most wonderful place on earth." Delores was set back by this sudden rapture. The old nun explained: "That's where I was born. I knew an O'Flaherty family very well. We lived in Ballycastle back then."

"Why, that's where me husband's family live," Delores gushed.

"What's your good husband's father's first name?"

"Odhran; the same name as me husband's granddad."

"Saints be praised!" the old nun said, raising her hands and face to the sky. She waved her fingers. "Odhran O'Flaherty from Ballycastle. Praise the Lord, isn't it a small world? How old would grandpa be now?"

"He'll be in his seventies, I think. I've only seen an old photo, but it was brown and very cracked."

"Aye, he'll be the same age as me. Seventy-six last birthday. We went to the same school, you know. We sat in the same class. Bless his heart! Is he still alive?"

So engrossed were they, they didn't notice the fog descending. Suddenly it was total and they couldn't see a finger before their faces.

The old nun invited Delores and Fred to join her for Vesper's, but Delores declined the offer and they parted the best of friends. With a hand on her chest, the Sister had promised to personally tutor young Fred.

Lost in the fog, the normal fifteen-minute walk took Delores and Fred an hour to reach home. But Delores was pleased with herself for having had the courage to confront a teacher. And she couldn't wait to tell her husband about the connection with County Mayo.

But, more importantly, the meeting was a turning point in the education of Fred O'Flaherty.

SATURDAY 4 AUGUST 1943

Every Tuesday morning during the school year, Fred and his pal, Tommy, had marched half-a-mile, rain or shine, with the other boys to the public swimming baths. The school swimming lessons were compulsory.

Before entering the heated pool, the twenty-five boys had to first sit one behind the other in the fifteen-foot long bathtub sharing small squares of carbolic soap. If they were not well lathered, they stayed in the tub until they were. When considered clean, they stood under cold showers. Only then were they allowed to enter the swimming pool. Although the instructor was aggressive, Fred and Tommy always looked forward to Tuesday mornings. And as a result of their enthusiasm, and the strict regime, they were awarded certificates for swimming a full length of the pool.

On Friday 17th July, the school closed for the summer holidays, and, without money, they were deprived of the opportunity to swim. However, recently, they heard that the canal was a great place for swimming, at least in summer. And, being a costly tram ride away from the built-up area, it was isolated.

Fred regularly took advantage of one of the few benefits of having a tram-conductor father. On Saturday afternoons, he occasionally sat in the tram. Without paying, he travelled around Riverton until he was bored. And, on those excursions, he watched his father collecting money, punching out tickets, and, in his strong County Mayo dialect, frightening the life out of unruly children. He was proud of his father's authority. Sometimes, Fred was even allowed to ping the ticket machine; but best of all, when there was a double-decker tram in service, he'd sit upstairs with the smokers. And this day, his father was working on a double decker.

Fred and Tommy sat on the front wooden seat of the upper deck. From this elevated perspective they had a panoramic view of Riverton. It seemed that the shops lining both sides of Main Street went on forever. And at least three-quarters of them were open for business. Most of those shops not trading were closed because their owners were now wearing military uniforms and dispersed all over Europe and North Africa.

The continuing expansion of factories around Riverton had sucked in unskilled workers on an unprecedented scale. From a nineteenth century farming community of less than a hundred, the population of Riverton was now estimated at 14,300, less those 3,000 men fighting the Germans. The rental houses, built to accommodate the expanding workforce, were small, identical and so numerous that the council had run out of sensible street names. To meet the needs and wants of this congested district, hundreds of retail units had been built along both sides of Main Street. But now those shops still trading faced additional difficulties.

The shortage of goods to sell was matched by the shortage of money. In these austere circumstances, shopkeepers could no longer stand behind their counters and offer their produce at unaffordable prices. They had to be out and about checking their competitors' prices. And this wasn't difficult: they were all chalking the discounted prices on their shop windows, and trading twelve hours a day (but closed by church edict on Sundays).

Fred and Tommy stared down at the crowds and merchandise filling the pavements. Women and children avoiding each other as well as sidestepping the pots and pans, linoleum rolls, fruit and vegetables, flowers, and fish swimming in metal tanks stacked outside shop windows.

Tommy Timpson also lived on Primrose Street, just six doors from Fred's house. But Tommy's father was dead. Riven by consumption, he had wasted away. With five children – and Tommy was the eldest - the pressures on Mrs Timpson were etched in her face. Not yet thirty, she had lost all her teeth; her skin was yellow and her eyes sunken.

As a family, they were underfed and ragged. And their house reflected the same degree of destitution. The flagged floors of their two downstairs rooms were uncovered, and the once gloss-painted walls now a faded yellow. There was no furniture in the front room, just the smell of decay. And when the front door was initially opened, that peculiar dank smell leaked out. Fred's mother said Mrs Timpson had given up in despair, but his father called her a lazy cow. Fred agreed with his mother's assessment. Mrs Timpson always offered him a piece of toast when calling for Tommy on his sway to school. And he always politely declined the offer, holding his breath.

Like Mrs Timpson, Tommy never complained about their dire circumstances, but he was embarrassed when regularly sent home from school to have the bedbugs removed. Fred found this amusing, but didn't say so. However, he was careful not to get too close to Tommy in the mornings.

"Look, there's Mrs Pickles, our teacher," Tommy shouted, standing up and putting his head against the window.

"Wonder what she's doing in Riverton?" Fred queried, also standing at the window. "Do you think she lives near here?"

"Naw, she's just shopping. Probably lives where they've got gardens and flowers."

Fred and Tommy had just sat down when the rattling tram screeched to a halt. Suddenly stationary, it shook as simultaneously the cacophony of shattering glass and screams filled the lower deck. Fred and Tommy hurried down the winding steps.

"Blimey, a coal cart's come in through the window," Tommy shouted, putting a hand before his open mouth.

Fred's father was helping a woman along the passageway. Blood was dripping from her nose; she was crying. Bemused, and still seated below the broken window, an old man's lower body and legs were buried under a pile of putrid coke. The lorry had reversed into the side of the tram, pushing a corner of the flat-loader through the window. A sack of coke had split open, spilling its contents on the road and into the tram.

Tommy, ahead of Fred, pointed out of the window. A carthorse lay on the cobbled roadway, its body twisted inside the wooden shafts and two of its hooves sticking up in the air. It was shaking. Disconnected from the coal cart, the damaged tram was driven off the main line and along lines curving onto parallel rails.

Standing with the rest of the disembarked passengers, Fred and Tommy stared at the injured horse. Still on its side, and trapped by the heavy shafts, it was wide-eyed and frothing at the mouth. And then a small green van appeared with the word VET printed in white. A small man, wearing a long white coat and black bowler hat, emerged. He was carrying a short rifle. The crowd watched in silence as he put the barrel to the horse's head. Although anticipated, the gunshot caused the gathering to collectively lurch and gasp, but only one woman shrieked. Fred expressed surprise that the horse was still shaking when they departed on the replacement tram.

It was mid afternoon when they reached the canal and still pleasantly warm. But this section of the canal was a viaduct, too narrow for swimming and suspended high above an extensive network of interconnecting railway lines. Tommy said the height was making him dizzy.

In search of the wider section - that they'd been told existed - they walked away from the bridge, following the overgrown towpath. And then, just as the older boys had predicted, the canal widened out, perfect was swimming from one side to the other.   However, the black waters were partly shaded by a high and continuous factory wall.

Undeterred, they undressed and climbed into their one-piece swimming costumes, leaving their clothes in two neat bundles on their towels.

Sitting on the side of the canal, they tested the temperature with their feet. Not as warm as the water at the swimming baths, but here, unlike the public baths on Saturdays, there was no admission fee. And they had the canal all to themselves. Cautiously, they lowered their bodies into the stagnant water, but when their feet touched the silted bottom, debris rose to the surface. Unconcerned, they swam across to the comparative warmth on the sunny side of the canal.

For fifteen minutes, they laughed and splashed each other, but then Fred swam onto a large, pink carcass. Furless and without a head, it was suspended just below the surface. Panicking, they swam back to the towpath, hauling themselves out of the water as if being pursued by the dead dog. Anxious to remove every last drop of the polluted water from their bodies, they hurriedly searched for their towels and clothes. They walked up and down the towpath, but in vain: their belongings had mysteriously disappeared.

SATURDAY 15 JULY 1944

The Jones family lived in the house directly across the street from the O'Flaherty's. But they had arrived in Primrose Street six years before Joseph and Delores O'Flaherty. Mr Dylan Jones, educated for a year beyond the statutory leaving age of 14, had secured a job as an order clerk at the Indian Rubber factory on the outskirts of Riverton, a fifteen-minute tram ride away.

Both Megan and Dylan took great pride in their appearances. Every night Megan slept with her long black hair rolled in paper curlers, and covered her face in calamine lotion. In the morning, she sprinkled talcum powder under her arms. And, unlike her neighbours, changed her pinafore twice a week.

Dylan always kept his black hair short, parted in the middle and covered in oil. But he went to work wearing a black trilby. Having seen Humphrey Bogart in *Casablanca*, he always pulled down the brim of his hat over his right eye. One of the best-dressed men on Primrose Street, he always wore a black suit and the same white shirt and navy tie. Conscientious, he worked six days a week and never took holidays. However, and like his wife, his personality was complex: in the company of men, he was always softly spoken and obliging. But he showed only intolerance to his wife, as though he suspected something untoward but lacked proof.

Due to her introversion, Mrs Jones true inner-self rarely emerged; astonishing really for someone born in the Rhondda. As a child, Megan promised her pit foreman father that she would never leave the Valleys. It was Dylan who persuaded her. She wished she'd never gone with her parents on that fateful camping holiday to Ogmore-by-Sea, or more especially to the chip shop where Dylan was frying fish. It rained nearly every day of the weeklong holiday, but on the one day the sun appeared, she had sat on the beach with Dylan eating his dad's chips from a newspaper. Then they threw crumpled newspapers at each other playing catch-the-ball. And later she ran barefoot, laughing as the incoming tide followed her onto the pebbly sand. That was the best day of the week. She thought it would always be like that.

She was homesick for Wales. And she longed for the fern hills, Caerphilly cheese and the community spirit of the Valleys. But it was the traditions that Megan missed most: the sight of black-faced men returning from the pits, the sun glinting off their teeth, and the rattling tin Billy cans hanging from their belts; the all-male voice choir singing on winter Monday nights, their breaths visibly rising with the scales. Her father, grandfather and great grandfather had all worked in the same pit. There had been many accidents, she had to admit, but even when her grandfather lost his testicles after being kicked by a pit pony, her affinity with coal prevailed.

When Dylan and Megan moved to Riverton in 1924, they had great difficulty understanding their neighbours. And their neighbours also had difficulty understanding them. But in the realm of business, Megan was not as stupid as she appeared. Her aunt Gwenda had once rented a market stall in Pontypridd and, as a child, Megan had helped sell her aunt's homemade cakes. But Megan's entrepreneurial skills were aided by a Machiavellian cunning concealed by serenity, a soft voice and a refusal to argue. If ginger-headed Ralph Biddles, the coalman, hadn't opened his mouth in the Bull's Head, nobody would have known that Megan, in return for two extra bags of coal each month, had regularly made herself available on the kitchen floor. Fortunately for her, the stains and coal dust on the linoleum were easily removed with the mop; and her husband was teetotal.

Despite all those years of free coal, it was seven years before Megan conceived. Her ginger-haired daughter Blodwyn, weighing just over six pounds, was born 19 July 1931. Dylan Jones, narrow-faced and Methodist, nurtured Blodwyn with extreme care. At the chapel, she was taught right from wrong. Promiscuity was definitely wrong. But there was never a need to reinforce the preacher's sermons with threats of punishment. Blodwyn always put her hand on her heart and promised to respect God and chastity.

Mr Jones was particularly proud of his young daughter: she had been awarded the Brownie's *Skills Badge* before she reached eleven. And at twelve added the Girl Guide badges *First Aid* and *Sock*. And as a demonstration of parental love, she always darned one of her father's socks while her mother reluctantly darned the other. But, in search of praise, she learned to darn quicker and better than her mother. But she was in her teens when Fred first saw her naked body.

It had been exceptional hot. And the anticipated cooling down in the evening hadn't materialized. Delores insisted on accompanying Joe to the Bull's Heads and, worn down by the humidity, he reluctantly agreed.

While Fred's mother and father were lounging on cushioned chairs, enveloped in tobacco smoke and surrounded by pints of beer, Mr and Mrs Jones, were sitting on wooden chairs listening to Gwyndaf Thomas preach at the Wesleyan Chapel on Collybark Road.

In search of the erotic literature that he knew his father kept hidden, but read by candlelight when sitting in the outside lavatory, Fred had gone into his parents' bedroom. He looked under the pillows, mattress and bed. Nothing! But when he passed the window, he noticed a movement in the Joneses' bedroom directly across the street. Somebody was lying on the Joneses' double bed. Crouching down, he peered over the window ledge. Blodwyn was lying on her back with three pillows behind her head. She was as naked as the day she was born, except for the ginger hair under her arms and around her crotch. Fred couldn't believe his eyes. Because she was naturally overweight, he had no idea she had breasts like that.

With the back of his hand, he wiped away the steam building up on the window. Somebody was standing next to the bed wearing a striped shirt and black socks. To get a better view, Fred stood up and peered around the curtain. He had to refocus three times: it was Ernest Price, the boy who put the milk bottle on Joneses' doorstep at six o'clock every morning. Fred's heart was pounding as Ernest, still wearing his shirt and socks, climbed on top of Blodwyn and then pulled his shirt up around his waist. Fred gulped as he watched Ernest's naked pink bottom rising and falling. But he had no sooner started than he finished. Ernest stood up and hurriedly pulled on his trousers. Blodwyn sat upright in bed. She was looking up at Ernest and obviously saying something.

To look out of both eyes, Fred moved the other half of his head from behind the curtain. Blodwyn turned away from Ernest and looked straight at the window. She said something to Ernest; but, without following her gaze, he ran out of the room. Blodwyn walked slowly towards the window. Still naked, and with her hands on her hips, she put out her tongue. Fred went on his hands and knees and crawled out of the bedroom.

MONDAY 21 AUGUST 1944

It had been another hot day, and, for the Riverton inhabitants, the fear of bomb-laden German aircraft flying overhead had diminished. Their concerns were the V1 and V2 missiles that had been landing on London and the southeast for the past two weeks. Despite this unexpected twist favouring the Germans, the Pathe News films being shown nightly at the picture house were becoming increasingly positive. And most debated opinion concluded that the missiles did not have the power to reach the north of England.

The fear of being too far from a place to shelter in an air raid had been a constraint, particularly for households with children. In the early stages of the war, children had been restricted to playing on the street where they lived. Enemy aircraft had previously targeted the factories to the north of Riverton, and parents considered it safer for the children to play on the south side, where the public park just happened to be located. And it had a brick 'summer house' with built-in wooden seats. But it was open to the elements on the side facing the narrow river.

According to the tram driver's historical narrative, the park had been created nearly a hundred years before, in 1852 to be precise. Worried by the increase in the number of children with rickets, Riverton's then fledgling council decided to do what other councils had been doing since 1847. They created a park on land that couldn't be used for any other purpose. The undulating grasslands sloped down to where a river meandered lazily over natural weirs.

To create a sense of countryside within the surrounding bricks and mortar, the council manually widened the river to accommodate two swans. But two days later they disappeared. Fencing was erected around the river, and two new swans, with clipped wings, were installed on the 24 December, but they too disappeared the same night. The council then spent money on river trout, but they went with the flow and swam away. Frustrated, they gave up on the wildlife idea.

However, cheap labour costs enabled the council to landscape the riverbanks and plant trees. And they covered a flattened area with razor sharp cinders and installed hazardous playground equipment. Although many children were regularly being admitted to hospital with broken limbs and head injuries, the council had run out of money. Nevertheless, as a testimony to Victorian engineering, those same dangerous swings, seesaw, slide and roundabout are still in use in Riverton Park today.

As a hobby, Archie, the tram driver, had spent years in the Riverton library reading yellowing copies of the *Penny Weekly*. And it was from this source that he paraphrased the interesting article relating to fornication in a public place. According to the police report, at nine o'clock on the evening of 10 June 1892, Jeremiah Aspinal and Annabel Shaw were caught with their pants down. They were allegedly seesawing in that very same children's playground. The Watch Committee was reported as being incensed, and the very next month installed insurmountable black railings around the whole of the park's perimeter.

Bill Bradshaw, a veteran of the Second Afghanistan War, was employed as park keeper and provided with a whistle and a heavy stick. And every day of the year, ten minutes before sunset, the matching heavy gates were padlocked and not reopened until eight in the morning. Repainted gloss black every five years, these railings remained in place for 48 years. Unlike the railings, the lethal metal playground equipment was not removed to help the war effort.

In 1940, the War Cabinet, faced with an embarrassing metal shortage, and with an urgent need to make bombs and bullets, requisitioned all iron gates, railings and non-essential metals. This had very little impact on the residents of Riverton as very few had gardens, or anything made of metal, other than old bikes and the pitted knockers on their front doors. However, when the park railings and gates were removed, it did offer opportunities for those activities first identified in 1892. But, as most men were away at war, they were opportunities missed. That is until 1944.

A short walk from this accessible oasis of shady nooks and overhanging trees, the enemy, offering tangible evidence of British success in Europe and North Africa, now inhabited Riverton's very own Italian POW camp. At first, few knew of its existence, but word soon spread among the hair-netted, meat-filling women at Todd's pie factory on Hay Lane.

Often ignorant of young children's capacity to absorb information – or just careless - parents and grandparents repeatedly, but unwisely, discussed, in their presence, the latest gossip. And when parents whisper, their children are more attentive. Mrs Packer, who also lived on Primrose Street, was rumoured to fraternize with the 'Ities' – as the Italian prisoners of war were referred to. She was, therefore, often the subject of street-corner debate. Thirty-year old Mrs Packer looked - to Fred and his pals, at least – much older than her declared age. Having children under the age of sixteen she was, as the War Act allowed, excused from work.

Thin, stooped, bespectacled and always with the look of having lost something, she did not seemed to be the sort of woman in search of passion. Nevertheless, she dutifully hurried to the school to collect her young children and then confined them to the house. She was a doting mother, buying comic books, puzzles - and even a monopoly game. But there was a method in this expenditure.

At first, her neighbours couldn't understand why, on warm summer evenings, she wore the same heavy red overcoat. Always carrying a wicker basket, they at first assumed she was doing some late shopping.

Walking south from Mrs Packer's house to the park could be measured in minutes. Walking north from the POW camp to the park about the same. At dusk, it was here in the municipal park that international relations took on a new meaning.

Like the dogs and cats, the children of Riverton had, from a young age, a licence to roam - but under strict instructions not to interact with the opposite sex. It was decreed by government, church and society that babies born out of wedlock brought shame on the family and, accordingly, were officially identified as 'bastards'. With little motor traffic, and with most (male) child molesters now conscripted, the kids were free to roam – but only within those parameters that allowed them to be home before dark.

And after school, the park was the perfect location for the boys to carry out their war games - especially in the remote and overgrown corner where the park ended against a moss-covered stonewall. Here, the river arrived though a dark tunnel under a road bridge, bringing with it an unexplained smell that few could tolerate. The seclusion suited Fred and his pal Tommy.

Concealed in the heavily laden lower branches of an ash tree overhanging the riverbank, the two ten-year olds hid from the perceived enemy. Each with a water pistol, they were ready for any attack from the Germans or Italians.

"Enemy!" Tommy said, as a man wearing a pale grey uniform walked down the grassy bank. He was walking directly towards them.

"I'm not ready yet," Fred replied, moving to a thicker branch. "I'll tell you –"

"Keep quiet, Fred. There's a real Itie coming...."

They couldn't believe their eyes. They'd only ever seen these POWs at a distance on the road encircling the park; never walking on the grass. And now they were almost in touching distance of an enemy soldier.

The man sat down on the long grass and took a black and brown packet from his trouser pocket. With his little finger curled, he carefully plucked out an oval-shaped cigarette. Fred, whose grandfather polluted his houses with the same stinking Pasha brand of Turkish cigarettes, nudged Tommy and pointed to the slim packet in the man's hand. Drawing deeply, the Italian blew a perfectly formed circle and the expanding ring of grey smoke slowly rose up into the green tree. Had the POW watched its ascent, he may have seen Fred and Tommy holding their noses.

"Look, Fred, is that..." Tommy whispered.

"Yeah!" Fred acknowledged.

"What's she doing down here?" Tommy asked, quietly scratching his head.

The POW stood up, greeting Mrs Packer with a kiss on the cheek. Putting down her wicker basket, she withdrew two thin grey towels and laid them down end to end on the grass. The Italian nodded his head towards the cigarette packet in his hand, but she declined the offer.

"In't it a nice day," she said, removing her red overcoat and placing it on the basket.

Holding his hands out, as though about to play an accordion, he raised his shoulders and turned the palms of his hands to the sky. Pulling back his face muscles, he proudly exposed his neat white teeth. He pointed a finger at the red coat, and raised a thumb.

Thinking he was expressing admiration for her dress sense, she smiled: "It were a Christmas present from me -" she began, but stopped in midsentence.

Pointing to the coat again and then to himself, the POW replied: "Luigi."

Mrs Packer shook her head so violently that her round-framed, black spectacles slipped own her nose.

"No, I can't give it you, Luigi. It's me best coat," she said, pushing the spectacles back up her nose.

Luigi did the accordion-playing gesture again and shrugged his shoulders. Inhaling deeply on the end of the cigarette, he threw away the stub. He pointed to the towels and then to himself again.

Getting concerned by his demands, she looked for a clue in his eyes. She had only met Luigi once before, and that was in Siforiana's ice-cream parlour where her friend had introduced him. He wasn't bad looking but there was something sinister about the way he stared. His small, close-together eyes and a permanent frown on his narrow forehead were not endearing. His skin was also darker than most of the Italians seen around the park. And he was tense, certainly not relaxed like Antonio, her regular lover, but now confined to barracks after a packet of Durex had been found during a routine camp search.

Betty Curran, her forty-year old, pie worker friend, who also lived on Primrose Street, had passed Luigi on to Mrs Packer. 'Bit of a 'andful but a good 'eart,' she had said. The arrival of hundreds of Italians had been a blessing for Betty. A short, ugly, humpbacked spinster in search of romance, she regularly visited Siforiana's, or walked around the camp's perimeter. All her life, ignored as an oddity, she was now enjoying numerous liaisons.

Luigi took another cigarette from the packet and struck a match on the sole of his boot. He put the cigarette in his mouth and held the flame before his face without lighting the cigarette. Through the flame, he stared at Mrs Packer. Now tense, she was relieved when he finally lit the cigarette and blew out the match. He offered her the cigarette, but she shook her head. He put an arm around her waist. Anticipating a kiss, she put her face close to his and closed her eyes. Turning his head away, he put the cigarette back in his mouth, inhaled and then blew another perfect smoke ring.

Tommy and Fred couldn't take their eyes of this courting ritual but couldn't understand what was going on.

Releasing his hold on Mrs Packer, he bent down and spread her red coat on the towels. Straightening up, he smiled broadly and stuck out his chest. Mrs Packer, now thinking she understood, responded: "I thought you was after me best coat." She forced a laugh.

Still holding the cigarette in one hand, he wrapped his other arm around her waist. He offered her the cigarette, but she again shook her head. After another quick drag on the cigarette, he held it above his head, and rubbed his nose on her cheek. The two boys couldn't make out where his interest lay.

"Amore," Luigi sighed.

"Amore," she replied.

"She can speak blinkin' Itie," Tommy whispered.

After inhaling very deeply once again, he released his hold on Mrs Packer. With the cigarette in one hand, he put the forefinger and thumb of his other hand in his mouth and sucked loudly. Thinking this was an Italian lovemaking ritual; she did the same. Frowning, he studied her face but smiled again. With the now wet finger and thumb, he squeezed out the burning end of the cigarette and put the stub back in the packet. With the packet back in his pocket, he drew her closer to him again, pushing a leg between her legs. Slowly, he lowered her until she was lying on the red coat.

"Amore," he said again, but now with an unusual amount of breath. Looking down at her, and with his mouth open, he let his jaw drop and half closed his eyelids. He sighed again.

Mrs Packer, now comfortably on her back, put her hands behind her head. Kneeling, Luigi tried to force her legs further apart, but she resisted, explaining: "Luigi, you Italians are fast. Don't rush me, you'll be givin' me 'iccups. I've not long since 'ad me tea."

But Luigi was impatient and, putting his mouth to her neck, began sucking. She relaxed and saliva dribbled from the corner of her mouth. With a sleeve of her coat, he wiped it away. Breathing heavily, she watched as he lowered his trousers. But then her attention was drawn to a movement in the tree above their heads. She looked at Luigi, now searching inside his underpants, then again at the tree. She screamed, pointing to the face staring down from between a cluster of leaves. Luigi sprang to his feet and, struggling to get back into his trousers, looked up. Tommy jumped down and ran up the incline with partly-dressed Luigi chasing after him.

"Come back, you leetle swine. I sleet your throat," Luigi shouted, trying to hold up his trousers.

Had he been properly dressed, the POW may have had no trouble catching the ten-year old. But Tommy also had the advantage of knowing the warren of back streets and alleyways that surrounded the park.

By the time Luigi returned, Mrs Packer and her possessions were gone. Fred, now higher in the tree, watched as Luigi, with English expletives Fred had yet to learn, stamped on the ground where the grass had been previously flattened. Lighting the unfinished cigarette, he blew another circle of smoke. Fred held his breath. Muttering incoherently, and much to Fred's relief, Luigi, with his head bowed, slowly walked away.

MONDAY 7 MAY 1945

'The war is over!'

When they heard the announcement on the wireless, Joe and Delores danced around the kitchen. Other than in bed, it was the first time they had made physical contact in ten years.

Overweight from unhealthy lifestyles and, consequently, breathless, they sat at the table and reminisced about the past five years of war, with Joe reflecting on the passage of time.

"It doesn't seem five minutes since the war started," Joe said, pouring the remains of a bottle of beer left over from Sunday night. "Well, it doesn't seem like that to me. Seems like a lifetime –and we was nearly killed!" Delores replied, high pitched but courageously taking the cup from her husband's hand. She put her thin lips to its rim.

Joe didn't react to the provocation. Of course, in normal circumstances, Delores would not have gone anywhere near his beer. But these were not normal circumstances. And Joe was feeling generous, perhaps with a shade of guilt. Neither Delores – nor anyone else, for that matter – knew that he might have been responsible for the bomb landing at the top of their street. But, fortunately, that was the only bomb that ever fell on Riverton. Delores was so excited she couldn't stop talking.

"And you, an Irishman from across the ocean, out risking your life three nights a week. Standing out in the rain and cold, protecting us English."

Joe had returned his Air Raid Warden uniform and accessories weeks ago but loved to talk (exaggerate) about his acts of 'bravery' when he patrolled the night streets. But, of course, he never mentioned to Delores that since 1942, the Bull's Head had been serving drinks all through the night, catering especially for the thirty local wardens in need of refreshment.

As a badge of honour, Joe retained the Warden pin-badge, now in the left lapel of his tramways-issue, black, serge jacket. He was equally proud of the badge in his other lapel, representing ten-years service with the

Norwester Corporation. But the related wage rise had been deferred for at least twelve months.

Despite this setback and hardships of the past five years - and the rationing and food shortages that seemed to be going from bad to worse – it had not been all downhill for the O'Flaherty family: they've had a few strokes of good luck.

Joe's warm-hearted, youngest brother Eamonn, had also deserted the peat bogs, moving north of the border to Belfast. Working as a packer at Gallaher's, he never forgot any of his siblings' birthdays. And – as usual on his birthday – Joe received a small package of tobacco.

But more importantly, four months ago - on the morning of the second of January, to be precise - Delores's eighty-six year old paternal Granny was found in the backyard. She must have just put the washing out on New Year's Day when she slipped on the ice. Her grey long johns and red flannelette nightshirt were still hanging from a string stretched across the yard. Like Granny, the garments were frozen stiff, and, like her face, they were covered all over in gorgeous blue and white crystals.

"She'd probably still be alive if you hadn't given her that bottle of gin for Christmas," Delores had complained, standing beside the open grave.

"It's God's will, Del," Joe whispered, while secretly agreeing with her assessment.

"She was a lovely woman; do out for anyone," Delores's Dad had said, wiping his nose with the sleeve of his black overcoat. "Anyways, Delores, I'd like you and Joseph to have me Mam's old sideboard and some of her bedding."

It was a blessing: Delores had been storing their few clothes in double-sided, brown, cardboard boxes. But the two blankets and a pink quilted eiderdown were the real godsends for the O'Flaherty family. In the weeks before Granny's death, and to keep warm, they had been sleeping in their day clothes. And there was an added poignancy: as a small child, Delores had often snuggled under that quilt when sleeping-over.

Every night since the old lady was found frozen stiff, and before she pulled the quilt up over her face, Delores prayed for Granny's soul.

'It's more than four months since Granny died," Delores said, putting the kettle on the gas ring.

"Seems like yesterday," Joe replied, again expressing his condensed perspective of time.

"She'll never know we won the war."

"Don't suppose she'd have bothered one way or the other – as long as she had her gin."

"Joseph!   What have I told you: don't go being disrespectful to the dead!"

Joseph shrugged his shoulders and reached across the table. "Where's me bleedin' beer?" he shouted, looking in the empty cup.

But she ignored the question and, taking the cup from him, put it in the white enamel bowel in the sink. "You know what day it is, don't you?"

She could always tell when he was thinking: his eyes rolled around under his shut eyelids. After a long pause, he suggested: "We won the war day?"

" It's our Fred's Eleven Plus exam day. I hope all this excitement doesn't upset him, Joe."

"If he don't pass, nobody will."

39

"Your probably right! I don't know here he gets it from," Delores said, rinsing the cup under the tap.

"From me! Obvious!"

Conscientious as ever, Joe went to work on the three to eleven shift, eagerly looking forward to a pint at the Bull's Head during his early evening break (the bus was on an hourly circular route and the terminus was conveniently outside the pub's door. Driver and conductor were entitled to eight fifteen-minute rest periods each eight-hour shift). And, as planned, he had his first pint fifteen minutes after the pub opened its doors at six o'clock. After completing another tram circuit, just after seven he was back at the pub – but now standing elbow to elbow after fighting his way through the crowd. He'd never seen so many customers before. And he didn't recognize anyone.

When the tram returned to the Bull's Head at 8.15pm, his worst fears were realized: it seemed like all of Riverton were either in the pub or standing outside on the pavement. They had even congregated in the middle of the road. Determined, and ringing the bell of the ticket machine hanging from his neck, Joe pushed his way through the compacted bodies. But by the time he reached the counter, they'd run out of beer. Edna, now on the customer's side of the bar, and obviously having helped reduce the stock, threw her arms around his neck and kissed his cheek. But that was no compensation, and Joe returned to the number seventeen tram and filled his pipe with Gallaher's Irish Cake tobacco.

TUESDAY 8 MAY 1945

Although the war with Germany came to an official end yesterday when the Germans signed an unconditional surrender in Reims, France, the surrender was reinforced in Berlin by further signatories today. In the interest of caution, the Allies chose not to end the state of war with Germany – but, for the inhabitants of Riverton, this was academic. Hostilities had ended, and that was all that mattered.

Joe had a restless night: two pints of bitter were not enough to keep him asleep until mid-morning. He was downstairs before the children and, to his surprise, didn't have a headache. And when Delores reminded him that the government had declared this a Bank Holiday, he felt more alert than he had felt in years.

The newspaper shop was opposite the Bull's Head, and Joe was pleased to see draymen manhandling wooden casks of beer and lowering them on ropes into the pub's cellar. But otherwise the streets were empty and most houses still had their blackout curtains drawn. The newsagent complained about the lack of customers, saying he thought they'd have been dancing on the streets.

"Are you working today?" the shopkeeper asked.

Joe shook his head and, seeing the pub's recently appointed manager talking to a drayman, crossed the road.

"What time will you be opening, boss?" Joe asked, sensing signs of delirium tremens.

"Same as usual Paddy. Twelve o'clock."

"I thought with it being a special day, you'd be opening early."

The conversation continued for several minutes, but Joe sensed he was getting nowhere. With the change of management, there had been a change of policy. No stopovers after closing time, and no early opening. It would be another three hours before he could have his first pint of the day.

When he returned to the house, Delores was bent over the sink quietly performing the weekly laundry. And the children were still in bed. Sitting in the fireside chair with his feet resting on the end of the fender, Joe opened out the *Daily Express*. A moment of pleasure, he thought, smiling to himself. No work today; peace and quiet; a few pints to look forward to. Perfect! But one by one the children appeared, at first still half asleep and wearing their nightshirts. And one by one they demanded breakfast. Delores dried her hands and cut four thick slices off the loaf of bread. With the four pieces thinly covered with congealed fat from the frying pan, she returned to the sink, pouring a cupful of bleach into the laundry bucket. It was a weekly ritual with a nauseating smell that always caused Joe to retch. Then the children began arguing. It was as though Joe wasn't there. He went upstairs and lay on the bed.

The sun was shining through the bedroom window, warming the room nicely. He was beginning to relax again, but holding the newspaper above his head was making his arms ache. With the paper covering his face, he fell asleep.

It was the banging, scraping and raised Welsh voices from the street that disturbed his sleep. He went to the window. Dylan Jones and his wife Megan from the house opposite were trying to push a table through their front door. Side on, two of the table's legs were on the street, the other two still behind the door. Mrs Jones was red in the face, but this didn't stop her husband from cursing her.

"It's too heavy, Dylan," she replied, meekly. Her forehead deeply furrowed, she lifted the bottom of her pinafore and wiped the perspiration from her face.

Watching his neighbours struggling with the table, Joe couldn't help smiling. But others were arguing on the street below his window. He couldn't see what was going on, but that conversation was also very heated. One of the voices sounded like Mr Butler who lived next door with his wife and daughter Ethel. Joe put his forehead to the glass but still couldn't see what was going on below. Back across the street, the table was now upright on the pavement. And then the door next to the Joneses' house opened. The young couple living there had moved in after Delores's granny froze to death in the backyard. The couple carried their smaller table out onto the street without any difficulty. Perplexed, Joe hurried downstairs.

"They're getting ready for the street party," Delores explained. "We'd better start moving ours."

By midday, the odd assortment of tables had been positioned end-to-end and covered with red, white and blue crepe paper. On the cobbled roadway, the tables were unsteady and the covering of crepe paper repeatedly blowing away. But the latter problem was resolved by broken bricks, aided by plates of fish-paste sandwiches and bowls of jelly and powdery custard. Responding to a shrill whistle, the children of Primrose Street sat along two sides of the tables.

Although Fred was a reluctant participant, he sat, at his mother's behest, beside his three siblings. Sitting opposite Fred, and reflecting the geography of their respective homes, Blodwyn put a thumb to her nose and wriggled her upright fingers. Fred turned his head away but couldn't help feeling she was still watching him. To cancel out the image, he studied the parents standing in close proximity to their corresponding children. He wondered why, living in the same street, half of them he had never before seen. And then he caught sight of Mrs Packer standing on the doorstep of her house. Her friend, forty-one-year-old Betty Curran was standing beside her, stony faced and defiant in the face of neighbourhood hostility. Wearing a grey, plastic see-through raincoat, with her arms crossed over her chest, Betty reminded Fred of Quasimodo in *The Hunchback of Notre Dame*, currently showing at the Essoldo picture house.

Despite the warmth of the day, Mrs Packer was also wearing a topcoat, the same red overcoat she wore on her regular visits to the park. But she had outgrown it. To compensate, she held the two sides of the coat, pulling the fabric before her - but the posture couldn't hide her protruding stomach. Mrs Packer's pregnancy wasn't news to Fred. He had heard his mother and father discussing the hearsay that had originated out of Betty Curran's own mouth.

Betty had accompanied Mrs Packer to the off licence where they purchased a pint of London gin for fifteen shillings. The two women then took the tram to Mossbank, entering the abortionist's house, as pre-instructed, by a backdoor.

The thin old woman who invited them into the kitchen, asked the pair to sit down.

"Who's 'avin' it done?" she asked, smiling and obviously toothless. Mrs Packer held up a hand. "'ave you got the bottle?" she continued, taking a cup out of the sink.

With the end of her faded pinafore, she wiped the inside of the cup and placed it on the table.

Mrs Packer produced the bottle from her shopping bag, and asked: "Is this enough?"

"Are you on't tram?" the old woman asked, curling her thin lips. Mrs Packer nodded. "More than enough. You'd better get drinkin'. Do you want a cup of tea?" she asked, looking at Betty. Betty said she would prefer a drop of gin. Frowning, the old woman placed a second cup on the table. "I'll go and get me daughter."

Alone, the two women studied the surroundings. The kitchen was small, bare and dirty, nothing like what had been described by one of Betty's workmates at the pie factory. Betty poured the gin into the two cups.

"Cheers, love!" Betty said, holding up a cup. With a weak smile, Mrs Packer did likewise.

The old woman, carrying a child-size, metal tin bath, returned with her daughter. She put the tub on the floor near the sink.

"It's this one," the old woman said, pointing a finger at Mrs Packer.

"Call me Cyn," the daughter said, fastening the back strings of a white, plastic apron. Fat, with red cheeks and grey hair, she was the opposite in appearances to her mother. She studied the two women while holding a kettle under the tap. She put the kettle on the stove, struck a match and lit the gas ring. 'Have you got sommat fer me?" she asked, rubbing a thumb across the four fingers of the same hand.

"How much, did you say?" Mrs Packer asked, putting a hand in her coat pocket.

"Thirty bob!"

Mrs Packer searched inside her thin purse and produced a folded pound note and ten shilling coins.

"Have you done this before?" Mrs Packer asked, concerned by the woman's unkempt appearance and shabby state of the kitchen, but, before the woman could reply, Betty interjected.

"I told you, she did Rosemary from work."

"That's right. I'm a professional. I won't be a minute."

With the money in her hand, the woman left the room but returned almost immediately. She asked Mrs Packer to stand and remove her coat.

"You look more than two months to me," Cyn said, running her hand over Mrs Packer's stomach. After a slight pause, both Mrs Packer and Betty Curran shook their heads. "Get stripped off, then."

When the alert whistle on the kettle blew, the abortionist emptied the boiling water into an enamel bowl and added cold water. After testing the water's temperature with her elbow, she emptied the content into the tin bath. She repeated the exercise several times before asking Mrs Packer to sit in the tub.

Sitting in the hot water, her legs outside, and her feet on the stone floor, Mrs Packer drank the rest of the gin in the cup. The abortionist poured more water into the tub.

"It's too hot," Mrs Packer cried.

"'otter the better!" the woman shouted, and spread a stained bed sheet on the floor beside the tub.

Twenty minutes later, red faced and perspiring, Mrs Packer was helped out of the tub by Betty and the abortionist. Lying naked on the sheet, she was instructed to spread apart her legs and raise her knees.

As Betty had contributed half the cost of the bottle of gin, she wasn't going to miss out on a boozy afternoon, and drank as much gin as Mrs Packer. Nevertheless, and much to Mrs Packer's consternation, the abortionist asked Betty to stand by in case of emergency. But it was Betty who failed to prevail. It wasn't the scald marks on Mrs Packer's haunches, but the thin end of the wooden spatula slowly disappearing and the ensuing trickle of blood that caused Betty to faint.

'We was right pissed. Lucky we didn't get nicked by cops,' Betty was alleged to have told Sylvia, her new lodger. Although vowed to silence, Sylvia told Mrs Pratt, who told Mrs Porter who then mentioned it to Fred's mother.

Obviously, it was unnecessary suffering and thirty shillings down the drain. But worse, Mrs Packer's was now ignored and ostracized by most of her neighbours - including Lillian and Sheila who were still enjoying the company of Italian POWs. 'Can't blame the Ities,' they allegedly told her. 'You should have watched the calendar.' Now seven months pregnant, Mrs Packer's dilemma was etched in her face. According to Betty Curran, the telegram Mrs Packer received that morning had just one line: 'ARRIVING SATURDAY LOVE BRIAN.'

SUNDAY 4 NOVEMBER 1945

For the duration of the war, and for obvious reasons, bonfires and fireworks had not been allowed. And although most of the children under the age of twelve were unlikely to remember those prewar bonfire nights, their parents were determined to make up for those missing years. And each street was competing with surrounding streets. Committees were formed, duties allocated, and the cost of fireworks shared.   On Primrose Street, Fred's mother, Delores, provided the brown sugar, black treacle and syrup, and Tommy's mother pledged to make the toffee.   Mrs Butler, the O'Flaherty's next-door neighbour, promised to supply potatoes for baking.   And Mr and Mrs Jones, living across the street, said they would provide the chestnuts for roasting.

As far as the children were concerned, this was interference: their main priority was to have the biggest fire.   For that purpose, they had already spent many evenings and weekends collecting wood, and, in Primrose Street, it was now stacked like a pyramid in the middle of the cobbled road. But they needed more burnable material, and wood was scarce, an essential ingredient for igniting fires in domestic hearths. Most of the year, householders stored their wood in the backyard, unwilling to part with it for a communal bonfire.   Like all the other children of Riverton, Fred and Tommy decided it was their prerogative to acquire it by stealth.   But first they would make a final tour of the park, railway cuttings and, that last resort, neighbours' backyards.

After school and at weekends, ten-year-old Emily Openshaw often followed Fred.   Infatuated, she regularly offered him sweets, but he wasn't interested. And although she went to a different school and lived in the next street, she volunteered to help build the Primrose Street bonfire. This was an unusual request for a girl to make. For a girl living in another street, it was unheard of. However, in pursuit of acceptance, she was willing to compromise.

"If you let me log-in with you, I'll show you me thingy," she said, pointing a curled finger at her crotch.

Fred and Tommy thought about this proposition before agreeing she could join them. It wasn't the crotch; they needed somebody to act as a lookout.

In search of wood, the three children wandered down back alleys, climbed over spiked railings, and slid down steep railway embankments. They climbed in, and under, railway wagons parked in the sidings. As a diversion, Fred and Tommy raced breathlessly through the municipal park. Becoming more serious again, they climbed trees, trying to shake down branches. But those efforts were unsuccessful. They contemplated the wood yard on Lilac Street, but dismissed the idea. The fence was too high and covered in barbed wire.

"Do you want to see it now?" Emily asked, annoyed at being ignored for so long and craving attention. But Fred said they had more important things to do. Still empty-handed, they agreed it was now time to risk searching backyards.

The backyard of each house on Primrose Street was separated from the next by a wall, and from the back entry by another wall but topped with coping stones sloping on two sides. And these black edging stone continued uninterrupted, even bridging decaying yard doors.

Tommy followed Fred as they walked perilously along the slippery copingstones. But most neighbours had, as usual in the weeks leading up to Guy Fawkes' night, concealed their portable property. Emily remained on the ground, ready to alert them should an adult appear.

Near the beginning of the war, small air-raid shelters had been built in a few backyards. No longer required for their original purpose, these buildings were now used as secure storage units. Wood gatherers usually ignored those backyards. However, a plank of wood had been lying on the roof of one shelter. Fred led the way, crawling from the wall onto the adjacent flat roof. Sodden and long, the plank was too heavy for Fred alone to move. And through the kitchen window, he could see a man and woman in conversation. With his arm, he signalled for Tommy to keep down and move alongside him. Waiting for the people in the house to move away from the window, they lay on their stomachs watching.

Although the room was in semi-darkness, they both recognized the heavily built man with a thick drooping moustache and wearing a black cap. They'd often seen him wearing that same cap with the shiny peak when cycling to work. The man was gesturing and shouting at the slightly built woman wearing a floral cotton dress.

"It's Mr Philip, the train fireman," Fred whispered.

"Yeah, I know," Tommy replied, "but that looks like Mrs Baker, except her hair's different."

"She's bleached it," Fred affirmed

Fred and Tommy knew the fireman too well; he was bad tempered, somebody to be avoided. And he lived with his wife in the last house on the street. They also knew Mrs Baker's husband, a soft-spoken man who also worked on the railways, but as a signalman. But he didn't seem to be in the room.

The man removed his black serge jacket and placed it on the table in the middle of the room. The sleeves of his grey shirt were already rolled up tightly above his elbows, and his thick arms were covered in black hair. With one hand holding the halter of Mrs Baker's dress, he wagged the forefinger of the other hand before her face.

"I'll kill the bastard if…" His voice, initially audible, trailed away.

"You lot still up there?" Emily shouted from the back entry.

Still lying on his stomach, Tommy rotated his body until his head was leaning over the wall. He raised a forefinger to his lips before whispering: "Quiet, there's going to be a murder!"

Mr Philips released his hold on Mrs Baker's dress, and, bending as if in supplication, gripped the hem of her dress and lifted it. She willing raised her arms above her head, allowing him to remove the dress. Braless but wearing large white knickers, she stood motionless.

At that moment, Mr Philips looked out of the window, but without raising his gaze above ground level. Distracted by Mrs Baker removing his cap, he scratched his head and put his mouth to her ear. He then disappeared from view before reappearing in the backyard. Fred and Tommy pressed their bodies to the shelter roof. Standing in the lavatory, and with the door open, Mr Philips whistled while peeing.

Without flushing the lavatory, but still whistling, he stepped back into the yard and re-entered the house. Back in the kitchen, he undid his thick belt and dropped his trousers. With Mrs Baker bent over the table, he stood behind her, his naked posterior to the window. Although amused by the fat man's shaking bottom, the wood was more important. Quietly, Fred and Tommy slid the plank to the edge of the flat roof and down into the entry.

"You've been blinking long enough," Emily complained.

With the length of wood resting on their shoulders, Fred and Tommy debated whether to tell Emily what they had just seen. But, deciding it was not something a girl should hear, chose not to. They also declined her repeat offer for them to see her thingy. They were far too excited by this acquisition.

SATURDAY 4 MAY 1946

Surprisingly, Mr Packer had not divorced his wife, as neighbours predicted. And, although nobody saw Mrs Packer for a month after her husband's return, he was - also to everyone's surprise - occasionally seen out with the baby infant. Nobody ever learned what excuse she had made, but the baby's mental condition may have contributed to his acceptance of another man's baby. Although dark of features and hair, its pointed head couldn't be attributed to any specific nation. But, as Betty Curran once whispered in Mrs Packer's ear: 'he's got Antonio's eyes'.

Despite the war having been over nearly a year, a few housewives were still waiting for news of their missing husbands; others knew their soldier husbands would never return. But many of those servicemen who had returned had brought a new burden to bear on their families - and society. For Mrs Porter, events had been mixed: the electric-shock treatment had been concluded the previous year, and Mr Porter was alive but seriously injured and being nursed in a French hospital.

Two years earlier, in 1944, Jack, the Porter's only son, had failed his eleven plus examination and been installed in the local secondary school. Conversely, Fred O'Flaherty had been successful and was in his first year at the grammar school. However, despite the year difference

52

in age - as well as now living in different streets - Fred and Jack had resumed their friendship and occasionally played street football or street cricket, especially at weekends.

The long, brick-built air raid shelter that the council had erected between two long rows of brown terraced houses dominated Daffodil Street. The communal shelter was now neglected and occasionally flooded. And those neighbours living in its shadows complained it was an eyesore and reduced the daylight reaching their houses. However, Mrs Porter, sanity now returned and looking like a different person, didn't complain and couldn't be coerced to support calls for it to be demolished. 'It's somewhere for the kids to shelter when its raining,' she argued. This independence of thought, and her recently acquired preference for emulating a certain film star, did not endear her to some of her female neighbours. Worried that her manufactured new looks and unpredictability may attract those un-enlisted husbands still living in Riverton, she was often the subject of gossip.

In thick white chalk, Jack had drawn three lines on the shelter, representing his goal area; and Fred's task was to kick the ball past Jack. Hitting the wall represented a goal.

"Goal!" shouted Fred, as Jack's mother appeared on the street struggling with a large, round, wicker basket. She put the grocery-laden basket on the doorstep and searched inside the deep pockets of her mustard-coloured overcoat. Looking up at the darkening grey sky, she withdrew her hands, one holding a key. With the palm of her other hand upright, she looked at the sky again.

"You're going to get wet, you two," she called out. "Do you and Fred want to come with me to the pictures this afternoon?"

Jack turned to Fred and shouted: "Yeah!"

"Come on in. I'll make some butties," she proposed, picking up the basket.

"Come on, Fred," Jack said, kicking the ball towards Fred.

But Fred was more circumspect and looked across at Mrs Porter. Since moving to Daffodil Street six years earlier, she had changed the colour of her hair: formerly short, untidy and black, it was now long, blonde and falling straight down over one side of her face. It was obvious to Fred that she was now paying more attention to her appearance and, like his Aunt Breda, copying the appearance of the famous film star Veronica Lake. Mrs Porter was now also plucking her eyebrows and redrawing them with a black pencil – just the way his aunt did.

Although he enjoyed going to the picture house, Fred was hesitant and didn't immediately agree to the invitation. The memory of that day when Mrs Porter showed him the sword rarely entered his head. But her invitation today had triggered a recollection. However, it had started to rain, and, after all, he'd be with Jack. He called out:

"What's the picture, Mrs Porter?"

"*King Kong*!" she shouted. "It's about an ape."

"Should I go and get some money off me Mam?"

Mrs Porter said that was not necessary as she'd been to the Post Office that morning.

The afternoon film show had already started when they arrived in the small auditorium, and, in the flickering darkness, Mrs Porter led the boys towards the front row. Those seats were the cheapest and had the advantage of an uninterrupted view of the screen. The disadvantage was the angle of view. After a while, the neck had to be rested by bringing the head forward and screwing up the forehead.

The rain had stopped by the time they emerged in the daylight, and Mrs Porter suggested Fred join them for chips and peas. The chip shop was next to the picture house, and Mrs Porter joined the short queue while the two boys went to advise Fred's mother of the arrangement.

This was the first time Fred had been in Jack's house on Daffodil Street, but the front room looked similar to the Porter's previous house on Primrose Street. Fred followed Mrs Porter and Jack past the brown corduroy settee that also dominated this small front room, and he shivered at the memory of that encounter six years earlier when Jack's mother sat on that very settee holding the sword. He turned his head away from the settee, glancing at the sepia picture of an old lady, shawled and sitting on a rocking chair. Then his attention was drawn to the small cast-iron fireplace below the picture. The paper covering the walls was different: less oppressive than the dark brown lincrusta paper that covered the parlour walls of their previous house. Although on a much larger scale, the pink roses adorning the walls were similar to the colourful flowers on Mrs Porter cotton dress. Fred stopped, feeling an urge to turn around and run out of the house, but Jack took his arm.

"Hurry up, Fred, I'm starving."

As the brown settee dominated the front room, a large square table took up most of the limited space in the rear room. The bare-wood table was positioned against the wall concealing an enclosed staircase. A square, brown wireless sat on the rear of the table close to the wall. This small reflective Bakelite box looked modern and strangely out of place in a room where everything seemed of a previous century – except for the HP brown sauce bottle and three birthday cards, one with 35 printed on its cover. In the narrow space between the table and the large black fire grate, a brown rug provided an illusion of comfort on the otherwise stone-flagged floor. The three mix-matching, straight-backed chairs were pushed under three sides of the table.

The area under the four-paned sash window was fitted with a low, white, stone sink and, to its side, a narrow stove stood on four long curved legs. The white enamelled oven door, like the deep sink, was badly chipped, revealing its dark underside.

"Sit down, Fred," Mrs Porter said, drawing out one of the chairs. "Don't like cold chips, do we, Jack?"

Stretching up on her toes, she ran her hand along the high wooden mantelshelf above the open fireplace, collected a box of matches and lit the gas ring. She then put a pan under the cold-water tap; half filled, she put it on the hissing red flames. Dutifully, Jack collected three plates from the floor-to-ceiling cupboard built between the fireplace and the wall separating the two rooms. From an inbuilt draw under the table, Mrs Porter produced three forks.

"Did you like the picture, Fred?" Mrs Porter asked, distributing the chips and peas across the three plates.

Before Fred could answer, Jack said: "It was too sad."

"Yes, thank you, Mrs Porter," Fred replied, politely. He watched Jack pour brown sauce over his chips.

During the meal, they talked about the film, but then Jack said it was also too tame. He said he preferred *The Outlaw* with Jane Russell.

"Have you seen it?" Fred asked, leaning his head towards Jack.

"Twice!"

"But you have to be sixteen, don't you, Jack?"

"Went with-" he replied, pointing a thumb at his mother. "You vouched for me, didn't you?"

Mrs Porter smiled, nodded, and continued to eat her chips.

"Do you think I could get in to see it, Jack?" Fred asked, putting his fork across the plate.

Jack looked at his mother, and she smiled again. She stood up, carrying the three plates into the backyard. On returning, she put the plates and forks in the sink and suggested they all go up stairs and play find the parcel.

Fred followed Jack and his mother into the front bedroom. He was impressed: it was not what he expected after seeing other rooms in the house. The floor of this front-facing bedroom was covered with large alternating green and cream squares, and the linoleum was undamaged. But it was the stylish wardrobe and matching dressing table bathed in the low afternoon sun that surprised Fred. Both pieces of furniture were similarly cross-veneered in light walnut with smooth, rounded edges. And all the matching gilt-button handles were intact. The dressing table was equipped with two drawers each side of a kneehole and connected by a slim central drawer. The stained and faded top acting as a storage area for Mrs Porter's hairbrush, comb and numerous small bottles. Positioned in front of the window, its tall, three-piece mirror provided some privacy from the houses across the narrow street. And a kitchen chair provided Mrs Porter with somewhere to sit when making-up her face in front of the central mirror.

"Hot or cold? Now, you two, guess where the parcel's hidden," she said, sitting at the dressing table watching their reflections in the mirror. She applied lipstick while Fred and Jack move around the room.

"Give us a clue, Mam."

"Ice...cold...warm...warmer," she declared, as Jack and Fred moved together around the room. "Hot," she shouted as Jack stood before the wardrobe.

"Let's see what's hiding in here," she said, opening the wardrobe door. Reaching up to the inner shelf, she withdrew a large brown envelope. "Close your eyes." Slowly, she withdrew two magazines. Holding them up, she exclaimed: "Look what I got you - from America." She handed a copy to each boy.

'*Sunshine and Health*," Jack shouted, reading the titles. "Where'd you get 'em?"

"Never mind where I got them; I got them!"

"Off that Yank, didn't you?" Jack complained, his response disappointing his mother. "You said you weren't seeing him any more."

"He's only a friend. Anyway, I bought them from the mag shop on London Road," she said, removing her shoes. "Go and read them in your room."

"You just said they came from America," Jack replied, slightly raising his voice. Taking the magazine from Fred's hand, and in a gesture of defiance, he threw it on the bed. Ignored, he turned to Fred. "Come on," he said, making for the door. "Looks like she's going out again."

"You don't expect me to stay in every night, do you?"

"You went to the pictures this afternoon," Jack shouted, stopping by the door and forcing Fred to halt behind him.

"That was for your benefit. And that's all the thanks I get."

"I know where you're going, you're going to see that feller."

"No I'm not. And where I go is none of your business."

Fred followed Jack into his bedroom; surprised at the way Jack had spoken to his mother. Sitting on the edge of the single bed, Fred looked over Jack's shoulder at the pictures in the magazine, fascinated by the naked women.

"Where's your mag?' Jack asked, holding his copy to his chest.

"You threw it on the bed, Jack."

Instructed to collect it, Fred went into the front bedroom. Mrs Porter was standing naked. Although she had a dress in her hand, she was slow to cover her body. His excitement was tempered by embarrassment. He apologized.

"Here you are, Fred," she said, now holding the dress before her and handing him the magazine. "I've told Jack these are to go before his dad comes home. Ask him if you can have them. He's got loads!"

With the magazine in his hand, Fred sat beside Jack. He began to repeat what Mrs Porter had just said, but Jack said he had overheard.

"OK, you can have them next week, but you'll have to do a swop. What've you got?"

SUNDAY 12 MAY 1946

By agreement, Fred was to call on Jack and make the exchange. In preparation, he had packaged his collection of 98 foreign postage stamps. But he was troubled by Mrs Porter's naked image that unexpectedly, and repeatedly, crept into his mind. He was embarrassed and reluctant to call on Jack. And where would he keep the magazines without his parents finding them? The more he thought about it, the less inclined he was to make the exchange.

However, and more-or-less without thinking, he walked towards Jack's house - but turned around again, and, with different thoughts crowding in on him, wandered the streets. He walked along Main Street looking in shop windows. The window of the bicycle shop was now stocked with the latest models, including the Eagle, the bike that his mother promised to buy him when she won the football pools. He stopped to look at the smart suits in the menswear shop window, his reflected image superimposed on a grey pinstriped suit. He promised himself a suit like that after he finished school and got a job. He walked on, recalling the mangled bikes and shredded suits lying in the road the day after the bomb dropped. Only the former second-hand shop remained unoccupied, its door and window spaces now sealed by sheets of plywood. He walked down to the park, sat on a bench, and watched the children in the playground. Back on the main road, he called in Siforiana's milk bar and ordered a large glass of Vimto. Struggling with his conscience, and trying to decide whether to return home or call on Jack, he slowly walked back to Daffodil Street.

Mrs Porter, in fluffy slippers and wearing the heavy, brown dressing gown, opened the door. Frowning and clasping the front of her gown, she put her head out and looked up and down the street. She didn't speak.

"Is Jack in, Mrs Porter?"

"He's out playing cricket. Didn't he tell you?" she retorted, continuing to look over his head.

"He asked me to call round today," he replied, handing her the small package of stamps.

"You kids! What's this?"

Concerned by her changed and aggressive attitude, he stepped back. Her staring eyes reminded him of the day she showed him the sword. Standing on the pavement, he explained he had come to do the swop for the magazines.

"You'd better come in a minute," she snapped.

Hesitantly, he followed her, bending as they walked under the damp washing hanging from the wooden ceiling rack. He watched her stub out the lipstick-stained cigarette end that had been left burning on an ashtray on the table. Although, as far as he could see, not dressed beneath the dressing gown, she had obviously taken care to apply make-up and fashion her hair. And she'd taken the trouble to pluck and redraw her eyebrows.

She repositioned a chair from beside the table to the front of the tall wall cupboard. Leaning behind him, she picked up the wine glass and small bottle of sherry from the table. The Lux soap and perfume on her skin mingled with the smell of sherry on her breath and tobacco smoke in the atmosphere. But these smells were competing with the damp laundry on the airing rack.   Standing on the chair, she put the bottle and glass on the top shelf.

"This is to stop Jack swigging it. He's a little bugger. You're all little buggers!"

Fred couldn't reconcile the change in her behaviour. She seemed like a different person, and he was afraid.

Still standing on the chair, but now on her tiptoes, she reached further inside the cupboard and produced a brown paper package.

"I don't want these in the house when Mr Porter comes home next week. And don't let your Mam and Dad find them." she said, leading him by the hand to the front door.

The sky matched his mood as he hurried up the street. He now had magazines that he would have to hide - but he had nowhere to hide them. Although living just three streets away, he would normally have to walk along the busy, shop-lined Main Street which provided a junction for the many long streets of terraced houses. A narrow entry running parallel with the main road offered a quicker alternative route, but, littered with dustbins and dog excrement, it was usually avoided. But it also offered a degree of privacy. Standing on a concealed backdoor step, he opened the package. He was disappointed: there was only one, and it was the same magazine he had looked at several times, both in Jack's house and in the air-raid shelter. He felt cheated, angry with himself for making a swop without seeing what he was receiving in exchange for his valuable stamps. Disturbed by two youths walking past the alley, and feeling uncomfortable, he threw the magazine in one of the dustbins. He recognized one of the voices: it was Phil Pratt who also lived on Primrose Street and usually walked to school with Jack. Standing on the street corner, he watched Phil and his friend stop at Mrs Porter's house, and then knock on the door. The door opened and they stepped off the street.

MONDAY 20 MAY 1946

Fred stood on the same corner of Daffodil Street for more than an hour. He had taken a double lunch break from school, curious to see a man who the local paper had described as a war hero: a man who had lost a leg on the last day of the war. There were other reasons he wanted to see Mrs Porter's husband, but he wasn't sure what they were.

Since reading the article in the *Riverton Times,* Mr Porter had been creeping into Fred's imagination. But it was the picture of the man he remembered vaguely from before the war. He could recall the tall, slim man, dressed in navy overalls cycling to work, but not the face. Former subconscious thoughts were now rising to the conscious level. Rumours relating to Mrs Porter were circulating but Fred put them down to Phil Pratt's boastful imagination.

As Mr Porter's anticipated arrival had been reported in the newspaper, he expected the street to be lined with people, buntings, and balloons – perhaps even a brass band. But the street was empty. Convinced he had either got the time or dates wrong, he was about to return to school when a black cab arrived in the street. It stopped at Mrs Porter's house, and a man with only one leg and dressed in navy blue suit – but hatless - struggled out of the cab's back door. Hesitantly, on two wooden crutches, he shuffled across the pavement. Before the door opened, the cab had moved away.　Fred couldn't see who greeted the war hero but assumed it would have been Mrs Porter.

MONDAY 5 JULY 1946

Fred's first year at the new school had produced mixed results, and those low marks had been in and around the few weeks of his visits to Jack Porter's house.　In the two months since he last visited Daffodil Street, his marks had improved dramatically and were close to where they had been for the first seven months.　In May, the teachers and his parents couldn't understand the decline on his weekly reports, but his mother was especially relieved.　She had purchased his expensive uniform on a one-year weekly instalment plan.　However, Fred knew what the cause was, and promised himself not to waste any more time looking at magazines with naked women.　He had been too preoccupied with thoughts of a sexual nature.

Fred was feeling more contented with himself, pleased to have formed a friendship with Patricia, another first year pupil at the grammar school.　Living on two sides of the same district, their relationship had evolved from travelling home from school on the same tram to sharing sandwiches in the school playground.　In the five weeks of their friendship, she had encouraged him to join the Unitarian Church's youth movement.　He enjoyed the weekend sporting events and Monday's bell ringing lessons, but refused to join her at the Sunday morning Bible classes.

Standing at the entrance to the church's spiralling stone staircase, and dressed in a pink cotton dress with white sandals, Patricia said it was too hot for going up in the belfry.　Fred, still in school uniform, readily agreed.

Taking his hand, she said she would show him the shallow river at the back of the church where 'blood suckers' attach themselves to the legs and feet of anyone brave enough to paddle in the slow-moving, shallow waters. Fred was familiar with the leaches, but in the adjacent public park where the same river continued to flow after journeying beneath the road bridge. He chose to plead ignorance.

Despite its ancestral name, the Victorians had seen to it that only one river remained in Riverton, and it flowed through this ancient graveyard before disappearing underground and remerging in the valley of the undulating park. The same park, he recalled, where Mrs Packer, Betty Curran and other local women used to lie with the Italians.

Whereas the public park's grass - on the other side of the high wall - were occasionally cut, this burial ground was neglected. The long grass and riverside bushes created a wilderness unmatched in a district that was otherwise constructed in bricks and concrete. Although close to the park, the graveyard was surrounded on three sides by high dry-stone walls and fronted by the church. This was a wasteland that he didn't know existed. And the ancient, leaning gravestones added another layer of mystery.

Careful not to stand on any graves, they wandered between the crumbling and disorderly head stones, reading, where still legible, the inscriptions. They competed as to who could find the oldest date, and expressed compassion when they came across a memorial to a child.

"Do you know this was where dissenters chose to be buried?" Patricia asked.

Fred had no idea what she was talking about. "Dissenters?" he asked, anxious to learn.

"Dad said they didn't like being bullied by the Anglican Church, and about God being three things, or something like that."

"How does your Dad know?" Fred asked.

"He and Mum come to church services every Sunday. They don't think God exists as three things. What do you think?"

Fred thought about the question, then explained his understanding: "I always thought God was three parts. At junior school they said He is the Father, the Son and the Holy Ghost."

"Well, I'm afraid I don't see how one person could be father and son – and a ghost."

"Look at this writing. All these little children!" Fred said, steering her away from a possible argument.

"Isn't it sad that some do not have a full life," she said, bending down to read the inscription, "and can't enjoy beautiful evenings like this."

"I don't want my family to ever die," Fred said, leaning down to read another inscription.

"Neither do I," she replied, dabbing her eyes with an embroidered handkerchief.

They asked each other questions about the past; questions about each other's family that they could answer, and abstract historical questions that neither could answer. They wondered why the graves were not all in lines as in the new cemetery just a mile away; wondered how all those dead people had made a living and where they had lived? They questioned how they had died.

"Do you think they had wars in..." Patricia began, but paused, having difficulty reading the inscriptions on a tall memorial stone. "... in 1881?"

"Dad says consumption kills most people," Fred replied. "Look at this: all the same family buried in 1918."

She shuddered, wrapping her arms around her own shoulders. "Let's find some blood suckers."

Stepping down the slight incline, Fred and Patricia sat by the narrow river upturning small boulders with twigs off a tree. Being with a girl in a concealed location, and without any of those sexual thoughts that had recently plagued him, he felt proud of himself and protective of his new girlfriend. And instead of being looked down on, he was being looked up to.

Distant voices and the rustle of long grass alerted them to somebody approaching from the church.

"Quiet, Fred. It might be the Reverend; he sometimes comes down here for a walk," she whispered.

Hidden by the embankment, they crouched down and listened. There were two voices, and although too distant to hear what they were saying, they were getting closer. Lying on his stomach, Fred raised his head a little, looking over the inclining bank. A tall woman with a man in military uniform was walking towards them. The woman was carrying a mustard-coloured coat over her arm but walking unsteadily on black, high-heeled shoes. As they drew closer, Fred had to look twice: it looked like Mrs Porter; and the man looked like a soldier – but it couldn't be them: Mr Porter had only one leg and he was thinner, taller and white. But as they drew closer, his suspicions were confirmed. It was Mrs Porter with a black American soldier. And the coat was the one she wore regularly and hung on a nail behind the front door. Fred broke out in a cold sweat, fearful of an encounter. But then the couple stopped by a large headstone. Mrs Porter pointed to the church building, partly obscured by the gravestone, and her companion nodded.

"Is it the Reverend?" Patricia whispered, lying next to him but keeping her head down below the brow.

Fred didn't answer immediately. Speechless, he watched Mrs Porter carefully stretch her coat out on the grass-covered grave beneath the tall headstone. The soldier, dressed in beige shirt, trousers and with a matching tie tucked inside his shirt, removed his soft hat and slipped it into an unbuttoned breast pocket. Standing close together, the American put his lips to hers, but the interaction was brief. Intently, Fred watched as she rubbed her hands up and down the front of the military trousers.

"It's a woman with a Yank," he whispered. "Keep your head down."

But Patricia raised her head and exclaimed: "A black man! In Riverton!"

"Ssh! Keep it down," Fred said, putting a finger before his mouth.

Holding the American's hand, Mrs Porter lowered herself onto the coat and re-arranged her skirt that had risen above her knees. But the American knelt down, pushed the skirt back and began stroking her thighs. He watched the American roll her skirt back to expose the edge of her white knickers. Fred couldn't see the American's face but could clearly see Mrs Porter's with that same patronizing smile that he remembered. The man then put a hand between her legs.

"He's fumbling her!" Fred murmured, inaudibly, and Patricia, now lying at his side and watching events unfold, asked what he said. Self-conscious, he didn't answer.

"What are they doing?" Patricia asked, naively, Fred thought.

Mrs Porter arched her back, putting her weight on her upper back and feet. Still smiling at the American, she wriggled her lower body, at the same time lifting the tight black skirt above her waist. Her companion bent down and removed her knickers.

Patricia put her mouth close to Fred's ear and whispered: "Why'd he put her panties in his pocket?"

Fred turned to Patricia, unsure whether to be frank or evasive. He looked at her face: her eyes were wide and her mouth open. But before he could answer, the GI lowered his trousers and underpants to his ankles. Patricia put a hand across her eyes, but kept her fingers apart.

"What's he doing, Fred?"

"I think they're making love."

"If the Reverend comes down they'll be for it. Doing that on a grave! Isn't that disgusting, Fred!" she whispered, but her word were lost as the church bells started to ring.

Fred looked at Patricia looking at the couple. He was excited by what was going on and wondered if it had the same effect on her. He was tempted to ask her, but dismissed the thought immediately. He returned his focus to the copulating couple, but the American was already standing and peeling off the condom. He threw it to the ground. Mrs Porter lay inert, looking up as the man dressed himself. With one hand to the ground, she slowly raised herself to her feet, put a hand in his pocket and pulled out her knickers. Bending down, and deliberately smoothing down her skirt, she looked up at the man. She said something to him, but he shrugged his shoulders. She shook her overcoat and draped it over her arm. Unsteadily, she followed him towards the church.

Uncomfortable about following close behind them, they sat quietly looking at the slow flowing river, but not with any interest in leaches.

"I've never seen one of them before," Patricia said, thoughtfully.

"All men have them, Patricia."

"What?"

"Willies!"

"Not that! I've never seen a black man before. Have you?"

Fred conceded he hadn't, but said a Red Indian lady served behind the counter in the glass shop on Main Street.

"A real Red Indian, living in Riverton?" she asked, her eyes opening wide in astonishment.

"When we were kids, we used to go and look at her through the shop window. She never said anything. But one day, she got annoyed and came out to ask what we were staring at."

"Did she tell you off?"

"Not really, but I asked her if she was really a Red Indian, and she said her father was the son of a Sioux chief who came to England with Buffalo Bill, but never went home."

"Wow! What does she look like?"

"She has long black hair in a pigtail, and brown skin. She looks just like those squaws in the cowboy pictures – but she's very thin. I'll take you to see her, if you want."

"Can you see her through the window?"

Fred thought about the question. "No, it's now full of stuff. Sometimes I go there and buy putty for Dad. She doesn't say much, unless you ask her something. Me Mam knows her. I think she's called Bessie."

"I'll have to tell me Mam and Dad. And I'll tell them I also saw a black man. Will you tell yours, Fred?"

"Don't tell them what he was doing," Fred warned.

"Of course not, silly," she replied.

"Have you seen a willy before?"

Avoiding the question, she became serious: "They had no respect for the dead, did they, Fred"

But, determined to get an answer, he repeated the question. After a pause, and now chuckling, she said: "Peter Smith showed me his when he was seven. But it didn't look like that man's. It was only tiny."

Fred established that Peter Smith was a cousin with whom she had been evacuated to Wales during the blitz.

"Did he see yours?"

"We'd better be going, Fred," she said, ignoring the question and standing up. She dusted the dry grass off Fred's school jacket.

Fred stood beside her, momentarily distracted by thoughts of the Porter family. He always thought Jack was making it up about the American. His thoughts then turned to Mr Porter, wondering what he would do if he found out. He was also wondering how Mrs Porter knew about this hidden graveyard.

"Have you seen that woman in church, Patricia?"

"Never seen her in me life, and hope I never see her again. Doing that on a grave is unholy."

Fred couldn't agree on that interpretation, but Patricia was adamant and said God, having seen them lying on a grave, would be furious.

"He may not allow them in heaven when they die," she concluded, with some emphasis.

Having been force-fed the Bible at the Catholic junior school, he couldn't agree with her assessment, and explained: "There's nothing in the Ten Commandments about standing on graves, but what that woman did was sinful."

"Just the woman? What about the man, they were both lying on the grave?" she argued.

"In Genesis, marriage is established by God. Therefore she's broken the seventh Commandment."

"How do you know she's married?"

Fred didn't answer immediately, unsure whether it wise to admit, at this late stage, that he knew her.

"I think she's a neighbour."

"A neighbour? Gosh, and she's married?"

He reverted to the Bible again, reminding her that it wasn't a sin to stand or lie on a grave, just disrespectful.

Patricia was impressed by his biblical knowledge but couldn't agree. She maintained that what they did on the grave was an insult to the persons buried there... as well as to God.

In silence, they walked through the graveyard, Patricia now engrossed in thoughts of death and religion. But Fred was still thinking about Mrs Porter and the afterlife. He couldn't envisage any redemption for someone like her. In his mind, he went through the Ten Commandments; confident he, personally, hadn't broken any of the written edicts, but not convinced he was totally innocent of some other breach. He decided to reread the Bible that evening.

SATURDAY 5 OCTOBER 1946

Fred and Patricia waited patiently in the queue outside the art deco frontage of the Essoldo picture house.   The sky was a mixture of fast-moving clouds, some pale grey, wispy edged and high enough to catch the last salmon-pink rays of the setting sun. But below those soft-looking clouds, heavy black clouds were swirling in from the west.   And then the rains came.   Huddled together, Fred held his raincoat over their heads. Slowly they edged forward until they were sheltering under the glass-panelled canopy, standing just a few yards from the entrance and pay desk.

Inside, they were jostled and pushed as they searched for two seats together. They were lucky to find two adjoining seats off the middle aisle and not too far back.

As with other new arrivals, steam was rising from their wet clothes, but many of those seated watching the film had been there since the afternoon, choosing to view *Gone with the Wind* all over again.   Fred and Patricia sat holding hands, enthralled by the vibrant colours on the huge screen and the romantic music filling the auditorium.

Their friendship had blossomed since their first date in July. And Fred knew she had been good for him. Patricia had an aura of purity that he had never seen in any of the other girls in Riverton, and she had a gentle voice. And, like him, she was curious about the meaning of life. 'Why did God put us on earth?' she often asked, not abstractedly but seriously questioning religious creativity.   And she often answered her own questions with suggestions such as

'Love for people' and 'to create man in His own image'. But Fred didn't always agree with her religious theories. Without saying so, he thought they were superficial hand-me-downs like those he had heard at his mother's knee. Or one-liners from the Bible that had been bellowed from the pulpit in an effect to keep dwindling congregations awake. He thought that Patricia, having attended a non-church junior school, lacked the in-depth religious knowledge that he had acquired during his six years at a school with an attached church. Her philosophy that Unitarianism was superior to the Trinitarian understanding of God – and which, she said, made more sense than Fred's Catholicism - annoyed him. And when Patricia argued that there was only one God, not three, he again tried to explain that he agreed there was only one God but that God was the whole of three parts: the Father, Jesus the Son, and the Holy Spirit. Although Patricia poured scorn on such an impossible concept, he refrained from argument. Fred recalled how it had taken him several years before he could get his head around the idea, and the revelation only came after Sister Margaret 's simplistic comparison with the sun. Fred restated the Sister's analogy of the one sun providing heat, light and radiation, Patricia said she could now see his point of view. On the subject of religion, Fred soon recognized that Patricia was more open to reason, willing to listen to another person's point of view, and less dogmatic than himself. 'I must tell Mum and Dad about that,' she had exclaimed, excited that the sun could be used to explain something so profound.

Patricia's willingness to change her mind contrasted with his unwillingness to accept an alternative religious point of view. He respected his religion above all others, but only in the sense that he respected his parents above all other parents. He sensed that respect could be hierarchical and imposed on the subservient from above - but refused to develop this idea, afraid of where it might lead.

He admitted to himself that he had been too compliant at school; too willing to accept religious ideologies without asking questions. But at that school, he reflected, questions were not encouraged.

Since changing from a church school to a non-church school, an inner conflict had developed in his head between the real world that he could see, touch and smell, and the metaphysical, that of the church and Bible. And it was one thing for the priest to preach 'giving as next to godliness' but it was all one sided. It was his parents who gave the priest a shilling every Friday night. And the day his mother had to borrow from a neighbour in order to leave 'Peter's pence' on the doorstep was etched on his memory. The theological concepts of Catholicism were now in direct conflict with his humanity studies at grammar school.

As much as he cared for her, he couldn't help thinking that Patricia's worldview was still dominated by naivety and innocence. And when he explained the meaning of the Genesis text 'Be fruitful and multiply', he was chastised for thinking naughty things. In reality, thoughts of sexually related subjects no longer afflicted him as they did before he got to know Patricia. He was content to be in her company without touching her body, or imagining her undressed. Sitting next to her in the picture house was the highlight of his week.

To fund the expenses of this courtship, Fred was sharing a newspaper round with another boy. As a latecomer, he had the unenviable job of delivering the morning papers. In the beginning, he was delivering the papers during daylight hours, and once he had learned how to navigate the labyrinth of similar-looking streets, the job became less stressful. But Fred still found it difficult getting out of bed at five o'clock and having to walk the dark and unlit backstreets.

It was still raining when they left the picture house. Had he been alone with these holes in soles of his shoes, Fred would have felt miserable walking home in the rain, an element that also intensified the gloom that pervaded every aspect of life in Riverton. But in the company of Patricia, he saw only beauty in the rain-soaked, silver-grey roof slates and glistening, black cobbled roads. His wet feet were suddenly unimportant. Linking arms, they hurried under his raincoat.

"That was the best picture I've ever seen," Patricia said, "but I don't think that little boy should have been hurt."

"Killed!" Fred said, taking hold of her hand.

Patricia Johnson lived to the east of Riverton, where the streets were fewer and three-bedroomed houses had been built in pairs. And each of those semi-detached houses had a small front garden. This was misconstrued as the posh side of Riverton. Unknown to Fred, these were council-owned houses.

Standing by the still-in-flower rose bush, and sheltering under Fred's raincoat, she allowed him to kiss her cheek. Hurrying up the garden path, she stopped to wave back. With a finger on the doorbell, she hesitated and turned around: "I forgot," she shouted, putting a hand across her forehead. "Mum and Dad want to know, can you come with us to the theatre on Friday?"

FRIDAY 11 OCTOBER 1946

As arranged, Fred took the number 210 tram and walked across town to the Monk Repertory Theatre. He stood beneath the four tall Corinthian columns fronting the round white building. Patricia had only given him the time, date and place. She hadn't mentioned the name of the play, and he had forgotten to ask. However, the black and white poster pasted on the wooden hoarding announced: *A Midsummer's Night Dream* by William Shakespeare. Although still only in the school's second year, he was familiar with the author, having read and memorized all his sonnets from a book at the local library.

"We're here, Fred," Patricia shouted, hurrying alongside her mother.

Not wanting to appear inquisitive, he didn't ask the whereabouts of her father, assuming he would be following.

Fred had never before been inside a real theatre with red velvet seats and a wide stage. Patricia sat between her mother and Fred, but kept her hands on her knees, careful not to let her mother see any physical contact between her and her boyfriend.

The large, round ceiling lights in the auditorium were electric and very bright, contrasting with the heavy black curtain hanging above the stage. Fred looked around: all the seats in the small theatre seemed to be occupied by people, like himself, wearing their Sunday-best clothes. And there was a pleasant smell, like that of fresh lemons. To enjoy this agreeable fragrance, and for a moment forgetting where he was, he held his head back and breathed in deeply. Patricia turned to him and smiled.

Fred put a hand to his mouth, pretended to cough, and then whispered:

"Where's Mr Johnson?"

"He works here. That's why we get free tickets," Patricia explained, holding a hand to the side of her mouth. "He's the stage manager."

When the curtain went up and the house lights went down, Fred was slowly carried into another world, a world of make believe where extraordinary things could happen. He had a sudden urge to climb up on the stage and escape into this strange new world.

At the interval, Patricia's father joined them in the cafeteria. He was not as smartly dressed as he had been when Fred had visited the house. On those occasions, he usually wore a checkered shirt, tie and a brown sports jacket with leather elbow patches. Fred was surprised at this change in his appearance. The open-necked plaid shirt and rolled up sleeves set him apart from everybody else in the room. And a thin grubby booklet was sticking out of his shirt's breast pocket.

Sitting at a Formica-topped table, Patricia's father asked Fred what he thought of the first half of the play. Fred was genuinely fascinated by what he had just seen and heard, and said so – and that impressed Mr Johnson.

"Yes, it's a lovely play to produce, so full of imagery," her father added. "Did you like the scenery?"

Patricia and her mother sat at the other side of the table talking about their respective days.

Fred replied in the affirmative: "...and especially the bank where the wild thyme blows..." Mr Johnson smiled, impressed by the correct quotation from Oberon's edict to Robin. But reflectively and trancelike, Fred continued:

"...Where oxlips and the nodding violet grows..." and flawlessly recited the following eighteen lines.

"You acted in this play at school?" Mr Johnson asked, exchanging quizzically looks with his wife and daughter.

But mentally, Fred had been walking through that magical garden of luscious Woodbine and sweet-musk roses. "I'm sorry; I was just thinking...No, I haven't been in the play."

"But you've obviously read it," Mrs Johnson said, politely trying to extract information.

Fred felt uncomfortable attracting so much attention, and couldn't understand why they thought he was familiar with the play. Memorizing a few lines was a normal function; at least that was what he thought. He didn't think having a super-retentive memory, first identified by his mother, and later, Sister Margaret, was that unusual.

"I heard Oberon say it," he said, breaking the silence.

"When?" her father asked, looking at his wife for further support.

"Tonight!"

Not convinced, Mr Johnson pulled the thin booklet from his shirt pocket. Forcing back the pages, and still holding them apart, he put it before Fred. Leaning towards him, he asked:

"Can you memorize the epilogue for me?"

"Go on, Fred," Patricia urged.

He didn't like being the centre of attention at the best of times, but in front of Patricia's parents it made him even worse: he blushed, felt nervy inside. He didn't expect to be tested. And the people sitting at the next table were now taking notice. Then that familiar feeling came over him. He wanted to run away.

But encouraged further by Patricia, he removed his spectacles, wiped them, then replaced them. He put his face close to the page.

"This?" Fred asked, pointing to the last lines of the play.

"Yes, beginning 'If we shadows have offended'.

Fred read the passage, and her father withdrew the script, holding it in a way that Fred couldn't see the page. Unhesitatingly, Fred recited the sixteen lines that he had just read.

Not knowing what to say, Patricia and her parents waited for someone to say something sensible. Eventually her father broke the silence.

"What are you going to do after school?"

"University, I hope."

"Studying what?" Mrs Johnson asked.

'Don't know, but I don't want to work on the trams."

Patricia and her parents laughed, but Fred didn't think what he had just said was funny.

"With a memory like that, you should think about becoming an actor.' Still smiling, her father turned to his wife: "By the way, love, they phoned this afternoon. I got that job."

SATURDAY 12 OCTOBER 1946

Sheltering from the rain, Fred and Patricia sat in Siforiana's ice-cream parlour, slowly sipping frothy milkshakes through straws. The whole place had been refitted since their last visit. Even the name outside had changed from Siforiana to MILKBAR.

Three white tables with four matching chairs to a table now filled most of the area between the counter and the two glass windows and door. And, for comfort, the green plastic-covered seats were now padded. Mr Siforiana, in a long coat, white like the rest of the furnishing, stood behind the new chrome-fronted counter.

"How you lika the new place, eh?" Mr Siforiana asked, putting his hand on a lever attached to the wall. "Nice? Well watcha this."

He pulled down on the lever, and the external tubular-glass 'MILKBAR' sign flickered into life, intermittently switching itself on and off. And when it was on, it threw as much red light into the seating area as it did on the street. Fred looked at Patricia and couldn't help smiling as she changed from red to white to red. But it was a shallow smile: she had just explained that her father had got a job at the Memorial Theatre. She said Dad was moving first, and the rest of the family would follow in November. They were going to live in a rented house near Stratford-upon-Avon.

"Why don't you putta some music on, eh?" Mr Siforiana asked, pointing to the new illuminated jukebox in the corner of the narrow room.

Bodies touching, they leaned on its glass top reading the list of available records. Patricia chose *Till the End of Time.* Fred put a threepenny bit in the slot.

"Do you like Perry Como?" Fred asked, stirring the froth in his glass with the straw.

"Yes! Till the end of time, that's for you and me, Fred." With a tear in her eye, she continued: "I'll writc everyday."

She hid her face as the door opened. But Fred looked up; it was Mrs Packer, still wearing the same red coat, but it now seemed a size too big. She was carrying her infant son. Although little more than a year old, the infant had thick hair. But the hair couldn't disguise the misshapen head: pointed and too heavy for its neck to support, it flopped from side to side. Dark skinned with black hair and eyebrows, the infant had the features of a much older child. Fred wondered again how Mrs Packer had explained the birth to her husband and how he had reacted. But of greater concern, he wondered if the attempted abortion had caused the disfigurement and possible brain damage.

MONDAY 3 FEBRUARY 1947

Fred couldn't help thinking how odd it was that it was Mr Porter who now had a psychological problem. But unlike Mrs Porter's unexplained mental breakdowns, his was the result of war damage. It was the constant fear of standing on another mine that plagued him when in a public place. Walking along the street was a very slow process: he had to first test the ground before him with one of his two wooden crutches.

But Mr Porter was not the only damaged former soldier living in Riverton. They were numerous and visible. Those without physical disabilities, but mentally scarred, stood on street corners or sat in the municipal park. These, the less informed claimed, were malingerers; while those, like Mr Porter with missing limbs, attracted sympathy. But Mr Porter's disabilities were complex and his shuffling attracted ridicule from young children. He became known as the 'creeper'. For all her apparent faults, Mrs Porter seemed to have a compassionate side: she was often seen walking by her husband's side.

Less visible on the streets of Riverton than the recently damaged veterans were those war-wounded ex-servicemen who fought in the 1914-18 war. With appalling injuries and inability to earn a proper wage, the survivors were now middle-aged, or older. But neglected and underfed, they all looked very old. Ignored by society, they spent most of their lives indoors. However, some of those damaged former military men from the First World War were an integral part of Riverton society. And Fred usually encountered them on his journey to and from school, or when running an errand.

Fred and his pals bought their 'penneth' of peas from Mr Turnbull's chip shop next to the picture house. But for adults, peas were only supplied with fish, chips, or both, and usually wrapped in unread newspaper. And although the sixty-six-year old proprietor had lost the top of his skull, he always wore a neat white wig to cover the metal plate. He never overcharged.

On his way to junior school, Fred had to pass the Lilac Street wood yard where Cedric Swanson worked. If not sawing wood, he always waved. It was at the Battle of Gallipoli, Christmas Day, 1915, that nineteen-year-old Cedric lost his nose, half his face and an eye. He was lucky: the same Turkish sniper shot dead the man by his side, or so he said. Fifty-one-year-old, Cedric operated the large, electrical rotary saw. The company purchased the machine in 1939. Before then, he cut the wood with a handsaw, but never sustained an injury.

Fifty-three-year-old Andrew Jackson, who lived seven doors from Fred's house, was unemployable. As a

Second Lieutenant, age nineteen, he returned from fighting the Germans in East Africa unscathed by battle but with a rare medical condition. With uncertainty, it was diagnosed as sleeping sickness.

According to Fred's mother, when Andrew returned to Riverton, his father washed and dressed him, and his mother fed him. But when his father died in 1939, his mother, then sixty-nine, took over all duties. Although he appeared frozen – except for his trembling right hand - he could shuffle along when gently pushed and guided from behind.

Weather permitting, he stood on the doorstep wearing a purple cardigan, neatly pressed grey trousers and purple house slippers. His shirts were always white, but collarless. Although Andrew was unable to talk or communicate in any way, Fred knew he could hear because he could see the hint of a smile in the man's eyes when, on his way to school, he greeted him.

Riverton, like many other districts, was now home to disabled soldiers from two wars with Germany. And Phil Pratt's father, who also lived a few doors from Fred's house, was a casualty of the Second World War.

Phil Pratt's father had lost both full legs and had spent two years in a London hospital. He returned home in 1944 with just a head, a body and two arms. Resilient, he made portable wooden steps that enabled him to reach the sink, climb up on the bed or onto the toilet seat.

Before the war, Mr Pratt had been employed as a carpenter on the railways, but he didn't complain when he wasn't offered re-employment. Instead, he used those old skills to build a portable trolley: a square of wood with a roller-skate wheel at each corner. On its surface, for comfort, he glued a piece of patterned carpet. And Monday to Friday he travelled on the tram to the city centre, usually assisted on and off the platform by the tram's conductor. Adept and now no longer self-conscious, he sold books of matches outside the train station in the morning and evening, and at the entrance to the three-story emporium during the day.

On the city street, he had become a familiar figure, well respected for his fortitude and warm personality. But it was a cold winter and his hands were frostbitten from pushing himself along on his wooden trolley. Perhaps unable to stand the cold any longer – or simply defeated - he returned home at midday. In the evening, he was found hanging: he had put a rope around his neck and fastened it to the tap above the sink. He had then pushed himself off his portable ladder.

FRIDAY 7 FEBRUARY 1947

Despite the snow lying thick on the ground and clinging to gnarled branches in the churchyard, more than a hundred mourners filled the unheated church. Many genuinely moved, a few curious to see the size of the coffin. Most of those attending the service were neighbours or customers from the Bull's Head – the local pub where Mr Pratt had occasionally enjoyed a pint of mild beer.

Fred and his family sat on the row behind Mr and Mrs Porter. Fred's father asked Mr Porter how his leg was, and Mr Porter said he could still feel it. Mrs Porter then made a point of turning and talking with Fred's mother. Within hearing range of Fred – but talking as though he wasn't there - he heard her ask how he was doing at the grammar school. He felt uncomfortable, childlike. He was angry that she was talking about him as though he were a little boy. He felt like knocking the black taffeta hat off her head and kicking it down the paving-stoned aisle. He had an urge to pinch that part of her body pushing between the polished wood bench and backrest. He wanted to lean across and shout: 'shut up and be respectful in church'. Listening to her conversing with his mother made him extra uncomfortable. He couldn't help wondering what his mother would say if she knew Mrs Porter had given him that magazine. But foremost in his mind was the image of Mrs Porter standing naked.

Mr Porter whispered something in his wife's ear. She turned to face the altar and put her head close to his. Mr Porter had a hand before his mouth. Certain he had seen Mr Porter glance at him, Fred worried he was talking about him. He'd heard his mother – quoting Mrs Porter - say that Mr Porter had become difficult to live with since losing his leg. Fred's father thought it was something to do with women protecting women. At a personal level, Fred felt profoundly sorry for Mr Porter, but loathing for his wife. Seeing them together reminded him of the graveyard and Mr Porter's ignorance.

Fred suddenly realized he was holding a battered, black-bound Bible. He couldn't recall lifting it up off the support behind Mrs Porter. Returning the Bible to the sloping support, he studied her back. It seemed broader, but he reasoned it could be the padded shoulders and the thickness of her dark grey coat. And it was obvious that she no longer bleached her hair: the hair showing under the small hat was a mix of colours but mainly black, just like it was when he was in short pants. Her skin was now grey, and her features had a stern look about them. In less than a year, she seemed to have aged.

As usual, his thoughts were irrational and wandering. He wondered if she was still seeing the American soldier. He imagined somebody bringing flowers to the grave and finding that condom. The thought made him smile. He mentally compared Mrs Porter adultery with Patricia's purity. During all the time he knew Patricia, he had not been allowed to touch her body, not even on top of her coat. His thoughts returned to Mr Porter. 'Does he know about the Yank and those rumours? Well, Ivy, does he? Does, he?' Fred shuddered at the thought, a combination of the low temperature and solemnity of the occasion. Unexpectedly, Mrs Porter half-swivelled her body around and smiled at him. Fred didn't know where to look.

"Please to hear you're doing well at the grammar, Fred. Do you like it?" Her voice was now soft, nothing like the last time she spoke with him.

He avoided making eye-contacted and, showing the palms of his hands, raised his eyebrows and shoulders. "It's okay."

"By the way," she continued, "have you seen our Jack, recently?"

Fred was surprised by the question; he hadn't seen him for weeks, maybe months. "No, I haven't seen him for ages."

Mrs Porter didn't reply, but turned towards Fred's mother. "Isn't it sad about poor Mr Pratt. He was such a lovely little man."

MONDAY 28 JULY 1947

Word got around that they were going to pull down the long, brick-built, air-raid shelter standing in the middle of Daffodil Street. It had been erected just six years earlier to offer the public protection against German aircraft. Although enemy planes had regularly droned overhead, only one bomb and small fragments of twisted molten metal had ever fallen on the streets of Riverton. But, as treasure, the children had eagerly collected the shrapnel, a valuable commodity for trading with other children. It was more valuable than the back-issue editions of the Beano, Dandy and Hotspur comics – but of equal value to a large piece of Meccano or three, internally-coloured glass marbles.

Solidly built of red bricks that looked almost new, and with fourteen-inch thick walls, the shelter's external appearance was misleading. Its interior had suffered from recent years of neglect and misuse. With no drainage facilities, and with unsealed entrances at both ends, the rainwater that ran in off the street remained. And, since the war's end, it had become a convenient dumping site for rusting pushchairs, broken bicycle wheels and any rubbish that had no value and was too big for a dustbin. The built-in wooded bunks and benches were buried under the weight of garbage. Furthermore, during the dark hours, strangers used the shelter as a public lavatory. By the end of 1946, the local children no longer used it as a shelter on rainy days. The dank stench had become unbearable and was leaking out and into surrounding houses. Responding to public demands, on Wednesday, 5th February 1947, the two entrances had been bricked up, and the building listed for demolition.

When the large yellow bulldozer arrived on Daffodil Street, those neighbours not working lined the street and cheered. A woman, fat, turbaned and wearing a pink pinafore, waved a small union jack. The foreman, distinguishable from the boiler-suited and cloth-capped workmen by his dark blue suit and black trilby, walked authoritatively down the street. Waving both arms, he ordered the crowd back. Satisfied, he turned and raised a thumb. Slowly the wide bucket at the front of the bulldozer rose level with the driver's head.

The first impact with the building caused no damage, but the second impact on the same area not only fractured the wall, but also brought down a huge chunk of the concrete roof. The third strike pushed part of the wall inwards, and dozens of rats scrambled over the fallen bricks. The crowd parted as the swarm ran knowingly towards the back alleyway at the top of the street. It was an hour later before they found gnawed human bones.

From teeth records, the remains were identified as Jack Porter's. The Coroner's inquest could not determine the cause of death, but the date of the death was recorded with reasonable accuracy as between Tuesday 4 February, the date he went missing, and Wednesday 12 February. The air-raid shelter's only two entrances were bricked up on the 5th. This calculation was made on the assumption that he could not have survived in total darkness without food and water for more than seven days.

MONDAY 11 AUGUST 1947
The service and internment for Jack were held at the same church and graveyard as the arrangements for Mr Pratt. But the mourners were fewer - less than two dozen.

89

Fred, with his mother and sister, followed Mrs Porter and the coffin into the church. She was wearing the same dark grey coat but now with a black armband. A black chiffon scarf tied in a knot beneath her chin covered her head. Wearing her usual high-heeled shoes, she walked unsteadily towards the altar, faltering at the entrance to the first row. Helped by the undertaker, and with a hand on the waist-high Bible rack, she edged along the continuous seating. She beckoned for Mrs O'Flaherty, Fred and his sister to join her on the front row.

An ardent supporter of the Pope, Mrs O'Flaherty, was, by nature and religious indoctrination, an enthusiastic dispenser of sympathy. It was she who had regularly shared a double seat with Mrs Porter on the five-mile tram ride to and from the hospital. It was Fred's mother who held her hand while she underwent electroshock therapy. But that was years ago and as soon as Mrs Porter's mental depressions had stabilized, Mrs O'Flaherty was surplus to requirement. Although only thirteen, Fred now construed Mrs Porter as not only deceptive, but also a clever manipulator of people,

Sitting next to Mrs Porter, Fred's mother apologized for her husband's absence due to work. Mrs Porter responded by saying her husband was at the hospital that day having a new prosthetic limb fitted. Fred, listening to the conversation, wondered why the hospital visit could not have been re-arranged for such an important event.

In the two weeks since Jack's remains were found, Fred had heard various stories about his death. One claimed he had gone into the shelter for a pee and been attacked by rats. Another source claimed he had disturbed a tramp sleeping in the shelter and been stabbed by him.

This second theory had some traction: last January, an unkempt man had occasionally been seen hanging around the shelter. Others blamed aliens from another planet, a rumour started by Fred's youngest brother who swore he saw white lights flashing when he walked past the entrance the night Jack went missing.

The service was short, and after the coffin had been lowered – and, still standing by the grave - Mrs Porter, wiping her eyes, invited the mourners back to her house for drinks. Most declined, the day was too nice for sitting indoors. And Mrs Porter still had a reputation, especially among the women living in and around Daffodil Street. Fred made an excuse saying he had some homework to do, but Mrs Porter, now having difficulty standing, put her hands on his shoulders and reminded him he was Jack's best friend.

Fred couldn't reconcile this statement with reality. Their friendship had always been transient, at best. He was more than a year younger than Jack, hadn't seen him for months, and had never really liked him. Those past interactions with Mrs Porter were now weighing heavily on Fred's conscience. And she was obviously no longer creating the illusion of allure.

"You must come for a teeny-weeny sherry," she said, putting a hand before Fred's face and making an incomplete circle with a forefinger and thumb.

The smell of sherry on her breath confirmed what he was thinking: she was drunk! But up to this stage of the proceedings, her utterances had been controlled and reasonably articulate. But her female friends saw only a mother grieving for a lost son. And thoughts of those rumours about American G.Is and others – well, they were dismissed as nothing more than malicious gossip.

The curtains were drawn when they entered the house, but being of a thin material, they allowed some light into the parlour. But this didn't stop one of the mourners exaggerating the situation.

"Turn the bloody light on," the man with a strong Scottish accent shouted, "before ah break me bleedin' neck."

Mrs Porter crossed the room and switched on the light but left the curtains drawn. Fred looked around. The only change to the room he could identify was a small glass-topped table with four metal legs. It was situated between the corduroy settee and fireplace. A dozen assorted glasses and two bottles of sweet sherry – one two-thirds empty - had been randomly placed on the glass top. Fred recognized the flowers painted on one of the small glasses, and his thoughts flashed back to one of his previous visits.

"Help yourselves. It's on peg leg," Mrs Porter said, sitting in the easy chair under the window.

With two hands, she held a large white handkerchief over her lower face. Still standing inside the front door waiting for those before him to move forward, Fred watched the handkerchief move in and out in time with Mrs Porter's breathing.

Enid Salmon, the Scotsman's wife and Mrs Porter's sister, dropped herself heavily onto the settee and, looking at Mrs Pratt, patted the adjacent cushion. She repeated the exercise, looking at Fred's mother. With the settee fully occupied, she turned her head, looking behind at the three people left standing behind the settee. Her eyes settled on Fred.

"Can you bring the chairs in, love. We'll need...one for me hubby, and one for you, and you. That's...How many is that, Jimmy?"

It was also obvious to Fred that Mrs Porter had not been drinking alone.

"Three!" the Scotsman calculated. "How's that for a man who left school at fourteen?" Enid burst out laughing. "They said I'd never get anywhere, and they were bleedin' right."

Mrs O'Flaherty and her daughter held down their heads; Fred had to suppress a smile, and Mrs Pratt coughed - but Enid's laugher intensified. Mrs Porter kept the handkerchief before her face.

"They're in the kitchen!" Enid shouted, but Fred was already passing through the connecting door.

"He knows, he's been here before," Mrs Porters said, now using the handkerchief to wipe her nose.

Mrs Porter noticed Fred's mother's surprise, and quickly added: "With our Jack." Smiling weakly, she tucked the handkerchief up the sleeve of her coat.

Fred's sister followed him into the back room. He noted the tall cupboard was now white, but some of the paint also patterned the stone floor and edge of the fireside rug. Nevertheless, Fred was impressed: the white paint and large easy chair in the corner made the small room brighter, more comfortable.

"Thank you, young lady," Enid's husband, Jimmy, said, bowing as he accepted the chair. He dragged it across the room and placed it beside the small table. But before sitting down, he looked at Mrs O'Flaherty: "Am looking for a new missus. Is your daughter still single, by any chance?"

Fred's sister blushed, and Jimmy's wife stood up and declared: "He's yours for sixpence! Okay, tuppence! No? I'll take a farthing."

Mr Salmon filled seven glasses with sherry, but Fred and his sister declined his offer and remained seated behind the settee.

"Got a fag, Ivy?" Mr Salmon asked, leaning across and passing her a glass of sherry.

Mrs Porter, still wearing the heavy overcoat, put the drink on the floor beside the chair. Taking a slim, multi-coloured packet from her coat pocket, she tapped its base. The tips of four cigarettes appeared. She put one of them in her mouth and passed the packet to Mr Salmon.

"Thought you were a Craven A woman," Mr Salmon said, accepting the packet. "Can I take one for later?"

Mrs Porter agreed, but her verbal response was morose: "Craven A, Woodbine's; they're all the same to me."

Fred watched her strike a match and put it before the cigarette. After lighting the cigarette, she continued to watch the matchstick blacken and bend. Indifferently, she blew it out when it had burned close to her fingers. She threw the remains of the match into the hearth. Enid put the sherry glass to her lips and emptied the content.

Mrs Porter's sudden plunge to a lower level of melancholy was obvious, and Mr Salmon, trying to lighten the atmosphere, quipped: "It's not the cough that carries you off, it's the coffin they carry you off in." But his humour was misguided. Tears rolled down Mrs Porter's cheeks.

Enid stood up and put an arm around her sister. "That was stupid, you old sweaty sock, talking about coffins."

Mr Salmon apologized and put one of the cigarettes in the top pocket of his stained and shiny black jacket, passing the cigarette packet to Mrs Pratt.

"I'm all right, Love. I know he didn't mean harm," Mrs Porter said, and Enid returned to her seat.

Reminded of the gravity of the occasion, the conversation dried up. In silence, the five adults sucked on their cigarettes. Relaxing as they inhaled, they stared at the ceiling; stared at the linoleum-covered floor; stared at their cigarettes - stared anywhere except at each other. The room soon filled with smoke.

Enid broke the silence: "Our Jimmy's in the clear now."

"In the clear?" Mrs O'Flaherty asked.

"He's not wanted now. He's done his time," Enid explained, looking at her husband. He smiled back.

"He was a deserter!" Mrs Porter said, holding her cigarette between two fingers at the side of her face. Noticing Enid's furrowed brow, she added: "Or sommat!"

Enid responded indignantly: "A conscious objector!"

Only Fred or Siobhan could have corrected the malapropism, but neither bothered. Mrs Porter watched the ash building on her cigarette.

Mrs Pratt and Mrs O'Flaherty made their one small glass of sherry last the forty minutes the wake lasted. Jimmy and Enid drank most of the whole bottle and, arm-in-arm, left the house in tears. Mrs Porter was on her third glass but now looking long and hard at Fred's mother. The unblinking gaze was unsettling, reminding Mrs O'Flaherty of those hospital visits.

"We'd better be going," Mrs O'Flaherty said, turning to look at her children but also to avoid eye contact with Mrs Porter. Fred and his sister stood up.

"Mr Porter did it, he killed my boy."

Mrs Pratt and Mrs O'Flaherty gasped, with Mrs Pratt putting a hand to her own throat. Fred and his sister looked at each other and sat back on their respective chairs.

"No!" Fred's mother said, quietly. "He wouldn't do that."

"He wouldn't," Mrs Pratt concurred, putting a splayed hand across her chest.

After a pause, Mrs Porter continued: "He kicked him out of the house. He had nowhere to go."

This explanation seemed to confirm what Fred had heard from one of Jack's pals. Jack's father had evicted him from the house, but nobody knew why.

SATURDAY 3 APRIL 1948

It was three years since the war had ended, and the families of those men who had not returned from the war – but had not been officially declared dead - were resigned to them never returning. Two of Fred's grammar school friends were now fatherless – one officially and the other unofficially. However, for many families, those casualties of war were becoming blurred memories. And the conventions of family life were being reinstated, in some cases with unanticipated vigour: in droves, returning servicemen were divorcing unfaithful wives. But marriages were also rising to prewar levels, helped by the 70,000

English girls marrying American servicemen. But some English girls were, surprisingly, still marrying Englishmen. For example, the O'Flaherty's next-door neighbour, Ethel Butler, was betrothed to Albert Simkins, an apprentice bricklayer.

The few clouds that were in the blue sky were white and airy. It didn't seem like a Saturday afternoon. Fred was wearing a new blazer adorned with three silver buttons and a crown embroidered in gold thread on the breast pocket. It was a hire-purchase acquisition – repayable over 26 weeks - made by his mother for the occasion of Ethel's wedding. And his new trousers were bought on the same six-month repayment scheme. But, unfamiliar with grey flannel trousers, the coarse material was irritating his legs. He watched seventeen-year-old Ethel struggling to squeeze into her uncle's small Morris van. Although dressed all in frothy white, her pregnancy was obvious and her movements awkward.

After the church service, the O'Flaherty family walked with other invited guests the half-mile to the Co-op Hall. It was a large room situated above the related, multi-windowed emporium and had been booked by Mr Butler for a maximum of three hours. The only entrance to the hall was by a side-street door and a steep staircase – not wide enough to permit more than one person at a time.

Positioned in the middle of the vast open space, four long tables had been covered with white tablecloths. Each of the four tables had been set for twelve guests, six to a side. The paper plates supported diagonally cut sandwiches and a small meat pie, and, in the interest of hygiene, covered with paper serviettes. Two similar-sized, but uncovered, tables had been conveniently positioned along the wall by the windows. One table supported three crates of bottled beer, two bottles of sherry (one dry, the other sweet) and two large bottles of lemonade. Additionally, clear plastic tumblers were stacked in three piles.

On the adjacent trellised table, a tall, stainless steel tea urn had been carefully positioned with its spout extended over the table edge above a galvanized bucket. Also on that same table, a dozen white cups were upturned on matching saucers. Although the thick pottery appeared unbreakable, most of the cups had distinctive grey chips on the rims. For security reasons, the cups and saucers were all printed with the Co-op's 'C' logo in green.

As next-door neighbours to the bride's family, The O'Flaherty family was privileged and seated at the top table. The bride's fifteen-year-old cousin sat next to Fred.

"I'm Mildred," she said, by way of introduction. "What's your name?"

Fred wasn't listening: he was watching Mrs Porter who was sitting beside her one-legged husband. Her presence reminded him of the day she had shown him the military sword. Unbidden, images swirled around in his head. He wondered what happened to the German officer who had owned the sword. She was pulling the long blade out of its scabbard, inviting him to touch it. She was standing naked. Those were vivid recollections. He could only rely on hearsay for what went on after Jack's school pals entered the house that day. But he didn't believe what they said. It seemed too outrageous, even for someone as depraved as Mrs Porter.

"Are you asleep, or got cloth ears?" Mildred said, nudging him with an elbow.

"Did you say something?' Fred asked, removing his spectacles and wiping the lens with a paper serviette.

"Yeah! What's your moniker?"

"Me what?"

"Yer name. Specky Four Eyes?"

"Fred."

"Yer live next door to Ethel, don't yer?" she said, looking across the table at the bride, but Ethel was also preoccupied, watching her new husband across the room, his head held back drinking the remains of what was a pint of beer, obviously acquired elsewhere.

Fred nodded, but continued to glance the Porters through the side of his spectacles. Although sitting beside her husband, Mrs Porter seemed detached, self-absorbed, examining her painted fingernails, looking down at the plate on the table or the cigarette burning between her fingers. The Porters were ignoring each other, and ignored by those other guests on their table. In Fred's opinion, Mr Porter seemed more depressed than his wife – but, of course, he had good reason. Fred wondered why they'd bothered to come to the reception, spoiling it for those around them.   Having lost a son in such terrible circumstances, he felt sorry for both of them, but especially for Mr Porter.   With only one leg and psychologically damaged, he must be totally dependent on a disloyal wife. But then he thought of Mr Packer bringing up the son of an Italian POW. Mr Packer, otherwise unscarred by the war, was sitting on another table with his wife. They seemed to be getting on all right. But Fred wondered if that was just a front.   He also wondered how many other men were unwittingly bringing up other men's children.   Only mothers would be able to answer that hypothetical question, he reasoned.

The bride, still wearing her white finery, and sitting opposite Fred, shouted to her husband who was standing by the beer crates with two of his friends: " Will yer stop friggin drinkin' like that, Albert? There'll be nowt left."

"We brought these in from pub. What's the matter wi' yer," he shouted back. "Yer dad's got a load of nat's piss."

The bride's father left his seat and walked across the room.   Face to face with his new son-in-law, he put a hand on his shoulder and pushed. The confrontation was short and silent. Mr Butler calmly walked back to his seat next to his daughter, the bride.   With his two friends, the bridegroom crossed the room and descended the stairs.

Unconcerned by her husband's departure, and with her elbows on the table, Ethel leaned across towards Mildred and, with soft intonations, nodded towards Fred, and said: "Watch 'im, Mildred: 'e'll 'ave his 'and up yer clouts!"

Fred blushed. That feeling of escaping came over him. He looked towards his parents sitting farther along the same table. Fortunately they were out of hearing range.

Although only three-years younger than Ethel - and they had lived next door to each other as long as he had been alive - she had never before spoken to him other than to say "'ow do!" or "'pissin' down again!" He had, though, briefly heard her conversing with her husband-to-be that very morning.

Scraping his breakfast plate above the dustbin, Fred heard the whoosh of the Butler's outside lavatory flushing. Then there were footsteps and whispers. But he distinctly heard Ethel complain: 'Can't a go to the lav on me own? You want a quickie?' and then agree: 'All right but...' Although Fred quietly replaced the metal dustbin lid and crept across the backyard to be nearer the dividing brick wall, he didn't hear anything further, just the sound of a creaking door and a bolt being drawn.

"'ey, dad, when you gonna switch on the blinkin' gramophone?" Ethel asked, turning to her father.

Without responding, he stood up and walked to the small table in the corner of the room where, earlier in the day, he had placed a portable gramophone and a small stack of vinyl records. Selecting a Victor Silvester record, he put it on the turntable and pressed a button. Bending down, with an ear to the machine, he listened to the music before turning up the sound.

Smiling, and addressing the guests, he exclaimed: "In't it marvellous. We used to 'ave to wind these things up. 'ere, Ethel. Come and 'ave a dance wi' yer Dad".

And as father and daughter shuffled on the linoleum-covered floor, their neighbours and relatives clapped and cheered. Two women joined them, waltzing like professionals, their faces to the ceiling.

"Yer can turn that crap off," a voice shouted from the door at the top of the stairs. It was Albert with his two mates, all three holding fresh pints of beer. The three young men, similarly dressed in loose-fitting black trousers, long black jackets, white shirts with black bowties and lace-up black boots, slowly walked towards the gramophone. Albert carefully lifted the needle off the record and put the arm back on the support.

"What the bloody 'ell d'yer think yer playin' at?" Mr Butler shouted, and, letting go of his daughter, strode over to face his son-in-law.

"It was givin' us a 'eadache, Pops," Albert calmly explained, but Mr Butler was incensed and threw a punch, knocking Albert to the floor. Albert's two friends jumped on Mr Butler, but they were soon over-powered by six guests.   Ethel was confused: she didn't know whether to comfort her father or new husband – but chose to kneel by her wounded husband. Mr Butler rose to his feet, brushing off the thin layer of dust that had transferred from the floor to his new navy-blue suit.

"You didn't need to 'it 'im, Dad," she said, wiping the bloody from Albert's nose with the inside hem of her wedding dress.

Mr Butler stretched out a hand towards Albert and helped him to his feet. The two men hugged each other. With the music reinstated, calm was restored: it was as if nothing untoward had happened.

"Have you ever kissed a girl, Fred?" Mildred whispered. "Bet you haven't."

Fred thought about the question before responding. She was, he calculated, probably a year older than him. And, furthermore, she worked at Woolworth's on Saturdays.   Ignoring the question, he asked: "Why you wearing a long pink dress?"

"Because I'm a bridesmaid, stupid. Don't try to get out of it."

"Out of what?"

"Have you ever kissed a girl?"

"Maybe."

"When?"

"Years ago."

"When you were five?"

Fred was indignant. "What's it got to do with you?"

She put her lips to his ear and whispered: "You can come with me to the park after, if you want. We can feed the ducks."

"What with?"

"With these," she said, putting a folded sandwich in Fred's breast pocket."

The limited supply of alcohol was soon consumed, and when Mr Butler switched off the gramophone, the guests quietly drifted out onto the street. Although the sun was very low in the blue sky, it was still warm.

Putting her arm in his, Mildred led Fred down the sloping street leading to the municipal park. The two gates, recently reinstalled by the council, were both locked and chained. But they stood alone: the railings surrounding the park had yet to be delivered and installed.

"Push me higher, higher," Mildred shouted, as Fred stood behind her pushing the seat of the swing. When she thrust out her legs, her long, pink, satin dress rose to her thighs, revealing knee-length white socks and white knickers.

They slid down the slide, rotated with the roundabout, oscillated on the seesaw.

"Let's feed the ducks," Mildred said, pulling Fred by the arm.

They walked along the river to where it bulged between two shallow weirs, but there were no ducks. Fred picked up a stone and threw it across the water.

"Are you trying to make it skim?" Mildred asked, sitting on the grassy incline with her hands on her knees.

Fred nodded. She stood up. "You need a flat stone. Come with me, I want to ask you something."

Mildred led Fred by the hand, and guided him under the overhanging branches of one of the many riverside willow trees. Fred sat next to her, avoiding eye contact and looking out through a gap in the thick foliage at the darkening sky. "What do you want to ask, Mildred?"

"Do you want to put it in?" she asked, standing up and looking down on Fred.

"Put what in?"

"Your dick, in there," she said, pointing to her crotch. "In my pussy." She lifted the hem of her long dress above her knees.

"Hey, cover up: someone might see," Fred said, standing up and anxiously looking around.

"Nobody can see us in here. Get it out, Fred. Let me have a look at yours."

"I don't think it's the right place. It's too public, Mildred," he said, sitting down, but seriously tempted by the opportunity. It was the thought of Mildred telling Ethel that worried him. It could easily get back to his mother and father, he thought.

"Are you shy?"

"No, but what if the cops see us?"

His words didn't match his thoughts, and he turned his back to Mildred so she couldn't see the movement inside his trousers.

"Why are you turning your back on me?" she said, putting a hand on his shoulder and forcing him onto his back. "Well if you won't, I'll get it out," she said firmly, and unbuttoned his fly buttons.   "It's a bigger than I thought it would be. How old are you?" Fred ignored the questions. "You'll have to put it in quick before it goes soft."

Lying on her back, she pulled up her dress, removed her knickers and opened her legs wide. She instructed Fred to lie on top of her. But Fred was perplexed, questioning to himself how he could get his penis inside her when there wasn't a visible entrance? A depression surrounded by red hair was clearly visible, but it seemed to be sealed. He lay on top of her and tried repeatedly.   But each time, she squealed in pain.

"Where are you?" a gruff voice called out from nearby, accompanied by a barking dog.

They were sitting silently side by side when the white-bearded face of an old man appeared through the overhanging branches.

"Are you okay, love?"

"Piss off and mind your own business," Mildred shouted, with such venom that the stranger immediately withdrew and hurried away.

Mildred climbed to her feet and parted the branches. "He's gone, the nosey sod! Get it out, Fred! I'll wank you off like I did those two GIs."

'Two GIs?" Fred asked, but she declined to elaborate.

He stood up to double check they were now alone, but had a change of heart. The man's sudden appearance had confirmed what he already knew: there were always people in the park, even after sunset. And he had lost interest in her undeveloped body. Neither did he like the idea of doing it in such a public place and getting caught.

"Come on, get it out," she demanded,

Fred suggested they should be getting back before ten, but he was scorned for thinking she had to be home so early.

"I can stay out all night, if I want. Nobody cares. Anyway, are you still a kid or what?"

Fred made the mistake of arguing with her, and the more she belittled him, the more he wanted to disprove what she was implying.

"You won't tell Ethel, or anyone else?"

"Of course not. Do you think I'm stupid?"

"Well I don't want you watching."

"And I don't want you shooting your spunk on me dress, so there."

But some of the semen flowed onto her hand. She casually wiped it off on his trousers.

"Why'd you do that? They're me new trousers. And look at the grass stains on me knees. Mam'll go barmy!"

"Shouldn't have let it dribble."

Fred was annoyed, and they walked up the hill and back to Primrose Street in silence.

The spluttering filaments in the street gaslights cast shadows and leaked noxious fumes. But the pavement outside the Butler's house was illuminated by electric light flooding out of the parlour, bedroom window and the open front door. Music and voices suggested to Fred and Mildred that the party was still ongoing. In contrast, Fred's house was in darkness.

"Aren't you coming in?" she asked, standing in the pool of light outside the Butler's door.

"I've got to clean me pants," he replied, annoyed at now having to remove the stains off his trousers and underpants.

"Sorry, Fred! Put 'em under the tap," she suggested.

To his surprise, Fred found the front door ajar, but the house in total darkness - and yet the old settee in the parlour was creaking. He turned on the light.

"Turn that light out. I'm having a rest with your ma."

Fred did as his father instructed, but not before he had recognized Mrs Butler, the bride's mother, lying beneath his father. Although his father was still dressed in the suit he wore at the wedding, Mrs Butler was naked from the waist down. Fred went through into the kitchen, listening to the whispers and movements in the front room.

"We're going back to the party," his father shouted through the adjoining door.

Fred shivered when he heard the front door forcibly closed. He knew from the tone of the voice and the slamming front door that his father was angry. Satisfied that he was alone, he removed his trousers and underpants and draped them over the kitchen sink. After placing the stained areas under the cold-water tap, he rubbed them with the hard-bristled hand brush his mother used for scrubbing the kitchen floor. Satisfied the white stains were removed from his trousers and underpants, he was trying – unsuccessfully - to remove the grass stains from his trousers when there was a knock on the front door. Thinking it was his parents at the door, he threw his wet clothes into the cupboard under the sink. Somebody was repeatedly hitting the door. Standing behind the door holding a towel around his waist, he slowly opened it, peering into the darkness. Ethel, still in her bridal gown, pushed Fred aside and rushed into the house.

"Where are they?" she shouted.

"Who?" Fred asked, feigning ignorance, but guessing she knew about her mother's tryst with his father.

Ethel stopped in the doorway leading to the kitchen and turned. "Where's Albert?"

"Who?"

"Me bleedin' 'usband. That's who."

Fred shook his head and replied forcibly: "How should I know?"

Ethel looked down at the towel. "Are they upstairs?"

"Nobody's upstairs."

"You sure?" Fred nodded. "Where's your kecks?"

"I was getting ready for bed."

"You've been stuck up our Mildred, 'aven't you?"

"I haven't been stuck up anyone. I'm going to bed."

"Are you sure she's not upstairs with my Albert?"

"Last time I saw Mildred was when she went in your house about an hour ago."

"After you'd been stuck up 'er."

"No, I just told you."

'On your Dad's life?"

"Yes!"

Ethel walked slowly past him but then quickly turned, putting an arm around his neck.

"Let go! I'm going to bed," he responded, tired and angry at being abused in his own house.

Without letting go, she continued reflectively: "Wait till I see Mildred; the cow's pissed off with me 'ubby. I'll show the bugger what's good for the goose, is good for the gander."

Now with a firm hold on his neck, she led him the few paces into the room and forced him down on the rug in front of the tiled fireplace. Standing unsteadily above him,

108

she lifted her wedding gown up above her breasts. Beneath the gown, she was naked.

"Look at them, Fred! 'ave you every seen a pair of tits like that?"

In the subdued light filtering through the open door from the kitchen, Fred stared up at her breasts. She's right to be proud, he thought. They were sticking out as though inflated with a bicycle pump. He moved his gaze down to her navel. That too was protruding. Releasing hold of her wedding gown, she knelt beside him.

Fred was confused. What was happening didn't make sense. He couldn't understand why she was suddenly showing an interest in him. She usually ignored him, or spoke to him as though he were a child.

"Give us a kiss," she said, stretching out on the rug beside him.

It was then that he realized she was drunk. The smell of whisky was evident. Assuming alcohol had affected her judgment, he was in conflict with himself, afraid of touching her lest she didn't want that. When sober, she may be sorry, he thought.

But there was no ambiguity when she moved onto her back, lifted her wedding gown above her breasts again, and spread her legs apart.

"Put it in!" she shouted, using a similar expression to the demand Mildred had made earlier that evening. It occurred to him that Mildred had definitely been talking about him.

"I can't."

"Why?"

Fred ignored the question, and tried to rise, but she held him down.

"You've 'ad it off with our Mildred, 'aven't you? She was right!"

Fred pleaded innocence, and said he wasn't feeling very well.

"Get yer 'and down there and work me off."

The timing was unfortunate, for Ethel's orgasm coincided with her new husband parking his motorcycle outside the house. Fred's front door led directly from the street into the parlour - and the front door had been left open.

"Stuffin' me wife? Well 'ere's sommat else of mine-"

Although Fred recognized the voice of Ethel's new husband, and saw a boot before his face, those were the last memories he had of the encounter.

SUNDAY 4 APRIL 1948

Imprisoned between white sheets tucked tightly under the mattress, Fred stared through swollen eyelids at the ceiling and the bright neon strip above his head. He could hear footsteps and distance voices. He lifted his head, unsure where he was and suffering a headache, the likes of which he had never before experienced.

Beds lined two sides of the long room. And between the beds, steam was rising from two huge kettles on a central table. His head and left leg throbbed; his veiled vision made focusing difficult, and the smell of disinfectant added to his sense of nausea. He lowered his head on the pillow, half awake, half asleep, and pulled the sheet over his face. Slowly, very slowly, pieces of the puzzle began to fit together, but his concentration was interrupted by a woman's voice, at first quiet and inaudible but slowly becoming distinct.

"…Can you hear me? Wakey, wakey! Let me see…" she said, reading the metal clipboard that had been hanging at the end of the bed. "Frederick O'Flaherty, 1st April 1934. Is that right?" Fred didn't respond to the voice or the hand on his shoulder, hoping the woman would go away. She gently pulled back the sheet, letting out a little gasp.

"Oh dear, what have they done to your face?"

The nurse's face was above his head; too close for comfort - an invasion of his privacy. He wanted to go back to sleep and later wake to find it was all a dream.

"Have you got an aspirin?" he asked, running his tongue around his dry, swollen lips.

"Are you in pain?"

"Leg and head; they're very sore."

"I'll bring you something later."

"Can't you bring me some pills now? It's like a knife's been stuck in my head, and I think I've sprained me leg."

"Broken! The fibula may have to be reset tomorrow," she replied, ignoring the request for medication.

"Can't it be done today? It's hurting like mad."

"Today's Sunday, all day! Open your mouth, please." Fred obliged, and the nurse placed a thermometer under his tongue. "Close your mouth. That was a nasty accident you had last night. Don't worry; it's surprising how quickly these serious facial injuries heal. The doctor doesn't think there'll be any brain damage. But we have to be sure." She removed the thermometer, studying it without comment.

"What time is it, Miss?"

The nurse studied the small watch attached to her starched white bib. "It's just after six."

"At night?"

"Morning! The tea lady will be down this end in a minute," she said, unwrapping the bandage around Fred's forehead.

"How long have I been here?"

"They brought you in last night, covered in blood and half dressed, so I hear. Ooh, that's nasty! Gosh, they must have hit you with a hammer. And some of those stitches look loose. Saturday night staff shortage, I suppose! We'd better rewrap and wait for the doctor on his rounds."

He could now recall most the previous evening's events, and he wanted the ground to open up and swallow him. But he couldn't understand the nurse's reference to more than one person.

"It was one bloke," he said, reflectively

"Man and a woman, I heard." The nurse replied, re-bandaging the wound across his forehead. .

"A woman?"

"Man and wife," the nurse affirmed.

"No, no; I don't think so."

"No concern of mine: the damage is the same no matter who inflicted it. That wound needs tightening up or you'll have a scar for life from ear to ear. You're lucky they didn't break your nose as well as your leg."

"There was only one bloke," he again insisted.

"And they also gave you two right shiners... and a cauliflower ear. But, like I said, these things heal fairly quickly. Not sure about the leg, though. This ear's got some dry blood inside. Can you hear me?" she asked, covering his other ear with her hand.

Fred nodded; he wanted the nurse to stop talking, to go away. He wanted to be alone with his embarrassment.

"When can I go home, Miss?" The nurse smiled, but shook her head. "Did you say it was Sunday?"

"Till tomorrow!"

"I've got school tomorrow. I've got to finish me homework."

"Can you turn your head to that side? Good, that's fine. Tell me if this hurts, Fred?" she asked, wiping the inside of his ear with a cotton swab.

But Fred was pre-occupied, trying to recall more detail. He could remember hearing Albert's voice and what sounded like a scream. He could remember the boot before his face, but after that it was all a black void.

"How did I get here, nurse?"

"In an ambulance, of course. Here's Phyllis with the tea. See you later."

Fred declined the offer of tea, and lay watching the neon light above his head. He wanted to go back to sleep and perhaps wake up in his own bed, but his thoughts were too active to allow him to relax. It must have been Albert and one of his mates, he thought. And then a feeling of guilt crept into his analysis of events: 'Albert may divorce Ethel and cite me as the adulterer. I've ruined a marriage.' And then remorse turned to fear: what if Albert sues me for destroying his marriage? "Where will I get the money," he said aloud, forgetting he was not alone.

"What's that, son?" the old man in the next bed asked, lifting his upper body on an angled and fleshless arm. He leaned across the narrow divide.

"Sorry, I was talking in me sleep."

"That's all right with me, son, as long as you don't start fartin' like some of 'em in 'er. Can't get to sleep some nights."

"It's the bake beans they keep feedin' us," the equally old man shouted from the opposite side of the ward.

But his comments were ignored, and the old man in the next bed enquired if he'd been in a car accident. Fred shook his head and turned his back.

"They won't let you sleep in 'ere, son. It's worse than bleedin' prison," the old man shouted, "and food's no better."

The old man was right: at regular intervals, nurses carried out different functions on his body. And finally a grey-haired doctor arrived, accompanied by a nurse and two young women, both wearing similar long white coats. The nurse removed the bandage.

"Nasty!" the doctor exclaimed, looking close-up at the wound and then at the X-Ray film carried by one of the young women. Casually addressing the two young women, he continued: "One fractured leg, but no broken facial bones. Surprising, considering the external damage to the face. Do you know how many bones make up the face?" One of the young women raised her eyebrows and shoulders. He answered his own question: "Fourteen, and not one broken."

The second young woman asked if that included teeth, but she was ignored. The doctor turned to Fred. "You must have good bone density, at least in the head. On somebody else, an assault such as you suffered could have been fatal. All in the genes, all in the genes! Thank your parents when you see them."

"What about me leg?"

"The fibula is a thin bone that is easily damaged, especially when hit from the side. Do you know, ladies,

114

how much body weight the fibula supports?" Neither of the junior doctors responded, and, after a pause, he continued: "About seventeen percent. You are lucky it wasn't the tibia, young man."

"When can I go home?"

The doctor explained that Fred would need several more x-rays on his leg and head, and undergo a series of neurological tests over several days.

"We have to be sure there is no brain damage."

For most of the day, Fred stared at the ceiling listening to the mundane conversations taking place between the two old men in nearby beds. The old man in the next bed said he had terminal cancer, and the older man across the divide said he was always saying that and was really just a malingerer. Their conversations got heated and contradictory until Fred didn't know what to believe.

At seven o'clock precisely – and after the remains of the evening meal had been cleared – the matron opened the door at the end of the corridor. And those faces that minutes earlier had been peering through the door's glass panels led the stream of anxious visitors.

Fred's mother and father, dragging plastic chairs, walked up and down the ward twice before being led by a nurse to Fred's bed. Fred still had the sheet pulled up over his head. His parents sat at either side of the bed.

"It's us, Fred," his mother said.

"Are you all right, lad?" his father intoned.

Slowly, Fred pulled down the sheet and his mother let out a little yelp. The same nurse who had led them to the bed hurried across.

"What's the matter, love?" she asked.

"His face, his face," Fred's mother moaned. "Will it get better?"

"I'm sure it will!" the nurse exclaimed, unnecessarily straightening the blue and white bed cover.

"They made a right mess of it," his father remarked, casually.

"It was Ethel's bloke," Fred said, by way of clarification.

After a short pause, his mother said: "It were two of 'em."

Although his parents couldn't see the white of Fred's eyes, Fred could just about make out their blurred images through the swollen blue slots. He looked first at his mother and then at his father.

"Two of 'em, Dad?"

"That's right, lad. You've got some answering to do."

"Not now, Joe," his mother interjected.

"We've got to sort it out before they come."

"Before who comes?" Fred asked.

"I told you what they said when I phoned this morning. They're worried about thrombosis," his mother whispered. "He's got to remain calm."

"Are you talking about me?" Fred asked, pointing to his own face. His mother shook her head.

"Where'd you get the shirt, son?" his father asked, but Fred's mother explained that it was probably a hospital-issue nightgown.

Although he couldn't remember much after seeing that black boot approaching his face, he could now remember every detail of what preceded it. While his parents talked to each other across the bed, Fred was thinking about those events. He reflected on his father lying on top of Ethel's mother, and the coincidence of himself later lying by Ethel. For the first time he thought of the context: mother and daughter being had in the same room, one after the other, and by father then son. He wondered what the odds would be on such a thing happening. He also tried to analyze the circumstances leading to his confrontation. Why, he thought repeatedly, did I leave the front door open? And what was Albert doing coming into our house? If only…

Fred was glad when the bell rang and his parents departed. He wanted to sleep but he was continually disturbed by the nurse arriving with medication, and the orderly with tea, and other patients walking past his bed making banal jokes about his injuries.

"Jesus, look who's here: Frankenstein's monster."

"Bet the other fella's dead."

"You could audition for the Black and White Minstrels show."

When the overhead lights were turned off, the floor-level nightlights projected elongated green strips across the white linoleum. And the sterilizing unit on a table in the centre of the room pulsated with an orange glow, regularly dispersing steam with a disconcerting hiss. Fred began to imagine he was in hell. Everything had suddenly gone quiet, but then the old man in the next bed broke into song:

" Two lovely black eyes. Oh, what a surprise; only for telling a man he was wrong, two lovely black eyes."

"Silence!" a female voice ordered out of the semi-darkness, but by then Fred's head was under the sheet with his hands over his ears.

MONDAY 5 APRIL 1948

At 8am a heavily built black porter dressed in a fawn-coloured dustcoat lifted Fred out of bed and into a wheelchair. In silence, Fred was wheeled out of the ward, along a long corridor and into a spacious elevator, built obviously to take a bed and its occupant. The porter eventually broke the silence.

"Car crash?"

"Sort of," Fred replied, not wanting to get into a conversation with anyone.

Like the elevator, the radiography unit seemed ancient and far too large for its purpose: it was sparsely furnished with one long, rectangular table covered in a white sheet that touched the floor. A large black box affixed to two upright tubular steel rods, was suspended over the table. Standing by an open inner door, a young woman rotated an index finger, and the porter wheeled Fred to the table. With the porter's help, Fred was eased onto the table. After moving the black box above his leg, both she and the porter disappeared through an inner door, closing it behind them.

Alone with his thoughts, Fred tried to recall the journey from home to the hospital. He could remember hearing Albert's voice and the boot before his eyes, but that was all. However, pictures of earlier events kept recurring: he was cleaning the stains off his trousers, lying naked from the waist down on the rug with Albert's wife. 'My God,' he thought, 'Me Mam will find me trousers and underpants under the sink.' And then he thought of being brought to hospital half dressed. He was now convinced everybody in the hospital really knew what had happened to him and how he had arrived. They were being polite and only pretending not to know, he thought. The radiographer reappeared; repositioned the camera over his head, then disappeared again.

Later that morning, Fred was wheeled to a smaller room with another table, but this one covered with plastic sheeting. Stainless steel tubs littered the floor. Lying on the table and with his broken leg supported by a small trellis, wet bandages were wrapped around it, and with each layer the underlying white bandages solidified. His leg was now encased in white plaster of Paris.

By midday, he was finally being wheeled down the long corridor towards the ward. He was exhausted, aching all over and mentally dejected. He imagined everybody back in Riverton would be talking about him. What if the story got back to school...? He vowed to keep away from females for the rest of his life.

"Did you say it was a car crash?" the porter asked.

"Can't remember," Fred replied, in no mood for satisfying the man's curiosity.

"It must have been bad, looking like that and for the police to be involved."

"Police! What police?" Fred asked, trying to look up at the porter. "I haven't made any complaint."

The porter didn't reply. And by the entrance to the ward, turned the wheelchair sharp left into a small side room.

A uniformed policeman was sitting in a chair facing the door, his tall black hat balanced on his knees. Above and behind the policeman's head, a long, narrow, horizontal window provided the only light. The frosted glass sparkled in the sunlight, and its small block structure caused the sunlight to fragment, illuminating the room with acutely angled, but pencil-thin, shafts of orange light. The porter positioned the wheelchair facing the policeman and departed.

Fred looked briefly at the policeman, and then at his surroundings. Unlike all the public rooms and corridors, where the smell of disinfectant was dominant, in this room, the prevailing smell was of perspiration. The policeman said nothing, but alternated his gaze between his notebook, resting on top of his helmet, and Fred's face.

"Fred, Fred O'Flaherty?" he asked, breaking the silence. Fred nodded. "Leg hurt?" Fred nodded. "Headache?" Fred nodded. "Why'd you do it, Fred?"

"Do what?"

"You know what I mean."

"Don't know what you mean, sir."

The policeman stared at Fred for several minutes before referring back to his notebook.

"Is that what they teach you at that school?"

"What's that?"

"Disrespect for young women."

"We're taught to respect all women."

"Very good, Fred; very good. Then why'd you do it?"

"Do what?"

"Why'd you do it, Fred?" he repeated, but softly, pleadingly.

"Do what?" Fred asked again, but knowing what the man meant.

"A nice boy like you. Why'd you do it?"

"You mean Ethel?"

The policeman smiled and pointed his pencil at Fred's groin: "You're on the right track, son."

"She asked me to do it."

"Do what, Fred?"

"You know what I mean."

"No, I don't know what you mean, Fred. Tell me about it."

"She asked me to put it in."

'Put what in where, Fred?"

"In her thingy; her…fanny."

"Your willy?"

"Yes, no…, me finger."

"Make up your mind, Fred. Willy or finger?

"Both, she asked me to put both in."

"At the same time?"

"Yes."

"I've ever heard that one before, Fred. Still I don't know half of what you youngsters get up to these days. When I was a lad it was one or the other. Not both together."

"It was three."

"Three! Three what, Fred?" the policeman asked, his forehead narrowing.

"These three," he said, holding up three fingers.

"She asked you to put three fingers in her fanny? Hadn't she just got married?"

"I was at the wedding."

"A young innocent bride asking a fourteen-year old boy to put his fingers in her fanny?"

"She did, sir. She asked me to put me willy in, but I refused."

After another long pause, the policeman continued with the same slow delivery: "A sweet, little seventeen-year-old virgin asked you to do it on her wedding night?"

"She wasn't a virgin."

"How do you know?"

"She's pregnant, that's why."

"Jesus! That's even worse."

"She's sex mad. I heard her over the yard wall having it off with Albert the morning they got married."

"In the yard, in daylight, over the wall? Can you see through bricks and mortar?"

"No, but I've got good hearing."

"Isn't making love normal when a man and woman get married?"

"They weren't married."

"All this is very confusing and irrelevant. But from what you say, listening to people in the privacy of their homes...well, it makes me think you're also deviant. And you're asking me to believe that a young woman, married that day, asked you, a schoolboy, to put it in?"

"I'm telling the truth."

"That's what they all say."

"I know I did wrong, but she made me do it."

"Why did she attack you, then?"

"She didn't."

Pointing to the white plaster cast on his leg, he continued, frowning as though empathizing with Fred's injured leg:

"Still aching?" Fred nodded. "I broke me leg once. Fell off a bike. They don't half itch. I used to stick a knitting needle down. Does yours itch?" Fred shook his head. "Ethel did that; hit you with a poker."

"No she didn't. Why would she do that?"

"To get you off her?"

"She didn't hit me."

The policeman referred to his notebook. "She was stopped by her cousin, Mildred Butler. Otherwise you might not be here now."

"Mildred wasn't there. It was Ethel's husband who kicked me."

"And Mildred stopped him too, indirectly. Anyway, can't blame Albert? If it were my missus, I'd probably be very angry, too."

"I did wrong, but she encouraged me."

"Let's not go over that again, Fred. Do you expect me to believe that? The girl had just got married that day." With his pencil poised above the notebook, he continued: "Frederick O'Flaherty admits to raping Ethel Simpkins at... What time was it?"

"I didn't rape anybody."

"What time was it when you put your willy in?"

"I did not put me willy in," Fred shouted, trying to get out of the wheelchair.

"Sit down, Fred. You'll be breaking your other leg." After a long pause and referring to his notes, he continued. "What time was it, Fred?"

"After eleven, I suppose. But she made me to do it. I didn't want to."

"I'll call it 2310 hours. Is that okay?"

Fred didn't answer. He placed his chin on his chest and looked down at the policeman's boots. His thoughts were jumping all over the place. Irrationally he assumed the man's feet were probably the source of the sweaty smell filling the room.

Returning his pencil and notebook to his pocket, the policeman lifted his helmet, stood up and stretched his arms. Towering, he smiled then walked to the door where he stopped, turned and addressed Fred's back:

"I'll arrange for a juvenile officer to visit you tomorrow. Ask your mother if you can borrow one of her knitting needles, Fred."

It was a lonely and uncomfortable afternoon for Fred. He couldn't concentrate on yesterday's copy of the *News of the World*, and kept thinking about the unanticipated implications of what lay ahead. The unwieldy newspaper was full of stories about adultery and retribution, but the salacious narrative no longer titillated him. The articles merely reminded him of what the future may hold. And he didn't expect the evening to be any different: midweek visiting time was restricted to the period between seven and eight in the evening and for a maximum of two persons.

On Monday evenings, Fred's parents always spent four hours at the British Legion Club on Town Lane. It was the highlight of the week, and they never missed those bingo evenings, not even after they found Fred's great grandma encased in ice in the backyard.

At seven O'clock, he watched the visitors rush through the door, hurriedly dragging straight-backed chairs to the bedsides of the patients they were visiting. To avoid any embarrassment at being alone and a disfigured spectacle, he held the open newspaper before his face. He couldn't concentrate, wondering when the juvenile officer would be arriving.

"Hello, Fred."

He slowly lowered the newspaper. It was Mildred, standing beside the bed with a small bottle of Lucozade in her outstretched hand.

"What you doing here, Mildred?"

Mildred, like other first-time visitors to his bedside, also made an involuntary noise on seeing Fred's damaged face.

"I asked your mam if I could visit, and they said yes. Said it's okay 'cause they've got to go somewhere else this evening."

Mildred had arrived too late to claim a chair, and she stood beside the bed staring down at Fred's face.

"You can sit on the bed, if you want, Mildred. Just watch me leg. It's in plaster."

Mildred thanked him and put the Lucozade on the small, metal bedside cabinet.

"If you don't mind me saying, that bugger made a mess of your face. You were lucky you didn't have your specs on."

"Can't remember much about it, Mildred."

" Spoiled the party! Do you always read that paper, Fred?"

"Yeah, me Dad has it delivered to the house. Some old woman came round yesterday selling papers and stuff on a trolley."

"Me Mam says its full of dirty stories and prefers the *Sunday People*. She's old fashioned."

"How did you know I was in hospital, Mildred?"

"I was there! I watched them carry you out on a stretcher."

She explained that when she arrived back at Ethel's, the house was full of drunken parents, grandparents, kids.

"Everyone was smoking! Honestly, Fred, you could cut it with a knife. Albert said he had to go to the cig machine at the top of the street. He asked me if I fancied a ride on the back of his motorbike. It would have been as quick to walk, but I thought it would be good for me lungs, but when we got there he tried it on in the shop doorway. His breath stunk like a brewery. I told him to sod off, Ethel's me cousin. He made me walk back. No problem! As I was walking down the street, I saw him putting a chain on his bike. Then there was a scream. I saw him go in your house. I looked through your window and saw him kicking you. You know what happened next."

"No, I don't. What happened next?"

"I ran in your house. Ethel had a poker in her hand. Then your dad and some others arrived and everyone went bananas. You were flat out. She said you'd tried to rape her."

"I didn't rape her."

"I know. Our Ethel told me this morning. She said otherwise Albert would have killed her."

"She must have told the police," Fred suggested.

"No, it was Albert. I told her today that she's got to be truthful, or else I'll tell the cops. And I told her that Albert had tried to put his hand up me dress."

"What did she say?"

"Said I must have encouraged him, and she'll never talk to me again. Anyway, she went to the police station this afternoon and told them she'd made a mistake."

"Thanks, Mildred. I don't know how to thank you."

Mildred didn't respond immediately. She looked up and down the ward, then at Fred. A smile crossed her face. Putting her head closer to his, she whispered: "Do you want me to wank you before I go?"

Fred too looked around: there were no nurses, and all the patients and visitors seemed to be preoccupied. He

126

opened out the *News of the World*, spread it over the bedding, and then nodded. Furtively, she slid her hand between the sheets.

FRIDAY 26 SEPTEMBER 1952

Fred had to stand the large grey suitcase on its end to fit it under the stairs on the double-decker bus. It was a present from his mother for gaining a place at university, but far too big and heavy to be practical. The few clothes he had packed amounted to all his worldly possessions yet barely filled a quarter of the space. Sitting on a rear, inward facing seat, he didn't take his eyes off it.

It was only a short ride to the city centre, but a long, uphill walk from the bus stop to the railway station. The suitcase was not especially heavy, but, because of its size and shape, difficult to hold away from his legs. To reach the designated platform, he had to walk two hundred yards along the first platform, climb a steep metal staircase, walk fifty yards across an enclosed metal bridge and then descend another metal staircase to the third platform. By the time he reached that platform, he was breathless. Not wanting to miss the afternoon train - the next one was not until seven in the evening – he had arrived thirty minutes early.

There were double train lines on both sides of the raised platform but only one train standing stationary. The man with a long chain hanging from his black serge waistcoat had explained that this train had to go out to allow the next train, his, to come in. Sitting on the hard metal bench with his suitcase before his knees, he watched the men and women hurrying along the platform. Some jumping or skipping to dodge the steam that occasionally spurted out from between the train's wide wheels. A few cursed while others were embarrassed, but two young women jumped way from the jet of steam, threw their heads back in laughter and skipped along the platform. And some passengers left carriage doors open; others closed them. Fred pondered on how people respond differently to similar situations. But he was puzzled as to why only the two young women were amused by the hissing steam. He assumed one of them must have influenced the other's reaction.

The steam engine seemed to be in three parts with the sides of the middle section cut away. Standing to the platform side of this raised narrow section, the driver, wearing an oily black cap with a shiny peak, poked his head out of the side opening. He looked back towards the five connected carriages. There was another person standing behind this driver. He was leaning on a shovel and had a cigarette in his mouth. Although older than when Fred last saw him, he was still recognizable with his thick, drooping moustache. It was Mr Philips, the same stocky man whose naked bottom he'd seen seven years ago when collecting wood for the bonfire. Fred smiled at the recollection, but surprised he was still working on the railway. Shortly after Fred and Tommy had seen him with Mrs Baker, he had been imprisoned for assaulting her husband. The Baker family still lived on Primrose Street, but the Philips' family was evicted.

Farther along the platform, two men, also wearing similar caps and greasy overalls, loaded steel milk churns onto a porter's flatbed trolley. A third workman, smoking a pipe, sat on an isolated churn. He occasionally made silent hand signals towards the two other workmen.

The hissing steam and clanging metal churns were suddenly accompanied by the repeat slamming of doors. Fred watched the porter – the same man he had spoken with earlier - walk along the platform towards the engine. Having slammed shut the last of the open doors, the porter stopped beside the driver who was leaning out of the side of the engine. They both looked back towards the line of carriages. Apparently satisfied, the porter blew his whistle. Slowly, and like the seesaw in Riverton's public park, the long metal rods connecting the large wheels began oscillating. With steam now also blowing out of the front chimney and other orifices on the cylindrical engine, the train slowly moved away, creating a chugging rhythm all of its own.

Coinciding with the train's departure, the uniformed man with the whistle ascended the wide staircase. The bridge, an open weave of metal bars, interconnected with all four platforms. Fred watched him stroll leisurely across the bridge before descending to the next platform. He turned his attention to the three workmen now sitting side-by-side at the platform's edge, their feet dangling close to the railway line below. In unison, they lowered themselves, carefully stepping over two sets of gleaming metal lines before climbing up onto the next platform.

Alone, Fred took a slim book from his pocket. He studied the purple and yellow cover: *A Midsummer's Night Dream* by William Shakespeare. He turned back the cover to focus on the handwritten inscription: 'To Fred, till the end of time, love Patricia'. For a moment he was back in the brightly lit theatre sitting next to Patricia and waiting for the curtain to rise. But the cacophony of shoes and boots on unstable metal disturbed his brief moment of solitude. Men, women and a few children hurried down the metal steps and congregated on the platform.

But they needn't have hurried: the train was an hour late. Never having travelled on a train before – and not having anything to compare it with, and being compliant by nature - he wasn't concerned: it was an adventure.

Not only had he never travelled on a train before, he had never before travelled more than five miles from home. He had no idea all those separate carriages were all interconnected with a narrow corridor that allowed a passenger to walk from one end of the train to the other. But he wasn't going to explore the train, leaving his suitcase unattended. And he was sensible enough to choose a compartment next to the lavatory. Too big to put on the overhead string rack, he placed his suitcase on the opposite seat. As the train pulled away, he sat by the window and relaxed, so very pleased to have a compartment all to himself.

He took out his purse and counted how much money he had left after buying the one-way ticket. Of course, he knew exactly how much he had – and precisely how it was made up of pounds, shillings and pence – but he needed reassurance. At least, he reflected, the government was paying for him to study and live in Oxford. But for extras, he would either have to rely on the small amount of money he had saved in his post office account, or get another part-time job. He reasoned weekend work, if he could find it, would not detract from his university studies.

Feeling hungry, he opened the suitcase and unwrapped the four thick rounds of bread and cheese that his mother had packaged. Although outer-wrapped in a sheet of old newspaper, she had thoughtfully wrapped the actual bread in greaseproof paper. Holding a chunk of bread in his teeth, he carefully rewrapped the remaining three sandwiches and put them back in the suitcase.

Contented, and enjoying the luxury of being alone on an otherwise crowded train; he put his head back against the linen covered headrest and reflected on the past and the unknown future. He was quietly excited, but also apprehensive. He looked out of the window and saw his own reflection. His feelings were mixed: being the only boy from his school to ever go to Oxford made his mother proud, but it set him apart, and he didn't want to be unique.

The view through the window reminded him of home as the train raced past the concreted backyards of inner-city terraced houses lining the track, their brick-built privies plainly on view. Then the backyards changed to the small gardens of suburbia with sheds and flowers, and from suburbia to the green fields that stretched away to infinity.

He looked again at Patricia's hand-written message in the book. But his thoughts inexplicably jumped to plump Blodwyn lying naked on her bed. He shook his head, trying to dismiss her image, but she lingered and seemed to be laughing. He couldn't understand why his brain could so often appear independent, forcing unwelcome images. He stared at the book's cover. Suddenly, he was back in the theatre sitting next to Patricia. He closed his eyes.

After Patricia moved with her family to Stratford, they did, at first, exchange letters everyday; then once every week; then once or twice every month. And now it is only birthday and Christmas cards they exchange. But, as she had written in one of her letters, her father had done well, rising from stage manager to production manager. Additionally, he was freelancing as a set designer and making enough money to pay for Patricia's private education. Fred was pleased for her, but suspected this was why her letters became so infrequent.

After Patricia and her family moved to Stratford, Fred kept up his association with the social aspects of the Unitarian Church, but treating it more like a sports club than a religious organization.

Although he still hadn't fully mastered the technique of pulling the ropes of the heavy bells up in the belfry, he had becoming proficient with the hand bells. Every Monday, he climbed the winding stone staircase to the bell ringing room, and soon – due to his extraordinary memory – he was conducting the bell ringers. Within a few months of Fred's leadership, the hand-bells team was performing in the church hall and attracting large crowds. And, influenced by his visit to the Monk theatre, he had also joined the church's drama group. Every Wednesday, the group had sole use of the hall and its large stage.

It was just after Fred's fifteen birthday when, studying in the bedroom, his mother called:

"Fred, come down. Blodwyn wants to talk with you."

Fearing a confrontation, he shouted back that he was busy. But his mother insisted.

Standing on the doorstep, the elevation allowed him to match Blodwyn's height, if not her girth.

"Me Mam said I should go with you to the drama group on Wednesday," she said, smiling and confident.

This sounded like an order. Fred wondered how, when he'd hardly spoken with her before, she knew how he spent some of his spare time. And he wondered how she could stand there so brazenly when she knew he had seen her naked with the milk boy lying on top of her.

"It's only for men," Fred said, but quickly corrected himself. "Males!"

"Well isn't that funny. Me Mam's been to see Mr Jenkins. He said I can join, and said I should come with you on Wednesday night. So there!"

Fred wasn't going to question the information. Mr Jenkins was the caretaker and collected the members' weekly subscriptions.

After school on Wednesday, Fred asked his mother to go across the street and tell Blodwyn he was ill. But his mother shook her head and said her father would be angry if Blodwyn wasn't allowed to join him at the church hall.

Fred had long recognized that one of his weaknesses was acquiescence. Although he had occasionally displayed disdain, it was not in his nature to offend. But Blodwyn was now testing his resolve.

He was uncomfortable walking beside her on the main street. He felt intimidated by her confident swagger. And she was nearly three years older, two inches taller and probably a stone heavier. But what annoyed him more than her silly grin and naive way of expressing herself was the Girl Guide's blue beret sloping on the side of her ginger hair. He couldn't understand how anyone could be so shameless: he'd seen her naked on her parents' bed, but she wasn't embarrassed. He thought about reminding her of what he had witnessed, but decided to keep quiet.

Almost everywhere Fred went in the hall that evening, Blodwyn was sure to follow. When he sat down to listen to the evening's arrangements, she sat next to him. When he went to the toilet, she followed him and waited outside. But when she excused herself and made for the ladies toilets, he hurriedly went on stage. He had been instructed to place an extra weight behind the back wall of the new scenery. In the semi-darkness, he squeezed between the set and the stage's rear wall. Bending down to repositioned the weight, he was suddenly pushed against the brick wall. Blodwyn had an arm around his neck and she was pressing her body against his. He was finding it difficult to breathe.

"Get off," he croaked, breaking free of her hold.

"Quiet, or I'll scream," Blodwyn said, again pushing him back against the wall.

Her movements were surprisingly quick. She had maneuvered him into a position where he was now side-on against rear brick wall. And she was pressing her body against his.

"You tell anyone you saw me with Ernie and I'll cut your prick off," she whispered, her spittle hitting his ear.

He was trapped and concerned she was going to hit him.   But then he felt her hand unfastening his fly buttons. Her plump hand was warm, clammy and her embrace gentle, not what he would have expected from such a loud person. The voices of others in the hall below could be heard, but she appeared unperturbed and in no hurry to finish what she had started. He sensed she'd done this before, probably with Ernie Price, the boy who delivered the milk.

He had to admit, it was Patricia who taught him there are more important things in life than carnal knowledge. But, he conceded, when she departed so did his new interest in chastity. And, despite conflicting emotions, he was stimulated by the recollection of being abused by Blodwyn.

"Yes, this is the right one. Thank you!"

Fred opened his eyes, for a second not knowing where he was. A well-dressed, middle-aged woman stood in the corridor, framed by the compartment door. He could smell the perfume before she entered. He went to stand up, but, realizing his thoughts of Blodwyn had encouraged an erection, sat down again.

"Hello, Sweetie," she said, huskily. Sliding the door shut behind her, she threw the neatly folded *Guardian* newspaper on the seat by the corridor window. Watching Fred, she placed her brown leather briefcase on the rack above that seat.

Satisfied that his erection had subsided, he stood up. Muttering he was sorry for leaving the case on the seat, he went to move it but she assured him it was not necessary.

Leaning slightly forward, the tall woman peered through handheld spectacles at the number above each seat. She focused on the number above Fred's head and then at the small buff ticket that she was holding close to her face. Raising a gloved hand, she declared loudly:

"What the heck, there are plenty of seats, aren't there, darling?" And, with that comment, she returned to the seat by the corridor, crossed her legs and opened out her newspaper.

Fred opened the pages of his book, but was really studying this heavyweight newcomer. He had never before seen a woman so richly adorned. The string of white pearls hanging around her neck and the cream satin dress were in sharp contrast to the short black fur jacket and black pillbox hat with its attached mesh-veil hanging down below her nose. He looked down at her cream, high-heeled shoes. Not a scuff as one would expect to see on light coloured leather shoes. He let his eyes wander up her silk stockings to where the imprints of her suspenders were clearly defined on both sides of the tight-fitting dress.

Fred was impressed by both the quality of the woman's garments and colour coordination. In Riverton, grey or back were the preferred colours (or availability). He made a mental comparison with his mother and all those other poorly dressed women he knew. And, for the first time in his life, recognized that society was very unequal. He had always assumed that having a father who worked six days a week was indicative of the good life. But looking and listening to this lady, he began to question this assumption. In comparative terms, he reasoned, the people of Riverton may be the new poor - no different than the Victorian poor he had read about at school.

But the newcomer had been making her own discreet observations, and she commented: "I could never make sense of Shakespeare."

"It's my favourite play," he said, turning the cover towards the woman.

The woman held the back of her gloved hand to her mouth and coughed gently.

"I've got a sore throat, dear. Too much G and T, I suspect."

Fred was thinking that these upper-class people even cough differently when the door suddenly slid back. Fred looked up, and, from his seated perspective, the door space seemed filled by a man dressed all in black.

"Tickets, please!" the man demanded, touching the peak of his cap.

While Fred searched his pockets, the woman took a ticket from her briefcase and handed it to the inspector. He handed it back and look towards Fred.

"I think you used it as a page marker," the woman, said, returning her briefcase to the rack.

Fred flicked the pages and, smiling weakly, passed the ticket to the man.

"Third class! What you doing in here?"

Fred looked at the man, confused.

"I'm going to Oxford; to the university," Fred explained.

"Not in 'ere, you ain't! Get back to third or I'll 'ave you."

The woman reached up for her briefcase again and, extracting a small satin purse, unfolded a large, white, crisp five-pound note and handed it to the inspector.

"He's with me. I made the mistake. Please take the difference out of this."

After reprimanding the woman, the inspector stepped back to the corridor and slammed the sliding door shut.

Fred thanked the woman and apologized, explaining that he had wondered why he had had the compartment all to himself as far as Stoke. He offered to pay her back, but she shook her head and smiled. With her back to him, she reached up to the overhead rack causing the hem of her dress to rise slightly above her knees.

He studied the silk-smooth legs, pondering if wealth and privilege had enabled this middle-aged woman to retain her good looks and shapely figure. He knew from listening to the two women in his household that stockings like this woman's were still expensive.

Sitting down, she ran her gloved hands over her thighs and knees, smoothing out the creases in the satin dress. Fred was fascinated: the cream-coloured gloves were obviously made of leather, but so thin they clung to her hands like a second skin.

"I do hate autumn," she said, almost as an aside and looking at the diamond bracelet hanging loose at her wrist. She then looked directly at Fred. "It's like life, darling: summer gone and only winter ahead. England is lovely in the summer, but less so when the cold winds of winter are blowing. Do you have a girlfriend?"

"In Stratford; my girlfriend's there."

"Are you going to see her?"

"We don't write so often…now…not since she moved there."

'That's life, dear: here today, gone tomorrow."

The woman's response was indifferent, and Fred sensed she might not be interested in anything he, a working-class youth, had to say. She probably spends most of her time with important people, he thought, and images of fat men smoking cigars and drinking champagne suddenly flashed through him mind.

"She goes to Rugby School," he said, reflecting on the tone of the woman's response and beginning to think she was depressed. He'd seen plenty of that back in Riverton. But the woman was suddenly alert and, leaning forward, exclaimed.

"What a coincidence! That's my old school, dear. She'll be kept busy with all those lovely young bulls bedding her."

If this was a reference to sex, it didn't seem to match Fred's impression of the woman. He thought the comment

138

coarse and insensitive, but couldn't help thinking she was probably right. But, determined to protect Patricia's honour, he said:

"She's not like that; she's a Unitarian. Anyway, I think she's left school."

"I don't know what one of those is, but I do know something about human nature. We're all programmed to fill the world with screaming little babies that pooh, pooh all over the carpet, the sheets and fill the house with the most dreadful odours. How old is she, dear?"

"Eighteen!"

"Yes, they throw most of them out at eighteen."

Fred turned the pages of the book on his knee, but was concerned it may appear impolite if he started reading. He kept the book open at the page with Patricia's inscription and looked up at the briefcase on the rack. More real leather! But he was thinking about what the woman had just said, and which hadn't crossed his mind until now on this train. Closing the book, he asked:

"How far is Stratford from Oxford?"

"You'll soon find out, dear: you'll be going past Stratford soon. Your first year?"

Fred admitted he was a freshman and that this was his first experience of travelling by train.

"You'll be telling me next you're a virgin." She waited for a response, but when none came, she continued: "Where you from?"

"Riverton, it's in Lancashire."

"Lancashire? Oh dear me! I hear they breed like rabbits there! Why, only last week a friend at the Women's Institute was telling me they even do it in the street there, and in daylight! Have you ever seen them doing that?"

Fred shook his head, but couldn't help smiling at the thought and the woman's stupidity.

"Not in the street but," Fred began, but paused. Not wanting to show Riverton in bad light, he decided against revealing the public park as a suitable location. "But I hear that's what they do in London."

"Probably, now we've got all these blackies coming in by the boatload. No, to be honest, I wouldn't really know; rarely get to London these days. I'm actually living in the country just outside Coventry."

Fred was pleased with his off-the-cuff remark. It had come out of his mouth without it being formulated in his head. And it fulfilled his endeavor to correct a misunderstanding. However, although he couldn't understand the reference to blackies, she seemed to agree with his contrived observation.

"What's your name, dear?"

"Fred," he replied, looking down at the book's cover.

"I don't like that. It sounds so common. Should it be Frederick?"

Fred looked up and nodded. "It wasn't my choice."

"Of course, it wasn't, dear. Some mothers have no idea about names, no taste - or anything else, for that matter. Having said that, I must admit my mother was different. She gave us both royal names. My brother's a Leopold, and I'm a Henrietta. I'll call you Frederick. Do you have the time, Frederick?"

"It's in my...in there," he said, pointing to the suitcase. "Do you want me to-"

"What a strange place to keep a watch! No, no, don't trouble yourself, dear. The trouble is, they make them so tiny these days."

She pulled back the left sleeve of her fur jacket. The face of the wristwatch was encircled with diamonds and the numerals so small that she had to hold her spectacles over the dial. She folded the spectacles, put them back in a slim leather case and stared across the narrow divide.

"Frederick, can I ask you a personal question?"

Fred was suddenly alert: he didn't like personal questions; since he was hospitalized, he'd erred on the side of caution. "About Riverton?" he asked.

"About you!" She paused for effect before continuing: "Had you been touching yourself before I got on the train?"

Fred was taken aback, shocked by the implication and her casual way of asking such a private question. He didn't answer but stared at the women.

"You were erect when I got on the train."

"No I wasn't," he lied.

"I know an erection when I see one. And you owe me a favour; don't you, dear?"

She stood up and pulled down the blinds on the three windows separating the compartment from the corridor. Sitting in the opposite corner, Fred wasn't sure what these actions implied, or where this conversation was leading. He didn't want to get involved with this woman. He didn't know anything about her, and she sounded privileged. But his thoughts were clouded: she had paid the extra for the first-class ticket.

Her agility reminded him of how Blodwyn had overpowered him behind the scenery at the Unitarian hall. But this woman must be in her forties, and yet, from a sitting position, she had stood up, closed the blinds, and was now on her knees undoing the front buttons of his

141

trousers. And, with her other hand firmly pinning him back to the seat, she buried her head in his crotch. Fred acknowledged to himself that she was bigger and stronger than him, and, ashamed to admit his only concern was somebody walking in off the corridor. He tried to push her away, concerned that she may cause injury with her teeth.

The sound of the train's movements had changed: it was slowing down. Through the intercom system, a porter's voice announced the next stop as Birmingham. But it was the sound of screeching brakes that prompted her to let go. Standing up, she looked in the built-in mirrors above the bench seats and touched her hat. Taking a small white handkerchief from a pocket in her fur jacket, she wiped her mouth and calmly returned to her seat. She sat with her gloved hands crossed on her lap, smiling, her eyes fixed on Fred. But he was uncomfortable sitting within touching distance. He looked out of the window as the train slowly drew level with a raised platform.

"Did you like that, darling?" she asked, standing up again and leaning over him to look out of the window.

Fred was annoyed that he had been so carelessly handled. She hadn't even removed her hat or gloves. But he was especially angry with himself for allowing her to dominate him. He was furious at his own penis for being out of synchronization with his brain. And, as he reminded himself, other females had also imposed their will by physical force. It seemed to be the history of his life. He recognized that he had to become more dominant. Irrationally, he thought of joining a gym to develop his muscles. His thoughts were chaotic. He didn't want to let her watch him refasten his fly buttons. Neither did he want to leave his suitcase unattended. He sat with the book on his lap.

Avoiding her with his face to the window, he thought back to what his mother had said when he was a child. If a lady is standing holding the handrail on the tram and you're sitting, you must stand up and give her your seat. When you walk on the pavement with your girlfriend, always walk on the side nearest the road. Never raise your hand to a lady. And always allow a lady to enter a room first. He had always agreed with these sentiments, and tried to follow her instructions, but suddenly none of this seemed to make sense.

Sliding the door open, Henrietta turned, raised an arm and waved her fingers: "I'm off to visit my Aunt Fanny. Bye, bye for now!"

Reflected in the window, he watched her leave the compartment. The train stopped with a judder. He crossed to the door, forcibly sliding it shut. Returning to his seat, he checked that his trousers were stain-free and to fasten his trouser buttons.   But three buttons lay on the floor.   He picked them up, wishing he had punched the woman, not only for what she had done, but for the predicament he now faced. Despite this feeling of revenge, he was glad the strange woman had left the train.   But her perfume still lingered in the atmosphere and on his clothes.

Afraid she may waive as she walked along the platform, he turned his head away from the window, but then noticed the briefcase on the rack. Carrying the case, he ran down the corridor to the nearest door. But the train was now slowly inching forward again. Forcing down the door's heavy window, he looked along the platform. Many of the disembarked passengers were still walking towards the stations exit.

"Here's your bloody case," he shouted, throwing it out of the open window onto the platform.

Returning to the compartment, he again closed the door and opened the three blinds. Breathing a heavy sigh of relief, he returned to his book, not to read – he couldn't concentrate - but to look again at Patricia's inscription. He sighed again, so very pleased at being alone. But then the door opened and Henrietta calmly returned to her seat. Fred couldn't speak and involuntarily pointed to the rack. But she didn't understand.

'"What's the matter, Frederick? Do you want some more?"

"I thought you'd got off," Fred stuttered, standing up, afraid of what was likely to follow.

"Did you miss me, dear?" she asked, smiling and relaxing back into the seat.

"You said you were going to see your Auntie Fanny," Fred reminded her.

"Fanny!" she said, pointing to her crotch. "Pee, darling."

"I thought you'd left your briefcase behind."

Henrietta looked up at the rack and then at Fred.

"Where's my case, dear?" she asked, anger making her voice deeper and threatening. "Don't play games with Henrietta."

Fred explained what he had done. Fearfully, he watched her expression change and the colour drain from her face. Slowly, she stood up and pushed Fred forcibly back onto the seat. She opened the narrow upper window to look back along the line, but the wind caught her hat and, as it blew away, it carried with it the wig she had been wearing. Fred's jaw dropped as he looked at Henrietta's short back-and-sides haircut.

"You're…a…fucking…man!" Fred cried, hauling his suitcase out of the door.

Panicking, he hurried along the corridor, stepping gingerly through the shaking inter-carriage connectors. When he could go no further, he dragged his case into a small lavatory compartment and locked the door. But the smell was overpowering. He put his foot on the round metal button secured to the floor, but the flushing water was ineffective: the paper and excrement simply rose to the level of the wooden seat. He watched as the water slowly drained away, leaving behind the waste.

With the suitcase standing on end against the door, and his knees pressed again it, he sat on the semi-circular wooden seat of the low-level pan. The train was gaining speed and the wheels were no longing chugging, they were high pitched and vibrating. And the carriage was rocking. He reached out and grabbed the handrail affixed to the sidewall. Somebody was knocking on the door, but he ignored it, concerned by the sound of the swishing waste beneath his backside. Still holding the handrail, he quietly raised himself. Whoever had been at the door had gone away, but it had unnerved him. Like the movements of the train, his moods were suddenly erratic, ranging from self-admonishment to anxiety and the dilemma of the missing fly buttons.

But he didn't relax until he heard the porter announce the train was approaching Coventry. And as the train began reducing speed, he allowed himself a smile at the thought of Henrietta trying to explain his tangled appearance.

With the suitcase angled for access, he opened it, careful not to allow the contents to spill out onto the wet floor. His gabardine raincoat was now crumpled, but at least it restored his dignity. However, being cautious, he ignored the attempts of others wanting to use the lavatory. The train made two more stops before he heard the porter announcing that the train was approaching Oxford.

It was dusk but warm when, on the final leg of his journey, Fred hauled his suitcase off the bus. The wide road was busy with traffic but there were few pedestrians. He walked alongside the iron railings protecting overgrown gardens fronting distant houses. Several blocks ahead, he could see the illuminated windows of a row of shops. He stopped under a lamppost to study the map he had received from the university. But he couldn't concentrate: he couldn't help thinking how stupid he had been not to realize Henrietta was a man. And he could still smell the perfume.

The house where he was to lodge was marked with a red cross on the hand-drawn map. The figure 4 had been inserted in the same ink and annotated beside the second house on the right side of the street when approached from the main road. And a row of six small squares had been drawn to represent shops, and underscored in pencil.

He continued walking, passing a church and a library, both locked and in darkness. Perspiring, he finally reached the row of brightly lit shops. The geographical layout of the shops matched the sketch in his hand, and they even reminded him of Riverton, but the fruits on display in the greengrocer's included produce he had previously seen only in magazines. And the women's clothes displayed in the adjacent shop were more colourful and stylish than what was on sale in Mrs Harvey's shop back home. And the dresses and coats were not laid flat on a shelf in the window but displayed on life-like plastic mannequins.

Turning the corner, he walked from the commercial brightness into domestic semi-darkness. Although there were several gas lamps on the street, they had not yet been ignited. But the street name on the black and white plaque attached to the side brick wall was legible. Satisfied he had arrived, but weary and perspiring inside his heavy raincoat, he put down his suitcase and sat on it. He wanted to regain his composure before meeting whoever was going to greet him in the house across the street. He looked at what was to be his home for the foreseeable future.

All the tall terraced houses lining both sides of the street were similarly constructed.   Of the six main windows fronting the house where he was to live, only two of the rooms were showing light. Taking a deep breath, he climbed the six stone steps leading from the street to a deep porch. He hesitated, and then knocked. He knocked again. A light shone through the stained-glass fanlight, preceding the sound of creaking wood.

The woman standing in silhouette was blocking out most of the light behind her. She appeared to Fred like the kind of confrontational woman he wanted to avoid. But her voice was pleasant.

"Hello!   I think we're expecting you," she said, looking at the piece of paper in her hand.

Fred introduced himself and followed her into the uncarpeted hall. A sturdy wooden banister separated the hall from the wide – but also uncarpeted - staircase. Everything about the entrance to the house seemed outsized, old and, confusingly, contradictory. The floorboards were worn, stained and creaked, but the small dolphins carved along the length of the bannister had a lustrous patina.

"My name is Miss Pugh. You're on the top floor, Mr O'Flaherty," she said, leading him up the first flight of stairs. "We have rules, of course," she said, stopping on the first landing. "No lights during the day, or after ten at night. And that's the bathroom and lavatory. You can take a bath once a week. Not more than five inches of water."

She stopped part way up the second – and also uncarpeted - staircase: "No ladies! I'll be serving tea and biscuits in the dining room from nine to nine-thirty."

On the second landing, and breathless, she stopped again, patted her chest then pointed to the door immediately at the top of the third, but narrower, staircase.

"Breakfast is between seven and eight. It's all there," she concluded, handing him the sheet of paper she had been carrying. Walking away, she did a half turn, sniffed the air, and said: "And no men visitors, either."

The room was just wide enough to accommodate the single bed and three-drawer cabinet. And for longer garments – and making him feel at home - a curtain was suspended from a wire stretched between the chimneybreast and the attic window. The straight-backed wooden chair positioned beneath the small window completed the furnishings.

Fred threw his case onto the bed. He had more pressing needs than unpacking his few belongings, and sat under the window eating another of his sandwiches. Feeling thirsty, and wondering about the time, he unwrapped the alarm clock - a rare gift from his father - that he had placed inside a sock and then wrapped in a rolled-up towel. After winding it and setting the alarm for seven, he put it on the chest of drawers.

On his way down to the dining room, and still wearing his raincoat, he stopped at the first landing and opened the door to the bathroom. He was impressed: it contained a huge bathtub, a washbasin on a pedestal, and a lavatory pan; all white porcelain - and with few chips. But some of the white wall tiles were missing and those remaining covered in web-like patterns. He was about to close the door when he felt a hand on his shoulder.

"Expecting rain, old boy?"

He turned and found himself face-to-face with a young man, probably about his age. The youth was naked except for a towel wrapped around his waist. He was carrying a small toilet bag.

"Sorry, just seeing where everything is," Fred explained, stepping aside to allow the stranger access.

"Not much to see, really, just antiques,' the youth said, in a refined voice, but continued in a whisper: "and that includes people."

Fred asked for directions to the dining room.

"Dining room? You mean the mortuary. First door off the hall! I'm Archie, second year medicine. And you are?"

"Fred, first year, reading literature."

"See you down there, Fred."

The dining room was barren except for a long wooden table and two benches of similar length to the table. And like the floor, the long table and benches were untreated wood, but like the banister, with a natural sheen. The dark green paint on the four walls still retained its gloss, but the once white ceiling was yellowing. Adding to the sense of neglect, the large, round, white ball hanging from the middle of the ceiling was internally speckled with black spots.

Unsure of procedure, Fred sat at the table opposite a mature man with a small mottled beard. He was dipping a biscuit in a white mug.

"You have to go to the hatch," the man said, pointing to the opening in the wall. "Ask for digestives," he continued, holding up the biscuit in his hand, "or else you'll get ship's."

Following the man's instructions, Fred walked to the serving hatch. It had been centrally constructed in the middle of the wall with a ledge wide enough to take two dinner plates. Through the opening, he was able to see into the adjoining kitchen. In contrast to the dining room, that room was brightly lit.

"Won't be a sec," Miss Pugh called, but out of sight. "Sugar and milk?"

" One sugar with milk, please. And can I have digestives, please?" he requested, deferentially and looking back to the table.

The bearded man, now holding the cup with two hands, was watching him. He winked.

Beyond the table, a large, bare window filled most of that wall, providing a view of the street. The wall by the door was covered in small famed photographs. Several of the pictures were sepia, two in colour and the rest black and white. He walked across the room to get a closer view. They all looked the same: young men wearing caps and gowns and identifiable by a printed name. There were only two pictures of female graduates.

"There you are, Mr O'Flaherty," Miss Pugh said, placing a plate of three digestive biscuits with a white mug of tea on the ledge.

Fred joined the man at the table and, in search of common ground, dipped a biscuit in his own cup of tea.

The bearded man, half-standing, offered his hand across the table.

"I'm a Duchesne," he said, smiling broadly. "Call me Jacques."

Fred didn't recognize the accent, but then he had never previously talked with a foreigner. Without realizing it, he raised himself into a similar posture and said: "I'm an O'Flaherty, call me Fred."

"That's a good Irish name. But, if you don't mind me saying so, you don't sound Irish."

"It's me Dad; he's from County Mayo."

"You will, no doubt, have been to your ancestral home?" Jacques said, in perfect English, but with his accent still evident.

Fred admitted he had never been anywhere until now, and had mixed feelings about taking up the place at university. "Dad said I'd be better off on the new buses."

"But university is a great place to learn and meet like-minded people. I wish I had had the opportunity. Here at Oxford you'll have the opportunity to meet people who may one day influence your life. Who knows, you may be one of the influencers. I'm not saying those effects will be necessarily positive, but statistically you'll be better off than your peers who didn't have the same opportunity."

"It all feels a bit odd, to tell the truth. I've had a bad day...travelling and all that."

"It's a brave new world."

"Aye, as Miranda says in the Tempest."

"Have you seen the play?

"I read it in the Riverton library when I was at junior school."

Breaking his last biscuit in half, Jacque smiled. "They last longer this way. Self-delusion! The art of allowing oneself to believe something that is plainly not true. But where would we be without it?"

"Isn't that the same as self- deception?" Fred asked,

"Yes, I suppose it is."

"Then it's dishonest," Fred suggested - the unbidden image of Henrietta flashing before his internal eyes.

"Tread carefully, for the world is full of trickery! Not my words, but Max Ehrmann's. Have you read *Desiderata*?"

Fred thought for a second about what the man had just said and nodded his agreement with the quotation. He then corrected himself: "I'm sorry, no, I haven't read it. I'm reading, or rereading, this." He pulled the folded Shakespeare script from his pocket. Have you read it?"

Jacques said he was very familiar with the play and, after a thoughtful pause, added: "You should read *Desiderata*. It's inspirational; Max is an underrated poet. Are you cold?"

Fred explained that buttons had come loose on his trousers and he didn't have a needle and thread.

"Torches, matches, sticking plasters, needle and thread; you young folk always forget the essentials in life. Wait there; I won't be a minute."

Jacques left the room, crossing on the stairs with Archie, the young man Fred had encountered earlier. Archie entered the dining room with a theatrical flourish. His blonde, wavy hair was now greased flat to his head but still crinkled. He walked straight to the hatch and shouted: "Digestives and tea, Miss Pugh for me and..." he turned, raised his eyebrows and pointed a finger at Fred. Fred shook his head, pointing to the one remaining biscuit on his plate. "...and Archie," he concluded, grinning and pointing a finger at his own chest.

Turning back to face the serving hatch, Fred was able to study this well-spoken, and now well-dressed, student. He was dressed all in black: blazer, poloshirt and trousers. And his black shoes were highly polished.

"Still raining, old boy?" he asked, sitting where Jacques had sat. He brushed aside the used mug and empty plate to make space for his own supper. "Well?"

"Lost a couple of buttons off me pants."

"We don't stand on ceremony here. You can walk with your cock out if you want. Nobody gives a damn... except," he said, pointing his head and a curled thumb at the hatch. He looked up at the man slowly entering the room.

The newcomer, perhaps in his early thirties, moved towards the hatch without lifting his feet. The man's head and body appeared inflexible, but his focused on what lay ahead was total. Standing erect and yet moving as though in a trance, he held his slightly trembling hands before him. But he was neatly dressed in a navy-blue suit with a white shirt, unbuttoned at the collar. And his black hair was cut short and parted over his left ear. He stood before the hatch, his fingers involuntarily tapping the ledge.

"Shell shocked...from the war. We've got two of them," Archie whispered, leaning across the table. "Came here in last May, straight from the asylum!"

Fred and Archie sat sipping tea, watching the man shuffle towards them. As he drew level, Archie raised an arm and declared:

"Evening, Arnold!"

But concentrating on the task of getting to the table without accident, Arnold, the former soldier, ignored the remark, but then stopped and, in anticipation, turned his whole body towards the door. Seconds later, Jacques re-entered. Arnold looked for a moment at Jacques, as though trying to recognize him.

"Hello, Arnold," Jacques said, but his greeting was also ignored, and Arnold shuffled to the end of the table, sitting by the window.

Jacques sat next to Fred, placing on the table a reel of black cotton with a needle sticking out of the thread.

"I'm sure your eyes are better than these," Jacques said, his two index fingers directed to his own eyes. "I always have great difficulty threading the cotton."

"Try wetting the end with your lips," Archie suggested, talking through a mouthful of biscuit.

Standing in the doorway, an obviously tall but now stooped man knocked on the open door. Also in his early thirties but dressed in a dark brown suit with a brown shirt - like Arnold's, unbuttoned at the neck - he waited.

"Come in, Felix," Archie shouted, raising his arm and bringing it back over his head.

154

Leaning forward from the waist, Felix walked unsteadily towards the serving hatch, his gait pedantic; the heel of each boot never moving beyond the toe of the other. But whereas Arnold's shoes never left the floor, Felix's boots did, but only fractionally.

With mug and plate, Felix sat opposite Arnold, but they didn't look at each other or acknowledge the other's presence.

From the inside pocket of his blazer, Archie withdrew a silver-coloured cigarette case. A row of nine cigarettes was held in position by a wide, brown elasticated band. He offered the open case first to Fred, who declined the offer.

"Go on, Fred, take one. Duty free from my Commodore uncle," Archie said, lifting one of the cigarettes and holding it before Fred's face.

"I don't smoke," Fred declared, apologetically.

"You're here to learn, old boy."

Convinced by Archie's comment and insistence, Fred accepted the cigarette and put it in his mouth.

Archie held the case before Jacques, who, taking care not to disturb the arrangement, plucked a cigarette and delicately held it between his fingers.

Archie stabbed the table with the end of his own cigarette, and then withdrew a metal lighter from his side pocket. The repeated rolling of the flint wheel with his thumb produced a strong smell of petrol before the wick burst into flame. He put the flame to Jacques's cigarette, then Fred's. He then closed the lid on the lighter - but immediately flipped it opened again to light his own cigarette.

"Not giving those Nazi snipers the opportunity to line up on the third light?" Jacques asked, his clenched hand before his face and extended forefinger pointing at Archie.

Sitting at the other end of the table, both Arnold and Felix stopped eating and turned their attention to Jacques.

"He's only joking," Archie shouted.

Without retorting, or a change of facial expression, the two ex-servicemen returned their attention to the table.

"Nazi snipers? In Oxford!" Fred said, coughing and shaking his head in a cloud of smoke. Although reasonably well read and with a brilliant memory, Fred's worldview was naïve, and his conversational experiences limited to Riverton street talk.

"They're like the Mafia, everywhere! Look, no bloody curtains. One of those Wolves could be on that roof over there," Archie said, standing and pointing towards the window.

The ex-servicemen stood up and looked towards Archie, then out of the window.

"Werewolves!" Jacques said, correcting Archie's mistake.

Archie stood up, and walked to the window. With a flat hand over his eyes, he looked out, paused, and then turned around. "Nobody there. Sorry, men, too much Benzedrine inhalant." He returned to his seat, and the two former soldier sat down.

Not knowing what the conversation was all about, Fred turned to Jacques and asked: "I thought werewolves were only in comic books?"

"Archie is referring to those Nazi fanatics, still living in the forests of central Europe," Jacques explained, flicking the ash from his cigarette onto the flat tin ashtray. Raising his voice, he continued: "Those two brave men probably know more about them than me."

But the two men ignored Jacques's invitation to add anything to the discussion. Arnold stood up, shuffled across the room, and placed his plate and mug on the serving hatch ledge. Felix did the same. Arnold left the dining room, but Felix stopped by the door.

"Okay, Felix. You can go. See you tomorrow," Archie shouted, and Felix followed Arnold up the stairs.

"They don't say much," Fred said, coughing and trying to stub out his cigarette in the ashtray.

"Miss Pugh said they were both traumatized in battle," Jacques explained, "and they're here to recuperate."

"From the damage done in the asylum, more like," Archie intervened, pointing to his own forehead.

"Where did you hear that?" Jacques asked.

"The horse's mouth! They were lobotomized! If you did that to an animal, it would be called butchery."

"It's been successful in some cases, or so I hear. I'm no expert." Jacques said, continuing to support the practice of surgically removing part of the front brain.

"My father doesn't agree, he thinks it is nothing more than experimental; plunging a knife into the unknown," Archie said, reaching across the table for the ashtray. "Just look at those two: perfect examples of how reality does not always measure up to theory. They'd be better-off put down."

"I plead ignorance and bend to both you and your doctor father's medical knowledge. But, I'm afraid, I do not agree with euthanasia. Isn't that what Hitler was doing to those unfortunates in Europe," Jacques said, lightly stubbing out the remains of his cigarette in the ashtray.

"They're a burden on the state," Archie argued, but with less emphasis, now realizing that his analogy was not only contrary to the Hippocratic oath, but, in the current, post-Nazi climate, likely to inflame opinion.

Jacques stood up and stretched his arms above his head. "And so to bed."

"I saw it in the West End, only last year," Archie declared.

"Saw what?" Jacques asked, standing by the serving hatch.

"*And so to Bed*. My girlfriend Dilys was in the play. Saw it three times. Didn't cost me a penny!"

Fred was impressed by what Archie had just said, but needed reaffirmation.

'Have you really been to London? And have you got a girlfriend on the stage?"

'She's my ex! Teenage sweetheart! And yes, I actually live in London, Kensington, to be precise. Where you from, Fred?"

Recalling his conversation with Henrietta, he decided to be economical with the truth.

"Northwest."

But Archie wasn't really interested where Fred lived, or anything else about him. His regional-accent, cheap clothing and unworldliness labelled him working-class: somebody who had attended a state school somewhere in the north of England. However, having travelled that route and still manage to get accepted by Oxford, Archie sensed an intellect that may be sharper than his appearance suggested.

"Is Jacques also at the University?" Fred asked, wondering how the older man, who had just left the room, fitted in to the scheme of things.

"Not sure; understand he's staying in Oxford for a couple of months. French writer or something abstract! Look, old boy, I'm off to the Nag's. Fancy a pint?"

Thinking about his limited funds, missing buttons and the headache he had experienced after celebrating his eighteenth birthday at the Bull's Head, he declined.

The clock on the chest of drawers was reading nine-thirty when Fred returned to his room. With half-an-hour of permitted light, he sat on the edge of the bed with his trousers across his lap. Archie's advice had been useful: at the fourth attempt he had threaded the black cotton through the eye of the needle.

Very please with himself, he turned off the light, but the moon was casting its beam across his pillow. He stood on the chair to draw the curtains, but there were none. He looked out through the small window. The slope of the ceiling had already informed him that this room was the one with the window on the roof. But he wasn't too concerned: he had a room all to himself, something the university said they couldn't guarantee. For the first time that day, he was beginning to relax, and the sight of the moon and a sky filled with stars seemed to connect him with Riverton. He thought of his father collecting money on the new bus, and his mother, knitting while listening to the wireless. He wondered what his siblings were doing. Exhausted, he climbed into bed, lucky not to impale himself on the upright spike of a broken spring.

SATURDAY 27 SEPTEMBER 1952

Fred arrived in the dining room fifteen minutes before breakfast finished, surprised to see that three of the four people seated at the table were new faces. He made the mental calculation that the two young men and young woman were probably also students. Archie was holding court. Two of the newcomers were sitting opposite him, the third to his right. Archie raised an arm and pointed to the bench to his left.

In response to Fred's question, Archie explained that, as usual on a Saturday morning, a taxi had called to collect Jacques. And Arnold and Felix were leaving the dining room as he walked in. He confirmed that the three new arrivals were first year students. Putting his face close to Fred's ear, he reminded him of what he had missed at the Nag's Head:

"The piano gets a bashing on a Friday night. Drunken plebs galore: singing, farting, working-class tarts with painted faces and showing their blotchy tits. Honestly, you'd think you were in bloody Bedlam. You must come with me next week. All it costs is the price of a beer. Think what you'd need to spend to see a freak show like that in the West End!"

What he had described sounded to Fred like what goes on every weekend at the Bull's Head back home in Riverton, but he wasn't going to say so.

"Aren't you afraid of someone beating you up?" Fred asked, recalling the fights that regularly occur in that other Riverton pub nicknamed the Blood Bath.

"All in the line of duty. I'm trying to decide whether eugenics is a good thing or a bad thing. Look, old boy, they're breeding like mad, filling the country with ill-educated morons. Civilization is in decline; we need to stop the rot."

"Yes, I agree," interjected the student on the other side of Archie. "They need sterilizing."

Archie turned his head and shook the student's hand. "Welcome to the club. We must discuss this next week. What's your name again?"

"Cedric!"

Archie turned back to face Fred: "I've been called back to London. Mother is having lunch tomorrow with the Chief Medical Officer. She thinks it will be good for my career. But, as I said, the poor man will probably be dead by the time I qualify.   But Mother will not take no for an answer. Excuse the double neg."

Archie, excuse himself, saying he had a train to catch, but would be returning Sunday evening.

Apart from Archie's adlibbing, there was nobody to formally introduce the new arrivals, and it seemed Archie was the only second-year student in the boarding house.

 Furtively, Fred studied the three newcomers, focusing on the young woman on the other side of the table. Her red hair appeared naturally curly, and her pale face shiny, as though it had just been scrubbed with soap and water. From her posture, it was difficult to tell if she was really as slim as she appeared sitting at the table. But she was doing what his mother had told him he must not do: she had her elbows on the table, resting her chin on her hands. Between long pauses, she was talking with one of the other newcomers, but he noticed that occasionally, through the open fingers at the side of her face, she looked at him.   When their eyes finally met, she moved with difficulty along the bench to face him.

"Hello, I'm Debbie," she said. "Would you like a sweet?"

Fred accepted the boiled sweet, talking while untwisting the paper.

"I'm Fred, and I'm reading literature.

"So am I; St. Anne's. What's your college? Where you from?"

During the fifteen-minute conversation, Debbie divulged ambitions, hobbies, favourite films, favourite books, and, openly, her own family history.

"I live with Mum and brov. Dad's in Norwich; nothing serious, just financial fraud. It's convenient because it's only a thirty- minute bus ride from Wymondham. But I do miss all those holidays. We even spent a week in Blackpool. I think it's in the northwest. Have you ever been there? It's fab!" But before Fred could answer, and without seeming to take a breath, she continued: "We must have visited most of the counties of England. Never got to Scotland. Dad said it was too cold. Oh, yes, we went to Berwick-upon-Tweed. He was using a bank there. Thought nobody would find it, but they did. But it may be in Scotland. Is it in Scotland? And we went to Torquay and Ilfracombe. But I prefer Cromer with its fishing boats and, those delicious brown crabs. I love crab paste - don't you? They never did find any of the missing money; you know why? Dad spent it all on holidays. And we always had new clothes. It was some company that pressed charges against Dad; by then he'd nothing left for a decent solicitor. I love going to the seaside."

Fred felt as though he had been on a tour of the British Isles, but had to acknowledge that, with the exception of Blackpool, he had never heard any of those other place names before.   But he wasn't going to be impolite.

"Now tell me, Fred, about all your holidays."

But Fred had to admit that he had never been on holiday nor travelled on a train until yesterday.

Cedric, overhearing the conversation and disdainful, nodded to the other newcomer across the table. Without comment, they left the room.

For the first time in years, Fred sensed he had met someone of his own age and with whom he could relate. And he liked her soft intonations and rising inflections; so different from his own sharp short vowels and guttural pronouncements.

"Would you like to go for a walk this afternoon, Debbie?"

"I'd love to, but I'm pretty slow," she replied, lifting her calipered legs over the bench.

Standing awkwardly, she reached down and collected her long walking aid from where it had been lying on the bench, unseen by Fred. He watched as she pushed her arm though the leather loop beneath the padded underarm support, her hand reaching down to the handgrip.

Fred intervened as she stretched towards a plate on the table. "Please, let me do that."

Having been sitting opposite Debbie, he hadn't realized she was disabled. He'd seen her only from the waist up: a pretty girl wearing a dark brown twinset of a high-necked jumper and matching cardigan - popular garments, even in Riverton. Suddenly he was interpreting her as a deformed cripple. She declined his offer.

Moving away from the table, she swung her right leg in a semi-circle, following that movement with her other, but more flexible, leg. Slowly, with her legs spread apart, she walked around the table with the bearing of a hesitant stilt-walker.

Although the heavy brown skirt reached down to her mid-calves, it didn't hide the narrow, vertical metal bars on both sides of both legs. But, from what he could see of those legs, the left one was discernibly fatter than the other. The metal supports were affixed to the sides and heels of brown lace-up boots, footwear that reminded Fred of what some of the old women of Riverton wore on Sundays.

Standing at the bottom of the staircase, Debbie then removed her arm from the leather loop and clasped the stick in the middle, holding it like a spear. Because she had to swing out her right leg, she asked Fred to walk behind her. With her left hand firmly holding onto the banister rail, she slowly ascended the stairs.

"This is my room," she said, pointing at a door on the first landing. "Number one!"

"That's handy for the bathroom," Fred suggested, inclining his head toward the door facing Debbie's room.

"Yeah, but it's a bit annoying when people pull the chain in the middle of the night."

That afternoon, with Debbie relying on arm linkage and her crutch, they visited the Ashmolean Museum, the angled autumn sunlight catching the sides of the four Iconic pillars of the portico. Fred was reminded of his visit to the Monk Theatre with its more elaborately pillared portico. He thought briefly of Patricia, wondering what she would be doing at that very moment. But the thought was fleeting, and Fred and Debbie were soon marvelling at ancient creativity and discussing paintings and artifacts with the same fervour that most eighteen-year old males back in Riverton applied to brands of beer and cigarettes.

In their different ways, they were both searching for new identities. Although Debbie had talked enthusiastically about her travels, Fred sensed that her constant references to other places – to the exclusion of home life - suggested all was not what it appeared. He wondered if those fond memories were artificial, created by her father to compensate after she fell victim to poliomyelitis. She spoke openly about the viral infection she contracted when she was twelve-years old and the subsequent treatment. She hardly mentioned her mother.

As they stood trying to make sense of ancient terracotta fragments, Debbie asked him about his own upbringing. He answered briefly but diverted her attention by saying he wasn't very good with jigsaw puzzles. He asked for her opinion of the display, and she willing offered her own interpretation of what the bits of broken stone probably represented.

But he thought about her question, and how, since the age of four, he had endured the indignity of having to share a bedroom with two brothers - and a sister on the other side of a hanging blanket. He recalled how getting, and staying, asleep had been difficult, especially if somebody in the family was suffering ill health, which seemed to be a regular occurrence. He recalled having to go to the public library to study, but where he was often nudged awake by one of the two librarians. After Patricia moved to Stratford, he thought of following her – but as the letters faded, so too did that aspiration. There were too many bad memories in Riverton; too many people who knew too much about him; too many adults still thinking of him as a child. He had decided he didn't want to work in a factory or for the corporation. Most of the children of Riverton, sooner or later, were wearing oil-stained overalls. He knew from his studies, and from the reactions of various teachers, that his memory was exceptional. And he had long since acknowledged that it was that attribute that got him to Oxford. But placid and undemanding by nature, he acknowledged his other limitations.

After climbing the sweeping steps of the museum, Debbie had to sit down and rest. She apologized for being a burden. But Fred wasn't seeing her like that. On the contrary, the more they talked, the more he was attracted. Not only was her speech delivery soft and melodic, it was now also less hurried. As though she was no longer anxious.

To reach the river, they had to take two buses. Helping her onto the second bus, they sat side-by-side on a double seat. Walking along the bank of the Castle Mill Stream, they linked arms. But, even with support on two sides, progress was, as she had predicted, painfully slow. They watched ducks sitting patiently on the water; black coots, with distinctive white bills, occasionally upending in search of food, surfacing and uttering their noisy kwoot calls. In the middle of the river, a lone swan paddled against the flow. Fred, never before having seen a real swan – or a coot, for that matter - was captivated.

They crossed a bridge, its mirror image reflected in the still water, and rested on a bollard beside a navigational lock. A small boat with two oarsmen pulled up alongside the bank, lifted their boat out of the water and carried it on their shoulders along the towpath. Beyond the lock, they lowered their boat and, with a wave, rowed away.

"We must do that sometime, Debbie."

But Debbie wasn't very enthusiastic. "If I fell in, I'd sink to the bottom."

Fred hadn't been serious, and Debbie was only joking, but nevertheless he felt guilty at having made such an unconsidered remark.

MONDAY 29 SEPTEMBER 1952

At breakfast, Fred and Debbie sat together and she went into more detail about her medical history.

"When I was first diagnosed with polio, they locked me away in hospital for two years. Said it would probably affect my brain. But I escaped; I proved them wrong. And they said I would never walk. But I proved them wrong again. Of course, I was in a wheelchair until three years ago. But look at me know, you wouldn't know if I didn't have to wear these things and throw my leg about. I must admit, Fred, I've never walked so far, or climbed so many stairs, as I did on Saturday." She explained that it had taken her until now to fully recover from all the walking around Oxford. Fred apologized, but she said she would not have missed it for the world.

It was registration day, and Fred, Debbie and the other students went their separate ways. All approach roads to the colleges were filled with crowds carrying paper bundles, some with briefcases. Fred had never before seen so many well-dressed teenagers out on the streets. He was overawed by the massive brown buildings, the arches, turrets and towers; the wide sweeping lawns cut like painted chevrons. It was like one of those ancient cities he had seen at the picture house. He was excited by all information he was receiving about layout plans, tutors and tutorials, lectures, and extra mural studies. And access to a library with thousands of books and scores of seats.

That evening, and by arrangement, on the way downstairs, Fred knocked on Debbie's door.

"Door's open, come in," she shouted, sitting at the dressing table.

This room was larger and better equipped than his, with a double size bed, a wardrobe, a small dressing table, and a washbasin with two taps. Unlike the rest of the house, the pine furniture appeared new but lightweight. And this room had a large window looking out onto the street. The view suggested this room was immediately above the dining room. Both their images were reflected in the single mirror attached to the dressing table.

"I'm almost ready," she said, brushing her curly hair with a large, silver-backed brush. But her efforts were not making any visible difference.

The top of the dressing table was covered with a selection of functional items, the most noticeable being a small silver clock, black vacuum flask and a candle standing upright on a saucer. Half burned, it was supported in its own melted wax. Not having seen her wearing make-up or smelling of anything but scented soap, he was puzzled by the array of cosmetics.

She was wearing the same matching brown cardigan and jumper but now with a woollen beige skirt. Noticing the gold crucifix hanging from her neck on a short chain, he asked:

"Are you Catholic, Debbie?"

"Don't believe!" she said, shaking her head. "If there's a god, why me!"

Fred recalled his discussions with Patricia on this subject and didn't want to get into a debate.

"We've got ten minutes," Fred reminded her.

Declining Fred's offer of assistance, she shooed him away and, with her left boot on the floor, pushed the chair far enough back to allow her to withdraw her outstretched right leg. With one hand on the dressing table top, she levered herself out of the low chair.

"I'm very independent and don't need nursing," she said, now softly and without malice.

Archie and Jacques had finished eating and were each enjoying a cigarette. The rest of the table was unoccupied. Archie raised an arm and pointed to the space next to him, but Debbie made the gesture of smoking then waived the same two fingers across her face and curled her lips. Fred shrugged his shoulders as he carried his plate to the end of the table by the window, sitting where Arnold and Felix normally sat. Debbie refused his offer of assistance and made two trips to the serving hatch.

Sitting facing each, Fred and Debbie began eating in silence. It was obvious to Fred that something had upset her and guessed it was his mention of religion.

"I'm peeved," she said, breaking the silence. After a short pause, she continued: "I've got to move into halls of residence. Because of my condition! Before I came here they agreed I could live outside the college. I've had enough of institutional living. You know I can walk, don't you? Don't you?"

Although Fred had already grown fond of her, his inner reactions were contradictory: he didn't want her to move, but he had to agree travelling to the college would be difficult for somebody like her.

"When?"

"Tomorrow; they're sending the college van."

By the time they had finished eating, they were alone in the dining room.

"Do you fancy a drink, Fred?"

"The hatch is closed."

"In my room, a sort of going away drink."

Fred was surprised when she produced a miniature bottle of Martell cognac from a drawer in the dressing table. She looked at Fred, assessing his reaction.

"Where'd you get that?" he asked.

"The offey! But we'll have to share the cup," she said, passing him the bottle and pointing to the vacuum flask. "Will you do the honours, please?"

Debbie had already packed most of her clothes in the open suitcase lying on the floor beside the bed. Standing by the dressing table, he emptied the cognac into the cup and watched her reflection in the mirror. Sitting on the side of the bed, and to avoid bending, she dropped a folded bath towel into the open case.

Sitting beside her on the bed, they took it in turns to drink from the cup, careful not to consume more than the other.

"What's all that make up?" he asked, pointing to the dressing table.

"Not mine, found them in the drawer. Can you put the cup back on the flask...please?"

Since dinner, Debbie's attitude had softened. Fred thought she was beginning to face reality, perhaps accepting that it would be impossible for her to travel to lectures and tutorials on a regular basis by bus.

As requested, he screwed the cup back onto the flask, but when he turned, Debbie was lying at an angle across the bed. Both her legs sticking over the edge, the right leg unbending and supported by the full-leg brace. Her left leg bent at the knee, the calf against the bed. Her skirt had risen above her knees; high enough to reveal that the two metal frames supporting her legs were not the same. The metal brace on her right leg continued up under her skirt with the side rails being strapped above and below the knee. But the brace on the left leg finished below the knee with just one – but similar – wide leather strap.

"I'm so tired. Can you help me undress?"

Fred stood at the side of the bed, unsure how to react to such an unexpected requested. But she broke the impasse by sitting up and leisurely unbuttoning her cardigan. The smile on her face suggested to Fred she was being mischievous. He thought how, in just a few hours, she had changed from being polite to austere and then tender, but now frivolous. Removing the cardigan, she folded it carefully and dropped it onto the suitcase.

"Are you going to help me?" she asked, taking hold of the hem of her jumper, releasing it and symbolically raising her hands above her head.

Fred put one knee on the bed and took hold of the hem of her jumper. He hesitated, wanting to be sure he hadn't misinterpreted her request. But she sat passive, a smile in her eyes.

"Are you sure you want me to take this off for you?"

She nodded her agreement, and he gently pulled it over her head. She wasn't wearing anything underneath;

her breasts were much larger than he had imagined. She pointed to her skirt.

"You want me to help you with this, too?"

She didn't immediately reply but unfastened the belt buckle at her waist, allowing the leather belt to hang from the side loops.

"Be careful with my right leg," she instructed, laying her head back on the bed.

She lifted her backside, and Fred slowly pulled the skirt down and over her leg braces and boots. Holding the skirt, he didn't know where to look – but he had the urge to look down on her semi-naked body. He glanced at her pink satin knickers, at her legs, then at her breasts, finally moving his attention to her face. Everything had happened so quickly, and the body lying on the bed seemed so pathetic. He thought of her in composite terms: she had the innocent face of a thirteen-year old girl, the right leg of a ten-year-old, the left leg of a footballer - but the body of a twenty-five year-old beauty queen.

"This one unbuckles here," she said, patting a hand on the upper side straps of the full brace on her right leg. She pointed to her lower legs and apologized for the inconvenience. "I'm so sorry to trouble you, but there's the straps and the laces of those awful boots."

He unlaced the ankle boots, and, with unspoken permission to observe, studied the two leg braces. With just one strap, the half brace on her left leg looked straightforward.   However, the right leg brace looked complicated: it stretched from beneath her right buttock down to the stirrup attached beneath the boot. It had a wide, three-buckled strap around her upper thigh and two other straps, one above and the other below her knee. She edged herself back further onto the bed until she was satisfied that both legs were fully supported on the bed.

The half-brace was, as he thought, easy to remove. And, as instructed, he placed it on the floor beside the bed. Neither was removing the second brace as difficult as he had imagined it would be. The complication was in his mind as his fingers brushed her flesh as they worked at the buckles. The soft white padding lining the top of the full brace was marked with red stains. Finally, he peeled off her white ankle socks.

With the second leg brace also on the floor, he looked more closely at her legs. The right leg was not only thinner, it was shorter than the other leg, and her right foot pointed down instead of at right angles to the leg. But Fred was alarmed at the condition of the skin running just below the frill of her satin briefs: it was raw and weeping, marking a red circle around her upper thigh where the bucket-type support had carried her weight. He felt an acute sense of guilt for having encouraged her to do so much walking and stair climbing. Surprisingly, the thigh, like the calf of her left leg, was unusually muscular; not in any way deformed.

"Don't look," she instructed, but not as an order, rather as a coy admission of modesty. But then with urgency in her voice added: "Quick, light the candle and turn out the light. She'll be knocking on the door."

While he was lighting the candle on the dressing table, he watched her reflection in the mirror. Sitting up and bending forward on the bed, she wriggled out of her briefs. When he returned to the bed, she was lying with her head on the pillow, her body uncovered but with her back to him. In candlelight, he stood by the bed, unsure what to do next.

"I'm asleep," she whispered. "You'll have to wake me."

"Can I get on the bed with you?" he asked, still unsure of her motives.

"Yes, I told you, you'll have to awaken me," she said, smiling and half-turning her head to face him.

"With my clothes on?"

Debbie had not made anything clear. He thought she might be treating him as a friend, an able body helping somebody who is not. He didn't think a girl with a disability and painful and leaking abrasions would want anything other than rest. She looked angelic; like one of those girls proud of her virginity.

"It's up to you." She turned her head away.

He hurriedly undressed, leaving his clothes on the floor where he had dropped them. But he then hesitated: he didn't want her thinking he was excited.

She was still lying with her back to him and he was now looking down on the back of her head. He climbed on the bed, and, testing her reaction, ran his hand down her back, stopping at her lower back. She was receptive. He lay next to her, their bodies exchanging heat. She asked him to be gentle. Carefully, he moved his left arm underneath her body and, with both arms wrapped around her, cupped her breasts. For several minutes they lay still, both relishing the warmth of the other's flesh. She sighed, turning, with difficulty, to face him.

"It's been like months," she murmured, putting the palms of her hands on his chest. She put her mouth to his and they held their lips together for a minute. Her tongue caressed his face before moving inside his mouth. And then she withdrew it, inviting him to reciprocate. They rocked from side to side as their fingers searched each other's body. She sucked his ear while he sucked at one of her rigid nipples. With a hand behind his neck, she lightly forced his head down towards her crotch, releasing hold only when his face was buried in her red pubic hair. She writhed, experiencing a mild orgasm.

Fred repositioned himself until their lips were again touching. For a moment they lay silent, holding each other, content to relish the moment by looking into each other's eyes. Slowly, Fred moved her onto her back. But, unexpectedly, she reached behind her head and, lifting the pillow and arching her back, placed it beneath her backside.

With her lower body now raised above the bed, she moved her left leg, indicating for Fred to similarly move her paralyzed right leg. With both legs spread apart, Fred put his hands to both sides of Debbie, raising himself above her before carefully lowering his body. It was an easy entry, too easy, Fred thought, momentarily.

For a few minutes they lay side by side, each with their own private thoughts. She had not been the virgin he had imagined her to be. Logic was slowly replacing lust: he had obviously been preceded by many others, and now sensed his performance was probably being compared. But he also sensed she was caressing herself. She wanted more, but while his mind was willing, his body was exhausted. Gently he repositioned her until her legs were over the edge of the bed. Climbing off the bed, he knelt between her legs. Her upper body twisted and she began moaning again. Still breathing heavily, the moans turned to sobs and simultaneously she was urinating. Saturated, he looked up to her for an explanation, but she was crying. Unaided, she pulled herself fully onto the bed and climbed under the blanket.

"Are you all right, Debbie?" he asked, spitting out the urine and wiping his eyes.

Slowly, she peeled back the blanket and, to his surprise and relief, emerged smiling.

"Of course I'm all right. You've just hit my gee spot; the first time in years.

TUESDAY 30 SEPTEMBER 1952

Fred had crept up to his attic room in the darkness, and, forgetting to set his alarm, had overslept. He looked at the clock: at least breakfast would be served for another twelve minutes, and, at this time of day, he didn't have to stand in line at the bathroom door.

On his way down, he noticed Debbie's door ajar. He knocked softly, but there was no reply. Wondering if she too had overslept, he eased the door open and looked inside. All Debbie's things had been removed, and the bed had been remade. He deliberated, looking at the bed and trying to relive some of last night's experience. The smell of burnt candle lingered. He hurried down stairs, convinced she would still be in the dining room.

Only Jacques remained seated at the long table, reading an old copy of the *La Monde* newspaper.

"Bonjour; good morning, Mr Fred

Fred responded in French but continued to the serving hatch

"Have you seen the time, Mr O'Flaherty?" Miss. Pugh asked, standing on the other side of the hatch.

"Am I too late?"

"You would have been in two minutes."

With his boiled egg, buttered bread and mug of tea before him, he sat opposite Jacques.

"Not much for a working man," Jacques suggested, looking over the top of the newspaper.

"It'll do me. I like eggs; anyway, I'm not that fussy about food."

"At home in Paris, we don't have handles on our cups. We use two hands. Do you know why? It keeps warm our hands in winter."

Trying to appear casual, Fred asked Jacques if he had seen Debbie that morning.

"Debbie? Debbie?"

"The girl with the irons on her legs."

"Ah, yes, the very pretty mademoiselle! I saw her being helped into a van, a university van. Must have been...an hour ago," He looked at his wristwatch. "Yes, an hour ago."

"Did she have her leg irons on?"

"Why, yes, of course. They must be there always; must they not?" Fred shook his head and screwed up his face. "It must be very painful, having to sleep and bathe like that," Jacques said, folding his newspaper and putting it in the side patch pocket of his brown corduroy jacket. "I wonder, are they connected to the bone?"

"Did she leave a message for me?" Fred asked, his mind bizarrely flashing back to Riverton and Mrs Porter's brown corduroy settee.

Looking towards the window, and pensive, Jacques shook his head. "I didn't speak with her. Franklyn Roosevelt also wore leg irons. I think he had been afflicted with polio? Do you think that happened to...Debbie?"

Fred didn't reply; he shook his head, wondering how he would be able to contact her.

"Waiting for my taxi. I'm going to the Playhouse theatre. Can I give you a lift?" Jacques said, walking to the window.

Fred explained that he didn't have anything official until Wednesday.

"Lucky for you," Jacques said, returning to his seat at the table.

"Like this?" Fred asked, holding the mug with one hand on the handle and the other wrapped around the opposite side.

Jacques smiled. "No, in my house we don't have handles, as I said. We have bowls. I think we get more for our money. What does your father do for a living?"

Fred related the story of how, when on warden duty, his father had nearly been killed by a falling bomb, but also adding that he was a conductor on the buses. Jacques smiled, waving an imaginary baton. Fred shook his head.

"Collects the money."

"A very important job, too."

"Is the Playhouse a proper theatre?"

Jacques thought about the question before replying.

"If you mean actors talking to each other on stage but using somebody else's words, yes, it is a proper theatre.

"Shakespeare?"

"I suppose so, but I don't think he is in this season's repertoire. I'm only here until next week. A colleague and I have been preparing a teaching project that colleges can use - a programme that will eventually bring more realism to the stage, we hope! Our aim is to introduce the method as Stanislavski did for the Russian theatre at the beginning of the century.   There is not enough flexibility in stage performances here, or in Europe.   I'm sorry, this is all probably technical."

When Jacques had began speaking about his project, Fred was thinking about other things, such as visiting Debbie's college. But as soon as Jacques mentioned Stanislavski, he had his full attention. Jacques lit a cigarette and, for a moment, both he and Fred slipped into their own thoughts. Jacques revisited the window, looking out.

"The taxi is not usually so late."

"Didn't Stanislavski direct some of Chekov's plays?" Fred asked, reflectively, but knowing full well that he had.

"Yes, he did. But how did you know that?" Jacques's answered, genuinely surprised.

"I'm more familiar with Chekov than Stanislavski, but I do recall that Stanislavski wanted to explore the psychology of characterization.   He did this with three Chekov plays, at least that I know of."

"What were they?"

As Patricia's father had once interrogated him, Jacques was similarly questioning Fred's memory. He was convinced that Fred's knowledge about Russian theatre at the turn of the century would be limited to what he had already said.

"Uncle Vanya, 1899; Three Sisters, 1901 and The Cherry Orchard, 1904."

Jacques wasn't sure how to reply. He turned his attention from the street to Fred. They looked at each other.

"In   Russia?""Moscow!   At the same theatre Stanislavski had formed with Vladimir Danchenko. I think it was the Moscow Arts Theatre."

To himself, Jacques quietly repeated the three words; "Moscow Arts Theatre." But then asked: "How do you know all this?"

"The library near home. I had to do me study there because I had nowhere else to do it."

"Couldn't you study at a home?"

Fred was describing the drawbacks of sharing a bedroom with two brothers and a sister when a car horn hooted. Jacques's looked out of the window, but returned his attention to Fred.

"What's your ambition?"

"I think I'd like to be a stage manager, like somebody I know. They had a nice house and a garden in Riverton."

"Would you like to come to the theatre with me? There somebody's I would like you to meet."

The taxi stopped outside the wide front doors of the theatre, but Fred wasn't very impressed by what he saw. Except for the glass doors it didn't look at all like the theatre back home with all those Greek columns. And it was just part of a terraced row, like the multi-windowed Coop store on Riverton's main road.

He followed Jacques through the foyer and into the auditorium. Except for the wide stage, everywhere was in darkness. As they walked down the sloping aisle, Fred's eyes slowly became accustomed to the dark. He looked around, surprised at the large number of plush, red seats and impressive balcony. The two younger men on the stage were both dressed in loose-fitting, dark, crewneck jumpers. In contrast, the third person, a middle-aged man, was wearing a smart silver-grey suit with a red cravat tucked in the neck of a while shirt. Both young men were seated at a small table holding open books but listening to the older man standing before them.

"Sorry, Larry, the taxi was late," Jacques shouted.

Larry, the man on stage wearing the cravat, put one hand above his eyes and, half stooping, looked down to the seating area. With his voice resonating through the theatre, he responded: "Only just got here myself, Jacques."

Fred sat in the front row, watching and listening as Jacques and Larry debated while directing the two younger men. Much of the language being exchanged on stage was either incoherent or beyond Fred's comprehension. The onstage conversations were being noted in Jacques's thick notebook. Larry talked about a new acting school in New York that was based on the Stanislavski system, but Jacques dismissed it, claiming the American director, Israel Strasberg, was promoting mumbo-jumbo at the expense of articulation.

"Audiences still need to hear and understand the dialogue," Jacques argued.

Fred sat wondering why he had been invited. He was also feeling uncomfortable in the unheated auditorium. But when Jacques called time, Fred was thankful the proceedings were coming to an end. The two younger men jumped down from the corner of the stage, disappearing into the darkness.

"Time for lunch," Jacques shouted, shaking a cigarette out its packet. "Come on up, Fred."

Puzzled and stiff from sitting three hours in the cold, Fred slowly climbed the short staircase at the side of the stage.

"Larry, let me introduce my friend, Fred, Fred O'Flaherty whose father is a famous conductor in...Where is it, Fred?

"Riverton. But he's only on the buses; used to be on the trams."

"Ah, yes, Riverton." Jacques turned to Larry: "But Fred's father collects the money."

Larry laughed, extending his hand. "It's money that makes the world go around."

"Fred has a photographic memory. He's read Shakespeare and Chekov. And he acquired his knowledge from books in a public library, unprompted!" Jacques explained, promoting his fellow lodger's impressive memory and interest in theatre, a subject that both Jacques and Larry revered.

"Self-motivation! Wonderful! Wonderful! Let's go for some chow and you can tell me all about it, Fred" Larry said, leading Jacques and Fred down the same short staircase.

It suddenly occurred to Fred that Larry was the same man he had seen on the silver screen at the Essoldo picture house. A famous actor! And here he was, not only shaking hands with him, but also going for lunch with him. Larry led the way through the darkened auditorium.

"I haven't any money with me," Fred whispered to Jacques.

"It's on expenses," Jacques whispered back, raising a hand to the side of his mouth.

There were few customers in the Red Lion, but as the man with a white apron tied around his waist led the trio to a secluded corner, one customer stood up and declared: "Cry God For Henry! England and Saint George!"

Larry smiled, patting the man on the shoulder.

Seated, Larry turned to Fred, asking him if he recognized the line the man had just uttered.

Without hesitation, Fred answered: "Henry the Fifth."

"Do you know which act?" Jacques asked, putting his notebook on the floor beside the chair.

"I think it is...act three."

"Bravo!" Larry shouted. "It's not an easy play to learn. I was having sleepless nights."

"He wants to work in the theatre, Larry; as a stage manager."

Larry asked Fred what he was reading at Oxford, but then queried why, if he wanted to work in theatre, he was reading literature and not drama.

"You should try to get in RADA, Central or some other school specializing in drama studies," Larry suggested.

Fred replied that before today, he didn't know there were colleges that trained actors for the stage.

"Larry looked to Jacques: "Educationalists seem to think drama is not important. Is it like that in France?"

"Probably worse," Jacques agreed.

"Which are the best drama schools?" Fred asked, seriously interested.

Larry suggested Central, his old school, but Jacques disagreed, quoting Las Copiaux in Burgundy. As though amused, Larry waved his hand dismissively. But becoming serious, he said:

"Do your studies and get into rep. You can learn your trade on the job."

But then Fred was forgotten. He may have been on another planet.

"The problem is, most actors today are still performing like they did on the Victorian stage. Lead actors want to look good and they think speaking nicely is sufficient. They are too stiff," Larry declared, at the same time acknowledging the gestures from new customers arriving in the pub.

"Concentrating on recitation at the expense of characterization," Jacques suggested.

"Precisely!"

Larry and Jacques discussed Stanislavski, Chekov and method acting'. Jacques said an actor playing a tree should think like a tree; playing a bird should think like a bird. And Larry concurred, but on the theme of a fairy. Despite what he had read about the theatre and playwrights, none of these acting ideas made sense to Fred. While Larry and Jacques were circling in the realms of artistic interpretation, Fred, listening in silence, was unable to apply logic to those hypothetical concepts. He wanted to test these theories scientifically and challenge their conclusions, but, erring on the side of caution, kept quiet.

OCTOBER - DECEMBER 1952

Three days after Fred had accompanied him to the Playhouse, Jacques departed the digs for the last time. His parting gift to Fred was a paperback copy of Max Ehrmann's poetry. Between the pages, Jacques had left his business card. On one side, *Jacques Duchesne, Centre Dramatique de l'est, Strasbourg* was printed in black. On the other side of the white card, the words 'Tread carefully, for the world is full of trickery' had been handwritten in blue ink.

That same week, and in search of Debbie, Fred visited St. Anne's College on four different days, but failed to find her. On the fourth visit, he had been warned by a uniformed official to keep away from the women's accommodation halls. In the following weeks, he regularly visited the Students' Union, but she never appeared.

Three weeks after she moved out of the digs, and while sitting on the upper deck of a bus, he saw her on the street below. His first reaction was to get off the bus and say hello, but commonsense prevailed. Since moving out, she hadn't tried to make contact, and she knew the number of the payphone at the digs.   And she seemed very happy walking on the arm of the young man.

In November, he saw her again. She was sitting behind the plate glass window of a café. She was smiling, looking into the eyes of another male companion. Preoccupied, she didn't see Fred walk past.

1953

Fred had heard talk of a pregnant student wearing leg irons, but it was Archie who, on the last week of Fred's first year at Oxford, confirmed it was indeed Debbie. She had been forced to terminate her studies and return to Norfolk.

During that first year, Fred had spent all his vacation periods at his parents' house in Riverton, but found the circumstances increasingly difficult. His parents were still the same unambitious people but he had changed: he was now reasonably learned and becoming ambitious.

Although the dining arrangements at his Oxford digs had been frugal, he had picked up etiquette from those other students who had been educated in the public school system. In the refectory, he had watched other students eat and adapted their styles. And both willingly and subconsciously, he had also developed their mannerism and pronunciations, stretching his formerly short 'a:' in bath and softening the 'oo' in book. He spent two shillings on *Received Pronunciation,* a teach-yourself-elocution book. His changed persona pleased his mother but annoyed his father. But his tendency to correct his parents' mispronunciations infuriated both parents and his siblings.

Fred's father, Joe, had long harboured secret ambitions for his four children. He wanted his daughter to be married before her twenty-first birthday and produce his first grandchild in her first year of marriage. He wanted his three sons to follow in the family tradition: drinking, smoking and swearing as regular members of the Bull's Head's community. And he wanted his three sons to follow in his footsteps working on the buses. But, he openly declared, Fred had been a disappointment.

The trams, having been sold or scrapped in 1949, Fred's father had, since then, collected fares on the buses, but his intemperance had, like the size of his girth, grown. And his drinking was not confined to beer in the Bull's Head. Since the Corporation had reinstated the annual pay increase, Joe was in the habit of also drinking Jameson Irish whiskey by the fireside. Otherwise, the O'Flaherty family lifestyle had, more or less, remained constant, with three of the four children still living at home. But psychologically they were being torn apart since Fred's sister declared her preference for girls, in particular Blodwyn who lived across the street. Although her father had proclaimed he was not having any 'bloody queers living in my house', twenty-three-year old Siobhan not only remained; she had moved into the front bedroom, sharing it with her mother. Joe was now sleeping in the back bedroom, separated from his wife and daughter by a wall, and from his two sons by the hanging blanket.

By the start of his second year of study, Fred was no longer speaking with a Riverton accent, but his savings had gone and he was forced to take a part time job working Saturday evenings at the Red Lion. He had secured the one-day-a-week job because the manager remembered him having lunch with Larry.   And when being interviewed for the job, Fred had not denied he was Larry's nephew.

Kitted out in a smart black waistcoat, white shirt and black bowtie, he was taught how to dispense draught beer, recycle spillage, and mix cocktails in a chrome shaker.

Dora and her mother, Rhoda, were regular theatregoers and, due to the Red Lion's proximity to the Playhouse, also frequent visitors to the pub. Restricted by middle-class convention, they had a special regard for actors and their nomadic lifestyle.

Sitting on bar stools; their expensive high-heeled shoes resting on the metal footrests, Dora and her mother often discussed the most personal things - and in some detail.   And, like most customers in a public house, considered the staff as deaf, or, at best, inconsequential.

Dora, he overheard, was a hotel receptionist working one of two rotating shifts six in the morning and ten at night. Her mother, now divorced from Dora's wealthy father, had received fifty thousand pounds in alimony and the family home in Woodstock, something of a record, she had said, for the Oxford divorce court.

They were both always immaculately dressed, but Rhoda seemed slightly overdressed in satiny black fabrics, as if to avoid being overshadowed by her very attractive daughter. But the mother hadn't lost her looks. Fred thought she looked closer to thirty-five than her forty-five years. And, from their numerous conversations, he knew both their birth dates – and had noted them in his diary.

The perfumes they wore were not cheap, but Rhoda preferred musk-based scents, while Dora's preference seemed to be more towards floral fragrances. Similarly, Rhoda also wore diamond earrings and a four-carat diamond on her wedding-ring finger while Dora favoured a simple one-carat ring, which he imagined to be an expensive engagement ring. In contrast to Rhoda's preference for glitter, Dora wore soft muted colours. But it was Dora who shone brightest.

Although Fred knew more about them than they realized, there were two uncertainties in his mind. They didn't look like mother and daughter. Rhoda always wore a broad gold clip to hold back one side of her gloss-black hair. Conversely her daughter's honey-blonde hair usually hung down two sides of her face. And he wondered why Dora's fiancée was never mentioned.

Both women kept their small evening bags on their laps. Rhoda's black with inset white beads and a short gold chain; Dora's plain white satin with a short silver chain. But Rhoda rested the rigid brown box of Sobranie cigarettes and small silver Guilloche lighter on the counter.

Rhoda usually ordered the drinks, but they were both slow drinkers and never consumed more than two drinks after the theatre. Rhoda preferred the longer Tom Collins but Dora went for the vodka martini. And, when ordering, they called 'waiter'. This annoyed him; his name wasn't waiter, or Fred, for that matter. It was now Frederick! As a name, he now conceded, Fred had working-class connotations.

He was in his second month at the Red Lion when he overheard the manager in conversation with Rhoda and Dora proudly recounting the day Larry had enjoyed lunch in the Red Lion. "With his nephew," he had said, pointing to Frederick. After that evening, Rhoda and Dora referred to him as Frederick, and occasionally tried to engage him in conversation. But he was usually too busy and dedicated to be anything other than courteous. And he didn't want to disturb the misconception.

DECEMBER 1953

It was the first week in December; decision time: was he going back to Riverton for his Christmas break, or staying in Oxford and paying the out-of-term-time accommodation with his own money? The thought of spending two weeks watching his father drinking himself to death was in a different category to sleeping on the settee in the parlour. Nevertheless, the dual thoughts dismayed him in equal measure. But it was the idea of constantly being aggressively reminded by his father that he was wasting his life 'at that place', and turning out to be 'a right little snob' that upset him. During his father's outbursts, his mother often tried to intervene but that only resulted in a heated argument between the two of them. He had become an unwanted stranger in his own family home – but it was a two-way equation: Frederick's parents were not only working-class and insufferable; they had become an acute embarrassment. Then there were the neighbours!

Although the Butlers, still lived next door and were unforgiving, nobody knew what had happened to Albert, Ethel's husband. That information came as a great relief to Frederick. Nevertheless, he had to ensure Mr Butler was not on the street when he stepped out of the house. If he was about, Fred chose to leave the house by the back door. And he never visited the shops on Main Street. Riverton's public sectors had become no-go areas.

Rhoda and Dora were breathless when they arrived in the Red Lion. The show at the Playhouse had run longer than expected. Frederick stood obediently awaiting their order.

"That silly play went on far too long, darling. Can you hurry a TC and vodka martini," Rhoda said, hoisting herself up on the barstool next to her daughter, already seated. But Dora intervened.

"No, Frederick, please make it two TCs. I'm dying of thirst."

Although the two women were different in many ways, they both seemed to have trim figures with full breasts and, as far as Frederick could see, shapely legs. The most common factor was the sense of affluence they both exhibited.

"Where are you spending Christmas, Frederick?" Rhoda asked, flipping back the lid on the cardboard cigarette box.

"Undecided! Might stay in Oxford."

Dora asked where his family lived, but he was evasive, as usual when this subject arose.

"It's more than three hours on the train north.

"A long way to travel at this time of the year," Rhoda said, taking a pink cigarette from the box.

"And some trains are not even heated." Dora added.

"And if they are, they only warm the feet," Frederick admitted.

Rhoda pushed the box of cigarettes across the counter. "Would you like one, Frederick?"

"Not permitted on duty, but I don't smoke."

"May I?" Dora asked, turning to her mother while leaning across the counter, but then looking towards Frederick, enquired: "Why ever not?   I saw your uncle smoking in *Rebecca*,"

They asked what Larry was really like and what his plans were.   During his short time with the Larry and Jacques, he had been party to various snippets of information.   At the personal level, both men had been guarded in their discussions. However, being able to move back and forth between different customers, he could usually avoid answering questions. But, to the satisfaction of the two women, he related - and exaggerated - various anecdotes. He knew, for example, that Larry was working on a musical film, and that his wife had been suffering from depression.   Like a prizefighter, he was able to avoid questions by jumping in with a line then moving away to serve a customer or shake a cocktail. And the two women helped in this deceit by piling a question on a question. But little of what he said would have stood up to scrutiny.

While Frederick was serving another customer, Rhoda turned to her daughter and whispered: "Should we ask him to look after the drinks at our Christmas party?"

"You mean as a barman?" Dora asked, surprised by her mother's suggestion.

"You know how it is when we let them serve themselves."

Dora pondered the idea, quietly agreeing that their guests often abuse their generosity. "He presents well and seems very polite. But he may not be interested." After a thoughtful pause, she continued: "We do need a part-time handyman."

"Well, I hadn't thought of that. What a good idea. We could pay him... How much?"

But Dora was still sceptical: "We don't really know him. He might be a thief!"

"He's a student, and we know who his uncle is!" Rhoda exclaimed.

"Of course, we might be able to get his uncle to come over for lunch,"

"Dinner!"

But Dora still wasn't convinced that offering employment to Frederick would be a good idea. She suggested they first invite him to the house for lunch when they could engage him in a more meaningful discussion.

Frederick accepted their invitation to join them the following day – but only after being persuaded by Rhoda. Sunday was now the only day of the week when he could relax with a book and enjoy the comparative privacy of his attic room. Furthermore, he had recently invested in *The Complete Works of Shakespeare*, an expensive hardback book with more than two thousand pages. However, the thought of sitting down to a proper meal was enough to encourage him that the reward may justify the inconvenience of sitting on a cold bus on a Sunday morning.

His only tie – an old school issue - had been in his suitcase since he first left home fifteen months earlier, and it was badly creased. Similarly, he had washed his shirt in the bath but it was still damp and needed ironing. Fortunately, Miss Pugh had recently employed a sixteen-year old, live-in maid who, for a small fee, offered guests a laundry and ironing service. And May O'Leary, having travelled alone from County Clare, and already feeling homesick, sought comfort in anything Irish. And the name O'Flaherty was in that category.

Wearing a neatly pressed shirt and tie, Frederick sat on the upper deck of the bus with mixed emotions. He was curious why Rhoda and Dora had invited him for lunch. He was interested in their live style, but on cold days he preferred being alone with his books. He had that familiar compulsion to do an about turn, but fought against it, arguing internally that something positive may come out of the meeting.

There was no gate between the two large stone pillars, but the long drive was semi-circular and overhung by the naked branches of converging trees. The drive led to a large house but continued curving away in the distance.

He stepped inside the arched porch. Its walls had at one time been painted red but were now showing areas of bare brick. However, the colour difference was minimal; it was the difference between the gloss and matt surfaces that drew his attention to the paint loss. The heavy front door had two vertical upper panels of elaborately stained glass. The doorbell was attached to one of the two sidewalls, its white button inset on a pitted brass base. The brass letterbox was also pitted and similarly coated in green verdigris. He put a finger on the button but paused, studying the peeled black paint on the heavy door. These were not the symbols of wealth that he had anticipated, and, although four large windows fronted the house, the overall appearance was that of neglect.

Even at this late stage, he was having second thoughts. Did he really want to spend a couple of hours in the company of two people he knew only as customers? He wondered what he could talk about with two women whose conversations in the Red Lion related mainly to clothes, jewellery and food. And he anticipated they would be asking more questions about Larry. Convinced he would be bored, he turned to walk away - but then the door opened. Dora's smile was very welcoming.

"Hello, Frederick! Saw you through the window. Sorry to keep you. Just got in myself. Come in! Rhoda's late, but should be back from church any time now."

She wasn't dressed in one those elegant dresses that he was familiar with. She was wearing white shorts, a white sports shirt, and soft white shoes.

He followed her into the spacious hall, impressed by the central staircase leading to an open-plan balcony. At ground level, doors to both sides of the wide staircase led beyond the hall. Although worn in places, the thick blue carpet suggested quality and continued up the stairs. A badminton racquet was resting against the wall. She continued talking as she led him through the door to the left of the hall. A large, brown, leather sofa, a Moroccan-style coffee table and a tall mahogany cabinet comprised the furnishings.

"I'm just going to change. Won't be a tick. Please sit down and make yourself comfortable."

Frederick walked to the window and looked out. The grass beyond the driveway was overgrown and brown. And, stripped of their leaves by the season, the trees added to the sense of abandonment that pervaded the exterior of the house. But, in contrast, the furnishings – or what he had seen of them – implied quality, although slightly worn.

Dora put her head around the door, revealing only part of her towel-wrapped body. "Sorry, Frederick, if you'd like a drink, please help yourself. Just pull the front down." She pointed to the cabinet.

Alone again, and interested in its construction, he walked to the chest-high walnut cabinet situated in the corner of the room. He pulled on the gilt handle and lowered the upper front panel; simultaneously the top of the cabinet opened up. The front panel, supported by two long internal hinges, remained horizontal to the cabinet to provide, he assumed, a serving base. Mirrors lined the interior, multiplying the rows of drinking glasses on two glass shelves. He closed the cabinet and returned to the window. At that moment, a black Triumph Renown was driven past the window, its grill and protruding headlights gleaming. Still in view, it stopped outside a detached garage beyond the house, and Rhoda, wearing a broad-brimmed black hat and black cape emerged from the driver's side.

He tried to listen to the muffled conversation as the two women talked in the hall. But they were out of range. Wishing he'd stayed at home, he sat down, running a hand over the fine cracks in the arm of the antique leather sofa. Another five minutes past before Rhoda appeared, now without the hat and cape.. With her arms outstretched and smiling broadly, she approached Frederic. As he stood up, she put an arm on his back and her face close to his, offering her cheek. Having seen the ritual performed many times in the Red Lion, he knew what was expected on him. He brushed her cheek with his lips.

"Sorry to keep you, darling. One of those pre-Christmas sermons in preparation for the bigger event!"

She led Fredrick to the room on the other side of the hall, also overlooking the driveway. But this room was twice the length! And a cream fronted counter stretched from wall to wall at the opposite end of the room to the window. Three dispensing optics were fitted to the wall behind the bar. The floor was wood panelled, and fitted bench seats covered in green velvet lined the two long sides of the room. Frederick estimated seating for at least forty people.

"We call this the ballroom, Frederick dear. But we don't use it for dancing anymore. It was Dora's dad's idea. Anyway, it keeps the guests from the rest of the house. No carpets to stain in here! Empty space, really. Keep saying I'll refurnish it, but I don't know what we could do with it. I'll tell you about our idea later. You must be hungry. Did Dora give you a drink?"

Rhoda led Frederick to the conservatory at the rear of the house. A tall palm tree growing out of a large blue porcelain pot contributed to the exotic ambiance provided by four wicker chairs and another Moroccan-carved round table. Although similar in style to the table in the lounge, this table was full size. It was already set with three place mats and three wine goblets. The atmosphere was bright and airy, but the rear garden, like the front, was overgrown and obviously neglected. Dora, now wearing a white knitted jumper and black linen trousers, arrived carrying two bottles of wine.

"Sweet red or dry white?" she asked, holding the bottles before Frederick. "We've got more white in the fridge."

Frederick looked briefly at the labels, then at Dora. By the look of her hair, she recently showered, and the absence of make-up did not detract from her good looks. He expressed a preference for the dry white, but Rhoda suggested she leave both bottles.

Dora, still standing, filled the three glasses then left the room.

"You must tell me more about your uncle," Rhoda asked, but Frederick parried the request with a series of questions of his own.

"He's suffering from a cold at the moment. But tell me, what is the name of that tree, the one over there with the hanging branches."

As Rhoda admitted not knowing anything about horticulture, he changed the subject to religion. She again pleaded ignorance, but she was still describing some of the 'ghastly people' in the congregation when her daughter arrived pushing a serving trolley complete with an oil-heated chafing dish.

The lunch of Welsh rarebit was not what he had expected, but it was hot, and the wine appreciated.

Although the whole of the upper deck was a designated smoking area, the view was better than that on the lower deck. It reminded him of his childhood trips on the trams. And upper decks always provided a panoramic view of the landscape. Furthermore, the three glasses of wine and part-time job offer had provided inner warmth.

The hall was lit by a single light bulb, and May, the new maid, was on her knees scrubbing the floorboards. Her thick black stockings had been rolled down to form a tight band around her ankles. And, reminding him of Mrs Porter, her black skirt was tucked under the elastic of her knickers. She moved the water-filled bucket to let him pass. Walking on tiptoes, Frederick thanked her again for pressing his shirt and tie.

"Ssh! Miss Pugh's only just gone to bed," she whispered, putting a wet finger to her lips.

She needn't have reminded him. He knew Miss Pugh always took a nap between three and four on Sunday afternoons, and the silence suggested most resident did something similar.

"Aye, and I thank you, young lady, for imparting that important information," Frederick replied, confident in alcohol and putting on his best Irish accent.

May stopped scrubbing, and, craning her neck, asked if he would like a cup of tea. He said it was an admirable idea.

"I've nearly finished. Would you like it in your room, sir?"

He had hardly settled down in his chair when she knocked on the door. She had rearranged her stockings and black dress. And the small white apron hanging from her waist effected the transition from cleaner to maid.

"You know, May, this is the first time I've had a cup of tea in my room."

"You mustn't tell anyone, sir. If Miss Pugh finds out, I'll be for it."

Frederick swore not to tell anyone, and asked her why she had chosen Oxford and not somewhere like

Liverpool with all its Irish institutions. May explained that her Aunt Theresa had lived in Oxford for five years, working as a cleaner at the town hall, and promised to accommodate her.

"But then she had a new man move in, and wanted me out; can you believe that, now?"

Frederick noticed a tear in her eye. He stood up and put his arm around her. She responded by leaning against his body. Although he was only three years older than her, he suddenly felt protective, fatherly. But as she pressed her breasts against him, his paternal instincts disserted him. He moved away, not wanting to allow his body to dictate to his head, again. Expecting her to now leave the room, he returned to his chair and picked up the book. But instead of making an exit, she recovered her composure and sat on the edge of the bed. She crossed her legs, exposing the narrow band of white flesh beyond her long black stockings that were supported by broad elastic bands.

With her hands clasped around one raised knee, and looking at the title on the upright cover, she stated the obvious: "Is that about Shakespeare, then?" But before he could answer, she continued: "Is there any sex in it, now?"

Frederick explained that sexual references were plentiful but often abstruse. He asked her if she liked sexy books, noticing that her skirt had risen above the hem of her black knickers. She replied that was all she liked reading. With an older and less pious woman, he would have had an idea where the conversation was leading, but this girl had previously exuded persona of an orthodox nun. He dismissed her references to sex as the verbal adventures of a young girl. Pointing to the clock, he drew her attention to the time. She hurried out of the room.

That evening, he joined Archie at the dinner table. And, as usual, Archie related his Saturday evening exploits. The two ex-service men were seated at the far end of the table but, also as usual, seeming to live within their own private worlds. Frederick often wondered if the two ex-servicemen actually understood the various conversations around the table. He knew, for example, that they did show an interest when the subject of war was mentioned, but beyond that they seemed disinterested. Archie handed Frederick a copy of the *Sunday Times*. It was open at page six and folded back. A picture of Jacques filled a quarter of the page. Archie said nothing but waited for a reaction.

"Jacques! A Frenchman intelligence officer working as a spy for Great Britain during the war!" Frederick said, continuing to read, but conscious of being watched by the two ex-servicemen.

"A decorated war hero! But read on," Archie exclaimed, excited, as though learning the information for the first time.

Frederick read aloud the next paragraph: "Before the war, a leading director in French regional theatre, Jacques Duchesne, has been appointed as Director of the French National Theatre."

Archie and Frederick looked at each and then towards the two ex-servicemen, but the two men were again concentrating on what was on their dinner plates.

That night, Frederick lay in bed but couldn't sleep. He was reworking his many conversations with Jacques, looking for clues, but there was nothing. Miss Pugh had still not fulfilled her promise to put up curtains at the window, and the moonlight was filling the room. Eventually the thoughts were becoming intangible. He wasn't guiding them; some inner power had taken over, and he was drifting into a mist. He wasn't sure if he was dreaming when the door creaked open.

"I was having a nightmare. I was scared. Can I rest with you a few minutes, sir?"

Frederick sat up in bed, concerned as to how Miss Pugh would react if she found the maid in his room.

"You'll be in trouble if she finds out."

"She won't known. She asked me to make a cup of cocoa to drink with her barbitits."

"Barbiturates?"

"Yes, like I said, sir."

This answered a question that had long plagued him. 'So Miss Pugh didn't hear Debbie's moaning and shouting because she takes sleeping sedatives.'

Concerned by this intrusion and yet sympathetic to a young girl having had a nightmare, he agreed she could rest on top of the bed until she recovered her composure. But she immediately climbed under the blankets, forcing him closer to the broken mattress spring. It was only when he felt her hand searching inside his pyjama trousers that he knew her motives were other than psychological.

She was wearing a flannelette nightdress that seemed to stretch beyond her feet. But he was still debating with himself what do next. Logically, half his brain was calling on restraint. She hadn't attempted to lift her nightdress and this created a barrier between them. He just couldn't be sure what to do next. He wondered if this was the young girl's physical adventure, like her verbal adventure that afternoon? Was she simply curious about men's bodies the way he had once been about women's? Were her intentions one-sided?

For several minutes they lay like this, but then she whispered in his ear: "I've never been with a man before."

"Have you been with a boy?"

"Only playing doctors and nurses."

"Then you know how babies are made."

"But I wouldn't do that, sir. I've promised to remain like Mary, a virgin, until me wedding day, and if I don't keep me promise, God will surely know."

"Well, why are you holding me?" Frederick asked, putting a hand on her breast. But she moved his hand.

"Will you marry me if I let you?" she whispered.

Logic prevailed, and acknowledging the girl's naivety, pushed her hand away.

"You'll have to go back to your room. If Miss Pugh finds out you've been in here, she'll sack you."

"Promise, on your life, you won't tell her, sir," she pleaded; only now thinking of the perils of unemployment. Before departing, she kissed him on the cheek.

Frederick emptied the small case he had bought for carrying his books, and, from the list he had prepared, carefully packed his toiletries and change of clothing. Neatly dressed in his bar-staff uniform, he put on his raincoat and, with some trepidation, descended the stairs.

As he expected, there was a lot of Christmas Eve activity on the city streets, and the incoming buses were bringing in yet more unruly partygoer. Conversely, there were few passengers on the bus going out of town, and he had the upper deck all to himself.

The Triumph Renown was parked on the driveway when he arrived at the front door. Rhoda greeted him with the usual flourish and extended cheek. Both Rhoda and

Dora were wearing dresses that he'd seen before but now they seemed somehow overdressed. He couldn't decide if it was the extra jewellery or the domestic environs.

Rhoda led him to the bar in the ballroom. Bottles of spirits, wines and mixers were stored beneath the counter. Additional a bottle of gin and a bottle of whisky had been fitted to the dispensing optics attached to the wall. And rows of various sized drinking glassed were upturned on the bar counter.

"Everything is free, darling, but keep the measures on the small side. The optics have been recalibrated so you don't have to worry about those."

It was an hour later before the first guests arrived. The vicar, accompanied by his wife, ordered two gin and tonics. "By the way, young man, make them doubles and go easy on the tonic."

Early in the evening, Frederick was treated with contempt, a servant at their command. However, the situation slowly changed and houseguests began enquiring about Larry's health, marriage, and future plans. But towards the end of the evening, Frederick and Larry were forgotten: self-indulgence reigned supreme. And from his vantage point behind the bar, he was able to study the interactions of the middle and upper classes; the middle-aged and elderly. Sex, both conversational and physical, seemed to be the prevailing driver. Edgar, Rhoda's elderly doctor, blind in the left eye, spent most of the evening leaning on the bar, his young wife choosing to stand on his blind side. While refilling their glasses, Frederick observed, several male guests, standing to her left, running their hands over her shapely backside. And while the doctor was facing the bar placing an order, Frederick watched another man caress her left breast.

He overheard whispered assignations being arranged, scandals being divulged, infatuations being disclosed. He watched breasts being squeezed, genitalia fondled, backsides caressed and, later, looking out on the garden, the young doctor's wife on her knees and her face in the crotch of Rhoda's youthful-looking solicitor.

It was after midnight when the last guest departed, and Rhoda and Dora helped Frederick clear the mess. The pre-arrangement was that he would be sleeping in the guest room. Standing at the bar, Dora poured herself a glass of wine.

"Anybody else for a nightcap?" she asked.

An hour later, and feeling the effects of the whisky Rhoda had been feeding him, Frederick asked for directions to the guest room. Looking at each other, the two women smiled.

"One for the road, I say," declared Rhoda, holding up an empty glass.

At two o'clock, and relying on the bannister rail for support, Frederick unsteadily followed Rhoda up the stairs and along an unlit corridor.

The lighting from the two bedside lamps was pink and subdued but offering enough light for Frederick's befuddled brain to deduce this was a very feminine guestroom. Peach coloured eiderdowns, their lace frills almost touching the white sheepskin rugs, covered the two double beds. And each bed had a side cabinet that matched the bleached walnut dressing table standing elegantly on four Queen Anne legs. The dressing table was situated against the wall and between the entrance and the door leading into the connected bathroom. Feathery, white dressing gowns were draped over both beds. Unsure of his ability to stay upright, he sat on the edge of the nearest of the two beds. Stroking the satin-covered pillow, he asked:

"Where do I... schleep?"

"This is your bed, dear," Rhoda explained. Pretending to yawn, she put the back of her hand to her mouth. "We're sharing because the other rooms are being decorated. If you are shy, you can undress in there," she suggested, pointing to the open door of the adjacent bathroom.

"Are you schleeping...." Unable to complete the sentence, he pointed to the other bed. He was not only struggling to unscramble his confused perception of the situation, everything was suddenly unreal, out of focus.

"Yes, if that's what you want?" she said, turning off both bedside lamps.

It was a white mist that passed through the open door of the bathroom. Through the haze, he could vaguely see two women, but they crossed the room and disappeared into the bathroom. Sitting in the darkness, he waited for the second sound of flushing of water to follow the first, but the door opened. In the light from the bathroom, he watched the two women put their hands behind their necks, but they were having difficulty. They approached him, turning their backs, but then retreated. Then their dresses fell forward of their shoulders. They stepped out them, but their bodies and breasts were still covered by one-piece silver corsets. They hesitated, but then unclipped the suspenders and rolled down their stockings. Slowly, they removed their knickers before wriggling out of the elasticated corsets. They stood before him naked. He had an urged to grab hold of their breasts, but wasn't confident of standing and was unsure which pair to go for. The two images wrapped themselves in the white dressing gowns.

Standing, he took two steps before falling to his knees. He looked up: Rhoda was now standing above him, and the mist was clearing. She was smiling, holding out her hands to him. With her assistance, he sat on the chair by the dressing table.

"What's… this?" he asked, smelling the cup she was holding before his face.

"Warm water with vitamin A," she explained. "Antidote to alcohol! This'll clear your head."

Although he was now alternating between single and double vision, his brain was still confused by alcohol. Nevertheless, he knew from his conversations back in the digs that detoxification was a natural process. Archie had regularly explained that there wasn't an artificial method of accelerating the conversion of alcohol to acetates and other molecules.   Although snippets of logic were creeping through the veil of cognitive dysfunction, he was not yet ready for debating with Rhoda – or anyone. Instead, he drank the liquid.

"Aren't you getting undressed?" she asked, climbing into the nearest bed.

He turned around. There were two heads on two pillows. Cautiously, he rose to his feet and slowly entered the bathroom, closing the door. Standing at the washbasin, he held out his tongue. But there were also two heads reflected in the mirror. And both tongues were coated with yellow fur. He put his fingers to his cheeks and pressed down. His four eyes were bloodshot.   He filled the washbasin with cold water and submerged his head until he could stand the pain no longer. Shaking his head, he looked in the mirror again, relieved to see only one reflected image.

Feeling a little sharper, he reconsidered Archie's theories about alcohol and its remedies but couldn't reconcile the two. For some unfathomable reason, he imaged the doctor kissing his wife when they got home. Sluggishly, he undressed, and entered the shower cubical. Now recalling Archie's theory about stimulating blood flow to repair damaged nerves, he alternated the taps between hot and cold. But, as it proved impossible to control the hot tap, he remained under the cold water. Feeling revitalized, he scooped up his clothes in a bundle and returned to the bedroom. Lying on her side, and illuminated by the light from the bathroom, Rhoda was still awake. She threw back the covers, exposing her body. Naked, she appeared much bigger than when dressed.

At their insistence, he spent the rest of his vacation with Rhoda and Dora, never knowing with whom he was going to bed, or waking up with the next morning. Mother and daughter obviously had a roster, but there was no obvious pattern and never any arguments. But those were duties above and beyond the implied contract. If it wasn't raining, he worked in the garden or cleaned the car. If it was inclement, he polished the 'ballroom' floor, cleaned the bathroom's tiled walls, or helped with the laundry. The visiting part-time charlady worked only ten hours a week, but her duties did not extend beyond vacuuming, dusting and polishing. The more strenuous cleaning activities were left to Frederick.

It was the money and free board that kept him going, but the morning and night sexual activity soon became an imposition. He enjoyed his relationship with Dora, but her mother's demands were often unnatural. Nevertheless, with the thought of money at the forefront of his mind, he persevered. However, he also had some preparatory study to do. He decided to return to his digs.

Working Saturday nights at the Red Lion had had a greater impact on his study time than he had at first realized. At the beginning of his studies, he had been convinced that having a brilliant memory was enough. But, into his second year, he recognized that memory alone was not a substitute for coherent analysis. He was beginning to understand what his tutor meant when he said no essay was so good it could not be improved upon. And, his regular mantra: 'Any idiot can exceed the limitation rules', convinced Frederick that he had some catching up to do.

MONDAY 4 JANUARY 1954

Returning to the routine of his attic room was strangely comforting, like returning home from junior school to a bowl of cereal and milk. He stood at the front of the line waiting to collect his dinner. May, standing in the kitchen, put her head through the serving hatch and whispered:

"I've got something for you?"

Frederick was curious but disinclined to allow the relationship to develop as it nearly did when she visited his room on the second occasion. She was obviously naïve, vulnerable and - especially disconcerting - likely to disclose everything in the confessional box, he reminded himself. And Miss Pugh, a middle-aged spinster, had occasionally displayed signs of puritanism. However, he did have soiled materials that required laundering. He reasoned, if he could keep May sweet, but at arms' length, she could be useful.

He was in his pyjamas when May tapped on his door. He held the door ajar.

"What is it, May?"

" I brought you a little gift," she said, handing him a small package neatly wrapped and tied with a ribbon. "Merry Christmas!"

Before closing the door, he watched her tiptoe down the stairs. Sitting on the edge of the bed, he unwrapped the package. It was a small bottle of Old Spice aftershave. Feeling guilty for having misconstrued the maid's intentions, he vowed to return the gesture.

SATURDAY 9 JANUARY 1954

Jimmy, Frederick's tutor, recommended Woolworth's on Cornmarket Street as a good place for buying low-cost gifts. Unsure what a suitable present would be for a sixteen-year-old girl, a sales assistant recommended Eau de Cologne.

Saturday was also the day that Miss Pugh did her weekly shopping, and, catering for so many residents, it usually took her all afternoon. And during her absence, May busied herself with the week's laundry. Having neatly wrapped the Cologne in Christmas paper, he hurried down the stairs.

Barefoot, May was in the washhouse at the rear of the house, the sleeves of her white blouse rolled up and the small white apron replaced with a black plastic pinafore that reached the floor. Wiping her hands, she threw her arms around his neck and kissed his cheek. He returned to his room with rare thoughts of compassion and goodwill.

Unrelated to his area of study, Frederick was now borrowing books from the university library relating to psychology and philosophy. He was privately studying cause and effect and other areas linked to motivation and the human condition. Why, he was constantly asking himself, does sex have such a powerful and constant influence on human activity, more than on any other species? But, in search of other truths, these private studies were not confined to gonadic drivers. He read Jung, Freud and other author's, but couldn't agree with Freud's principal premise that memory – or suppressed memory – can be the underlying cause of some mental disorders. Nor could he agree that unlocking those memories, real or false, could restore rationality. As conceptualized as Freud's theories appeared, they were less intrusive than the lobotomy the two ex-servicemen had endured. But, conversely, he had to agree the electric shock treatment Mrs Porter had undergone had provided short-term benefit. But then he questioned his own conclusion: perhaps her transition was an illusion shaped by appearance alone?

It was the letter he received from his mother informing him that Mrs Porter was dead that got him reading about psychoanalysis. She had thrown herself under a train, not a tram or bus as she had often threatened. He had mixed feelings about the news, but it came as no surprise. The surprise was that it had not happened sooner. He had never, in any sense of the word, considered Mrs Porter to be normal. Her polarized moods were too extreme. And he could never agree with his mother's constant contention that her depression was caused by her husband's aggressive behaviour. Nor, in face of the evidence, could he understand how his mother could reach such a conclusion. It was common knowledge that Mr Porter was away in Europe when his wife was undergoing electric shock treatment. Frederick pondered, as he had so often in the past: would his mother's theory remain constant if she knew what he knew? This led him to think how some opinions are formulated without any supporting evidence. But he had to acknowledge that if everybody knew everything about their friends (and their friends' private thoughts), friendships wouldn't survive.

Frederick considered the relevance of family conventions and the Statute and Canon laws that Mrs Porter chose to ignore. He couldn't understand why she had been so determined to operate outside the law of state and church. Perhaps, he thought, her wants had been so dominant that she refused to be bound by those rules that enable society to remain cohesive. He wondered, was it innate lawlessness, mental derangement, or a sex drive so commanding that her sense of morality was repressed? Perhaps all three, he thought. But he couldn't be sure. He had read that Carl Jung cited ancestral input through the genes. He agreed with much of what Jung wrote, but questioned the complexities and reliability of multi-generational research.

From his own childhood observations, he recalled how war had unexpected consequences for family life in Riverton. Most able men had been enlisted, and the town and surrounding villages were subsequently transformed into sexual deserts. But sexual deprivation had not affected all women in the same way. While some mothers had sought solace lying under American GIs or Italian prisoners of war, some mother's had resorted to treating local schoolboys as surrogate husbands. On the other hand, other mothers, imbued with a moral fervour stronger than their sex drives, had remained loyal to absent husbands. Or were they just fearful of the consequences – or simply deprived of the opportunity?

Frederick was beginning to think that Mrs Porter was a victim of her sex drives, the same way she had no control over her depression. She had certainly been more depraved than those other adulterous women of Primrose Street and Daffodil Street. She allegedly became a magnet for the local schoolboys who boasted openly about what they thought were conquests. Of course, if the stories they related were true, they were prey, he concluded. He accepted the premise that unique circumstances had led those women to different liaisons. And, in mitigation, they didn't know if their husbands would return from the war with Germany. But he still thought there must be a biological explanation for why some of those Riverton women behaved the way they did.

To fulfill their sexual needs, Mrs Packer, Betty Curran and several other women, he recalled, regularly lay in the park with Italian prisoners of war. And, although they didn't know it, the open-air fornications were more instructive to the boys of Riverton than any school lesson. But Frederick couldn't help wondering if unmarried Betty was also looking for a husband.   However, he couldn't apply the same reason to Mrs Packer. She had young children and a husband fighting the Germans somewhere in Europe. He concluded that nature is flawed and women are no different than men, often discussing their extra-marital liaisons. Like men, they are unknowingly driven by an inherent compulsion to procreate.

Mrs Porter's behaviour was outrageous, but it wasn't her sexual deviousness that concerned him, but what her true motive may have been for showing a young child a military sword. He couldn't help wondering if there was something more sinister on her mind. And, at that time, she was undergoing electroshock treatment. It was the razor-sharp sword and his vulnerability as a child that worried him the more he returned to that particular memory. He deliberated: could a mood change from low to high have occurred in the short time he was in the room with her?

In his extra-mural readings, Frederick was likewise searching for an answer to the question 'what is normal?' He had read the four Ds of psychiatric disorder, and concluded that the extra-marital activities of those Riverton women were, in his estimation, deviant. However, as some of those activities were also conducted in private, Freud may have argued they were normal. But could the same be said when Mrs Porter behaved like Claudius' wife Messalina - but with a preference for schoolboys and coloured GIs?   Mrs Porter's extra-ordinary conduct repeatedly undermined Frederick's use of Riverton housewives for testing the theories of Freud, Jung and others. Freud's emphasis on erogenous zones struck a cord, but it raised more questions than answers. Confused by all the conflicting theories, he decided to concentrate on literature.

SUNDAY 17 JANUARY 1954

A week and a day after giving May a belated Christmas gift, she arrived at his door with an armful of neatly pressed laundry. He had arrived in Oxford with all his worldly goods. And his washables included two sets of pyjamas, three shirts, three underpants, and three pairs of socks. Miss Pugh's employment of a maid had been a blessing. He accepted the bundle of laundry with a genuine expression of gratitude. Smiling, and smelling strongly of Eau de Cologne, May remained standing at the door. She had obviously changed into her smart maid's uniform to make the delivery. She broke the silence.

"Do you want to pay Miss Pugh or me? If you pay me, there'll be a discount."

"How much?" he asked.

"Half price! There's me bill."

He invited her into his room and she sat on the edge of the bed, as before, crossing her legs. She noticed Frederick looking at the uncovered skin just above her long black stockings. When he turned to search in his raincoat pocket, she revealed more flesh.

"If you close the door, I'll tell you something very important," she said, putting the money in the pouch pocket beneath her small apron.

"Did you go to mass this morning?" he asked, closing the door.

"Of course! I went with me Auntie Theresa, and she said if I want to keep in with God, I can have sex as long as you put a rubber on your Micky."

Although taken aback by the statement – and concerned she had discussed him with her aunt - he didn't

214

want to show it: "Well that counts me out: I don't have a rubber."

"Well I do, from me auntie!" she said, holding up a small white packet.

But Frederick questioned the idea: "I thought using a rubber was condemned by our church?"

"Aye, so it is. And the Father said I must not listen to me auntie."

Just as Frederick feared, she was also holding nothing back in the confessional box.

"You must not tell him anything about me," Frederick warned, noticing more flesh.

"I won't tell him a ting," she promised.

Neither needed to discuss the matter further, and they both undressed themselves.

"You'll need to watch the broken spring," he reminded her as, with her bottom in his face, she climbed on the bed.

Frederick had never used a contraceptive before, but May had obviously been instructed by her auntie on how to unroll it.

It was only in the morning that he noticed the speckled blood on the sheet. Concerned by how Miss. Pugh would interpret the stains, he used his toothbrush and a cupful of water to remove them. And that night slept in a damp bed.

1954

And for the rest of the academic year, every Sunday afternoon she faithfully delivered his laundry, and they spent ten minutes avoiding the damaged spring on his bed. But, try as he might, she always insisted he wear a rubber.

He soon learned that when May made a decision, only her aunt could change it. And every third week she gave him half-a-crown out of her laundry money. Obediently, he visited the barber's shop and purchased a packet of three condoms for that same sum. The arrangement was perfect for both of them. On his last Sunday at the digs, she cried, but he promised to write.

During his first year living and studying in Oxford, he had occasionally thought of Patricia, then living in Stratford upon Avon. But by the end of that year, she was a distant memory, and he thought only of Debbie, wondering how, wearing leg irons, she would manage bringing up a child (subconsciously thinking about paternity). During his second year, he was perplexed that he had perfect recall of Debbie's body, but not of her face. However, egocentricity had replaced compassion, and his only concern was his own future.

Half way through that second year, he had carried out a self-assessment study. A degree in literature may offer opportunities in journalism, teaching, or even in the peaceful confines of a library. But in none of those areas – except perhaps in a library - would he be able to fully use his one real talent, his memory. He decided only an actor could make use of a perfect memory. In search of advice, he wrote to Jacques Duchesne at the Strasbourg address. A month passed before he received a reply, not from France but from London. The reply he received was promising: Jacques was living in London where he was teaching one day a week at a drama school. He was also working as an associate director at the Shakespeare Theatre.

At Jacques' invitation, he was invited to London to audition for a place at the school.   Much to Frederick's surprise – but suspecting Jacque's influence - he was accepted.   And the education authorities agreed that funding could continue with study fees paid direct to the drama school, but for only one year, the third and final year of his grant.   Accordingly, he advised the university he would be terminating his studies at the end of the second year.

With Jacques assistance, he secured a one room flat in London, half a mile from the drama school but close enough for him to save on the expense of public transport.

The curriculum was different to what he had anticipated and experienced at Oxford.   The hours were more like his school days, starting at nine in the morning and finishing at four, occasionally late in the evening.   The intellectual demands were less but the physical activity more intense and the study more varied.   At first he was nervous standing before his fellow students and reading from a script.   Their criticisms of his delivery annoyed him, made his hands shake.   He was embarrassed and careless in the free movement classes. He hadn't expected to be taught basic ballet steps, fencing and deportment.   Nor had he expected to spend hours learning how to breathe.   He thought that was a natural process.

"How do you think you can carry a thirty-line soliloquy if you can only fill a quarter of your lungs, the way you lot do?" the instructor had shouted.   "You will learn intercostal-diaphragmatic breathing if you learn nothing else. You will be able to send your voices to the back of the Albert Hall when I've finished with you.   And get the tension out of your shoulders, hum on em to clear the sinuses; I don't want you talking through snot. And do as Hamlet says: speak the speech, I pray you, as I pronounced it to you – trippingly on the tongue…Do not saw the air too much with your hands…and beget a temperance that may give it smoothness."

Filling the full capacity of the lungs was not as easy as he had imagined. Neither did the speech training come readily. Although fellow student at Oxford had influenced him, his southern pronunciations were loosely built on northern foundations. He was disadvantaged: most of the drama students were from London and Surrey, naturally using those vowels favoured by the school. But when ordered to learn a page of script and recite it the following day, he excelled. The script trainer began lengthening the number of lines, but Frederick never made a mistake. Nor could she catch him out with long Shakespearean soliloquies. His retentive memory soon became the talk of the drama school. But he couldn't relax when performing before other students.

"You'll never make it, if you walk around like a plank of wood," the instructor wailed, and Frederick didn't argue, he knew there was a lot of truth in the criticism.

Although Jacques worked at the school one day a week, he was engaged only in training third year students. Occasionally he looked in on the first year students. And, once a week in the cafeteria, he sat with Frederick discussing method acting. Jacques repeatedly reinforced the importance of not simply reciting lines, but believing you really are that character; or a tree, if playing a tree! He implored Frederick to get beneath the skin, or the bark: "Can trees think? If they can, what do they think of the way we treat them?"

1955

For the first six months of his drama studies, he borrowed library books on Chekov, Stanislavski and the works of Renaissance and Greek playwrights. He read prodigiously. And, in the privacy of his room, he also exercised, touching his toes, stretching his body, doing press-up and rotating his head. He hummed on em to improve the resonance of his voice. And for a couple of weeks, he gyrated inside an old bicycle tyre he found in the cellar of his lodging house. When out walking, he practised breathing exercises and recited lines. He was desperate to succeed. But then he met Wanda, a Ugandan princess.

Walking along the embankment, and thinking he was alone, he recited both Desdemona's and Othello's entreaties to her father. He was using two voices.

"That's lovely, really lovely," the princess exclaimed, clapping her hands.

As Jacques had suggested, he had climbed into both characters and spiritually was somewhere in the Mediterranean. Oblivious to his surroundings, he had walked past the bench where she was seated. His response was a confused mix of pride and embarrassment. But he bowed spontaneously. It was that moment - that response - that informed him he was no longer the man he was: he was a confident actor, or so he thought.

"Are you an actor?" she asked, eating a cream cake.

Frederick sat beside her on the bench and described his circumstances. Wanda related her own profile. She explained that she was also student, but studying English at Queen Mary University on Mile End Road. She had travelled by tube train to watch the boats on the river. She claimed it gave her inspiration for her poems. It also reminded her of childhood holidays on the banks of Lake Victoria. She further explained that her family is from the Apac district where her father owned a farm.

Despite his studies at university and now at drama school, he was unfamiliar with African tribal conventions. When she said she was a princess, he mistakenly put her on a pedestal with British royalty.

Frederick was fascinated by her smooth black skin, tight curly hair and thick lips, and the delicate way she picked her nose (although he thought it unbecoming of her status). During their short conversation, he allowed his mind to wander from those superficialities to what lay beneath the multi-coloured kaftan. The wraparound robe was too loose for him to assess her body size, but he estimated her to be extra large. Not being fond of overweight people – he thought, based on his own domestic experiences, they had a propensity to perspire – he wasn't initially attracted to the young woman by his side. But a balance had been struck between curiosity and inference, and he was leaning on the side of curiosity. And Wanda, like Frederick, had an interest in opposites; she wondered if his body was different to black men's. And although she thought he smelled of milk, said nothing. She asked if they could meet again.

By appointment, they met the following Saturday at the Kardomah Coffee House on Piccadilly. He listened attentively as Wanda told him about Uganda's giant lake stocked with succulent tilapia and Nile perch.

"And it is named after your Queen Victoria!"

He was especially enthralled as she talked about the wild animals that roamed the jungles back home:

elephants, giraffes, buffaloes, chimpanzees, baboons, and crocodiles.

"We also have gorillas that live in the rainforest on the mountains."

And, in response to her question, he told her about the bomb that fell at the top Primrose Street.

July signified the end of his year of drama studies and government grant. He was left wondering how he would survive. But he had support: in April, a month after meeting Wanda, he had moved into her well-furnished, two-bedroom apartment in the east end of London.

At first, the arrangement had been based on economic factors, but within three weeks they were sleeping together. Although her backside was unusually large, it was only noticeable when viewed side on. And his initial assessment had been a miscalculation: the rest of her body was not extra-large, as he had at first assumed. In fact, with the exception of her ample breasts and protruding posterior, she was well proportioned.

But when they walked down Mile End Road they were, as a pair, looked on with curiosity. Heads turned, and neighbours talked in whispers, or behind their hands. Young children were more vocal and demonstrative. But the insinuations didn't bother Frederick and Wanda: they were in love. And, furthermore, he was no longer lacking confidence. Now age twenty-one and with three years of advanced education, he could walk with his head held high.

However, as the weeks past, his newfound confidence was slowly eroding. All his job applications to theatre directors were either being ignored, or rejected. There were simply too many applicants chasing too few jobs. Television work was limited but even then only available to union members, and, to become a member of Equity, the applicant had to first act professionally on the stage. He wrote to Jacques.

1956

Securing the job as an assistant stage manager at an out-of-town repertory theatre was, at first, a reprieve from queuing at the Employment Exchange. He was grateful to Jacques, but soon realized that assistant stage manager was a misnomer: he was managing nothing but a sweeping brush. It was demeaning; not what he expected after three years of poverty and studying various disciplines.

Helping set-up scenery, sitting in the wings prompting actors on stage, making tea and sweeping the stage - these jobs kept him busy. But the money was not enough to live on - and he had the expense of travelling to and from the theatre five or six days a week, sometimes twice a day. Occasionally he had a walk-on part, but that wasn't compensation.

He mistakenly assumed that everybody has the same mental capacity as himself. He simply couldn't understand why some actors forgot their lines after rehearsing for a week. And, as a prompter hidden in the wings, he was growing impatient with on-stage actors fluffing their lines in front of an audience. He was no longer willing to whisper reminders. Instead, he was bawling them out, much to the annoyance of the director but to the amusement of the audience. He was sacked.

In October, Wanda received a letter from her father. He demanded she return immediately to Uganda. He had become a leading member of the Uganda National Congress party. As Uganda was a British Protectorate administered under English law, they urgently needed somebody to produce promotional literature in good quality English. She replied, saying that if the UNC needed somebody capable of promoting their cause and with oratorical skills, she knew somebody with those qualifications. She recommended an English actor who had also studied at Oxford University.

JANUARY 1957

It was an oppressive heat that rushed into the aircraft when the door of the BOAC Comet clattered open at Entebbe Airport. Frederick cautiously followed Wanda down the steps and onto the bubbling tarmac. He looked around: not another white person to be seen. It was, of course, the first time he had been abroad, and he had boarded that aircraft at London Airport with fear and foreboding; and now he was wondering would he ever see England again?

From a distance, the Mercedes saloon car parked outside the main entrance to the airport looked impressive: gleaming black with chrome grill and a small UNC flag on each of the two front wings. Standing limp beside the big car, the old black man in a loose-fitting black suit and open-neck white shirt greeted Wanda with a half bow. He removed his peak cap, and, fanning his face with it, complained about the temperature in Entebbe. His gaunt and unshaven face matched his dishevelled appearance. But Wanda obviously knew him and exchanged words in Bantu. The old man loaded the two suitcases into the car's boot.

Although the interior cream leather seating was comfortable, it was badly stained and cracked, and the worn springs no defence against the rutted roads. The road connecting Entebbe with Kampala was narrow, dusty, congested with old lorries, and older wooden carts pulled by donkeys or cattle. Herds of cows and goats clogged the roads, and herders were slow to respond to the honking car horn. Some women, carrying heavy loads on their heads, gave the driver the 'v' sign. The road ahead was obscured by red dust kicked up by a huge herds of longhorn cattle, and, as they drew closer to the herds, noxious gases seeped into the car.

"Kupunga hewa, Okapi!" Wanda said, leaning forward, but the driver shook his head. "I asked him to change the air, but …" Wanda stretched out her arms and shrugged her shoulders.

"Where are we going?" Frederick asked, removing his tie and jacket; only now realizing why all those Africans at the airport were wearing loose clothing.

Wanda explained that Okapi, the driver, worked on her father's farm but had been loaned to the UNC. And Okapi was taking them directly to one of their offices in Kampala.

Back in London, Wanda had mailed to her father Frederick's curriculum vitae, and he had been offered the position of assistant Promotions Officer with the fledgling political party. His terms of office included airfare to Uganda, a small salary and a room in one of her father's hotels on Jinja Road. Wanda was to be similarly employed by the UNC, but as a press officer and living in her father's Kampala apartment, also on Jinja Road.

Perspiring, they were too hot and tired for conversation, and while Wanda slumbered, Frederick looked out of the car window. He was fascinated by the ever-changing landscape: a glistening lake, forests, endless savannahs, banana plantations, tree-clad mountains and shantytowns. Under thatched overhangs, men lazed outside isolated mud huts. Kneeling by streams, women washed clothes, or, naked from the waist up, themselves. And, on the unpaved streets of the villages, other women carried bundles of wood on their heads, or huge cans of water. A few carried their babies on their backs; one infant suckling at the long breast that its mother had slung over her shoulder. Men cycled on rusty old bikes, others pushed their bikes with bunches of bananas attached to the handlebars. But there were surprisingly few motorcars on the rust-red road to Kampala.

It was late afternoon when they arrived on Jinja Road. Frederick followed Wanda up the narrow staircase off a side street. The stairs led directly into a small room with three ancient desks. But it was well equipped with up-to-date technology, including a telex machine, Gestetner printer, portable Underwood typewriter, and a telephone. The only person in the room, a slim Ugandan man, stood up and, with a wide smile, greeted them. Immaculately dressed in European-style clothing, he bowed slightly to Wanda and looked over her shoulder at Frederick.

"May I introduce our business associate, Frederick O'Flaherty?" Wanda asked, stepping aside to allow the two men to face each other. "Frederick, please meet Mr Obote."

Struggling with their suitcases, Wanda walked with Frederick to the hotel, a two-story Colonial-type white building a hundred yards along Jinja Road. They had agreed that initially she would be staying at the apartment her father owned – fifty yards beyond the hotel - but which he only used when attending political meetings. However, there was an impediment unanticipated by Frederick and not divulged by Wanda. Since childhood, she had been betrothed to Amare, the son of another tribal leader, and her father regularly reminded her of this economic and inflexible commitment. But now westernized, Wanda promised Frederick she was not going to enter into an arranged marriage purely to satisfy her father's business interests.

Parting with a handshake, Wanda, giggling, continued along the clay road, leaving Frederick standing outside the hotel door. But he couldn't understand what Wanda found funny. He was alone in a foreign country, unable to speak the language and worrying about his safety. He watched her walking away, her broad shoulders and large posterior swaying rhythmically, as if in time to a beating drum. Apprehensive, he entered the hotel lobby.

1958

Contrary to Wanda's prediction, soon after arriving in Uganda, her father made the necessary arrangements with the father of Amare. Wanda and Amare were married the week before Christmas. Frederick was marginally disappointed, but by then he had settled remarkably well into his new life in Kampala. And having found his true vocation, he was putting all his efforts into promoting the Uganda National Congress in general and Mr Obote, one of its leaders, in particular; as well as learning Bantu and Swahili.

Frederick's academic study and drama training had been the perfect preparation for the promotional activities he was undertaking. He was not only producing promotional literature and advertising copy in the office;

he was also going out to tribal meetings throughout Uganda. And, now Wanda was a housewife, writing press handouts and wining and dining newspaper editors. It was also his job to arrange promotional venues, advertise the event, and address the audiences before the main speaker.

To encourage attendances, the implied threat of violence was tempered with incentives such as gifts of barbecued goat meat. But some meetings were not attracting enough villagers. He decided to employ the services of a singer/guitarists, and soon realized that promotional messages are more effectively communicated through music. The balladeer wrote the music and Frederick wrote the words. Attendances grew, but he was still not satisfied. The ballad singing was pleasant but lacked the drama necessary to attract larger audiences.

One evening, out on the town with his Ugandan-born colleague Duidi, he witnessed a ceremonial dance. It was wild, exotic, and breathtakingly sexy: just what was needed to stimulate interest in the UNC. By agreement with Mr Obote, and funded by the party, he appointed a drummer and three female Bakiga dancers to supplement the balladeer.

Mr Obote was delighted: party membership was increasing exponentially. The UNC committee was also praising Frederick's efforts: they stood to gain personally from the increased subscriptions. To enable him to get the Congress's message to all four corners of Uganda's 236.000 square kilometers, Mr Obote sanctioned the purchase of a 1942 Mercedes-Benz, ex-military lorry. And Frederick was elevated from compere to main speaker.

Having loaded the musicians and dancers onto the back of the open-top lorry, Frederick, with Okapi at the wheel, set off for the one-hour drive to the Buikwe District. This was to be the first test of the new promotional arrangement, incorporating singing, music, dancing, and gifts of red and blue beads. A full evening of entertainment wrapped around a speech that Frederick would deliver in English, Bantu and Swahili.

In a jungle clearing, Frederick helped the three skimpily dressed dancers down from the lorry. Climbing up on the lorry, and speaking through a loud hailer, he invited the villagers to the musical entertainment. Slowly, the natives arrived, forming a wide circle around the lorry where the guitarist and drummer had positioned themselves. And to the rhythms of the beating drum, the three semi-naked teenagers frantically jumped up and down, kicking up the dry earth and lifting their knees to their chins. Bending from the waist, they moved forward in a line, wide-eyed as though in search of prey. Shaking uncontrollably, their bodies glistened and their perspiration sprayed the encircling spectators.

The audience was ecstatic, clapping their hands, shaking their bodies and rotating their heads in time to the strident drum beats. And then the villagers started singing, dancing and snaking in and out of the trees surrounding the clearing. Frederick, dressed in flowing, white boubou robes and matching prayer cap, sat with the village elders. Self-satisfied, he could sense this was the beginning of something big.

The young dancers were as entertaining off stage as they were on, and Frederick was enjoying their company. After working late one night, he agreed the three extravert teenagers could sleep on the floor of his hotel room. But their chuckling and whispering was keeping him awake.

Concerned by these disturbances, he insisted they stop chattering and go to sleep. The silence that followed reinforced in him the sense of power he had acquired in just over year.

The following week, and after another late promotional show, Frederick and the three girls sat cross-legged on the floor of his hotel room. They laughed, joked, and drank maize beer. But, unlike the first night, when he had insisted they sleep on the floor, he had reluctantly agreed to their demand that they sleep on his double-sized bed. Otherwise, they argued, they would go back on the nightclub circuit. Anticipating a mélange of moist bodies and the smell of perspiration, Frederick said he would sleep in a chair. However, the girls formed a tight circle, whispering and, occasionally looking towards Frederick, now sitting on the chair and enjoying a glass of beer.

The three Bakiga girls were impetuous and had been brought up in a sub-culture where they had to fight for what they wanted. Nevertheless, there was an initial level of cooperation. Baba, the lead dancers, stood behind Frederick stroking his neck. Looking up at Baba looking down on him, he was distracted and suddenly he was being woman-handled by the three dancers. Spilling his beer, they lifted him bodily and dropped him on the bed. Relaxed, and enjoying the frivolity, he lay back smiling, his hands behind his head.

It was Baba - his favourite – who removed his cap and spectacles; the other two girls stripped him of his robe and shoes. Then they massaged different parts of his body. Stress-free, he was enjoying this new experience. But then, held down by two of the girls, Baba sat on his genitalia. That was a position he despised. Lying on his back, he had no control. When Baba dismounted, they stared down at his flaccidity. As he now recognized, making love with three athletic teenage girls was beyond any man's competencies.

Undeterred by his limp demeanor, they lay on him, rolled him over, and slapped his buttocks. It was when they tickled his feet that he tried to escape, but he fell off the bed and they fell on top of him. He couldn't move, couldn't speak, and he was hurting. Despite their young years, they were fitter and stronger, and he was beginning to panic. He felt he was losing consciousness and may die. But then they suddenly released him. Standing up, each with one foot on his chest, they outlined their demands.

"Now me now, Mr Frederick," seventeen year old, Betty demanded. "Then her, then her again!"

But Frederick had already far exceeded his normal capabilities and was facing a dilemma. As he couldn't now perform, two of the girls held him down while the third sat on his face. They took it in turns, only moving off his mouth after experiencing a double orgasm. His tongue was aching, sore and raw, and his lips swollen and cracked from the friction of the girls' prickly pubic hairs. He wanted to be sick, he wanted to sleep, he wanted to be alone. Sexually satisfied for now, like a bunch of clammy pythons, the three teenagers wrapped their sweaty bodies around him. And then they slept, four in bed, but in the morning they wanted more of the same.

WEDNESDAY 1 APRIL 1959

In the past, Frederick would have spent his birthday in the hotel's bar with his friends. Today, it would have been nice, he thought, to celebrate his twenty-fifth birthday quietly with his live-in girlfriend, sixteen-year-old Baba. But he was now a driven man, enjoying his work and with a competitive edge he didn't know he had.

Baba was still dancing with the Bakiga group, but would no longer allow her colleagues to sleep in his bed. 'Not now we are engaged,' she had declared, much to Frederick's relief. But he had not promised marriage and did not agree with her interpretation of their relationship. But he didn't want to do anything that interfered with their association: she was extremely nubile, adventurous in bed and liberal. And she did, as he requested, regularly shave her bristly body hair.

Back in January, Mr Obote had been elected leader of the National Congress party, and, as a result, Frederick's own status had risen. He now had a telephone on his desk and extra money in his pay packet. And he was now mixing with Uganda's elite. But the political transition had not been easy: there had been both internal and external disagreements at both political and personal levels. Some members of the Congress were not happy that a white man had been given executive status.

Accordingly, Mr Obote, his mentor and protector, had instructed him to widen the promotional campaign north to the border with Sudan and south to the Rwanda border. Now espousing social democracy as the only way forward, Mr Obote had issued an edict that the UNC must be all-inclusive, and embrace all ethnic minorities. To fulfill these edicts, Frederick had the UNC logo painted in big letters on both sides of the open-top lorry and ordered five hundred teeshirts printed with Mr Obote's smiling face.

With the vehicle loaded for more events, they left Kampala before dawn for the five-hour drive south to Kabale. Unfamiliar with ethnic and tribal distributions,

Frederick was simply using a compass and a map of Uganda to select target communities. Travelling south, they stopped off at various townships, promoting the UNC cause and distributing teeshirts to tribal leaders. Finally, they arrived at the Echuya Forest, the final venue of the day.

As usual, the road journey had been slow, and the temperature, for an Englishman, too high. At least he had a seat in the cab, but having to share it with the driver and Baba, who was menstruating and a reluctant participant. It was less comfortable for the rest of the entourage riding on the back of the lorry. However, and thoughtfully, Okapi, the driver, had provided cushions and fitted a waxed-canvas awning under which the two musicians and two of the dancers sheltered.

The Batwa tribe, an oppressed ethnic minority, was surprised that any political party should show an interest in them, and this intrusion into their jungle village was initially unwelcome. Carrying long spears and blowguns, they surrounded the lorry. Cautiously, Frederick stepped down, but the appearance of a white man in white robes and cap, and wearing metal-rimmed spectacles, heightened the tension. The pygmy warriors repositioned their spears, pointing them at Frederick's chest. Frederick was immobilized at the sight of these very short and heavily armed people. But Okapi climbed on the back of the lorry and threw back the awning. The two Bakiga girls stood up. And when Baba climbed down from the cab, the atmosphere changed. The Pygmy men were no different than other men. The sight of three attractive girls with their breast covered inflamed their imaginations. Amazed, they pointed their spears to the ground. And like the presentations at all previous venues, the afternoon show was a roaring success, with the pygmies dancing and singing. And after the show, they feasted on monkey meat, honey and berries. For the two years Fredrick had lived in Uganda, his diet had consisted of tilapia fish, chicken, goat and maize porridge, but he had never before eaten monkey. He had acquired a new taste.

Sitting with the village elders, Frederick ogled the naked breasts all around him, contemplating how huge some are on such little bodies. He also noticed that some of the tribe's dancing men were surprisingly well endowed. However, in moments free of distraction, he listened as the elders outlined their grievances. Their prime concern was deforestation by white men.

Frederick, now thinking like a politician, knowingly and unknowingly indoctrinated by a system that supports his needs and wants, promised to offer protection if they vouched allegiance to the UNC. He had no idea what deforestation implied and suspected the government may have an interest in this enterprise. However, in pursuit of increasing the membership of the UNC – and his salary - Frederick was now willing to lie, even sell his soul. Before they departed, he presented the Chief with a printed teeshirt.

MONDAY 30 APRIL 1962

In 1959, the UNC had split into two factions with Mr Obote leading one faction. The same year, the Obote group joined forces with the Uganda People's Congress with Mr Obote being appointed leader of the newly formed UPC. This day, Mr Obote was elected Prime Minister of Uganda. For his energetic support, Frederick was provided with a villa, maid and a sleek, black, 1961 Ford Zephyr station wagon.

Unfortunately, for Frederick's road show, Baba and the other two dancers had been seen by a Kenyan theatrical agent and offered work in Nairobi. Baba said she would return when she had made enough money. But Frederick wasn't too concerned. Free to choose a maid, he had appointed a seventeen-year old Rwandan beauty queen. The fact that she had no skills in housewifery was irrelevant. Large, dark brown eyes contrasted with her light brown skin. But Abbo Kaminba was intelligent and aware attractive female mulattos were a much sought after commodity. Anybody wanting to offer her employment had to be asset rich (and she had a preference for white men). Being white, with a villa, car, and plenty of money, Frederick fulfilled all her requirements. But Frederick, playing it cool, slept alone - the first night. The second night, after a dinner of champagne and grilled tilapia, he introduced her to his bed. The problem was she wanted to be on top.

TUESDAY 9 OCTOBER 1962

This day, Uganda gained independence from Britain. To celebrate, Frederick and Abbo spent the morning walking along the northern shore of Lake Victoria. And in the afternoon, they swam in the lake's warm waters and lazed under palm trees. In the early evening, they dined in the Ggaba Lakeside restaurant. They started with fish, tilapia that had been netted that morning. And, for main course, they had goat, its throat cut that very afternoon, its blood still wet, warm and splattered on the courtyard's tiled floor.

In just seven months they had fallen in love and were now effectively living as man and wife. Now twenty-eight, Frederick had decided that his hunter-gathering days were behind him. And Abbo had declared her abiding love, promising never to leave him.

1964/5

During the Christmas holidays, and thinking it would enhance his career, Frederick invited one of Mr Obote's senior advisers and his wife to dinner at his modest villa. The sixty-one-year took a liking to eighteen-year-old Abbo and, following her into the kitchen, offered her the opportunity to become his second wife. Although black, he outscored Frederick on the other three points. She accepted.

In compensation, Frederick was offered a larger villa and a new Mercedes-Benz 220 limousine. Black with double headlights on each wing and gleaning chrome hubcaps, grill, bumpers, and Mercedes's bonnet badge, it was a car normally only allocated at ministerial level. With cream leather seating and matching large cream steering wheel, it was the perfect car for attracting the young women of Kampala.

However, on Wednesday, 22 January, Frederick was kneeling in his car wiping the stains off the back seat, when the phone rang. It was Mr Obote. An army unit of black soldiers in Jinja had mutinied and they had taken several prisoners, including British military officers as well as the Minister of the Interior (who had gone to negotiate with the leaders of the coup). A tri-lingual speaker was needed to translate for the white soldiers of a local battalion being sent to overpower the black mutineers. The Scots Guards, it was explained, were currently travelling by road to Jinja.

In his new car, with an armed bodyguard beside him, Frederick sped along the dusty Jinja Road, excited at this opportunity to climb even further up the UPC salary scale.

Waiting for the arrival of the Scots Guards, he parked the car outside the army barracks of the rebels, the First Battalion of Ugandan Rifles. But his car came under immediate gunfire. A bullet went through the windscreen passing between Frederick and his guard and exiting the rear window. He put the car into reverse, sheltering behind one of the native mud huts surrounding the fort.

Acting as a translator between the mutineers and an officer of the Scots Guards, Frederick quickly realized that some negotiations were also going on inside the barracks between the captured Ugandan minister and his Ugandan captors. But little progress was being made. The chief negotiator, Lt-Col W. W. Cheyne, resisted the insurgents' demands for better pay, conditions, and a reduction in the number of white men serving in the Ugandan army. It was obvious to the Ugandan government that the white British military would not agree to the terms being demanded by the black mutineers. And desperate to avoid the mutiny spreading to other parts of the country, the Prime Minister of Uganda sent a serving black military officer, Idi Amin, to intervene. An agreement – albeit unsatisfactory from a British viewpoint - was reached: all the soldiers' demands were to be met. Amin blamed the British negotiators for the delay in reaching an agreement and, in particular, their translator. But the latter judgment was both unfair and bias. Frederick had done his best with the faulty loudhailer.

With a neat hole in both front and rear windows, Frederick and his bodyguard returned to Kampala. Back in the promotions office, and determined to retaliate for Amin's criticism, he circulated a press handout.

The following evening, the local white aristocracy feted him at the cocktail bar of the Holiday Inn hotel. The ebony-black barmaid, Gloriana, was also impressed by his bravery in taking on the Uganda army. So impressed, that she accepted his invitation back to his villa. But, more importantly, the British landed gentry were at last recognizing him as somebody who may be able to further their interests in a country in which they were now being downgraded, treated as guests. He was invited to a Saturday afternoon party to be held in the ground of the Charmingly Estate.

Still with the holes in the windows of his black Mercedes-Benz limousine, and dressed in his regular white robes and cap, Frederick made an imposing figure as he drove through the streets of Kampala. Pedestrians waved and, smiling, he waved back (and threw coins to the beggars). Car drivers honked their horns, and he honked back. However, his self-esteem was punctured when he drove into the wide enclosure of the 10,000-hectare Charmingly estate. Four Rolls Royce Silver Dawns, two all black, two cream and black, competed for attention with three all black Silver Wraiths. The black Cadillac with white walled tyres somehow lacked the prestige of the seven Rolls Royce saloons parked outside the main door.

The mansion was formidable: three story high and fifty metres wide. A tall, black male servant, in full black and gold livery, greeted him at the door. Standing behind the servant in the expansive reception area, seventy-nine-year-old Lady Charmingly, dressed in a see-through, silver-satin, day gown, held out her limp, brown-spotted hand. Frederick needed no introduction: his face had filled half the front page of the Uganda Argus that week.

Under a pseudonym, Frederick had supplied the newspaper with two photographs, one of himself and the other showing the bullet holes. And, on official UPC headed paper, he had written editorial copy describing Mr O'Flaherty as the hero who had resolved the military insurrection. As the Argus newspaper was produced in English, he assumed only the white community would read it. But Idi Amin, now Deputy Commander of the Ugandan Army, always read that paper. He was incensed that a Roman Catholic upstart could be taking praise for what had really been his achievement, and, as Amin's parents were Muslim converts from Catholicism, his fury was even more ominous.

"Mr O'Flaherty, what a lovely name! Did you know that my ancestors came from Ireland? No, of course not, it was so, so very long ago. Time flies! Do you mind if I call you Frederick?"

Lady Charmingly raise her other thin hand, and a little black maid - her protruding posterior lifting the rear of her short tartan skirt to reveal her long red knickers – hurried across the room. She bowed and, repeatedly stumbling on high-heeled shoes, led him through the large reception area to the large patio windows at the rear of the house.

The view was spectacular: a manicured lawn stretching as far as he could see, and seeming to reach to the distance mountains. On the extensive patio, and surrounded by white men, two black servants were serving drinks from inside an open-top, circular bar. Deckchairs were scattered randomly on the lawn and around the large swimming pool. Some of the canvas chairs were also bearing the weight of two people in various stages of undress and interaction. Some guests sat or lay on large towels, others sat around tables. All the guests were white and holding drinking glasses; all the servants were black, scurrying around the lawn or constantly mopping the pool's tiled surround.

Standing at the open patio windows and feeling isolated (he was the only male guest wearing robes and a prayer cap), he was wondering what to do next when a girl, dressed in complimentary white riding breeches and a white blouse, approached him. She introduced herself as Looloo Charmingly, Lady Charmingly's great-granddaughter. She said she had read about his exciting exploits and wondered if she could have his autograph. She explained that she had recently returned from boarding school in England and was now having a short holiday before joining a finishing school in Switzerland. Her peach complexion and the few freckles surrounding her little stubby nose immediately attracted him, as did her sun-bleached hair arranged in a ponytail.   But it was the partially unbutton blouse that commanded his full attention.   From what he could see of her breasts, he quickly estimated her age to be at least seventeen, perhaps eighteen. But he wondered why she was allowed to display so much flesh in the family home. For a second, his mind flashed back to the day his father had ranted at Siobhan, his sister, for wearing a dress that exposed her knees.

"Let me show you my horse, Mr O'Flaherty."

Her voice was soft, tuneful, like that of a much-younger girl.   But from her sun-bleached hair to her perfectly formed feet, she displayed an air of innocence. He felt excluded, but still undressed her in his mind. She led him beyond the crowded lawn towards the outbuildings.

Beside the path, and some way from the crowd, two people seemed to be lying beneath a large white towel. At one end of the towel, four feet were displayed, but at the other, only a man's head was visible. As they drew level, his heavily bewhiskered face broke into an embarrassed smile. Looloo raised a hand and wiggled her fingers.

"That's my Uncle George; I think he's having another massage," she said, at the same time pointing to a enormous redbrick building. "All the six horses are Mother's; it's her hobby. But she bought Canon for my thirteenth. She looks after him while I'm away."

The entrance hall of the building was big enough to house a regiment. A black thoroughbred stallion was tethered by a sturdy rope and standing in sharp contrast against a whitewashed wall. It turned its head, first looking at Frederick, and then lingering on Looloo. Beyond the wide chamber, individual stables lined two sides of a long corridor. Looloo casually picked up a brush and ran it back and forth along the stallion's side. Slowly, its prepuce began moving; Frederick assumed caused by the brush moving the skin. But then, unexpectedly, the head of its penis emerged from its sheath, slowly gaining size until it was almost touching the ground.

"What do you think of that, Mr O'Flaherty?"

But he wasn't thinking intelligently: he was unexplainably embarrassed, not for himself, but Looloo. He also felt somehow inadequate.

"It's big!" was all he could think to say.

"Mother sometimes mates him, but she says it can be very difficult, even though Canon can fill a champagne glass with his semen. As you know, the problem living near the equator is all the days are of similar length. In England we usually couple them after April when the days get longer and the mare comes into season."

Frederick wasn't really listening, he was watching the horse now urinating, and it was running like a river towards him.

"Follow me," she said, jumping over a tributary.

He followed her, zigzagging down the corridor, where, at each stable door, she stopped to pat a horse's extended head. The corridor led to an anteroom where hay was tiered against another whitewashed wall. She sat on the lower tier and tapped the hay beside her. Frederick sat down, anticipating another lecture on horse management.

"How old are you, Mr O'Flaherty?"

Frederick hadn't anticipated any personal questions. He'd rehearsed answers to questions about his heroic act outside the army barracks.

"Twenty-five," he lied, knocking five years off his true age, but unclear why he'd understated it. "How old are you?"

"Sixteen, and never been kissed," she replied, laughing and showing the metal braces on her teeth."

"Is that because of the braces?" he asked, but she seemed taken aback by the question. "I mean, why you've never been kissed?"

"I've had more kisses than you've had fried fish," she declared. "But I'm not kissing you. You're too old! I'll judder you - if you want, though."

"Judder?" he asked, genuinely puzzled.

Putting her fingers and thumb together, she made a circle and moved her hand up and down. "Massage," she said, further clarifying her meaning.

Thinking he knew what she meant, he thanked her for the offer but declined. He knew from past experience that one-sided arrangements do not really satisfy anyone, except, perhaps, the curiosity of an adolescent girl.

"Most boys like me doing that to them," she explained, sounding rather disappointed.

"How many," he asked, now confident of her meaning and hoping the situation could develop.

"Ten!"

"Is that all?" Frederick asked, trying to encourage further admissions.

She didn't reply immediately, and, from the contortions on her face, it was obvious to Frederick that she was reflecting on what she had just disclosed.

"Only one!" she answered, standing up and shaking the hay off her jodhpurs.

As they walked back to the lawn, she was quiet, reflective. Breaking the silence, he asked her if she rode her horse regularly.

"Only when I'm in Uganda," she answered, stating the obvious. "Don't you tell great-grandmother or anyone what I said, will you?"

Suitably convinced, she led him directly to the table by the pool where her mother, grandmother, and great-grandmother were all seated sipping a mixture of white wine and water through straws. Facing the mountains, and without turning her head, Lady Charmingly raised an arm. A black servant, dressed all in white with silver tassels hanging from the epaulettes on his black tunic rushed across from the patio. She ordered another bottle of wine with a fresh ice bucket.

The conversation did initially focus on the army mutiny but with occasional incursions into his life back in England. But as there was no intellectual depth to the discussion, he had the opportunity to consider the four generations of the one family sitting before him. There was a distinct similarity between Looloo's mother, grandmother, and great-grandmother. They were all, in descending order, thin to slim, and blue-rinsed grey to blonde. Looloo's mother was still handsome, but then, in predictable degrees, the ravages of time and sun were etched into the faces and necks of the two older women. Although thin, there didn't appear to be any muscle beneath the flesh of those two. Frederick thought it was like looking at the ageing process in accelerated time. He could envisage how Looloo would look as she aged.

"You know, Frederick, we are all very concerned about the future. Since Uganda became independent we whites feel we have become marginalized," Lady Charmingly complained.

"It just isn't fair, we built the country, after all," Looloo's mother lamented.

'Can you have words with Mr Obote, telling him of our concerns?" Lady Charmingly asked, passing around her opened tortoiseshell cigarette case. Frederick declined her offer and was mildly rebuked.

"Can I have one? I am sixteen," Looloo asked, but her mother said she must wait until she is eighteen.

Frederick was relieved to hear she was sixteen. Listening to her childish utterances, he had been having doubts about her age. He stood and, picking up the heavy table lighter, lit each cigarette in turn, fighting the urge to close the lighter after holding the flame to the second cigarette.   The three women sat back, inhaling and contemplating the future.

"Yes, I most certainly will," Frederick agreed, replacing the lighter in the middle of the table, and sitting down again.   But he wasn't really concerned about the welfare of the white aristocracy.   Unlike him, they hadn't been forced to work and scheme for a living.   He quietly despised the upper class, the antithesis of his own upbringing.   But he still wanted to be part of their world, especially Looloo's.

The servant arrived and gently replaced the steel ice bucket on the three-legged stand beside Lady Charmingly. He asked if he should uncork the wine bottle, and she nodded her agreement.   Nothing more was said until the servant was on his way back to the cocktail bar on the patio.

"The servants will be asking for more money next, like those black soldiers. God knows where it will all end," Lady Charmingly commented.   "It'll never be the same again!"

Before leaving the mansion, he left his phone number with Looloo, inviting her to lunch at his villa, whenever she was in the area.   However, it was Lady Charmingly who, the next day, phoned inviting him to dinner at the mansion.

The invitation had come too soon after the afternoon soiree for it to stimulate the sense of anticipation that the first invitation had produced. And it meant he had to go out and buy a dinner suit with all the necessary accessories.   He contemplated making an excuse, but then thought of Looloo and her inviting bosom.

The selection of dinner suits on display in the store was impressive. He had never imagined that an African town with such dire and endemic poverty would have a shop like Banda's, offering so wide a choice of expensive European clothing, both military and civilian. The sales assistant, a young black man with effeminate movements, insisted on being in the fitting room while Frederick tried on the trousers. But Frederick's concerns were unfounded: the assistant was a skilled salesman and concluded the sale of the most expensive tuxedo in the store.

For more than a year, Frederick had worn only robes and a cap, usually white. Wearing a white dinner suit with red cummerbund and red bowtie seemed unnatural. But standing before the full-length mirror in his master bedroom, he was encouraged by the reflection. Breathing in deeply, he expanding his chest and turned side-on to admire his profile. He then turned his back to the mirror and looked over his shoulder. Unrealistically, he felt that wearing a suit like this had taken him up another rung on the social ladder.

The usual assortment of expensive motorcars was lined up outside the mansion, but there were also several military limousines. Entry to the mansion followed a similar routine to his previous visit, but Lady Charmingly, now dressed in a flowing black gown speckled with silver sequins, put her cheek to his face.

Since Frederick's previous visit, coloured lanterns had been strung around the paved area, illuminating the patio where two black servants struggled to meet the demand at the circular bar. The atmosphere indoors and out was a mix of expensive perfume, tobacco smoke, clinking glasses and animated conversations. But beyond the terrace, the distant mountains, now a vague shadow against a dark blue sky provided the perfect backdrop for the flickering fireflies. In contrast to the human dissonance, the chirping crickets were harmonizing with the white specks peppering the night sky. Frederick looked around. Most men were dressed in black tuxedos, a few in military uniforms. The women were all wearing long satin dresses and holding long cigarette holders.

"Hello, Mr O'Flaherty."

He knew it was Looloo, but turned, feigning surprise.

"Looloo! How are you?" he asked in his best quality English and exaggerating the aitch, a breath sound unfamiliar to him until Oxford.

"I've asked great-grandmother to sit you next to me, I hope you don't mind?"

It was music to Frederick's ears. Since meeting Looloo, he hadn't been able to get her, and her tight cleavage, out of his mind. Unfortunately, the red evening gown she was wearing had a mandarin-collared neck.

"Everybody is so old," she moaned, clutching the long gold chain of her black evening bag. Briefly, he wondered if Dora and her mother still frequented the Red Lion. "I'm so very grateful to you for your confidence. If it got back to Daddy, I'd be for it."

Having seen only the family matriarchs, he asked the whereabouts of her father. She explained that he was spending a couple of weeks in Paris with his girlfriend.

"Girlfriend?"

"Yes, but Mother doesn't mind; she has a boyfriend. But he's not allowed here, of course."

Frederick asked if she minded her parents having other sexual partners.

"What do you mean, sexual?"

He sensed tension behind the question, and considered his response carefully.

"Like...man and wife."

"There's nothing to stop Daddy having several wives. But he chooses not to. He's a lawyer and works very hard for Great-grandmother's tobacco business." She looked at her watch. "They'll be calling us to dinner soon. Let me order you a drink." She called over the black maid wearing the same tartan skirt. "Would you bring Mr O'Flaherty a...what would you like?"

"Whisky and soda, please."

"I don't like whisky. You'll need to order something else, like gin and tonic. Is that all right?"

Frederick willingly agreed and, as he assumed, he had to share his drink. In mitigation, she explained that the only alcohol she was allowed to drink was white wine mixed with water, and then only with meals.

The sound of a gong reverberated throughout the reception and terrace areas, and Frederick, with Looloo on his arm, walked with the crowd to the banqueting hall. The hall was long and narrow with a table arranged for fifty guests. Each place setting had been diligently arranged with an array of sparkling crystal glasses, gleaming silver cutlery, and a nametag. And, as Looloo had suggested, they were seated side by side.

"Did I tell you I love your suit?" she said, beckoning for the black servant to fill their wine glasses. "It looks spanking new."

"Yes, it's been well cared for. I always have it pressed after I've worn it," he lied, carefully taking note of the silverware Looloo selected for the first course.

Half way through their hors d'oeuvres, she nudged his arm and whispered: "Do you know that man? He keeps looking at you." She pointed across the table.

"Don't point; he's a bad tempered so and so," Frederick whispered, recognizing Idi Amin.

Sitting diametrically opposite, the powerfully built Amin, in full military regalia, was sitting next to another black man, slimmer but similarly attired. Both men had arrays of medals on their chests. Amin was eating at an accelerating rate and repeatedly calling over the wine waiter. While continuing to eat and drink, he occasionally put his head close to his colleague's. On one occasion, with a hand before his mouth, he stared pointedly at Frederick. Concerned for his own safety, Frederick avoided making eye contact with the two men.

"I do find these things so very boring, especially when I'm surrounded by my family. You've no idea how restrictive it can be." She raised a finger to the maid.

Sitting so close to Amin, Frederick was feeling very uncomfortable. Distracted by their proximity, he nevertheless tried to generate conversation.

"Are you planning to go to university after finishing school?"

"No, no, no! I want to be like my mother, a lady of leisure, with a husband, a boyfriend and six horses."

By the time they got to the orange sorbet, Idi Amin was perspiring heavily, repeatedly burping, and mopping his face with a large khaki handkerchief. He stood up and, followed by his military associate, hurriedly left the room. Frederick was relieved.

Slowly, the guests left the table until only Frederick and Looloo remained. The two glasses of wine with water had put a pink tinge on her cheeks and relaxed her eyelids. To Frederick's discerning eyes, these features epitomized those most desirable elements of femininity: youthful innocence with sexual desire. He said as much. Looloo was appreciative.

"Do you really think I'm attractive?"

After consuming half a bottle of wine, he was not going to prevaricate. "Of course you are attractive, very attractive."

"Bet you wouldn't say that if you saw me in the morning."

Frederick said he would love to wake up next to her in the morning. She put a hand on his knee.

The conversation was going the way he wanted it to go, especially when she suggested they walk down to the stable to say goodnight to Canon. Still seated at the table, he deliberated with himself how he was going to keep his new white suit from becoming sullied on the straw.

As they left the dining table, they walked into Lady Charmingly. She took him by the arm, at the same time instructing Looloo to go to her room. Looloo didn't argue, but he could see she was embarrassed.

"I need to talk with you, Frederick. As I said the other day, we are very worried by the way Mr Obote is nationalizing industry. Please come up to my room. I have documents from Government House that I would like you to see."

The comments were more of an order than a request, and he meekly accompanied the old lady as she slowly climbed the wide staircase.

Her high-ceilinged room was part office and - although panelled throughout in mahogany - part bedroom. She sat at the roll-top oak desk and opened a draw, withdrawing a bundle of documents tied with red ribbon. He could see the cover was clearly stamped CONFIDENTAL. She stood up, gesturing with her hand for him to follow her. On the table, also in the middle of the office part of the room, she untied the ribbon and opened the bundle at the page separated by a leather bookmark.

"Look," she said, stabbing the page, "this is what they are planning to do with foreign-owned businesses!"

Standing by her side, he could see the unambiguous heading: 'IDEAS FOR NATIONALIZATION'.

"Did Government House send you this?" Frederick asked, putting his head closer to the document.

"Of course they didn't. Every page is marked confidential. Obote thinks he can do just as he pleases. I've spoken with David but he says he now has no jurisdiction in Uganda.

"David?"

"Sir David Hunt, the British High Commissioner, he was at the table this evening. Sorry I invited him. I know you are close to the PM. Can't you make sure our company is not put on any list?"

Frederick promised to do what he could, but he knew that amounted to nothing. It was the government that paid his salary - not Lady Charmingly's tobacco factory. And although he had never voted in his life, he was, like his parents, a socialist at heart. His real concern was how a confidential government document could have come into the matriarch's hands.

Sitting on the verandah of his villa, the ice cubes rattling in his tall glass of gin and tonic, Frederick reflected how he had prospered since arriving in Africa seven years ago. And just one man, Mr Milton Obote, had made all this possible. But his thoughts kept switching back to the leaked documents. By the process of elimination, he tried to imagine the type of person who could have misappropriated the confidential papers. It was unlikely a black person would support a white, aristocratic family. And that white family, like other wealthy white families in Uganda, had got rich on the backs of cheap black labour. He concluded it must be one of the British employees working in Government House. Or, perhaps, a Kenyan! He picked up the phone.

The Ugandan government's main concern was word of the proposed nationalization programme reaching the British government in London.

"The British are meddlesome and likely to use dirty tricks," Mr Obote reportedly told his cabinet colleagues.

Frederick was instructed by Mr Obote's office to make false promises to Lady Charmingly, and also to mix with other wealthy factory and farm owners living in and around Kampala. The security service would identify them and make access easy. Furthermore, the government would orchestrate it so that his status would be enhanced by images of him appearing with leading members of the government. He would be given the fabricated title of 'Sir'. This title, he was assured, 'will put you on the guest list of all the white and brown elite.' And all his expenses would be paid. However, he was instructed to wear only expensive European clothes. The suits, silk shirts and Barker brogue shoes would be paid for by the Uganda government. Slamming his fist on the desk, Felix Onama, the Minister of Works and Labour, instructed Frederick to find out if leaked documents were in other hands.

Within days of Frederick reporting the leak to the Prime Minister's office, stage-managed images were produced. He was photographed with the President and John Stonehouse, a visiting British Member of Parliament. And he was photographed kneeling before Mr Obote with a sword across his shoulder. As Frederick was in charge of promotions and media manipulation, he had no difficulty in reinventing himself.

After seeing a photograph of the fictional investiture in the Argus, Looloo phoned him. And Lady Charmingly even had Kabaka, her personal chauffeur, deliver Looloo to 'Sir' Frederick's villa. Frederick sent a message back with the chauffeur that he would drive Looloo home before six.

That afternoon, Frederick and Looloo drove to Lake Victoria, sailed on the blue waters, walked along the golden beach, and dined at Frederick's favourite restaurant, the lakeside Ggaba. After lunch, they lazed under the palm trees. Looloo was thrilled to be feted like this by a knight of the realm and, for once, treated like an adult.

Lying back and half-a-sleep, he was totally at ease with the world. But it was the combination of wine, heat, and her hand on his thigh that caused the movement in his trousers. It didn't go unnoticed.

"Are you thinking dirty thoughts?" she asked, but Frederick was, as usual when caught out, embarrassed. He sat up.

"What do you mean?" he asked, but knowing full well what she meant.

But then she interrupted the drift saying she would have to go to the ladies room to change her sanitary towels. Fredrick decided it was time to drive her home.

Weekly, for each of the following the three months, he was wined and dined at the homes of the factory owning elite. As a white knight, he was treated with respect, somebody they could trust and who may be able to help them.

Slowly, it was emerging that the leaked document had not only reached Lady Charmingly, but most of the privileged minority. The minister for works was furious accusing Akbar Nekyon, the minister of information, of incompetence – even complicity. Cabinet meetings were convened but usually ending without reaching a conclusion. But the matter came to a head when Frederick reported that Asian factory owners were accusing the Obote government of racial prejudice.

Finally, the head of security was instructed to carry out a purge of Government House. Within days, scores of bloated bodies were being pulled out of Lake Victoria. But the practice stopped when the owner of the Ggaba restaurant – also popular with government ministers – complained it was affecting his business. 'Nobody will eat the fish,' he grumbled. Although officials continued to disappear, their bodies – those not consumed by crocodiles and hippopotami - were now being washed up on the banks of the Nile.

During those summer months, while spying for the Ugandan government, Frederick met Looloo regularly for walks and the occasional lunch. But, contrary to his nature, his intentions had become honourable. Ever since she talked about menstruating, she had, in his eyes, become desexualized (he had once had a bad experience when one of his girlfriends had not been forthcoming, forcing him to discard two bed sheets and a pillowcase). Despite this close friendship, and since being 'knighted', he had insisted on being referred to as Sir Frederick. However, the week before she was due to fly to Switzerland - and while eating barbecued goat in the Ggaba - he withdrew his demand:

"Looloo, please call me Frederick."

Like most sixteen-year-old girls, she was thrilled. It was like being invited into a special men-only club.

He sensed her satisfaction, and considered the implications. If allowing her to refer to him without his title had nearly moved her to tears, how would she react if he invited her to his bed? During dessert, he continued undressing her in his head.

"You seem so distant, Frederick. What are you thinking?"

"I was thinking how much I am going to miss you. You've no idea what you mean to me."

"I'll be back for Christmas," she whispered, putting her hand on his. "And I'll bring back something for your stocking."

"Bring me your body and I shall pamper it with perfume and kisses."

She laughed, heartily, and he noticed the metal brace was no longer covering her upper teeth. He had always thought of it as a distraction, an impediment to kissing, a symbol of immaturity. In his estimation, she was now liberated, freed from parental chains and ready for sexual adventure. Under the table, he could feel her hand moving around his kneecap.

"I do prefer you in robes, Frederick. You somehow seem more accessible."

"Don't you like the Savile Row suit?'

"Of course I do; it's so very smart, but suits are what all Englishmen wear. I like it when you are different."

"When I get back to the villa, I shall make a point of changing into my Sunday best kaftan."

The late-afternoon sky was still an unblemished blue, but Port Bell, the only road linking the beach with Kampala, was a pitted dust track. Driving north from the lake, Frederick was reminded of that day when he first arrived in Uganda: then roasting in an old motorcar with faulty windows and unsure of what lay ahead. In contrast, he was now a key government employee sitting in air-conditioned luxury with an attractive sixteen-year-old heiress sitting by his side. And she was stroking his thigh. However, scantily dressed herdsmen returning from market with their unsold longhorn cattle impeded Frederick's haste.

With her head on his shoulder, she rested the back of her hand on his thigh and, with an action like squeezing an imaginary rubber ball, repeatedly curled her fingers. Knowing what the local gesture implied, he was encouraged and constantly sounded the car's horn. But the herdsmen were indifferent. Frustrated, he drove the car off the road and between two rows of banana trees.

Without exchanging anything other than a smile and a nod, she followed Frederick, scrambling onto the wide backseat. She pulled her dress up over her head and hung it on the back of the front seat. Half turning, she indicated for him to unclip the pink satin bra.

From being a demure young lady, she had become a wild animal. She was the first to reach an orgasm, and they lay in each other's arms. It was the banging on the side window that separated them.

The broad and pockmarked face of a black man was pressed against the glass, his bulbous nose flattened, his stick being waved like a weapon. Looloo covered herself with her dress. Frederick partly lowered the window. In Swahili, they exchanged words. Compensated, the old man walked away with the bank notes in his hand.

Although they both had questions to ask, at first they travelled in silence, still traumatized from the initial shock of seeing the staring face just inches away from their naked bodies. The orange sky had darkened before Looloo asked him what the man had said. Frederick explained that he was the banana plantation foreman and complained about the damage to his crop. What Frederick didn't tell her was he had also called Frederick the equivalent of 'a lucky sod'. Frederick's question was more personal: "I thought you said you had never done anything like that before?"

But Looloo simply smiled.

That evening, Frederick sat alone on his verandah trying to read government documents. The small print, as usual, was written in a confusing mix of English and Bantu. And its subject matter, listing foreign business owners still to be contacted, interfered with what he wanted to think about. Furthermore, the light from his mobile kerosene lamp was inadequate, its metal case creating patterned shadows. He put the papers on the small table by his side and picked up the brandy glass, quarter filled with Courvoisier. Dismissing the memory of the face at the car window, he tried to relive the afternoon's interaction with Looloo. He couldn't get to grips with how she could be so sexually experience and yet appear childlike in both mannerism and speech. She was obviously more intelligent than he had thought. He had seriously under-estimated her, and this supported his growing theory that intelligence is not something that is learned in the lecture hall. It's innate, he thought, like Looloo's ancestors who were able to manipulate the system and get very rich. But just as he recaptured the mental picture of her lying with her legs apart, that pot-marked face appeared in his mind again, and he couldn't dismiss it. He thought a good drink would clear this unwelcome image and put the glass to his mouth. At that moment, a bullet ricocheted off the table, followed by a second bullet thudding into the lamp. In total darkness, he fell to the floor, crawled along to the door and into the villa. He bolted the door and, sitting on the floor, phoned the police.

In the darkness, and waiting for the police to arrive, he crawled to the window. Still on his knees, he looked out between the slats of the horizontal blind. It was too dark to see anything other than the vague horizon between land and sky. And, fifty metres from the house, a natural barrier of tall grasses made a perfect hiding place in which a bandit could hide. The monkeys, disturbed by the gunfire, were scurrying and cheeping, but he was familiar with that sound.

Perhaps, he thought, it was an accident: a hunter firing in the bush. But would the two shots have been so close to each other? Yes, he thought, highly likely a hunter would fire off more than one bullet.

It was two hours later before the police car drew up outside the villa. Carrying powerful torches, the two uniformed officers walked briefly through the grasses, covering the area indicated by Frederick. Fifteen minutes later, they drove away; also suggesting it was a distant hunter. But, having recovered from the shock, he disagreed. He had not been sitting in the dark.

The Uganda government was still working towards its planned nationalization agenda, but Frederick had completed investigating the European elite and was now actively spying on Kenyan business owners. He was surprised, then, to receive a call from Lady Charmingly inviting him to a New Year's Day luncheon at her mansion.

Dressed in his latest silver-grey Savile Row suit and a new black fedora, he drove through the quiet streets and out onto the country road. He had set off in good time and could now drive slowly, reflecting, as was his wont, on how successful he had been. Only last night he had entertained at his villa a dozen Kenyans and their wives. He had also invited Amira, the Kenyan secretary who did some of his typing. He knew her tenure was coming to an end but there was no point in telling her, spoiling the festive occasion. Besides, she was attractive, vivacious and displaying that magical formula that he worshipped: a slim body with large firm breasts. And he knew they were real. At twenty-one, she was a little older than his current collection of Ugandan girlfriends - but she had so much else going for her. He tired to relive the memory.

His cocktail cabinet had been stocked for the occasion by central office. Any leftovers would, as usual, be collected the following workday.

By ten o'clock, he had gleaned all he needed to know, and every word uttered had been mentally recorded. He could relax, paying more attention to Amira and remove her from the clutches of the portly Kenyan who had sent his wife home early. Frederick put a mental asterisk beside his name and status.

Although Amira's father was Kenyan, her mother was Sudanese, and she had obviously inherited her mother's attractive features. Amira had lived in Uganda only three years, having arrived from Kenya with her parents, initially living in Kaabong. Her parents remained on the border with Kenya. But Frederick knew all of this. He was also in the business of collecting information. He even knew where her solicitor father worked.

In bed, she had offered more than he ever expected from a typist. Physically drained, he lay in bed until ten.

Sitting comfortably behind the steering wheel of his black Mercedes - now sporting a flag on each wing – he looked around at a landscape that never failed to thrill him: blue skies; grasslands; bananas, clustered and hanging from trees; pink geraniums by the roadside; the remote highlands shimmering in the midday heat. If only they could see me now, he thought, reflecting on what his parents and siblings would be doing at that moment. He decided it was time he wrote them a letter, perhaps sending them some money. After such a wonderful night, he was feeling charitable. But then he wondered if they were still living in the same house? They may have moved from Riverton! It was many years since he last heard from them, and that was when he was living in London. He decided he would definitely write when he had time.

He had been so busy thinking about one thing and another that he had arrived outside the mansion without realizing it. He was surprised to see that his was the only car on the wide drive, but assumed he was early. He checked his watch: yes, he was five minutes ahead of schedule.

The same black servant greeted him at the door. Taking Frederick's fedora, he led him out to the garden where Lady Charmingly was seated at a table, her cigarette burning on the end of a long ivory holder. She pointed to a chair, and the servant pulled it out for Frederick to sit on. Her attitude was aloof.

"We'd better get to the point: Looloo is pregnant," she declared, looking towards the distant mountains.

Fredrick needed a few seconds to get his head around the implied accusation before replying.

"Oh, I see, is she, um, having a baby?"

"You'll see for yourself."

"Is she married?" he asked, illogically but needing time to prepare the case for his defence.

His question was ignored, and they both sat silently contemplating the next move. But then Looloo and her mother appeared, quietly sitting at the table. Frederick looked at Looloo's stomach. She was obviously pregnant and it didn't take him long to estimate about three months. Looloo, now with her hands clasped across her stomach, avoided making eye contact by looking down at the table. But her mother didn't take her eyes off him. Lady

Charmingly continued to look across the vista to the Aberdare Mountains.

"What have you got to say for yourself, then?" Looloo's mother asked, leaning towards him. She put her head so close that he could see down the front of her loose blouse. She wasn't wearing a bra. He realigned his attention towards Looloo. She had clearly been crying.

"I beg your pardon, but what's that got to do with me?' he asked, relying on the notion that attack is the best form of defence.

"Tell him, Looloo," her mother demanded.

He looked at Looloo. Slowly she lifted her head until their eyes met.

"Tell him," her mother repeated, but now with more emphasis.

"It's yours," Looloo murmured, so quietly that her mother insisted she repeat the statement.

"Are you sure, Looloo?" Frederick asked, but it was Lady Charmingly who replied.

"Are you trying to make out she's promiscuous?"

Frederick shook his head, but, unwilling to admit paternity, turned to Lady Charmingly: "Ask her if she's made love with anyone else."

"How dare you?" her mother cried, putting her hand on the back of his chair and shaking it so violently that his spectacles fell to the table.

Although unnerved by the woman's strength, he was convinced that Looloo had had more sexual experiences than she was admitting to. "Well ask her," he repeated, replacing his spectacles.

In the silence that followed, the two older women looked at each other. Their pale features appeared frozen, disclosing nothing until Lady Charmingly closed her eyes and her heavy eyelids revealed considerable brain activity. She opened her eyes and looked directly at Looloo.

"If I think you are lying, I'll bring out the Bible. So answer me truthfully: have you been with other men?"

Looloo didn't answer immediately. She looked towards her mother, towards Frederick and finally towards her great-grandmother. With tears in her eyes she nodded.

Frederick sat back in the chair, the tension suddenly draining out of his body. He felt limp. He wanted to go back to his villa. He was proud that his assumption had just been validated. Although feeling slightly sorry for her, he was annoyed that she hadn't previously disclosed this fact to her family.

Frederick stood up, preparing to leave, but Lady Charmingly firmly asked him to sit down.

"Have you been with any other men - or boys – since you lay down with him?" Lady Charmingly asked, pointing a crooked finger at Frederick.

To his dismay, Looloo shook her head. He could feel the tension building up again and could do nothing to stop his shoulders rising up to his ears.

"That's enough proof for me," Looloo's mother exclaimed, putting her arm affectionately around her weeping daughter's shoulders.

"That doesn't prove anything. She may have been with others before me. And I didn't leave it in."

Lady Charmingly put her hands to her ears, and Looloo's mother clutched at her heart, both groaning. Looloo broke down in a flood of tears. The old lady raised a bony hand, and the black servant hurried across the lawn.

"Bring me a Bible, right now," Lady Charmingly demanded, and the servant rushed back to the house.

Frederick and the three women sat in silence, each looking in a different direction. He felt trapped, as though in a swamp, sinking and surrounded by crocodiles. Subconsciously, he felt the net was closing in on him. He had no idea where it was all leading. At an upper level in his subconscious, he was ready to fight: to disprove the allegation that he was the cause of Looloo's pregnancy. He had that feeling of old: the urge to get up and run. But he knew there was no place to hide. He was now too well known in Kampala to do that.

"There you are, ma'am," the black servant said, putting the large, black, leather-bound Bible on the white table. "Is there anything else, Ma'am?"

Without looking at him, Lady Charmingly shooed him away with the wave of a hand. She pushed the Bible across the table to where Looloo was sitting. From her small purse, she withdrew a neatly folded linen handkerchief. She shook it loose and passed it to Looloo.

"Spit on your hands then wipe them with this."

Looloo did as she was ordered, but, with her head inclined, stared down at the ground.

"Is this really necessary, Grandma?" Looloo's mother interjected. But her question was ignored.

"Put your right hand on the Bible," the old lady continued." Satisfied, she asked: "Did you do it with any other men... or boys... last year?"

Looloo nodded, and Frederick began to relax again. But the two older women did not appreciate his involuntary exhalation, and Lady Charmingly stared long and hard at him. When she screwed-up her eyes, he knew there was more to follow. Speaking slowly, she continued to question her great-granddaughter, leaving the critical question until last.

"When did you lie with Jasper?"

When she admitted making love with her nineteen-year-old cousin, he thought he was now in the clear, but then, with her hand still on the Bible, Looloo was unexpectedly specific.

"It was the sixth of June, in a field at the Wyeminster Horse Trials. I'm so sorry, so sorry. Will you forgive me?"

Frederick didn't need to do a mental calculation. He knew that he was up to his neck in the sludge and at any time now could sink below the surface.

Lady Charmingly thanked Looloo for being so honest, then turned to Frederick.

"You may go now. You will be hearing from our solicitor."

Frederick remained seated in his chair for a moment, trying to catch Looloo's attention, but she turned her head away.

The sky was still sapphire blue as he drove back to Kampala, but his mood was black. Although Looloo had turned her back on him, he nevertheless let hypothetical scenarios cross his mind. 'If they insist I marry her, would I agree?' he thought, and then reasoned that marrying into the Charmingly family, with all its wealth and prestige, could lead to greater things. But he knew this scenario was unlikely to materialize, and that realistically the future looked bleak.

As Lady Charmingly had promised, eight days after that fateful meeting he received a letter and a contract from her Kenyan solicitor. The demand was unequivocal: Frederick was to pay the travel costs to and from London, and maternity expenses at St. Mary's Maternity Hospital in Paddington. After the birth, he would pay maternity benefits for sixteen years. Furthermore, he was to pay for the disruption to Looloo's education. He would not be permitted to see, or make any claim, on the child.

Concerned that Looloo's pregnancy could force him into bankruptcy, he sought advice from Duidi, his friend and colleague, also working at Central Office. Duidi Lumu, was a senior military adviser working on counter espionage. However, he agreed to pass the paternity order to an assistant working on the possible nationalization of foreign owned businesses. Duidi reassured Frederick that one letter was all that was needed to quash the order.

And, as predicted, Lady Charmingly's solicitor withdrew the order, citing compassion and a misunderstanding. Her solicitor also pledged his support for the Obote government and apologized for any inconvenience. Despite the reassuring narrative, Frederick ensured that the Kenyan solicitor's name was on the list of undesirable aliens.

Although there was no concrete evidence to prove or disprove the accusation, it was concluded that Kenyan officials had been responsible for the dissemination of confidential government documents. And all Kenyan nationals were to be expelled from senior government positions.

About this time, it was rumoured that Mr Obote was selling arms illegally to Congolese rebels who were fighting the Congolese government. In return, the rebels were paying with the international currency of gold and ivory. It was further alleged that the newly appointed Commander of the Army, Idi Amin, was Mr Obote's chief negotiator.

Frederick, as an arms-length confident of the Prime Minister, was instructed to write editorial copy discounting the rumours. To counterattack, he was ordered to promote Mr Obote's caring policies and egalitarian principles. Frederick was naturally sympathetic to Obote's socialist principles, and did what he had become good at since arriving in Uganda in 1957: reconfiguring truth and illusion. As a reward, Mr Obote presented him with a heavy gold ring incorporating the symbol of the Christian fish.

Sitting in his air-conditioned lounge, Frederick sat admiring the ring on his finger while contemplating the ups and downs of life in Uganda. He asked Rita, his latest Sudanese girlfriend, to refill his brandy glass.

1969

In 1966, Mr Obote had appointed himself President, as well as Prime Minister of Uganda. And, much to Frederick's delight, the party lurched itself still further to the left. His cherished leader was now effectively harnessing the powers of a dictator. All of this was favourable for genuine Obote supporters like Frederick. And he was using his PR skills to make the new President aware of his loyalty.

In 1967, and for his ten years of devotion to the party, Mr Obote had personally presented Frederick with a ten-ounce ingot of pure gold. And since that day it had been stored in the wall safe in his bedroom, concealed behind a signed photograph of a smiling Mr Obote.

Never a week passed without Frederick thinking of those roads that lay before him in 1952. Had he not gained that place at Oxford; had he not met - and been helped by - Jacques Duchesne; had he not studied drama - but more importantly, had he not met Wanda, life would have been so very different. For more than twelve years he had lived the good life, slept with more black women than most black men shake hands with in a lifetime. He was beginning to think he was invincible, but then recalled the four-year-old child he had never seen. He did know mother and child were now living with Looloo's – now divorced - father in London. Although he often thought of them both, he agreed with his inner-self that family life would have been too restrictive.

For Frederick's thirty-fifth birthday, Duidi, his friend at the office, had secretly arranged a birthday party at the Holiday Inn Hotel.

All the guests were black and government employees, but, as in most dance hall scenarios, there was self-imposed segregation. Most of the men were standing at the long bar, shoring up their courage. While the females sat coyly at tables encircling the dance floor. But each group was discreetly studying the other group. Duidi had ensured that the invitations were weighted towards young, attractive females, especially those who used skin-whitening creams and straightened their wiry hair. He had a preference for white girls.

However, the fluorescent ceiling lights in the cabaret room were new and subsequently emitting maximum illumination. As a consequence, the ultra-brightness had the effect of making those black faces with whitening cream appear yellow. And the low-level ceiling fans made oil-straightened hair flutter like fireflies.

Off duty, Frederick was dressed casually in his white robe and cap. By taxi, he arrived with Duidi expecting a quiet night enjoying a weekend drink at the hotel's bar. But, when they entered the cabaret room, the guests all stood up, greeting him with the appropriate song. Frederick was taken aback, but he was disappointed to see so many yellow faces. He preferred the black girls black and with naturally curly hair either braided to the scalp or plaited.

As the evening wore on, alcohol flowed, limbs loosened and perfumes were overwhelmed by sweat. Frederick, the only white man in the room, studied the girls around the dance floor. This was his kind of evening: attractive young women shaking their bodies as though at a voodoo ceremony. Being a 'Sir', single, well paid and owning a villa, a Mercedes car, and – as he had put it about – being a close confidant of the President of Uganda, he was usually in demand. And he was also birthday boy. Choosing a woman tonight, he thought, was like fishing with a large net in a bathtub filled with perch. But as the evening wore on, he narrowed his objective to a single target.

He didn't recognize the attractive, but bespectacled, young woman sitting in a corner with Namata. He was immediately attracted to this stranger, the only female in the room not wearing skin whitening cream.

Namata worked in the General Service Unit headed by Akena Adoko, Mr Obote's cousin. Frederick was on good terms with the secret police and regularly cooperated with Akena in identifying undesirables. Using the indirect approach, with Duidi and one of the waiters in tow, he joined the two women at their table, ordering a bottle of champagne. Namata congratulated him on his birthday and introduced the two men to her friend, Mugisha. Frederick sat beside Mugisha, leaving Duidi to engage with Namata. But the more he learned about this stranger, the more inclined he was to look for new quarry.

Frederick always found ultra-intelligent women more concerned with their brains than men's bodies – but not necessarily their own. And once their heads had risen into the intellectual stratosphere, he contended, they soon lost interest in sexual intercourse - with men, but not necessarily with women. Heterosexually, they became observers rather than participants; fearful of subordination, he argued when debating the subject with his colleagues at the office.

As a renowned lover, his government colleagues always listened to Frederick's advice on carnal subjects. Young stupid women were much better lovers, he often remarked over a beer, but once they were educated, their animal instincts reduced in proportion to their learning. And after the age of thirty, sex with men was perfunctory. However, he was willing to concede that genes and parental influences could not be discounted.

Mugisha explained that, like Namata, she had studied at Manchester University but acquired her PhD at London School of Economics. Negative thoughts were creeping in on him: she looked to be in her early thirties, and when she said she was an economist, he sensed he definitely had to move on. But at that moment, the sound of repeated explosion made everybody stand up and clap.

"Did you arrange the fireworks, Duidi?" Fredcrick asked.

"Don't sound like fireworks to me," he replied.

It was when the banging grew louder, more repetitive and holes began appearing in the ceiling that women started screaming. Panicking, and with arms waving irrationally, most of the men surged towards the door. But soldiers in the reception area, firing out of the building into the street, forced them back.

Like the majority of the guests, Frederick and his friends sheltered under a table. Kneeling next to Mugisha, he inhaled the expensive perfume she had sprayed liberally around her long neck. The close-up view of her short curly hair, neatly braided in tight rows was striking and, with her spectacles on the floor, she appeared even more beautiful. Clinging to his arm, intellectual superiority was no longer her priority. Frederick was suddenly the alpha male and she the subordinate, if not gamma, female. He now had a clear view down the front of her dress and was impressed by what he saw.

The gunfire was constant, occasionally interrupted by loud explosions that shook the building. With bullets ricocheting around the room, and plaster falling from the ceiling, nobody moved from where they hid. Everybody in the room was now silent, afraid of being shot, afraid of attracting attention, afraid of dying.

It was an hour later before the gunfight was concluded. Armed Ugandan soldiers, unnervingly issuing orders by waving their rifles, led the guests out of the hotel. Frederick agreed to escort Mugisha home.

Her apartment was on the top floor of a building that he drove past regularly on his way to Government House. It was probably the most exclusive apartment block in Kampala. Leading him into the large lounge, she threw her silk white scarf over the back of a white sofa and dropped herself forcibly onto the multi-layered black satin cushions.

"I need a drink," she said, kicking off her black high-heel shoes and pushing her spectacles up onto her hair.

He was surprised by the quality of the furnishings. Everything seemed new, very modern, and very expensive. He was moved to comment.

"I like your furniture," he said, running his hand along the leather sofa's broad back.

"It used to be a cow," she replied. "Can you pour me a stiff one, please?"

Three bottles of liquor and half-a-dozen glasses were neatly arranged on the low white table. He looked at her.

"Well?" she asked.

"What would you like?"

"A good question! Sorry, I haven't got over the shock. We could have been killed. Scotch, two fingers, neat! And help yourself."

He partly filled two glasses, handing one to Mugisha.

"Bathroom?" he asked, and she pointed to a door.

As he expected, the bathroom was also ultramodern, and he began to relax as the urine poured out of his body. But he couldn't help wondering how she, a working girl living alone, could afford the luxury of a penthouse apartment.

With a glass in his hand, he sat down next to her. For a few seconds they allowed each other space to savour the whisky and reflect on the day's events. Mugisha was the first to speak.

"Who do you think the rebels were?"

"Ugandans opposed to all the good work our President is doing."

"Good work?" she said, laughing out loud as though he had just told a funny joke. But he couldn't understand the response. It didn't match reality.

"New schools, new hospitals, new roads, airport development. Some factions don't want a unified country,"

"But isn't he banking tax receipts in his personal bank account?"

Although suspecting what she said was true, he objected to the supposition. Mr Obote had treated him with nothing but kindness, and Frederick was not going to criticize the hand that once fed him ten ounces of gold.

"Do you think it could have been those Congolese rebels trying to get their money back for dodgy weapons?" she asked, throwing one of her arms over the backrest.

The conversation was now too probing for Frederick's liking, and he wondered how she could know about the weapons deal. He was beginning to suspect she might be more than an economic adviser. He finished the rest of his drink, preparing to phone for a taxi. But then she put her hand on his shoulder.

"You can stay, if you want."

It was unusual for him to decline such an offer, but he was still internally agitated by the attack on the hotel. And the more he thought about the situation, the more the events didn't make sense. There were no soldiers in the hotel when he had arrived, and what were they doing there anyway? He stood up to leave, but then she also stood up, asking him to follow her onto the wide balcony. He stood by her side looking down on the empty streets below.

There was no traffic movement and the traffic lights had stopped functioning.

"It's too dangerous for you to go out."

The bedroom was even larger than the living room, but whereas that room was black and white, this room was a blaze of colour. A large rectangle of red and blue lights had been built into the ceiling and surrounded a mirror, roughly the size of the bed it reflected. Additionally, a white wall-light was focused on the bed. Fascinated, he made a mental note to order a similar lighting scheme and ceiling mirror for his own master bedroom.

Naked, unabashed, and with one arm beneath her head, she lay on the white sheet watching him climb out of his robe. It was obvious to Frederick that this was a familiar routine for Mugisha. She even had her legs slightly apart. Slowly, she lowered one arm until her hand rested on her pubic hair. As much as he loved African women, he disliked this bristly aspect of their anatomy. But he wasn't to be deterred.

The coloured lights painted wonderful patterns on her ebony black skin, and the bright, white spotlight cast shadows around the curves of her sensuous body. But there was nothing adventurous in her interactions: she preferred to be side-on looking directly into his eyes.

In every detail, she was beautiful and her perfume exquisite. It was as though his body was, of its own accord, reacting to her loveliness and unwilling to be separated from it. Although she was moaning, he continued making love. Never in his life had he performed so well. He felt proud, confident that it was all part of his ongoing maturity. 'She'll never forget this night,' he thought.

Frederick spent the following weekend relaxing or reading, and, with a smile, occasionally reminding himself of his recently acquired prowess. However, being pragmatic, he concluded the long-lasting effects of that night with Mugisha must have been aided by something he ate that day, and, from memory, made a list.

The newspapers provided wide coverage of the gun battle at the Holiday Inn, but explanations were absent. The men attacking the hotel were simply referred to as rebels. He knew the editorial had been censored – but didn't know by whom, and the editors were not forthcoming.

When he arrived at the government office on Monday morning there was a very unusual atmosphere, almost frivolous: clerical officers were standing outside their offices talking with other staff members. When he walked past the typing pool, it seemed as if all fifty-three typists were either talking or laughing. There was none of the usual clickety-clicking of typewriters breaking the silence. As he entered the executive suite, Duidi called him into his office.

"Look at this!" he said, handing Frederick a coloured photograph.

Frederick studied the picture while Duidi watched him closely. It was Mugisha, in bed with one of Mr Obote's senior advisers. Both naked and lying on their sides. It was the same bed; the same position that she said she preferred.

"Recognize her?"

"Shit!" Frederick exclaimed, suddenly feeling a cold wind blowing down his back.

'There's probably a copy of this in your mailbox."

The next day, further photographs arrived in the mail.   Naked beside Mugisha, Obote's Second Medical Officer, Ernest Mateke, was lying on his back.

"Look, he's holding his cock and smiling at the camera." Duidi couldn't contain himself and bent double, his arm across his waist.

It was Wednesday before the compromising photographs of Frederick arrived. And his nakedness was now also on public display. The prints had been sent to every department of Government House, including the President's office.   Fortunately, Mr Obote found all the pictures amusing and put a blanket ban on media publication. But Frederick and those other victims were, nevertheless, humiliated.   Duidi, promised to make immediate enquiries.

He phoned Namata for a background check on Mugisha. But she said, until recently, she had not seen her since their student days. She had simply phoned, asking if she could attend Frederick's birthday party.

Convinced that Mugisha was working for one of the opposing political parties, Frederick drove to her apartment.

He paused outside the door, trying to let his anger subside. He put a finger on the button and pressed. He could clearly hear the doorbell chiming inside the apartment - but also muffled voices. The door opened. It was Idi Amin, naked except for the white bath towel wrapped around his wide waist.   He looked down at Frederick and laughed, overpowering laughter, his stomach and ample breasts shaking like jelly.

It was later established by the CPU intelligence unit that Amin was behind the attempt to undermine Obote's government. There was also a rumour – but no evidence - that Amin was implicated in the armed attack on the Holiday Inn. Furthermore, the Chief Medical Officer had blood and urine samples of the Second Medical Officer tested. He had complained that he had a permanent erection and couldn't leave the house. Test showed that the SMO had been overdosed on either Rubiaceae or Alliaceae, or both! These potent local plants have powerful aphrodisiac qualities, the report concluded. But Frederick refused to accept this as an explanation for his own prowess that night.

Idi Amin, wide-eyed and laughing, apologized for Doctor Mateke's dilemma, saying it was a prank, and if they can't take a joke, married men shouldn't being putting it around. The President sympathized with the morality aspect but thought it rich coming from a hedonist with several wives and a harem that, it now transpired, included Mugisha.

Amin, as the Commander of Uganda Military, had been promoted far above his intellectual capabilities. He was now too powerful and unpredictable for confrontation. Obote had evidence that Amin was supporting the rebels. But he also had evidence that the British government was trying to undermine the Obote left-wing agenda. Prime Minister Harold Wilson, worried that Uganda was moving closer to communism, considered the uneducated – but pro-Western - Idi Amin a more suitable replacement.

But Frederick's personal fortunes were mixed that year. The photographic incident was soon forgotten (by most) but some of the typists in the office were impressed by what they saw and regularly stayed over at his villa. And then, in August, he was introduced to Pope Paul V1.

But after the Pope departed, the rebels were using more sophisticated weapons, gangster using more daring, and street violence endemic. And then, in December, an attempt was made on Mr Obote's life. Politic opponents were barred from office, thrown in jail, or fed to the crocodiles and hippopotami. Frederick's workload increased.

1970

This was a better year: after the banks were nationalized, Frederick enjoyed a twenty-percent salary increase. Although shop prices were increasing by a considerably higher percentage, this had no effect on senior government executives. In fact, their purchases were discounted below cost. Of course, to offset this, traders simply raised their prices for the common people, increasing baby foods by thirty percent - but Frederick didn't have to worry about that. He was now paying less for his champagne than he paid a year ago. Nor did he, as a promoter of government policy, have to worry about the chronic shortages. 'Grow your own food in your backyard,' he wrote in one of his press handouts. Mr Obote was impressed by Frederick's ingenuity.

On the downside, Idi Amin's ambitions had been increasingly on display. As the commander of all Uganda's military he was now confrontational at a political level. Frederick sensed this threat to Obote, worried that a change of leadership would impact negatively on his own future, perhaps life! He knew from the face-to-face meeting at Mugisha's apartment that Amin had never forgiven him for claiming to have resolved the army riots in 1964. After laughing uncontrollably, Amin had raised his fist and shouted: 'you are nothing but a stinking interpreter. Fuck off back to England.' Frederick had hurried back to the elevator. At that moment, he knew he had to do something about Amin's increasing belligerence.

To that end, for a year and a half, he wrote numerous articles, some openly denouncing Amin for not doing more to quash the rebels; in others praising the incumbent leadership. The articles were regularly published in newspapers written in Bantu, Swahili, and English. And Amin was reading them.

At last, Mr Obote took note of what Frederick and others had been saying: Amin's control over all the military must be ended. Consequently, Obote reduced Amin's authority and declared himself head of all Uganda armed forces. Frederick was relieved and continued to enjoy the good life, living off his tax-free expense account and banking his salary.

What a wonderful life, he thought, looking down on his latest girlfriend, sixteen-year old typist, Natasha Mukasa, her head buried in his groin.

JANUARY 1971

Frederick opened his eyes: the sun was streaming through the mosquito net, creating myriad shapes on Natasha's face. Her breathing was shallow, and her lips slightly parted. However, his head was aching from the previous night's party and it was water and aspirin that he needed more than anything. He contemplated the day ahead: he had to shower, breakfast, dress for work, and he was already late. He had to make an excuse for Natasha arriving late in the typing pool. At that time of day, sex was not a priority, but the vision of the sleeping beauty by his side was tempting.

And the President and leading Members of Parliament were away in Singapore.

He gently lowered the starched white sheet to look down on her breasts. Her black nipples, occasionally moving out and in, suggested to Frederick that she was dreaming of him. He wanted to climb into her thoughts to find out what he was doing to her. Trying not to wake her, he lowered the sheet further to her rounded thighs. Sitting up, he stared down at her black body, slim, but firm and rounded. She opened her eyes, smiling and held out her arms. They held each other, and she wrapped her hands around his back. But somebody was knocking on the door.

"Who's there?" he shouted, frustrating by the intrusion.

Pulling on his robe, he coolly greeted Duidi on the doorstep. But Duidi was breathless, agitated, shaking.

'There's been a coup!" he stammered.

But Frederick refused to accept that such a thing could happen.

"Impossible! Mr Obote's in Singapore." Frederick countered.

"Turn on the radio."

Frederick switched it on. Natasha, with the bed sheet wrapped around her body, joined them listening to the echoing voice on the radio announcing a military takeover and declaring that Mr Obote had been deposed. He would not be returning to Uganda. The announcement was dispassionate.

Entebbe, the main international airport in and out of Uganda, was closed. Military roadblocks were set up on all major roads. Armed soldiers patrolled the streets and also installed as overseers at all media outlets. Curfews were imposed. Kampala was under lockdown. But the bad news for Frederick was left until last. Mr Idi Amin would be taking over as acting military governor, and all close allies of former President Obote would be barred from office, some arrested.

"We'll have to fight them," Duidi said, his voice cracking with emotion.

"I knew it! I knew it! That bastard Amin must have been planning this for years," Frederick roared, and, deciding there was no time to change from his robe into a suit, put on his cap.

The two men embraced each other. They knew they were key players on the losing side and now faced relegation. Natasha remained seated, unsure what all the fuss was about. They agreed to meet at Government House and remove all their confidential files.

Duidi drove off first, saying he would see Frederick back at the office. With Natasha by his side (she also worked in the same government building), he followed Duidi along the winding country lane. But at the junction with Jinja Road, soldiers, some armed with Sterling sub-machine guns, surrounded Duidi's car.

Frederick and Natasha sat watching as Duidi stepped out of his car to confront one of the soldiers. He was waving an arm, as though in anger. The soldier ignored him, reading the papers he had just taken from him. Duidi snatched back the papers, but the same soldier pushed him to the side of the road and fired several bullets into his body. Natasha screamed, but Frederick put his hand across her mouth. Crazy thoughts were crowding in on him. An hour ago he was considering making love, and now he was facing death.

He looked in his rear mirror, preparing to reverse and race back to the villa, but a lorry was up against his rear bumper. He instructed Natasha to pass him a bundle of documents from the glove compartment. The same trigger-happy soldier was waving, beckoning him to move forward. He hurriedly flicked through the papers. Extracting a card, he put the rest under the seat.

He moved the car slowly forward, his heart thumping inside his chest. He knew if he didn't appear calm and behave politely, he would also finish his days on the grass verge alongside Duidi. He ordered Natasha to open her blouse and 'show your tits and keep smiling'. The soldier demanded Frederick's identity papers. Natasha leaned across to greet the soldier, ensuring he had a good view of her bosom. They were so perfectly formed that the soldier couldn't take his eyes off them.

"Jambo, sir! Good news for all of us this lovely day," Frederick said, a broad grin across his face.

More concerned with looking at Natasha's breasts, the soldier looked only briefly at the crumpled and yellowing card. But then he turned his attention to Frederick.

"Party official, eh!" he said, throwing the card into the car. He raised his rifle and pointed it at Frederick's chest. "You get me big pay rise, or else I take your woman." But before Frederick could answer, the soldier burst out laughing. "Go on, piss off, mzungu."

As he drove along the dusty road, the horror he had just witnessed was constantly being re-enacted in his mind. He wondered about Duidi's body: would they bury him, would they tell his family? He also dwelled on his good fortune: the old UNC card had been issued when he first arrived in Uganda fourteen years earlier. But he realized he was also lucky that an idiot had examined the card. It was not only old, the party ceased to exist more than ten years ago.

Armed soldiers were standing outside the doors of Government House and also those of Parliament; others were standing at major road junctions. Trucks loaded with more armed soldiers were heading south towards Entebbe. Frederick turned off the main road, following a back lane before eventually stopping behind a row of bushes.

"What do we do now?" he said, more to himself than Natasha.

But she suggested they drive to Mityana village on Lake Wamala where her parents owned a smallholding. He knew the village, it was about an hour drive west, but he couldn't see the logic in driving so far out of town. He reflected on recent events: perhaps Duidi might still be alive if he hadn't argued with that soldier. And although he personally felt threatened, Amin, as military leader, would now be too busy to be interested in a former government promotions officer. He decided to return to the villa by back lanes and drive across the grasslands.

Having followed a circuitous route, he approached the villa from the rear by driving through a banana plantation. He stopped the car on the edge of the open space. Between the plantation and the villa, the grassland offered no cover.

Although a hundred metres away, the army markings on the camouflaged truck parked on the villa's driveway were clearly discernible. Two soldiers were loading his furniture onto the back of the truck. But he saw no point in risking his life. He had money in the bank and gold in the safe, more than enough to replace the stolen fixtures and fittings. He decided to return after dark.

By moonlight, he drove slowly across the uneven grassland. The front door was lying on the ground. As he expected, the rooms had been stripped bare, and Mr Obote's signed photograph lay on the floor. Surprisingly, it was intact; the thieves' attention had evidently been drawn to the wall safe. But where the safe had been, a hole had been punched through the wall. All that remained in the house was the sheet that Natasha had wrapped herself in that fateful morning.

Although the porch furniture had also been taken, the soldiers hadn't ventured into the rear garden where Frederick's gardener kept his tools in a small shed.

With a spade - and a torch from his car - he drove to the junction where Duidi had been shot. As anticipated, they'd left Duidi's body on the grass verge, but there were also five more bodies, all men, their clothing stained by their own blood and covered in flies. He buried Duidi in a shallow gave, covering the other bodies with vegetation.

He agreed with Natasha's proposal to travel to her parent's farm near Mityana and wait for everything to settle down. But first he had to withdraw all his money from the bank. That night, Frederick and Natasha slept on the villa's floor, protected from the mosquitoes by the one bed sheet.

To reach the bank, he returned by the same back lanes to downtown Kampala. There now fewer soldiers on the streets. And other than the armed militia standing outside public buildings, everything seemed surprisingly normal, but the queue at the bank stretched into the street. When he finally reached the counter, the cashier checked his account. She asked him to wait while she went to the back office. She returned to advise him that all government employee accounts were temporarily frozen, by orders of the military. She suggested he try the following day.

There were no blockades nor military on the road to Mityana and, with his foot hard down on the accelerator, it took them less than hour to reach the town. But to reach the hamlet on the edge of Lake Wamala, they had to follow a narrow dirt track weaving through the forest.

Natasha parents were primitive; living in what she referred to as an enyumba: a hut built like half a coconut and made of mud and wattle. Hens, goats and a pig roamed freely around the clearing before the house. Her father, bare footed and wearing a ragged grey skirt and matching shirt, bowed his head in greeting. He smiled widely, revealing just two teeth. Frederick wondered briefly how such an ugly man could have produced such a beautiful daughter.

That evening, Frederick tried sleeping in his car, but with the windows closed it was too humid, and with them open, he was invaded by mosquitoes. For the rest of the night, he slept uncomfortably and alone in a small hut used to store animal feed.

The next day, he returned to Kampala, dropping Natasha off at the hostel where she lived during the working week. Armed soldiers were still on guard outside major buildings, but now also at the door of the British High Commissioner's Office and the government–owned Bank of Uganda. They were checking identification cards. Using a public phone, he called the bank. But the voice on the other end of the line reported that his account had been one of those appropriated for military expenditure. As the de facto owners of the bank, the military junta now had direct access to all bank accounts and safe-deposit boxes. They also had payroll records of all government employees, including age, ethnicity, and home address detail.

Within twenty-four hours, he had gone from being comparatively wealthy to being virtually penniless, from being renowned to being a fugitive. He still had his car, the money in his wallet and the robe he stood up in – but that was all. He phoned the office of the recently appointed British High Commissioner. He had occasionally sat beside Richard Slater at private dinner parties, but the line had been disconnected.

He sat in his car, looking at the fuel gauge while planning what to do next. He had a full tank of petrol, more than enough to get him to Entebbe airport, and enough money in his wallet to buy a plane ticket to Cairo. From there, he hoped, he would get consulate assistance back to England. Natasha had been helpful but he had no intention of spending another night with scavenging rats. He removed the two flags from the car's wings.

Where he saw blockades in the distance, he circumvented them by driving over fields, through plantations or into the bush. When he overtook military convoys he put a thumb up, and the smiling soldiers waved back. But as he drew near to the airport he could see the road ahead obstructed by army trucks. He turned off the road, but not before he had been seen by one of the soldiers manning the barricade. In an open topped jeep, and firing small arms repeatedly, they followed him across fields and up and down the valleys. He knew the route south: campaigning for the Obote party, he had twice visited the

Kabale area. Unable to keep up with the six-cylinder Mercedes-Benz, the driver of the jeep fired off a final round before turning back towards Entebbe.

Worried the military could reappear driving something more powerful, for an hour he kept his foot on the accelerator and followed the road south. He didn't stop until he reached Kayabwe, the last village before the wide but narrow bridge spanning the Katonga River, a major tributary of Lake Victoria. He pulled onto a farm track to consult his map and compass, the travel aids he had relied on to arrange his promotional tours. Both Tanzania and Rwanda share Uganda's southern border. As the Tanzanian border was considerably closer than Rwanda's, he decided to head for Tanzania. Although he overtook several troop convoys, also travelling south, he encountered no checkpoints.

Almost out of petrol, reaching the town of Masaka came as a great relief. There were no soldiers on the main street, just a few retail shacks selling pottery, meat and a bicycle repair workshop with a petrol pump outside its open door. And the petrol was cheaper than in Kampala but rationed. The owner complained the soldiers who passed through earlier had taken most of his petrol and refused to pay. Frederick was satisfied the eight gallons he purchased would be enough to get him to Nsunga, the Tanzanian border town. Beyond the petrol pump, and standing in isolation, a wooden hut with a corrugated tin roof advertised cooked rice and cabbage. The thought of eating in such a decrepit place appalled him, but he couldn't be sure when he would have the opportunity again.

Seated by the open door at one of the three rough-hewn tables in the unlit cafe, he spread out his map. What he hadn't considered was the distance from the border to the capitals of Rwanda and Tanzania. The café owner leaned over his shoulder to look at the map. To Frederick's surprise, he was Tanzanian and spoke English. The café owner explained that while it was only about 70 miles to Tanzania, it was more like 1000 miles to its capital, Dar es Salaam. In response to Fredrick's question, he estimated Kigali, the capital of Rwanda, to be less than 300 miles, but couldn't be sure. Distracted from the food on his plate, it was only when Frederick took his eyes off the map that he noticed the maggots wriggling in the remaining rice and cabbage.

His map only extended beyond Uganda's borders by a few miles, and, undecided between the two countries, he parked his car under a tree and switched on the radio. He had hardly slept the past two nights and needed to rest. He sat back, his eyes closed, vaguely aware of the military music that was still being recycled. And then the music stopped, abruptly interrupted by a news announcement: Obote was now officially in exile, living in Tanzania. There, he thought, is where he must go. His thoughts drifted back to the events of the past two days: he realized he had not given careful considerations to all the options. He could, he reflected, have gone by boat from Jinja straight down Lake Victoria to the Tanzanian port of Mwanza. He accepted he should have known the airport would be guarded by Amin's men, and acknowledged to himself that there was now no turning back. But the newsreader continued, declaring that all international borders were now closed until further notice. That, he thought, explains all those southbound troop movements.

The shock of seeing his friend murdered - and the repeated attempts on his own life - had sharpened his wits. Although tired, he was analyzing his options with unusual clarity. There was no longer a politic party for him to promote, and Obote wouldn't be in a position to employ anyone. Those days are over, he conceded. He had neither the money nor inclination for a thousand mile trip to Dar es Salaam, and it would be taking him east instead of west. Reassessing the available options, he decided only Rwanda's Kigali Airport offered a possible escape route – providing he could find petrol and a way across the border.

Repositioning the map, he put a finger on Echuya, the rainforest linking Uganda with the Rwanda border, and, talking aloud to himself, declared: "Batwa!"

Troubled by the news report, and without thinking of possible roadblocks, he drove straight into Mbarara, the next town south. A truck loaded with soldiers was parked across the road. One of the soldiers, holding a pistol in one hand and a clipboard in the other, jumped down, demanding identification papers. Frederick produced his old party card, and the soldier put his revolver in his hip holster. Running a finger slowly down his list, a shot rang out. The soldier fell to the ground. Reaching for his pistol, he fired towards the direction of the gunshot. The six soldiers standing on the back of the army truck also sprayed the surrounding undergrowth with bullets. Frederick reversed, and driving around the truck, accelerated down the bumpy road. He kept one eye on the rear-view mirror, thankful nobody was following him. He'd lost his old party card, but escaped with his life – again!

He got as far Rubanda, a hamlet just twenty miles from the Echuya Rainforest; and there he ran out of petrol.

With most of the money he had left in his wallet he bought an old Raleigh bicycle from a grateful villager. But, as he was aware from a previous visit to Echuya, he had to find his way around Lake Bunyoni, a large stretch of water between Rubanda and the rainforest.

For the first time that day, he was confident he wasn't being followed, and as he cycled along the rough track around the lake, he again began to rationalize. All his actions the past two days had been reactionary. He had been too preoccupied looking in the rearview mirror. He had become paranoid, seeing imaginary army trucks through the shimmering heat haze. The track that he was following was primitive and full of potholes, but he kept his eyes to the ground, intrigued by the variety of birdsong.

Stopping to rest, he sat by the lake watching a white pelican skimming the surface, its wide wings extended, their tips curled like black fingers. By the water's edge, and looking like a baby heron, a white egret also searched for fish. Its proximity suggested it was not familiar with the folly of getting close to humans.

He lay back, thinking of England, tempted to sleep and perhaps wake up to find it was all a dream. He was back in Primrose Street, as a child, watching the usual Sunday rain run down the window. His father, hidden behind a large newspaper; his mother bent over the sink, his siblings fighting. Smoke from the coal fire and his father's cigarette combining with ammonia. In an orderly line, he was marching from St. Aloysius Convent School to the nearby church. He wondered if his name was still carved in the old desk. And what had happened to all those school friends? Probably still in Riverton, he presumed.

The blood-red sun, magnified by its low trajectory, seemed to be sitting on top of the distant rainforest. But it was slowly sinking, and the melodious bird song was now accompanied by a cacophony of chattering and squealing monkeys and other wild animals. They were noisily announcing the waning of another day.

Desirous of sleep but watching the sinking sun, he reluctantly climbed to his feet. Taking one last look at the lake, he mounted the rusty bicycle. At least he could now see his destination. But a hundred yards ahead, banana trees skirted the curving path, stretching for what looked like miles. Free food, he thought. However, cycling with his eyes to the ground, he failed to see the army truck straddled across the path on the bend. It was the ricocheting bullet that alerted him to the danger. And it was the same truckload of soldiers that had stopped him in Mbarara. He quickly made the assessment that they had circumvented the lake in the opposite direction, and that they intended to kill him. Fortunately, he had drawn level with the banana plantation.

With his heart again thumping in his chest, he cycled into the compacted trees, spurred on by the bullets whistling above his head and ripping through the vegetation.

While it was obvious a truck could not drive between the trees, he was frightened they may pursue him on foot. Although there was no indication he was being followed, he continued into the dark, overgrown interior; now having to push his bicycle. At last satisfied he was alone, he sat down eating a banana, confident that somebody was looking over him. He made a bed of banana leaves, and, with large spiders crawling over him, slept fitfully until dawn.

At first light, he retraced his steps to the track, and, confident the army lorry had departed, cycled desperately towards the forest. The sky was pure blue, the birds singing, and the temperature perfect. However, he was puzzled. Since his last visit to the region, the track leading to the forest had been widened and the potholes suggested it was now much used, and by heavy vehicles. Probably by the banana farmers moving their produce to the markets in the north, he presumed. But, as he left the lake and plantation behind, the reason became obvious. A wide swathe of forest had been removed, and heavy machinery was standing idle in the clearing.

Although the original approach to the Batwa settlement had been destroyed by deforestation, he could, thanks to his infallible memory, remember the compass bearing. Wearily, he pushed his bike through the thick undergrowth, lifting it over entwining branches, eventually reaching the clearing, but it was barely recognizable. There was only scorched earth where the round thatched huts had been. Near exhaustion, he pushed his bike deeper into the forest, following a narrow path, but it led only to an impenetrable mass of entangled, moss-laden tree roots. Silently and unexpectedly, three spear-carrying pygmies dropped from the trees and surrounded him.

With his hands tied behind his back, and the older pygmy pushing the bike, he was led further into the jungle. Two hours later, they reached a second clearing, but now with the familiar cluster of mud huts and small fires surrounding the main, central log fire. Although there were no signs of life, he knew from previous visits that many more armed tribesmen would be watching. And, just as he anticipated, the rest of the tribe slowly emerged, encircling him. But then Kintu, the elder 'first man', wearing the teeshirt with Mr Obote's faded image, entered the circle and threw his arms around Frederick.

In Swahili – some of the tribe spoke Swahili as well as Rutwa, the primary Batwa language - and pointing to the teeshirt, Frederick explained that the army had forced Mr Obote to flee Uganda. He went on to describe how the military had then confiscated his own property and murdered young men, including his friend. To reach Kigali, his ultimate destination, he explained, he needed help to circumvent the rainforest. But Kintu replied it would not be possible. His scouts had reported hundreds of soldiers manning the border on both sides of the forest. The only way into Rwanda was through the rainforest itself.

Although apolitical, it could be argued that this particular tribe of pygmies leaned towards the former Obote regime. Not for economic or social reasons, but because no other political organization had ever entertained them with music and dancing girls, or made a gift of a teeshirt to Kintu. And the printed face on the shirt had become, by association, a friend. By nature, musical and immodest, they vividly remembered the three Bakiga dancing girls and talked excitedly about the time they danced on the clearing with their breasts covered.

Frederick had arranged the promotional tours to the rainforest in his early days in Uganda, a time when he had no knowledge of the country's geographical or tribal make-up. He had simply used a map and a compass to select venues. But Mr Obote's assistant, to whom he was then reporting, said he was wasting his time and party assets.

He had argued the pygmies had no allegiance to anyone but themselves. However, Frederick had a feeling that those promotional trips to the southwest tip of the country could now prove beneficial.

Later that day, the tribe insisted on holding a ceremony to welcome him back, and they sang and, making two circles, danced around the central fire, the women on an outer circuit. They drank homemade banana beer; ate roasted monkeys and black beetles baked in honey. During the welcoming ceremony, Kintu explained what had been happening to their forest.

Shortly after Frederick's last visit, those same men who had been cutting down trees using hand saws, had brought machines to the forest edge. Within just a matter of days, they had cut down dozens of the 'sacred' trees. Incensed by this desecration, his men had chased them away with arrows. But it was the poisoned dart in the manager's heart that dissuaded the loggers from returning.

As forest dwellers, the pygmies naturally had no vehicles, and there were no roads through the virtually impenetrable rainforest. Kintu discussed Frederick's proposal with his two best guides, but they both agreed getting a bike through the forest would be impossible. Kintu disagreed, but nevertheless warned Frederick of the obstacles: swamps to traverse, mountains to climb, ravines to descend. And then there are the poisonous snakes. He promised to help Frederick reach the Rwandan border.

Sitting uncomfortably on a smooth log of wood, and perspiring in the high humidity, Frederick found it difficult listening to all that Kintu had to say. The main distraction was two of the four women sitting outside the next hut. The naked breasts of the two young women were firm and self-supporting. Conversely, the breasts of the two older women lay flat to their chests, stretching down and over their stomachs. However, his admiration was not just for the anatomy of the younger women, but also for their decoration. The two teenager girls were painting each other's breasts and stomachs with white dots, circles and lines. And when one turned and bent down, the other teenager applied similar decorations to her rounded buttocks. Like the men, they were wearing only a narrow strip of bark cloth between their legs, tied front and back to a vine belt.

Occasionally, he watched the two men completing his temporary shelter. In the space of an hour, they had assembled converging branches, overlaid them with mud, and tiled the roof with broad leaves.

By the time he crawled through the low entrance to his hut, only two old men were still sitting by the central fire. Smoking from long bamboo pipes, their glazed eyes and the fumes suggested they were smoking something stronger than tobacco. Thoughtfully, the hut builders had also laid a bed of leaves.

At first, he listened to the two teenager girls talking in the next hut and the occasional chattering monkeys and squawking parrots in the forest. And then there was a silence, disturbed only by the distant sound of tumbling water. He fell into a deep sleep.

It was children's voices and the cries of babies that indicated the start of a new day. Soaked in perspiration, and with every muscle in his body aching, he lay back staring at the bright green fungous already growing on the hut's internal framework. For a second, he wondered if it was all a dream, but his thoughts were perplexed. He wanted to remain where he was, alone and private, but he also needed to wash away the perspiration and freshen his mouth.

He crawled out into the daylight, standing with difficulty. His leg muscles had contracted from all the cycling, subsequent walking and, despite the bed of leaves, sleeping on the ground. But his mood was lifted by the blue sky visible through the broken canopy, and the fragmented rays of sunlight dappling the ground. Naked children were using vines as skipping ropes; other children chased each other around the clearing. Women were cooking, bent over numerous open fires. A woman was weaving a large rattan basket. The two teenage girls were sitting outside their adjacent hut with one cutting the hair of the other with a knife, and, with her fingers, picking out lice. But the girls were also watching him. He hobbled across, asking for advice about washing.

The girls introduced themselves: facially, Lewa seemed to be older than Maha, but their bodies were so similarly developed that it was difficult to tell. Lewa, put down her knife and, taking him by the hand, led him into the forest. It was only a short walk to the river cascading over a waterfall into a pool of still water.

Stripping off her bark-cloth G-string, she jumped in, waving for him to join her. Frederick removed his robe, but not his underpants, and followed her into the warm water. She suddenly dived beneath the surface, and, taking hold of his ankles, pulled him under. For ten minutes they splashed each other, and various illicit thoughts passed through his head. But he considered it prudent not to make bodily contact beyond what he had already experienced.

And he didn't know her age: her dainty stature - breasts excluded - gave her the appearance of a child.

Frederick was the first to climb out of the water. Putting on his robe, he removed his underpants, squeezed out the water and placed them on a rock to dry. Lewa had no concerns about being seen naked, and dried herself with broad leaves. Taking a slender branch, she frayed the end, using it as a toothbrush to clean her teeth. She made another brush for Frederick. Before they left, four women arrived to collect water from beneath the waterfall.

The rest of the morning passed slowly. Lewa returned to cutting Maha's hair, and those other women were still cooking, making baskets, or feeding babies at the breast. Lewa explained that the men and male youths were out hunting for meat.

It was mid-afternoon when the hunters returned. Some carried small dead monkeys tied to their vine belts; two others shared the weight of an antelope; another two, a six-foot python. In nets, the youths carried small prey including rats and tortoises. Later, the fur of the rats, monkeys and antelope was burned off, and the meat wrapped in leaves then smoked over the central fire. Sitting alone outside his hut, Frederick watch the cooked meat being cut up into small portions and distributed. According to Kintu, the hunt had been good, providing enough meat for two days. The tribesman who captured the python was entitled to distribute the portions, and he included Frederick in that share out. Lewa asked if she could cook it for him.

That evening, to accompany the meats, the tribe roasted termites, mushrooms and caterpillars. From cupped leaves, the women and children drank the energizing juices extracted from the kola nut. The men drank the alcoholic beer fermented from bananas or bamboo. But all the men and women smoked marijuana.

After the meal, Frederick sat with Kintu while Lewa returned to sit with her sister outside their hut. Kintu hinted to Frederick that Lewa was taking a keen interest in him, but Frederick dismissed the suggestion. However, when the Elder said that she was an arobo, a girl of marriageable age who is entitled to practice free love until the day she marries, Frederick was attentive.

"She can make love with whoever she chooses. This way," he continued, "is how a Batwa girl finds the man best suited to be her husband."

Although Frederick thought the selection process flawed, he had long been an advocate of free love.

It was the flash of lightning preceding the thunder that emptied the clearing. Then the rains came, constant, pounding the huts and bouncing off the ground like projectiles. And the thunder rumbled and boomed, and forked lightning lit up the whole forest. Frederick lay in his hut, occasional repositioning in an effort to avoid the rain penetrating the leaves. It felt as though the humidity had been sucked out of the atmosphere and replaced with cool air. Lewa crouched in the entrance, only appearing when the lightning lit up the sky, and then as a silhouette. She waited a minute, providing Frederick with enough time to either invite her in, or refuse entry.

There weren't enough leaves to make a comfortable double bed, but Lewa spread them out so they could lie side by side. She wasn't wearing anything other than raindrops. Frederick held her in his arms, and when face-to-face, her feet reached only down to his thighs. This was a new experience, and although he had spent many years making love with black women, Lewa was presenting a new challenge: she was not only short but also physically proportionate to her height. He was afraid of putting his full weight on her small body. But he needn't have bothered: she was experienced. He had been misled by her small mouth and diminutive appearance.

When Frederick opened his eyes, he was alone and lying in a mist. There was none of the anticipated sounds of activity. He stepped outside. A heavy fog had descended on the camp, and he could barely see the adjacent huts. Although he had spent many childhood days walking through thick fog, back then in Riverton it was not wet and clinging. Assuming everybody was still sleeping, he walked through the bush to the river, but, as he drew closer, the sounds of children and babies grew louder. Naked, the women of the camp were standing in the river washing their children and themselves. Not wanting to impose himself, he wandered further downstream, disturbing Lewa who was lying beneath a young tribesman. With broad smiles, they acknowledged his presence but continued to make love.

For seven days, Kintu and some of his men discussed how they could help Frederick reach Rwanda by walking through the forest. Once there, he had reasoned, he could cycle the two hundred miles to Kigali. But pushing the bicycle through the forest would be unprecedented, a challenge, even for the most experienced tribesman. Many parts of the rainforest were also hostile territories inhabited by other tribes. And, as Kintu repeatedly warned, he would face hazardous mountain passes, concealed ravines, poisonous reptiles, and many other dangers. But when Kintu wasn't involved in discussions with his tribesmen, Frederick pushed him around the clearing on his bike.

Finally, it was agreed that two of the best hunters would accompany Frederick through the jungle. That night, the villages held a farewell party with more feasting, drinking and dancing. But Frederick noticed Lewa was lying with her head on a different tribesman's naked lap. Although suffering mixed emotions, he was relieved she hadn't selected him as a husband.

The next day, and before sunrise, he left the village in the company of the two tribesmen. Wearing his robe and cap, and with his compass hanging around his neck, he pushed his bike through the undergrowth.

For protection in the rain forest, both hunters wore material made of tree bark, waterproofed by bees wax. A square piece of cloth with a hole in the centre provided a waterproof cape. Layers of vine wrapped around their waists supported their long skirts. Several strings of beads hung down to their waists. And, as though sheared from the same pattern, their heads were shaved, except for a small round mound of hair left uncut but shaped on top of their heads. The older man carried a machete and a small bow with four equally short arrows, as well as a large pouch for carrying the foods they would harvest as they trekked.

Before leaving the camp, Frederick had watched the older man make poison by mashing the seeds and root of the strophanthus vine. The arrowhead were then coated with the poison and protected by thick leaves secured by vine twine. The younger man carried a spear and a net. The forest would provide their daily needs.

For several hours, and in semi-darkness, they struggled through the dense undergrowth without seeming to make any progress. There was no consistency in the terrain: the mountain they were climbing was scarred with treacherous gorges, some perpendicular. They walked along narrow pathways obviously carved out of the mountainside by the ancestors of the two hunters leading him to Rwanda. They jumped from stone to stone across a raging river, passing the bike from one to the other. They struggled up the opposite side of the gorge. And Frederick pushed, dragged and carried his bike.

In a line, Frederick walked behind the older man who was slashing at the undergrowth. Slowly they ascended until the blue sky became partly visible through the green and yellow canopy. And then the older man stopped, put a hand before his mouth and whispered.

"Nyani!"

Frederick understood this to translate as monkey, but when he looked through the branches, silently parted by the older man, he felt in imminent danger. He was standing just a few yards from where a massive gorilla was lying on its back chewing on a bamboo shoot. Although the three men made no sound, the silver-backed gorilla rose to its feet, and, looking in their direction, roared and beat its chest. It made a sudden charge towards them, but then stopped. The two hunters stood their ground, but Frederick retreated and had an involuntary bowel movement. The hunters had obviously known what they were doing. From the smiles on their faces, Frederick assumed they had created the situation for their own amusement. Apologizing, they collected soft leaves and helped him clean up.

At last on level, but densely covered, ground, the older man pointed out areas of interest. They stopped for a moment to study the enormous honeybees' nest high in a tree. As they continued walking, the younger man pointed to another nest but partly concealed in the decaying base of a dead tree. But they weren't searching for honey; it was meat they needed for their evening meal. They continued forcing their way through the crowded vegetation and climbing under or over the gnarled roots of massive trees.

Being abundant, the monkeys were the easiest animals to catch - but not when high in the trees, out of reach for short arrows. By late afternoon, however, the monkeys were descending in search of food. With his bow loaded, the older man began stalking with his thin legs bent at the knees, as if to make his small stature even smaller. Then, much to Frederick's dismay, the first arrow brought down a small monkey. Screeching and wide eyed, it fell to the ground but, with the arrow sticking out of its hip, staggered into the bush. The younger man jumped on it and snapped its neck. The exercise was repeated and, with three dead monkeys hanging from their waists, Frederick followed the two men deeper into the forest.

It was while they were sitting on their haunches eating cooked monkey that the noise, like that of a forest fire, made the two hunters jump to their feet. The younger man took hold of Frederick's elbows, forcibly lifting him. At that moment, the head of a wide column of marching ants appeared at their feet. The three men retreated to a safe distance.

"Siafu!" the older man shouted.

Frederick had read articles on this subject in the *National Geographical* magazine. Back then, he thought the article fictional when it estimated that a column contained as many as fifty million giant ants, and that they killed and ate anything that remained in their path.   He was now mentally conceding that it wasn't exaggeration. The three men watched the dense column of giant ants flowing like a brown river. Without pausing, they devoured the remains of the dead monkeys as they passed over them.   It was an hour later before the tail of the fast moving column had disappeared into the undergrowth.

After a restless night sleeping on the massive trunk of a fallen tree, they set off at dawn, stopping only occasionally to collect nuts and berries. By the time they reached the swamp, Frederick was suffering sporadic muscle cramps.   Nevertheless, he was determined to continue, confident that once he reached the Rwandan border he could cycle to Kigali in three days. It was while the two tribesmen were waiting for Frederick to finish vomiting at the edge of the moss-covered swamp, that the older man raised an arm. He put an ear to the ground.

'Tembo," he shouted.

Frederick was surprised: nobody told him there were elephants in the rainforest. But then the pounding and trumpeting grew louder. A herd was heading towards them, crashing through the undergrowth. The two tribesmen waded into the swamp, followed by Frederick holding the bike above his head. Standing in water up to their waists, they watched as three elephants charged through the trees before stopping in shallower water. There they submerged their trunks, blowing out the water they had inhaled. The older man explained that tree ants had probably climbed inside their trunks while the elephants were eating. Inattentive, the three men failed to see the crocodile gliding just below the surface until it was almost upon them. Frederick brought his bike down on its snout. However, it wasn't the bike that killed the crocodile but the spear in its side. Back on dry land, the two tribesmen debated while Frederick examined his bike.

Emerging above the forest canopy, and standing on a ridge above another deep ravine, they stopped to consider the best route down. Briefly, Frederick studied the horizon: the sky was pale blue and a few, pure white clouds floated above five distant volcanic peaks. It was a serene view, contrasting with the dilemma that they now faced. They had to descend a vertical cliff face. And the only way down was by following a narrow, zigzagging path.

Frederick had never been keen on heights, especially if there is nothing to hold on to. He asked if there was an alternative way. The older man shook his head. Standing as close to the edge of the precipice that his acrophobia would allow, Frederick determined it would not be possible to climb down with the bike. The two pygmies talked between themselves. And then a shot rang out, diminishing in volume as it repeatedly echoed across the valley. Speechless, the older man and Frederick watched as the younger hunter fell over the edge. Somersaulting through the air, his hunting net billowed out behind him. But before he had hit the rocks below, a second shot rang out. Frederick and the older man fell to the ground. Wondering what to do next, Frederick lay still, waiting for instructions.

"What shall we do?" he whispered, and waited, but there was no response.

Raising himself onto his hands and knees, he was crawling towards the tribesman when further shots began echoing up and down the valley. Lying flat again, he covered his ears as bullets whistled over his head and ricocheted off the ground. Assuming the gunfire originated on the other side of the valley, he crawled behind the older man. Without lifting his head, he shook the man's shoulder, but then realized the man's intestines were exposed and his lower body drenched in warm blood.

"Are you okay?" he asked, without thinking, but not knowing what else to say.

With the dead man lying between him and the valley, Frederick cautiously looked over the body. It took him a few minutes to distinguish the soldiers from the vegetation on the opposite ridge. Unless, the Ugandan army had suddenly changed its uniform colours and style, he concluded, those shabbily dressed military men were not Ugandan. Probably Rwandan, he assumed, protecting their border.

Although Fredrick had a perfect memory, his brain was rather slower when it came to analysis, and occasionally irrational when separating essentials from trivia. His first reaction was to avoid the blood slowly seeping towards his white robe – he didn't want to arrive in Kigali covered in blood. His second thought was what does he do with the hunter's body? And the third concern: how to avoid being shot. He looked around: some of the hunting weapons were within reach. And luckily, he thought, the older man was carrying the provisions of roasted meat, nuts and berries. Having slithered away from the leaking blood, he waited until dark, and then, by moonlight, returned to collect the weapons, and supplies. Trying to avoid the dead man's staring eyes, he pulled the cape up and over the man's head and unwound the vine rope from around his waist. Finally, he closed the hunter's eyes, said a prayer, and apologized for having to leave him unburied.

Sitting on a flat, white rock he contemplated his next move. He looked at the sky: not a cloud and a full moon. It was almost like daylight. He walked along the ridge looking for an alternative descent. But every time he looked over the edge, he was overcome by a terrible urge to jump out into space.

That night, in the foetal position, he slept restlessly on the smooth, flat rock, covering himself with the dead man's cape. Anticipating daybreak, he watched the thousands of stars move across the black sky until only darkness remained. And that darkness seemed impenetrable until a loom of soft orange light illuminated thin clouds, streaking away as though fearful of the coming day. A bad omen, he thought, but then, slowly, a turquoise backdrop to the rim of an enormous sun replaced the mother-of-pearl sky.

Sitting on the same rock, and eating nuts and berries, he felt abandoned, blaming the hunters for lack of foresight and for his current predicament. The dead body lay just a few feet away and it was already beginning to smell and attract insects. He said another prayer, asking God to protect him from falling in the abyss. But before he had even finished eating, he could see movements on the other side of the ravine. The military were still there!

Pushing the bike, he hurried back to the shelter of the forest, utterly confused and disorientated by the murders and the predicament he now found himself in. Alone in a dangerous jungle, he was nevertheless determined to find his way back to the Batwa village. He felt it was his duty to advise Kintu of the two deaths. And then he would leave the rainforest, cycling by road around the forest to Rwanda and risk facing the border patrol.

Since leaving the camp with the two tribesmen, he had taken regular compass readings, and mentally noted the variable characteristics of the forest. With this information, he was not as lost as anyone with a lesser memory would have been. All he had to do was to follow compass readings opposite to those he had noted on his way south. At least those were his thoughts, but he soon discovered it wasn't as simple as that: those forest characteristics were replicated thousands of times. All he could do was to keep walking. And for six hours, following a northern compass bearing, he cut and pushed his way forward without resting; but the stomach cramps were returning and his feet raw and painful.

On the banks of a stream, he sat with his lower legs in the cooling waters as he tried to wash off the fungus that had grown on the backs of both hands. The stream was speckled by the sunlight filtering through the green canopy. In this tranquil glade, he was reminded of the summer evening spent with Patricia behind the church. He could remember every detail: snapping the twigs from a tree and searching for leaches in the babbling brook. But then Mrs Porter's image appeared, lying on a grave and.... It was a hissing sound that fractured the memory. He looked around. The blue triangular head and pointed horns separated the viper from the undergrowth. Although he knew these snakes were deadly, he also knew they were nocturnal and generally lethargic in the day. Afraid of moving, he sat staring at the snake, and the snake stared back, ready to strike at the first sign of movement. Hardly breathing, his mind blank but focus total, he watched as the snake eventually turned around, slowly disappearing under a rock.

Hurrying away from the stream, he sat on the trunk of a fallen tree to examine his feet. The pea-sized lumps that had appeared before he left the camp had spread to his ankles. And the skin surrounding these swellings was now festering. Furthermore, he had developed a fever that was affecting his perceptions: he was occasionally walking in circles.

It was the following day when he noticed smoke rising above the trees. He struggled in the direction of the smoke and shouted until hoarse. But the pain in his feet had become unbearable. He was lying on the ground covered in ants when the Batwa hunting party appeared. Slung like a dead animal to a bamboo pole, two of the hunters carried him back to the camp, a third pushing his bike.

After listening to his story, Kintu arranged for two men to go to the ravine and try to recover the bodies. He also called for the shaman.

For the fever, the shaman provided syrup of cayenne peppers mixed with poison ivy, and for the fungus on the backs of his hands, a lotion of crushed garlic and citronella oils. And after a close examination, he said the growths on his feet and ankles were 'chigggers'. Sharpening his knife on a rock, he further explained that sand fleas had burrowed into his feet where they had laid their eggs. Without losing the smile on his face, he went on to provide a prognosis.

"They travel through the body, drink blood, eat lips, eat eyelids. Death!"

The shaman gave him the bark of a banana tree to bite on. He then sliced the skin above the lumps and scooped out the insects and their eggs. The dozen wounds were cleansed with a mix of citrus juice and moisturized beeswax. Although his feet were now unlikely to rot further, the shaman explained, they would need to be cleansed daily and any infestations occurring in the future cut out.

Sympathetic to their guest's plight, Kintu promised Frederick an orphan girl to assist in the daily cleansing of his feet. She would remove any new infestations, and also take care of his needs such as cooking, washing and waste disposal. And, grinning, he informed Frederick that Dembe was of marriageable age. But Frederick was in no mood for humour, and didn't know what that implied. He expressed his gratitude but said he must leave the camp as soon as he was fit to travel.

Despite his protestations, later that day, Kintu brought Dembe to his hut. Wearing just the traditional loincloth, she stood with her head slightly bowed, her eyes focused on the ground. At just fifty inches tall, she had the sad demeanor of a ten-year old girl who had just been told off for being naughty. Frederick sensed she had not volunteered. Still traumatized by the infestations, he was unsympathetic. And, furthermore, her features did not impress him: her nostrils were very wide and her lips unusually thick. But his real concern was that a child would be incapable of providing the necessary medical attention. Kintu smiled and, pointing to her large naked breasts, assured him that she had removed chiggers many times and was a grown woman of sixteen years.

Although still suffering from the after-effects of the fever and shock of the flea invasion, his thoughts were becoming more lucid. He was regularly debating with himself about his options. Travelling to Rwanda through the forest was, of course, no longer possible. He thought about the risks of returning to Kampala. But how could he get there, anyway? It was too far to cycle, and cars don't move without petrol. But, he had to admit; the Mercedes was probably long gone. And how would he survive in Kampala without money, work, or somewhere to live? He'd be shot, he thought. At least here in the forest he had food, shelter and a young girl, a kind of nurse, willing to care for him until he was fit to travel. Then he would cycle around the forest and, avoiding roads, find a way across the border into Rwanda.

Dembe was proving to be a good nurse and a willing housekeeper. Additionally, and to avoid infestation, she regularly shaved his head, beard and body hair. But, negatively, she had the grin of a rhesus monkey. And, although they shared a hut (with two sleeping areas), Frederick was repulsed by her appearance and had no interest in her sexually. Nevertheless, her warm personality more than compensated for her lack of height and ugly face, and they were now good friends. He conceded he had underrated her ability to harvest herbal medication, food, and dispose of human waste. And he acknowledged that she had nice breasts.

At first, he ignored the small lumps that appeared on his legs, convinced they were ant bites. But as they grew in size and began festering, he complained to Dembe that she had not removed all the sand fleas. She disagreed, saying they were worms living inside his body. She went to collect the shaman but was told by his son that he was up on the mountain collecting plants. This naturally had a bad effect on Frederick's frame of mind. He couldn't sleep that night, dreaming of worms eating him from the inside out.

The next day, the shaman examined Frederick's legs. He agreed with Dembe: it was a worm infection. And once again, he produced his knife, opening the largest swelling. Carefully, he wrapped the head of the thin worm around a stick, slowly rotating it. But Frederick had fainted before the entire three-foot wriggling worm had been fully extracted.

To avoid ingesting worm larvae in the future, the shaman advised him to only drink from the nearby river. And, to Frederick's consternation, explained that to reach his skin, the emerging worms had burrowed through his intestinal wall into the stomach cavity. He apologized, claiming there were too many worms for him to remove with his knife. Dembe would remove the remaining smaller worms. She was reminded to remove them slowly by carefully rotating the worms on a stick. If not fully removed, the shaman warned, they would reinvigorate and, in such circumstances, migrate under Frederick's skin to the stomach and scrotum, feeding on his testicles. Finally, he warned that applying water to the partly exposed worms encourages fertilization of eggs buried beneath the skin. Frederick was distraught.

The sand fleas, and then worms, that had invaded his body, convinced him that he would have to get back to civilization sooner than later. He acknowledged to himself that living with the tribe was fraught with all kinds of hidden dangers. And he accepted that he had no inbuilt immunity to the many infections prevalent in the rainforest.

The Batwa tribe was not entirely isolated from Ugandan society. Occasionally they exchanged surplus meat for tobacco, cannabis and those vegetables not available in the rainforest. The closest Ugandan village was where many farm labourers and their families lived. At Frederick's behest, Kintu enquired if those villagers had any information about the military border patrols. Kintu's report was not encouraging; anyone trying to illegally cross the border was shot. Frederick had to acknowledge that, until the border patrols were relaxed, he had to remain with in the forest.

1972

After Dembe had removed the last of the worms, he regularly joined her in the forest. She taught him how to distinguish between poisonous and edible mushrooms; which plants had medicinal properties and their peculiarities. She identified the birds with the most flesh, and how to (preferably) trap them in a net. She spent hours teaching him to throw a spear. Finally proficient, he speared a small wild pig and, hanging from a bamboo cane, they proudly carried it back to the village. Although still only seventeen and diminutive, she had the strength of a man and the ability to de-hair or skin a large animal in preparation for roasting. And Frederick was no longer squeamish about killing birds and animals, nor about eating beetles and other insects. He finally acknowledged it was all about conditioning.

But it was not all hunting for food. To Frederick's surprise, Dembe used parts of the animals for domestic functions. She separated and gently heated animal fat. From the renderings, she made soaps, skin balms and candles.   She also used it to start fires and as a waterproofing agent.   And, when plentiful, she also used beeswax to make less offensive-smelling candles and likewise scouring agents.   She had also used beeswax as a germicidal aid when she had treated his feet and leg infestations. There were numerous other applications.

But seven months after thinking he was clear of invasive sand fleas, worms and other infections, he began experiencing severe head and muscle pains. His skin and the whites of his eyes turned yellow. He was feverish and vomiting.   Perspiring heavily, and with no appetite, the shaman diagnosed yellow fever.   Promising a cure, he mixed a concoction of limes and herbs. For four days, Dembe force-fed him the thick brown mixture and applied and reapplied wet poultices to his head and body. On the fourth day of infection, blood began trickling from his nose, eyes and ears. The shaman expressed grave concerns. But Dembe wouldn't admit defeat, forcing him to drink water every hour, and controlling his temperature with wet leaves.   Contrary to the shaman's negative prognosis, he slowly recovered. And Frederick recognized that without Dembe's unfailing attention he would not have survived.

The latest illness had left him physically weak. And the natural energy and ambition that had driven him to success in Kampala was gone. He now had neither the energy nor inclination for trying to get to the border.   And he no longer had the bike to rely on as mode of transport. Marauding monkeys had visited the clearing early one morning, and the bicycle, leaning against the outside of Frederick's hut, was a unique attraction.   Although Dembe heard the animals, and chased them with a cane, it was too late: they had shredded the tyres. But Frederick wasn't as angry as she anticipated.   Without realizing it – and contrary to his own expectations. - he had become accustomed to living with the Batwa, and was even chief guest at Lewa's wedding.   And, reinforcing this tribal bond, Dembe had made him realize that there are more important things in life than sex.   But, as usual, he was having conflicting ideas.

1973

It was not out of compassion, but out of a genuine love for the girl that he asked Dembe to marry him (she was also six months pregnant). As an outsider, he still had to formally request Kintu's approval. On the first day after the first full moon in July, Kintu waved a bamboo stick with feathers attached to the tip. He then declared Frederick and Dembe married. And the singing and dancing went on until dawn.

Married to a tribal member, he was now considered an associate tribesman, but not fully integrated. That could only happen when he had increased the size of the tribe. And three months later, he was accepted as a mutwa, a full member of the Batwa tribe.

It was on the sixteenth of October, that Frederick and Dembe's son was born. She thanked the moon for blessing her fertility, the forest for sustaining them, and Kintu for allowing her to marry an outsider. And that night, the tribe sang and danced again. But, unexpectedly and as a result of the birth, printed pages of the Bible were now appearing before Fredrick's inner eyes. He was suddenly finding comfort in the religion that he turned his back on after junior school. He made rosary beads with groundnuts and, determined to share this awakening, preached Catholicism to the village children.

As a member of the clan, tribesmen taught him how to make banana and bamboo beers, and how to make a bow and sharpen arrows. They taught him how to build a house from branches, mud and grass. And Dembe taught him how to make and use smoke to ward off the bees when collecting wild honey from low-lying bees' nests (she collected honey and wax from the nests in the upper branches). But more importantly, she introduced him to various herbs that would enhance both their lives.

To enable him to work harder, she collected the stimulants mairungi and kola nuts. To enhance his performance in bed, she harvested cola acuminata. And, as she enjoyed long sessions, she searched the banks of the swamps for albizia gummifera to prevent early ejaculation; a condition he had been experiencing recently. Frederick blamed the lack of spermicidal control on friction caused by the bees' wax she was inserting in her vagina. Nevertheless, he was appreciative, but puzzled, that a young girl would have such expert botanical knowledge relating to sexual matters.

However, he didn't dwell on her reproductive knowledge, and came to understand Batwa philosophy. In the jungle, there is honesty that was absent in Riverton. The natives appreciate that the body is simply a vessel, and faeces a natural emission from that conduit. Good human waste is not to be despised but used as an effective fertilizer. Sexual intercourse is for procreation or mutual pleasure - not for self-gratification. Breasts are not for covering up in shame, but to be proudly displayed like, for example, the genitalia of the tribe's proud dancing men.

But breasts are primarily for feeding infants or the sick. And children bring renewal and vitality to communities. They must be cherished and protected from the few deranged tribesmen who practice cannibalism and roam the forests. For the first time in his life, Frederick was protective and concerned for others. He was no longer the naive fly being drawn into the female spider's web.

Mother and father were proud of their cream-coloured baby, and named him Joe. And although the baby had its mother's dreadful features, Frederick was a loving and caring father. Every day – sometimes three times a day - he lay Joe on his back, lifted his legs and wiped his bottom clean with young banana leaves. And if there was the slightest sign of a rash, he applied creamed beeswax.

1975
As hunter-gatherers, Dembe and other villages continued to teach Frederick new skills. Mbo Tki, Kintu's eldest son, taught him how to carve a spear from a branch. He also taught Frederick how to make poisons for the darts and how to blow them through a pipe, and – but more especially - how to avoid inhaling prior to blowing. And by watching Dembe, he had learned how to create fire by rotating a stick. Although he couldn't get the hang of sending smoke signals, he soon learned how to make love the pygmy way. For the first time since arriving in the jungle, he was confident and enjoying life.

1976
As usual, Dembe was out hunting for food with Mbo Tki, Kintu's heavily tattooed son. And, contented, Frederick lay in his outdoor hammock with infant Joe sleeping beside

him. Since he had been introduced to the bark of the Iboga tree, he had become addicted to its psychedelic properties. They added colours, sounds and smells to his memories.

He recalled some of those married, voracious Riverton women, but dismissed them in a blue vapour. However, Betty Curran lingered. As a midget, she would have fitted in nicely with the pygmies. In a loincloth, and naturally humpbacked, she was dancing around the campfire. But she too disappeared in a puff of smoke.

The uninvited image of Ethel was more difficult to erase. She was lying on her back, naked with her protruding belly button sitting atop her firm and dilated stomach. A baby's head was slowly emerging from between her legs. He tried to shake off the image, but it persisted. The baby was laughing. Her new husband was peering through a window, showing his teeth and waving his fist. Frederick clenched his eyes and shook his head.

Mildred appeared. She was sitting on the hospital bed, her warm hand under the sheet. Searching deep into his subconscious, he still couldn't recall where the semen went. It was a puzzle, but at least the nurse hadn't complained about stained sheets. Despite Mildred's preoccupation with sex, she also had moral values that he found attractive. He was indebted to her.

Contrary to Dembe's instruction, he dozed off, but quickly shook himself awake, checking young Joe was all right. Looking down at the sleeping infant he thought of Looloo. He estimated their child would now be ten. A sense of sadness overcame him. But then he was back in Riverton, standing at the front window on Primrose Street.

Fat Blodwyn, lying under the milk-delivery boy, crept into his thoughts, and he couldn't help smiling. There she was, suddenly standing naked at the window with her tongue out. He could even see her ginger pubes. But then she had him behind the stage scenery, squeezing the life out of him and his genitalia. It wasn't easy escaping her clutches, but he managed to redirect his thoughts from Blodwyn to Patricia.

Patricia was one of the few girls in Riverton to command his respect. She was the only one who kept her breasts under wraps. He wondered if her decency values were innate or conditioned in the family home? He speculated how she may have reacted on her honeymoon. He genuinely hoped it was pleasurable, but nevertheless felt cheated.

According to what she had told him, Debbie had also been nurtured in a caring family environment, and yet, despite her leg irons, seemed to be in sexual overdrive. Her doting father spent all that stolen money on her, but it did nothing to quench her sexual wants. The more he thought about it, the more he was convinced that conditioning was only part of the story. He agreed with Jung's theory that it was also in the genes. He thought back to his father lying on top of Mrs Butler, the woman from next door. He asked himself why had he so regularly consented to the amorous overtures of sex-mad females? Was it his dissolute father's genes that were flawed, and which he had inherited? But it was a freak of nature, he thought, that two unattractive and stupid people, such as his parents, could produce such a handsome and intelligent son. And he could only blame himself for allowing those predatory females free access to his body. He should have been stronger.

May was standing at the door, her little white apron contrasting nicely with her black skirt and thick woollen stockings. She was holding a little giftwrapped Christmas present. She undressed and climbed on the bed, her surprisingly broad and white posterior before his face. Like all those women in the past, he wondered what became of her. Fleetingly, Rhoda and Dora overlapped his thoughts, but he felt exhausted just thinking about those two.

Henrietta, waving a wig, was chasing him down the corridor of the train. Sitting on the lavatory seat, he put his feet up against the locked door. He could hear the rotation of the wheels and feel the shaking of the carriage. Henrietta was banging on the door, demanding to be admitted. He instinctively put his hands to his ears.

His thoughts meandered to the three dancing girls, taking turns to sit on his face. He coughed, clearing his throat. The recollection was too vivid and made him wince. He thought of Mugisha and her shiny black body. He was lying on his back looking up at the ceiling mirror. Holding a large camera, Idi Amin was looking down, laughing, his fat stomach shaking.

Then he thought back to his days in London and Wanda. Wrapped in swathes of brightly coloured fabrics, she was sitting on a bench beside the Thames picking her nose. A flash of light crossed before his closed eyes. Why hadn't he thought of her before? She, or her father, could have provided refuge in Kampala. He was furious with himself.

But his anger and self-loathing abated when Dembe and Mbo Tki arrived home carrying still-warm, young antelopes on their backs. Such a wonderfully devoted and caring wife, he thought, comparing her with all those loose women of his pre-marriage days. He smiled, thinking how lucky he was to have married such a trustworthy and industrious woman, and to have such good friends, as the Batwa and, in particular, Kintu's son, Mbo Tki.

But since living in the Echuya rainforest, a related question had troubled him. He was puzzled as to why married white women are so adulterous, but pygmy wives trustworthy, dedicating their vaginas to their husbands?

1977

He had been relatively free of infections the past few years, but in February he contracted malaria. For three months, the shaman treated him with a brew of sweet wormwood, limes, cinnamon, chirayat and vernonia amygdalina. And Dembe again nursed him and cared for his personal needs, disposing of his urine and excrement, and delicately washing his body.

By April, he no longer had to rely on her for those personal tasks, but felt he had forever been dependent on her, the shaman, and Kintu's caring son. He knew he was not the man he was when he arrived in the forest six years earlier. He no longer had the energy to walk alone, but Dembe helped him cover the short distance between their hut and the clearing where he taught English to the children and adults. And from memory he recited Shakespearian monologues.

Although teaching, and occasionally holding Bible lessons, he had to rely on Dembe and Mbo Tki for his daily needs. Together they hunted for monkeys and warthogs. And when hunting alone, Dembe caught birds in traps, and - but in breach of tribal edicts - climbed the vines of massive trees to collect honey and beeswax.

But in his heart, he wanted to return to civilization, taking his family with him. However, he acknowledged that travelling to England was impossible. The only safe haven, he reasoned, was the forest, the one place where they could survive without money. But, he had to acknowledge, he was vulnerable to the endemic diseases. He now had an overwhelming sense of responsibility for other human beings, and, deep in his soul, an inborn confidence that Jesus Christ would take care of him and his family. To visually support this religious reawakening, he made a cross and let his hair and beard grow long. Nevertheless, deep in his subconscious, there was a glimmer of hope that one day he would again sleep in a proper bed, dine at a table and wear a Savile Row suit.

1978

For the seven years he had lived with the Batwa pygmies, he had been constantly plagued by different infections, but recovered. But he had never fully recovered from the malaria infection. Nevertheless, with the shaman's medication, and Dembe's assistance, he had remained an active member of the pygmy community. The class sizes had more than doubled as adults and children of other nearby tribes began attending his lessons, attracted by the Bible stories.

1979

In April, news reached the Batwa tribe that Idi Amin had been deposed and fled the country. The slaughtering of innocents ended. A Presidential Commission had been established and it was planning to reinstate Milton Obote as Prime Minister.

Kintu broke the news to Frederick who was lying in his hut. The malaria parasites had never left his body; they had simply lain dormant in his liver. But recently, the efficacy of the herbal-based medicine had diminished, allowing the parasites to awaken, multiply and reinvade his blood stream.

But he wasn't despondent; he knew that if Obote became leader again, he would send the troops to bring him and his family back to Kampala. He would have the best medical treatment. He would recover his car, have his villa repaired, redecorated, furnished. In the evenings, he would sit on the porch with Dembe and his son by his side. And, for the pygmy communities, he would demand proper healthcare and brick-built schools. He knew he had a lot of persuading to do, but was confident of Mr Obote's support.

'Yes,' he thought, 'he will need me again to handle all the publicity.'

1980

On the 17 December, Milton Obote was reinstated as President. Three weeks earlier, Kintu had died, and his son, Mbo Tki, appointed temporary First Man. Partly educated by Frederick, and having listened to his stories of life in Kampala and England, he had ambitions beyond the forest. As a young man, he had also been responsible for setting up that trading relationship with a non-pygmy community twenty miles north east of the rainforest.

Many of those Ugandan villagers working on the banana plantations also grew their own vegetables, a few cultivated cannabis plants and tobacco leaf. In exchange for these commodities, the pygmies continued to barter with meat. But surplus meat was not always available. And this was why the woodcutters were able to return to the forest.

While Kintu was alive, - and at Mbo's instigation - the Batwa had a struck a deal with the lumberjacking company. Kintu had agreed to a peace deal. In exchange for Ugandan currency, they would allow a certain number of trees to be cut down. Frederick's warning that such an arrangement would ultimately lead to total destruction of their habitat was ignored.

John Jepson, the new manager of the timber company, was an Englishman who had lived in Uganda for twenty-five years. Mbo regularly visited the industrial site to monitor the woodcutting, and the more trees they removed, the more shillings Mbo received. It was during one exchange that the manager learned of the white man living with the Batwa. And he was astonished to learn that it was the once well-known Frederick O'Flaherty. During Milton Obote's reign, he had read much about Frederick, the only white man wielding political power after Uganda's independence. Mbo agreed to arrange a meeting.

Frederick was excited at the opportunity of speaking with an Englishman, but daily his immune system was breaking down. Weak, thin, perspiring, unable to stand, Frederick was lying inside his hut when the manager arrived. Frederick listened attentively as Amin's flight to Libya was described. But he found it hard to believe that Britain had a woman Prime Minister. The manager agreed to try and arrange for a doctor to visit the camp. And true to his word, the manager returned the following week with a doctor. After that visit, things moved quickly.

Frederick spent a week in a Kampala hospital, but the malaria was so advanced that he needed his blood removing and detoxifying before returning cleansed to his body.   And the hospitals in Kampala were either ill equipped, or with a waiting list too long to guarantee his survival.   While he was in hospital, the lumber company arranged hostel accommodation for his wife and son and, much against Dembe's wishes, provided them with suitable clothing.   But it was the British High Commissioner who organized transportation to London, where Frederick underwent the plasmapheresis procedure.

Frederick said it must have been somebody in the hospital who alerted the press to his nine years living in the jungle, but, like riding a bike, manipulation of the media, once learned, is a skill never forgotten.   And the media reporters were visiting his bedside, fighting between themselves and bidding for his story.   Although he sold the press rights to the *News of the World*, he ensured the contract did not include television appearances and radio interviews.

Ten days after arriving in London, his blood had been filtered and the malaria parasites removed, and he was discharged from hospital.   With media payments, and an advance of several thousand pounds, he and his family rented a four-bedroomed house in Wimbledon.   For the next six weeks, he sat by the window, either looking out on the Common or thinking about writing a memoir.   The appearances on television and interviews on different radio stations were inconvenient but lucrative.   But then the media became more interested in his pygmy wife and half-pygmy son.   Soon 50 inch tall Dembe, wearing a loin cloth and carrying a spear, was appearing on television chat shows alongside 90 inch tall Christopher Greener.   Circus and zoo owners were queuing up, offering her and her equally weird-looking son work in their freak tents. Barnum & Bailey sent their agent from New York. But when they wanted to dress up his wife and son as monkeys, Frederick decided enough was enough. With money in the bank, he decided if was time to see the sights. In one month they visited all the tourist attractions of London, and as soon as the final cheque arrived from the newspaper, he bought a gold-coloured Rolls Royce.

Joe O'Flaherty, Frederick's father, was, as usual on Sunday afternoons, sitting in the parlour reading the *News of the World*. Sitting close to the radio in the back room, Delores was listening to Family Favourites. Both having recently celebrated their 75th birthdays, they were now living frugally but still under the same roof on Primrose Street.

When Joe retired in 1970 he had a reasonable pension, but inflation during those ten years had average 15% annually, reducing his company pension to £3 a week (the state pension for the two of them totalled £43.50 against the average weekly wage for one person of £110). Joe blamed the Labour party, Delores was adamant it was the unions' fault. But, it could be argued, that erosion of his company pension income extended Joe's life: he could no longer afford Jameson's whiskey. And he was now only going to the Bull's Head for an hour on Sunday lunchtimes. But, he complained, it was a waste of time: most of his old drinking mates were dead, and the pub was full of stupid young men. In a similar vein, Delores lamented most of their former neighbours were also now dead, and young people had taken over the street.

"Look at this, Del; another O'Flaherty!" Joe declared, walking into the back room carrying the newspaper. "I wonder if he's one of me brothers' lads?"

Dolores put her face close to the picture but said she couldn't see without her spectacles. Joe picked them up off the mantelpiece and handed them to her.

"Frederick O'Flaherty! In't it funny: that's what our Fred was christened."

"It's not our Fred, is it?" Joe asked, leaning over her shoulder.

"Our Fred? Looks more like Jesus Christ! Our Fred's been dead years," she replied, handing back the paper.

Joe, returning to the parlour, stopped in the doorway and turned. "How'd you know?"

"Cos we'd haven't heard from him for twenty-three years, that why."

1981

Two months after arriving in London, media interest had waned. A white man living in the jungle was no longer news: his story had been told and it was now more of academic interest. But academics were not willing to pay for it: instead they were gleaning their information from the newspapers.

Although still living in the four-bedroomed house in Wimbledon, it had become increasingly difficult to pay the rent and rates. The business transactions in which Frederick had been persuaded to invest had all failed, and he had forgotten that the government wanted 60% of his 1980s earnings. To pay the back taxes, he had to sell the Rolls Royce, and they were now commuting by bus and by train.

But the public attention he once craved had now become intolerable: everywhere they went, people stared. And this attention was especially troublesome on the underground railway system where some male passengers were rubbing themselves up against Dembe, or fingering her private parts. And little Joe was traversing the carriages by swinging from handstrap to handstrap. Furthermore, their marriage had been declared invalid, and their son Joe registered as a bastard. They were finding official rulings intrusive, intolerable, and the crowded streets of London hostile and lonely. Frederick decided to return to Riverton.

1982

It was Delores who answered the door. And seeing what she thought were travellers trying to sell heather, she said her husband was Irish and a pensioner.

"We're here!" Frederick said, offering her the small bunch of flowers he had just purchased from the corner greengrocer. "It's me, Frederick."

Delores, her pink scalp now visible through strands of white hair, stared first at the long haired and bearded man standing on her doorstep, then at little Dembe, then at even littler, Joe; finally at the suitcase.

"Frederick?" she asked. "Frederick who?"

"Fred!"

"Back from the dead!" she gasped, putting a hand to the wall to avoid falling. "Joe, come here, quick!" she shouted. "It's Jesus... I mean Fred!"

Ten years ago, Delores had purchased, on a weekly repayment plan, a cream three-piece suite for the parlour. And Joe had removed the original, black, cast-iron grate and replaced it with a yellow tiled fireplace. The three trinkets positioned along the top of the fireplace were warm reminders of the happy holidays they had spent at Blackpool, Southport and Morecambe Bay. Delores removed the bed sheets that had been covering the chairs. Fred was impressed. But his father was speechless and sat on his favourite chair staring at Dembe and her son.

"We called him after you, Dad," Frederick explained.

Joe nodded, but, afraid of saying the wrong thing, kept silent.

"He looks like his mother," Delores said, extending her arms towards the child; but little Joe snarled and turned his back. "How old is he?"

Although the question was directed at Dembe, her vocabulary was still very limited.

"Guess, Mam?" Frederick asked, patting his son's shaved head.

"Three!" she replied.

"Nearly eight! We've got to register him for school. I was thinking about my old school."

Joe and Delores looked at each other, expecting the other to signal an opinion. After a pause, Delores agreed that would be nice, and questioned where they would be living.

"We were wondering if you could put us up for a while."

Delores looked at her husband, but, pretending to be preoccupied, he folded the large newspaper into a small square, pressing the edges. After another lengthy pause, Delores asked for how long.

"Till we get on our feet, you know what I mean?"

Although it was 23 years since they last heard from their son, as parents they felt obliged and reluctantly agreed to his request. They would accommodate Frederick and his family until 'you get on your feet'. During that period of transition, Frederick, Dembe and little Joe would, it was decided, sleep in the back bedroom, share the kitchen and be confined to that room for meals and leisure. Delores and Joseph would move into the parlour.

Of course, Dembe and little Joe were still not familiar with the niceties of suburban living. And this was soon to become apparent. However, Joseph and Delores listened intently when Frederick recounted his exploits in Uganda, but he had nothing to prove what he was saying was true, and his father didn't believe a word of it, suspecting Dembe was one of those foreign immigrants living in Tower Hamlets. But Frederick listened with keen interest as Delores updated him on their former neighbours.

"You know Mrs Porter died years ago, don't you?" she asked. Frederick nodded, her naked body jumping before his inner eyes.. "Well her husband's gone too. As you may recall, he only had one leg! Gangrene in the big toe of the other, they said. Your Dad thinks they saw him off; don't you, Joe?"

"Of course they did. You won't catch me going in a bloody hospital. They finish off all pensioners. It's all about money, lad. Mark my word!"

"Your Dad's right, you know. I've heard they starve old uns," Delores agreed.

"Is Blodwyn still living on the street?"

Delores was slow to answer, looking to her husband for permission to reply, but he answered the question.

"Aye, and living with that queer sister of yours."

'Because two women are living together, it doesn't mean they're queer," Frederick suggested, but the defence of his sister was met only by a grunt and the side of his father's face.

"Blodwyn's mam and dad are also in Riverton Cemetery," Delores said, trying to deflect the conversation away from her daughter.

"Aye, that was a funny one," Joe exclaimed, anticipating what was coming next.

"Megan's not buried with her husband; is she Joe?"

This was an invitation to complete the story, and Joe obliged: "She's in Ralph Biddle's grave!"

"Ralph Biddles? Can't place him?" Frederick admitted.

Joe pointed a finger at Delores, indicating for her to fill in the detail.

"Ginger hair before he went white! Of course, you wouldn't know that. Used to deliver the coal."

"Blodwyn's real dad, so I heard say in the Bull." Joe divulged, confident of his information.

"D'yer remember Betty Curran? They put her in a pauper's grave. But her friend, Mrs Packer, with her foreign-looking son, went on holiday to Naples. We never saw them again! And Mrs Pratt: she's still alive but living in a care home. Went to see her last year, but she didn't recognize me. Do you remember her son, Phil?"

"Yes, I remember Phil. His dad lost both legs in the war then hanged himself."

"Just spent six months in prison," Delores explained. "Mrs Pratt didn't have much luck, with one thing and another."

"Burglary?"

"`That stuff they smoke. What was it, Joe?"

"Dope!"

"Didn't know they did drugs in Riverton. What about the Butler family, Mam? Are they still living next door?" Frederick asked, thinking back to his confrontation with their daughter's husband.

"Oh, Mr Butler died years ago. Heart attack, I think. Mrs Butler still lives next door with Ethel and the youngest of Ethel's four kids."

" Did her husband come back then?" Frederick asked, genuine curiosity written across his face.

"Never saw him again. Did we, Joe?"

"Joe nodded, but without taking his eyes off young Joe, now sitting on the Victorian sideboard they had inherited from Delores' grandmother.

"Mrs Butler said it was never consumed."

"Do you mean never consummated, Mam?" Frederick asked.

"Sommat like that, Fred. I'm not that good with words these days."

"How come she's got four kids, then?" Frederick queried.

"Different fathers!" Joe replied, still watching young Joe.

"What's our Riordan and Patrick doing for a living?"

"Riordan's on the buses; drives a double decker."

"And Patrick?"

Delores turned to her husband, and he nodded his approval for her to answer.

"He's a window dresser. Works at the Coop," Delores declared, looking again at her husband. But he had returned his attention to the newspaper, and was again folding and flattening the edges.

"I must call and see Gran and Granddad Higginbottom tomorrow."

"You'll have go to the cemetery," Joe said.

"Me Mam and Dad went to heaven nearly twenty-years ago, Fred," Delores said, her mouth beginning to twitch.

"What you going to do for money, lad?" Joe asked, practical and direct as usual.

Frederick thought for a minute before answering. "I was wondering, Dad, do you have any contacts at the bus depot?"

"All dead or retired. Have a word with your brother."

"Yes, love, have a word with Riordan; he only lives up the street...number eighteen, in't it, Joe?"

While they were talking, little Joe climbed off the sideboard and disappeared from view. But, with the ballpen Joe used for the *News of the World* crossword, little Joe was drawing circles, dots and straight lines all over the back of the cream-coloured settee. Although Dembe expressed admiration, Frederick realized it could have consequences, and promised to remove the Batwa fertility symbols.

With a reference from Henry Simpkins (Joe's former manager, but also retired), Frederick was offered a job with Norwester Corporation as a bus conductor. And, with reluctant permission, he borrowed his father's industrial clogs. But while the wages were useful, residing with his parents was difficult.

When living in the rainforest, he had adapted well to the pygmy way of living, and that included making love. It was not the act itself, but the verbal noises that kept his parents awake. Little Joe, familiar with the wailing, always slept until daylight. However, immediately he awoke, he made those ultrasonic animal sounds he had learned in the jungle. And this always made the local cats and dogs react by howling and barking. Frederick and Dembe were both impressed by the way their son could communicate with animals, but Joe and Delores were at their wits end. Next-door neighbour, Mrs Butler, told Delores she didn't like complaining but strange noises were keeping her awake at night.

It wasn't the noisy lovemaking, but the howling cats and barking dogs that convinced the neighbours there was an antichrist living in Riverton. Unfortunately, *The Omen* was concurrently showing at the Essoldo picture house. Unsurprisingly, it was this supernatural film combined with pygmies living in the neighbourhood that generated the panic.

Although the rumour originated in Primrose Street, it soon spread to Daffodil Street and beyond. When Dembe and little Joe were seen on the street, grownups crossed to the opposite side. This odd behaviour was also apparent when they entered a shop: queues mysteriously disappeared.

This tittle-tattle reached the ears of the editor of the *Riverton Times*. Always desperate for something to write about, other than weddings, deaths and church fetes, he instructed the senior reporter, a talented writer of fiction, to cover the story. Living in the parlour, Delores answered the door.

"Hello, love. I'm from the *Times*. Do the pygmies live here?" he asked, pen in his top pocket, notepad in his hand.

"What d'yer want?" Joe asked, moving his wife aside.

"We'd like to do a feature about the two pygmies living here in Riverton."

"Go on, sod off! There are no pygmies living here," Joe shouted, his patriarchal instincts kicking in.

Anticipating events, the reporter put his foot in the door, but, because of his bearing, was unable to stay on his feet when pushed.

The same day, Frederick received a letter from the Riverton education authority reminding him that he had to arrange a school placement for little Joe. Delores was doubtful a school would accept a little foreigner who could not speak English and had a tendency to be disruptive. Frederick reminded his mother that his son had two English grandparents. Fortunately, Frederick O'Flaherty's name was printed in gold on the Roll of Honour plaque in the hall at St. Aloysius, his former infant and junior school. Accordingly, little Joe was enrolled.

On Joe's first day at school, Frederick and Dembe accompanied him. Although Dembe preferred to be free of clothing in the house, she realized that in public she had to conform by wearing an overcoat - but nothing else. However, because of her small stature, Frederick had been forced to buy child-sized clothing. But children's clothing is not made to accommodate large breasts, and this anomaly was obvious to other parent's waiting outside the school gate. Combined with their otherness, she and little Joe were the objects of whispers, giggles and pointed fingers. Some parents were amused, others fearful. Sensitive to this unwanted attention and ridicule, she wanted to return with little Joe to Primrose Street. Persuaded to wait, Frederick and Dembe painfully watched their little son being led crying into the school building. Turning to go home, they were confronted by a young woman with a camera.

"Say cheese," she shouted, before firing off several flashes and hurrying away.

It was Friday before the weekly *Riverton Times* dropped through the letterbox. Frederick and Dembe's picture was on the front page with little Joe and the school in the background. The heading, in bold black type, was concise: 'OMEN'. As was the subheading: 'Pygmies arrive in Riverton?' Although the article had one paragraph linking the film currently at the Essoldo with the strange noises, it also posed the question: 'do Pygmies practice voodoo?' The rest of the story discussed the likely impact of pygmy immigration on jobs, school places, hospitals, and pensions.

In the beginning, little Joe's odd behaviour was considered amusing, and when he scrambled up the drainpipe and sat on the school's sloping roof, the other kids cheered. But in the classroom, and unable to communicate, he refused to sit on a chair, preferring to sit on the floor. The Headmaster didn't know what to do. Health and Safety regulations had recently been introduced, and they worried in case he fell off the roof. And since the caning of hands and backsides had been outlawed, the teaching staff had no means of imposing discipline on a child whose language and behaviour they didn't understand.

Domestically, things were no better: Dembe and little Joe always ate with their fingers and, of course, preferred sitting on the floor. Frederick always sat with them. But, Dembe wasn't eating very much. Sensing she was unhappy, he asked her if it was the food. She said yes: she didn't like the meat and the way Delores cooked it inside an oven. Frederick was sympathetic, but explained most people in Riverton buy small pieces of flesh chopped off sheep or cows. But Dembe's sense of smell and taste were so refined, she could detect the meat the butcher was supplying was months old.

Dembe was desperate for fresh meat, and meat that still had its fur on. Knowing she preferred to burn the fur off on the fire, he tried to explain that such an idea wasn't practical inside a small kitchen. However, concerned about her deteriorating health, he promised to buy a rabbit.

The next day, he went to the butcher's shop. But the butcher said all wild rabbits had been killed off with the myxomatosis disease. He suggested the pet shop, but Frederick didn't like the idea.

"Try the slaughter house, then. Sometimes they get the odd small beast."

When he arrived home, Dembe was in the kitchen looking out of the window. The object of her attention was next-door's cat. It was sitting on the brick wall separating the two backyards. She turned to Frederick, the look of yearning lighting up her face. But Fredrick shook his head, explaining that some people in Britain keep cats as pets. Dembe asked why. Never having previously considered the question, he wasn't sure and shrugged his shoulders.

"Where's little Joe?" he asked.

She pointed under the table where their son was hiding. Indicating for the Frederick to follow her, she led him up the stairs and into the bedroom. The electric light cable and bits of plaster lay on the bed. She pointed to the hole in the ceiling.

The following week, when working on the afternoon shift, he went to the abattoir at daybreak, but couldn't find any small animals with fur. However, the foreman, with blood running down his white apron, suggested Smithfield Market. Again, he drew a blank, but Arnold Beckenstein said they had live rats in the cellar where they stored their potatoes. 'The rats down there are as tasty as barn rats. And you can keep all you catch,' he enthused. Again, Frederick wasn't keen on the idea.

Returning home on the bus, he sat on the upper deck looking down on the shops lining both sides of the road. But he couldn't identify any retailers from his youth. The former billiard hall was now a Mac Fisheries supermarket, and the pawnbroker's a video rental shop. Of greater relevance to Frederick's personal history, the fish and chip shop next to the Essoldo cinema was now a betting shop.

As a child, he knew the names of the hundreds of shops on Main Street; now they all had different names and were selling different things. It was like being in a strange town. Even the shiny cobbled roadways were now covered by black asphalt. He wondered if the tramlines were still there, buried for future generations to uncover.

The bus stop was just two blocks from Primrose Street. He walked along Main Street, trying to recall the retailers as they once were. He stopped outside what he thought was once Siforiana's milk bar. The sign above the door now read Tibb's pet shop. Despite the clutter in the window, for a moment, he was back in there with Patricia, leaning on the jukebox and listening to Perry Como. But this was also where they said their goodbyes. Now the place was unrecognizable.

In the window inside a small cage, a fluffy white rabbit put its twitching nose against the bars. It was looking up at Frederick as if in search of affection. He lingered, and the little rabbit began pawing the bars as though trying to make contact. It was then that he realized childhood conditioning is more influential than later experiences.

Out of curiosity, he entered the shop - but the physical conversion was beyond belief. Small cages were stacked high against two walls, many containing white mice, a few constrained yellow canaries. A puppy poodle lay curled in larger cage, but not large enough for the dog to move. On the counter, two glass containers respectively enclosed a green snake and an orange-coloured tarantula. The confused mix of smells and sounds reminded him of the rainforest at mealtime and compounded the sense of claustrophobia. The young woman behind the counter asked if she could be of service.

"I'm just browsing, thank you...but tell me, did this used to be a milk bar?"

"A milk bar? What's one of them?" she asked, her naked elbows on the counter, her prominent chin in her hands, and an amble cleavage exposed. For a moment, he was distracted.

"Siforiana's!"

"Don't know what they are, and I've been 'ere five years, love."

"What was here before you moved in?"

"It was Hilda's Cut and Curl. She's moved up the road. Bigger premises! Are you wanting to buy out?" she asked, straightening her back and lifting the snake.

Frederick wasn't listening: he was watching the long snake draping itself around the woman's neck.

"Do you want out?" she repeated, her painted fingernails tapping a rhythm on the counter.

An unexplainable sense of sadness overcame him. It was as if part of his history had not only been erased, but also vandalized. He thanked the shopkeeper.

But he couldn't accept the transformation: it was too dramatic. In denial, he stood on the pavement recalling the retailers on this particular block. He counted the shops from Primrose Street and had to concede Siforiana's milk bar was now Tibb's pet shop. With nostalgia sweeping over him, he felt an inner compulsion to reconnect with Patricia.

In need of a tangible connection with the past, he walked towards the Unitarian church. But the spire and belfry had disappeared, and the front of the building was clad in red and yellow plastic sheets. 'TOPLESS GIRLS EVERY SATURDAY' headlined the list of forthcoming attractions on the notice by the door. He walked around to the rear of the building where he had, one warm evening, sat by the brook holding Patricia's hand. But, like the spire, the gravestones and river had gone. The former graveyard was now a car park. He walked home, seriously troubled by the blatant desecration. Riverton had changed, and he felt uncomfortable.

It was also obvious to Frederick that Dembe was not enjoying life in England. He knew the unwarranted attention by strangers was a major factor, but he'd overlooked religion as a concern. In Echuya, the environment is the temple where the Batwa pray. That weekend, he took her to the park, but she said they were the wrong kind of trees – and not enough of them. Some mornings, she stayed in bed suffering hot sweats and dizziness.

On those occasions, Frederick or Delores took little Joe to school in the morning. In the afternoon Dembe would collect little Joe but only if accompanied by Frederick or Delores. Despite little Joe being only half the size of the other children in his class, he had twice the strength. Accordingly, when the home-time bell rang, it required two teachers to restrain him from heading for the drainpipe and to safely deliver him into the hands of his family. Anxious, Frederick took Dembe to the doctor's surgery.

The lady doctor repeated Frederick's pronouncements: "Hot sweats! Dizziness! She looks a bit young, but it sound like menopause. I suppose pygmies look younger than they really are. How old are you, miss?"

In Rutwa, Frederick reiterated the question. Of course, the Batwa tribe are not concerned about things like birthdays and age. He went back over their related history, and estimated her to be about twenty-seven.

The doctor admitted she hadn't previously had a pygmy patient and prescribed aspirin twice a day.

But the hot sweats continued, and, worried the aspirins weren't having any effect, Frederick went through a list of all the things they used to eat and drink when they lived in the rainforest. None of the birds and meats on the list was available in Riverton, but Frederick had noticed the pet shop was also selling tortoise. However, they both agreed tortoise was a delicacy that they only ate on special occasions. What puzzled Frederick, however, was the fact that he and little Joe always ate the same food and drank the same drinks as Dembe, but they weren't suffering hot sweats and dizzy spells. The list exhausted, he was beginning to assume that Dembe's condition was not physical but psychological. However, when Frederick was running a finger down the column of psychologists in the Yellow Pages phone book, Dembe turned to him and mumbled:

"Bangi!"

Frederick's face lit up. She had just shone a light in a dark room, and he shouted: "Marijuana!"

Marijuana was the only substance that they hadn't shared. But then his sudden burst of euphoria evaporated. It was plentiful in the forest but not in Riverton. That night, he lay in bed wondering where he could get a supply. And then he had another light-bulb moment: Phil Pratt!

The man opening the door was bald, stooped and with hollow eyes and yellow skin exaggerated by the moonlight. Standing to the side of the open door, he stared at Frederick but remained silent.

"Is Phil at home?" Frederick asked, suspecting he had the wrong address.

"Who wants him?"

Frederick, Frederick O'Flaherty."

"What d'yer want?"

"Does Phil live here?"

"Sometimes. What's yer beef?"

"No beef; I'm an old pal."

The bald man stepped out onto the doorstep, so close that Frederick could smell the tobacco on his breath. He put a hand before his eyes and stare long and hard at Frederick.

"O'Flaherty? Fred O'Flaherty from down the street?" the bald man asked, coughing up phlegm and spitting it into the road.

"That's me," Frederick confirmed.

"Seems ages since I last saw you, Fred. Been away?"

Frederick was shocked to see both downstairs' rooms bare and with gaping holes in the floorboards.

"Where's all your furniture and floorboards, Phil?"

"Suppliers! How do they expect yer to pay when yer in flamin' nick? There' no justice in this world, Fred. Country's gone to the bleedin' dogs!"

Without divulging too much information, Frederick asked Phil for his expert advice. Phil said he was no longer trading, but recommended a shebeen on Mossbank Lane. But there was a problem: they only allow white strangers admission if accompanied by a member. Furthermore, he explained, they don't open until after the pubs close. As a member, Phil agreed to accompany him on Friday night, providing Frederick paid his bus fare and bought the beer.

Mossbank Lane was in darkness, all the twelve shop windows were boarded, and the women standing in the shadowy doorways only noticeable because of the occasional orange pulse of light emitting from their cigarettes.

"Five quid, short time!" one of the women shouted, but Frederick and Phil ignored the sales pitch and hurried along the street to the row of gloomy terraced houses.

341

The ground floor window of the two-story house was also covered in wooden panels. And, like the street, dilapidated and in total darkness. Rubbish was piled high in the small front garden. It didn't look occupied. Phil pushed the bell. A deep voice said 'Yeah?'

"It's Phil, Phil Pratt," he said, his mouth close to the corroded intercom.

Five minutes later, the door, still on a chain, partially opened. Two eyes stared down out of the blackness. They followed the heavily built man up the creaking stairs and into a room illuminated only by one weak ceiling light bulb. This upstairs' window was also covered by wooden panels but nailed to the frame on the inside. Several men sat at three of the four small tables scattered around the room; another man stood between an antique double wardrobe and a bare trellised table. All the seven men in the room were black. Frederick, of course, was normally comfortable associating with black people. But these men were sullen and massive. He rightly sensed everyone in the room was watching him. The atmosphere, like the pervasive marijuana smoke, was intense.

"What you having, Fred?" Phil asked, trying to look tough with a cigarette hanging from his mouth.

Frederick looked at the long table but couldn't see any drinks or drinking glasses, but before he could answer, the hulk standing behind the table explained they only had pale ale. Phil ordered two. The same man opened the wardrobe door and, reaching down, produced two bottles and removed the caps with his teeth.

Attempting to impress the host, Frederick asked, in Swahili, 'how much'. But the barman leaned across the

342

table, took hold of Fred's lapel, and, in a singsong Caribbean accent, said:

"You takin' the piss? Me fuckin' English!"

Frederick apologized and, although the price was double the going rate, gave the man a tip.

"Got any hashish, Malik?" Phil asked, the cigarette still hanging from his mouth, but the smoke now irritating his eyes.

"No, only weed."

Each with a small packet of marijuana leaf in his pocket, they sat at the only vacant table. Drinking from bottles, they avoided making eye contact with any of the other customers by staring at the table. Frederick, anticipating that he would have to make future purchases, asked how he could become a member. Phil explained that, having made a purchase, he was now a paid-up member.

"See you tomorrow," Malik said, locking the door behind them.

Frederick was especially relieved to have emerged without incident. But Phil had other things on his mind.

"Do you fancy a bit of the other, Fred?"

"The other?"

"Short time, five quid!"

Frederick left Phil negotiating with one of the girls in a shop doorway.

Anticipating Frederick would keep his promise, Dembe stayed up waiting for his return. It was midnight when he arrived home and only Dembe was still downstairs. After smelling the leaf, she threw her arms around his neck. Unfortunately, Dembe had neither a pipe nor cigarette paper. But Frederick resolved the dilemma by borrowing his father's pipe. And that night, Dembe's temperature registered normal. But the next day, it was Frederick's father who was suffering dizzy spells and hot sweats.

In the rainforest, hygiene is, like the emptying of bowels and bladder, a public affair. In Primrose Street, defecation and urination was a private matter conducted inside a small, brick-built cubicle in the yard. And body cleansing was usually a once-a-week indoor ritual sitting tightly packed in a small tin tub. For the rest of the week, the galvanized tub hung from a six-inch rusty nail hammered into a wall in the backyard.

Like most toddlers, little Joe soon learned how to sit on the lavatory pan, but insisted on swinging on the hanging chain, repeatedly breaking the connection in the overhead, and difficult to reach, cistern.

Although the lavatory was installed when the houses were built in 1885, the porcelain pan was very substantial and made in Staffordshire by the renowned Thomas Twyford company. But Dembe found sitting on the pan a frightening experience. She said she was afraid of being invaded by a snake, and preferred to put some space between the water and her orifices. Therefore, she always squatted above the pan, her tiny and flexible feet clinging to the rim.

Of course, there were no snakes in Riverton, but her fears of vaginal or anal invasion were not entirely without substance. Mice and rats did occasionally navigate the sewage pipes, squirm under the U bend, and pop their little pink noses out of the water. Had Dembe closed the door, nobody would have known about her fears, but, understandably as a former forest dweller, she was claustrophobic. Frederick explained to his parents that it was just a question of time.

Although Frederick was doing his best to teach Dembe the ways of the English, it was a slow process. However, some traditions were easier to convert than others. For example, when they were living in Africa, Dembe mixed beeswax and lemon juice with fine shavings of dried figs in a wooden mortar. She then pounded the compound with a wooden pestle. Of course, it solidified if left to the atmosphere. Therefore, just before intercourse, she worked it between the palms of her hands until pliable. Having always complained that the pounding and plying made her arms and hands ache, she was an easy convert to the Dutch cap.

When they left the rainforest, Frederick's biggest concern was the pygmy practice of not wearing anything when menstruating; rather, such women bathed twice daily in the river. But his worries were unfounded: Dembe liked the soft feel of a sanitary towel so much that she took to wearing the extra long, 420mm, ultra-absorbent towels in place of the G-string.   But she hadn't taken to European clothing.

"Can you ask her not to walk around naked, Fred? Yer Dad doesn't like it," Delores pleaded.

"I can't make her change her way of life overnight, Mam. It's the way they dress."

But Delores was exaggerating in order to emphasis her own concerns.   Joe had never complained, in fact, before his pension was eroded by inflation, he used to regularly buy the *Sun* newspaper, just to look at the page three topless girls. And, anyway, Dembe always wore the towel inside her knickers. It was just her upper body and legs that she didn't like covered. And it was only when preparing meals that Delores was in the back room, or when Frederick's parents passed through the kitchen on the way to the lavatory or going to bed. Before Frederick and his family arrived, Delores always insisted that Joe smoke his pipe in the backyard, but since their arrival, she allowed him to smoke it in the parlour.

As a newcomer on the buses, Frederick wasn't getting any overtime; working just forty hours a week. This suited him, as on Sunday afternoons he could take his son to the park. While little Joe was balancing on the upper frames of the seesaw or swings, parents and other kids stood watching in awe. And little Joe would grip the bar with two hands, swing his body around it, and then fly through the air and land on his feet. And Frederick sat on the park bench, proud of his son's agility and soaking up the applause. But, much to little Joe's dismay, the park keeper had barred him from going near the duck pond.

However, while Frederick was living in the jungle, wages in England had risen to the point where the country could no longer sell what it was making. But, paradoxically, everything had suddenly become cheaper: half a billion Chinese were toiling eighty hours a week for a quarter of the money. Like falling dominoes, UK factories ceased trading.

For the leisure industry, this had three enormous advantages. Heeding the biblical warning (idle hands are the devil's workshop), the government was handing out wads of taxpayers' money to any entrepreneur with an idea that would keep the unemployed pacified. And cheap imports meant unemployment benefits were going further. Thirdly, the land where all those millions of Irish, Welsh and Scottish immigrant workers had once sheltered from wind, rain and snow was now barren. Benjamin Hardcastle's idea was paying dividends.

'Why don't you take Dembe and your son to Hardcastle's, Fred?" Delores suggested, desirous of a little peace and quiet on a Sunday afternoon.

"The cotton mill?"

"No, that shut down years ago. Hardcastle's Zoo. It'll make your son and missus feel at home," Joe suggested, looking over the top of the newspaper.

"It's where dye works used to be," Delores said, wrapping the mantelpiece trinkets in tissue paper and putting them in a drawer.

Just beyond the zoo's turnstile entrance in a narrow room, an old, lion was plodding up and down in a small cubicle, separated from the spectators by thick black bars. Urine-soaked sawdust and gnawed bones covered the floor of the small cage. The lion looked pitifully at little Joe, but Frederick warned his son not to make any noises that may upset it. But Frederick hadn't noticed the red and yellow parrot chained by a leg to a metal perch to the side of the walkway. Little Joe made a Batwa birdcall. The large parrot squawked, spread its wings, and tried to fly, but it could go no further than the short chain allowed. Repeatedly it was catapulted back to its perch. Battered, it clung to the metal bar, its wings flapping, its body twitching, and its beak clicking. Frederick hurried Dembe and little Joe out into the expansive outdoor enclosure, distracting little Joe with an ice cream cone.

Avoiding the birdcage, they visited the monkey house, and Dembe nudged Frederic, communicating with just a nod. But Fred shook his head. They watched children throwing screwed-up newspapers into the gaping mouth of the hippopotamus locked in a small outdoor pool. With a natural fear of vipers and pythons, Dembe and little Joe clung onto Fred's legs as they walked through the reptile house.

But the zoo was more than just animals living in small cages: shrewdly, Benjamin Hardcastle had installed amusement rides, penny arcades, cafes and many other money-making attractions. Little Joe, in a moment of parental distraction, disappeared into the black hole under a sign marked 'Ghost Train'. The mechanized ride was halted while a teenage operative searched the tunnels. Frederick and Dembe waited anxiously by the pay desk.

"Stupid foreign runt!"

Frederick turned. It was the ride's cashier looking out from inside the glass-fronted box.

"Watch it! That's my son." Frederick shouted, anger building on frustration.

"Sorry, mate. I thought it was a chimpanzee," the cashier replied, confident behind a locked door.

Incensed, and uncharacteristically, Frederick raised a fist and tried to gain access to the pay box. But the door was securely bolted from the inside.

"I'm going to report you to the management."

"I was only joking, mate. No offence meant."

Frederick stood looking at the face of the uncouth man behind the glass panel.

The cashier was also studying Frederick and, after a lengthy pause, said: "You look familiar, mate. From Riverton?"

"What's it got to do with you?"

"Did you once live on Primrose Street?"

"Living there now!"

"Is it Fred, Fred O'Flaherty?"

It was Tommy Timpson, and they reminisced about the old days, especially the time their clothes were stolen from the canal towpath. Tommy said he was a forty-eight-year-old orphan but married to Mildred Butler.

"Mildred! Not Ethel Butler's cousin by any chance?" Frederick asked, but not expecting it to be the same girl from his past.

"That's right; we've been married twenty-six years. Got three kids, all boys. One's in the army, the other two still at home, on the dole!"

While Frederick was mentally back in the park being jerked off by Mildred, Dembe, unnoticed, had also disappeared into the tunnel.

"Still living in Riverton, Tommy?"

"Yeah, got a council. They built them where that Itie camp used to be during the war. Three bedrooms, bath and indoor lav. All mod cons! What you doin' for a livin', Fred?"

"I'm working on the buses."

"On the buses! On the bloody buses! You're joking! Didn't you go to college down south? Bit of a let down, ain't it? Thought you'd 'ave been a doctor or sommat."

"Dembe!" Fredcrick shouted, noticing her absence.

"Your missus?" Tommy asked, pointing to the tunnel.

"Sort of."

"She's gone in there. They'll be okay. The electrics are off. Didn't know it was your wife and kid everyone's talking about."

"Talking about what, Tommy?"

"Between you and me, mate – and I don't believe it for one minute – they're saying there's been a curse on Riverton since they arrived. As I say, Fred, I don't hold with all that crap about pygmies bringing bad luck."

Of course, today's inhabitants of Riverton are no different to their forebears. Superstition has always been part of their psyche. And anybody who did not conform to this stereotypical concept of normalcy (white, uneducated and with a local nasal dialect) was considered abnormal. Coloured people were strange; pygmies, well, like the Loch Ness Monster, they were the stuff of fiction. Conformity was the key to survival in Riverton. But it be would be unfair to blame Dembe and little Joe for not abiding to the conformities imposed by ideologues over thousands of years. Before the Romans arrived in AD79, the inhabitants of Riverton, like the Batwa, didn't have washing machines, bingo, and cake shops. But in the 23 years Frederick had been living in Africa, British society had changed.

Unlike the Batwa, where free love was encouraged before marriage, in England it was encouraged after marriage. In the interest of balanced analysis, dancehalls and ladies hairdressers were established before Fred was born. And the history of promiscuity during the Second World War is well documented. But Frederick couldn't decide whether it was television, cinema or the GIs that had been responsible for the demise of modesty and reserve. Anyway, few would argue that the English veneer of respectability had been stripped away.

Ménage à trois was now a concept more English than French, and to promote this phenomenon, new factories had emerged and were mass-producing cosmetics, miniskirts, and bikinis - on industrial scales. Sex aids filled shop windows and supermarket shelves, all prioritized as essential commodities. Growth sectors evolved to service internecine conflicts between men, women, and the divorce courts. And those laws that had encouraged marriage – canon, sharia, and halakha – were now being questioned by homosexuality, atheism and the contraceptive pill.

But, returning to the subject of superstition, Delores O'Flaherty, born and bred in Riverton, was really no different to the rest of her neighbours. It was the family connection that had suppressed her acceptance of the supernatural theory. But an event that happened while Frederick and his family were visiting the zoo undermined that resolve.

Before Frederick left for Oxford in 1952, nobody living in Riverton had a motor vehicle. But now, old cars lined both sides of the back streets. And it was one of these cars that ran over the head of Ethel Butler's cat. That both the Morris Minor and cat were black added to the hysteria in next-door's household. It was Delores who found the cat in her backyard. It was wrapped in a copy of the *Riverton Times*.

After Frederick threatened to sue the *Riverton Times* for libel and racial aggravation, the editor issued an apology. But the damage was done. Those amateur photographers, who normally spent their free time photographing the homeless or other exotics at the zoo, were now lurking on the corner of Primrose Street or outside St. Aloysius School. At weekends, the curious were arriving in Riverton by bus and train. On the streets, children followed Dembe, and, crouching with their arms curled by their sides, grunted like monkeys. Seven-year-old children climbed on each other's shoulders to look through the parlour window.

It wasn't surprising, then, that Frederick decided to return with his wife and son to the uncomplicated world of the Batwa? And Frederick's parents moved back into the kitchen, living a peaceful and contented life for the next three years. Joe lived a little longer than Delores but suffered poor health due to asthma and arthritis. As a consequence, he was forced to move in with Siobhan and Blodwyn. Unfortunately, they confined him to the back bedroom for the remaining ten months of his life.

APRIL 1999

Frederick didn't know both his parents died a few years after he and his family moved back to Africa. But, being pragmatic, he would have considered it only natural: they were of a previous generation, obliged to make way for the next – at least as promulgated in the *Happy Euthanasia Annual,* a publication recommended to Frederick by a fellow student when living in Oxford.

When sitting in the mud hut while his wife picked out the nits in his hair and beard, Frederick often

352

philosophized about the meaning of life. He was fond of saying 'most of us are the result of a boozy shag'. So why, he concluded, should anyone want familial memories? They interfere with the more interesting ones. But he did think of his parents briefly last week when he celebrated his 65th birthday.

Although Frederick considered worshipping the trees, moon and sun as primitive, he could now accept the Batwa's right to perform their abstract ceremonies. People have to believe in something, no matter how ridiculous, he regularly reminded himself. Of course, he thought those people who could not accept the notion of the Virgin birth, resurrection and the Holy Ghost were naïve and infantile, but he never disclosed that opinion.

Dembe didn't say a lot, but usually seemed to be paying attention to what Frederick had to say. Occasionally, however, she drifted off into her own private thoughts. He did try to engage her by talking about Riverton, but her answers were always the same. She said she missed the sanitary towels and Dutch cap, but hated the English weather, stale food, meddlesome people, and crouching on the lavatory.

Little Joe, now twenty-five and fluent in English, moved to Kampala in 1992 where he is employed as a promoter of Mr Yoweri Museveni's NRM government. Unusual for a pygmy, little Joe grew to 62" and has skin a soft coffee colour, much admired by ladies the world over.

Earning good money, he bought his father's old villa and now lives there with his Sudanese first wife and Zambian second wife. Between them, they have six children. The infant, named Fred, now lives with Frederick and Dembe in the rainforest. Although little Joe has visited Rubanda, several times, he failed to locate his father's Mercedes Benz motorcar.

DECEMBER 1999

Surrounded by Mbo Tki, the old shaman and Dembe (carrying her grandson in a back sling), Frederick lay perspiring on three layers of banana leaves. He now knew his latest malaria infection was incurable and that he was dying. But he desperately wanted to be alone with his memories. Unfortunately, the misconception that dying should be a public event, was also an African tradition.

Fading in and out of consciousness, his history was being replayed on an internal kaleidoscope and impossible to arrange into an order of Frederick's choosing. He not only wanted to concentrate on selected sexual recollections, he wanted to reconstruct his relationship with Patricia, one of the few girls who had denied him access to her body. He tried to undress her, but the image was evasive and his recollection of her features too vague. Heads were being superimposed onto the wrong bodies.

He knew, from years ago, that an excellent memory doesn't necessarily stretch to recalling facial characteristics, voices or, for that matter, aid analysis. And the people standing around his bed were discussing him as though he were already dead. They were interrupting his private recollections. Of course, even if he had the strength, he couldn't really tell his wife she was interfering with his memories of other women's erogenous zones. To help recall, he desperately needed privacy. He wanted to lie in bed with Patricia, but it was Henrietta who was chasing him down a long corridor.

He was back in the stable on the Charmingly estate. The upper bodies of naked women were leaning out above the half doors. They were neighing, but their faces were blank. It was impossible to know who was who. He was searching for Patricia, but couldn't remember what she looked like. At the end of the corridor, a young woman was sitting on a square of hay. She was wearing white jodhpurs, black riding boot but topless. He ran to her outstretched arms. She pulled his head to her warm breasts. But it wasn't Patricia. He suddenly realized that love for her had been a childhood illusion, and her aura of purity had reinforced the misconception. At last, he had identified his true love. It was Looloo!

With his eyelids half closed, and through a veil of tears, he looked around. There was Mbo Tki, his truthful and reliable friend holding Dembe's hand. And, leaning on a walking stick, the dedicated shaman, now 89 and still working (he misdiagnosed the resurgent malaria as age-related infirmity). But then Frederick turned his attention to his dear wife, a tiny woman twenty years his junior, but a woman as honest and trustworthy as the day is long. He smiled, happy that he had not married a devious English woman. He pointed a finger at little Fred, whose head was just visible above Dembe's narrow shoulder.

"Little Fred," he croaked, barely audible.

Dembe, understanding his meaning, brought their infant grandson up and over her shoulder and held him out, within touching distance.

"Tread carefully, Fred, for civilized women are full of trickery," he whispered, trying to reach out to the infant, but now too weak to raise his hand. Passing little Fred to Mbo Tki, Dembe went on her knees and, in Rutwa, recited the Lords Prayer. Federick smiled; a smile of contentment, achievement. He closed his eyes.

Dembe stood up and wailed, raising her hands and, in Batwa tradition, warbled and waived goodbye. But then Frederick opened his eyes, and she went down on her knees again, shouting 'Resurrection!'

But Frederick was looking quizzically up at the shaman. Raising his eyebrows, he twitched his head slightly to one side. The shaman got the message and put his ear to Frederick's lips. With great effort, and slipping back into his native tongue, Frederick murmured:

"Why... are you small men so... well hung?"

But the shaman was baffled. 'Well hung' was an English slang term with no equivalent translation in either Rutwa or Swahili.

Disheartened by the shaman's failure to respond, Frederick closed his eyes for the last time.

The next day, Mbo Tki with other village elders carried his coffin through the thick undergrowth. Dembe, with grandson Fred on her back, led the mourning tribes up into the hills. That night, the villagers drank gallons of bamboo beer, ate a dozen roasted monkeys and sang and danced until dawn.

Living in the Echuya Forest, nothing is ever wasted, and while the villagers celebrated Frederick's life, Dembe and Mbo Tki celebrated his death. Sweating on Frederick's comfortable bed of banana leaves, they again made love, but now their shrieks were muffled by the encroaching woodcutting machines.

Ou oyetsiga niwe akuriire entanda_
The one you have entrusted with your food has eaten it.